L.M. LACEE

DRAGON'S GAP

Set Includes Stories 4 & 5 plus Love's Impulse

COPYRIGHT

Dragon's Gap Fantasy Romance Adventure
Set #2 4-5 plus Love's Catalyst
By L.M. Lacee
Copyright © 2012 L. M. Lacee.
All rights reserved. **Published by PrivotelConcepts**

MAIN TABLE OF CONTENTS

Be certain to check out the back of this book for other stories in the Dragon's Gap Series.

Ace & Harper's Story

Love's Impulse

ASH AND OLINDA

CHAPTER ONE:

The female dragon lay dying. There was nothing they could do to save her and the grief Commander Ash Battle felt at losing a dragon. Especially a female who was so young and heavily pregnant rippled through him and his Shields.

When Ash and his warriors had come upon the female, she and two male dragons were fighting a combined force of shifters and humans. They had obviously been fighting for some time by the number of bodies lying dead or dying. The male dragons had placed the female between themselves and the side of the mountain. Although it appeared as if a shifter or two had tried to snatch her from her position; she had retaliated and killed at least one. Another male had a knife sticking out of his thigh as he crawled away.

Within minutes of coming into range of the fighting, Ash's Shields had killed all but five of the attackers. Rowling, the unit's healer, rushed to the fallen female who had curled in on herself in what looked like excruciating pain. Ash slid to the ground next to her and took her hand in his, whispering she was safe and the Shields were there to help. She must have believed his words, because she gave a jerky nod when Rowling asked her permission to roll her over.

As gently as possible, they slid her onto a blanket, and yet she still screamed as blood poured from an open sword wound. Rowling shook his head in a silent reply to Ash's unasked question. Ash prayed the blade had missed the hatchling. Rowling slapped a bandage over the entry wound on the female's extended belly, then grabbed Ash's hand to cover the cloth. "Put pressure on that."

Ash pressed firmly against the pad covering the wound,

hoping to stem the flow of blood. Rowling worked fast, but it seemed like an impossible task to him. The males who had been fighting with her stood a little away, explaining to Ark and Axl, Ash's brothers that they were not with the female. They had happened upon her as she was holding the humans and shifters at bay. She had been outnumbered, and it seemed like the attackers were trying to persuade her to go with them rather than forcibly grab her. When she had called out to them, they had flown down and been attacked. Ash faintly heard Ark explain to the two wild dragons who they were. He quietly asked the medic. "What chance does the hatchling have?"

Rowling just shook his head again. And truthfully, with the amount of dark blood she was losing, Ash could see she was not long for this world. He had seen gut wounds before, seldom did they bode well for the wounded, and being pregnant, it was a miracle she had lasted this long. Rowling rumbled out. "I am going to save this hatchling."

"What do you want to me to do?"

"Talk to her, see if she will tell you anything."

Immediately Ash started talking to the female, and a few minutes later she regained a semblance of awareness. He begged her to tell him her name. She said it would make no difference to anyone. He told her it would make a difference to him. She caressed his cheek with bloody fingers and told him she had no family, no one to care whether she lived or died. He repeated it would mean something to him and his warriors, and again begged her to tell him her name. She once more smiled and shook her head.

Ash watched as Rowling performed an emergency caesarean. His first, he said, but he seemed to know what he was doing. A feeling of relief and triumph washed through the dragons as the medic successfully delivered not one, but two hatchlings. Their first startled cries touched each of the hardened male's hearts. Rowling offered to show the female the babies, but she refused, swearing they were not hers. Ash

11

found that hard to understand as he asked. "How can they not be yours? You carried them inside your body."

She tugged on his hand; so weak she could barely talk. He placed his ear near her mouth as she answered him, and what she said made him even more confused. "A gift. They are a gift." She gasped out. "Dragon's Gap."

"What about Dragon's Gap?" He demanded urgently. "Tell me what of Dragon's Gap?"

She smiled as her hand dropped away, and with her last breath, called out. "Goddess." Then she was gone. Her life force taken to the beyond. Every dragon there bowed their heads in respect and honor, reciting the Ancient blessing.

May you always have wind beneath your wings.

May you always remember you did not soar alone.

Ash sadly kissed her forehead in farewell before he wearily climbed to his feet with sorrow, clawing at his soul.

His dragon mournfully said. *She was a brave warrior.*

She was, she will be missed.

What name will she be remembered by?

We will call her Owena.

A powerful warrior's name.

Yes.

While he wiped the female's blood from his hands and face, sadness remained a hard knot in his chest. He watched as one of his Shields walked over with a blanket for the female. Rowling finished wrapping both hatchlings in blankets he had cut to size as he looked over at Ash and told him. "Ash, they have to go to the castle as soon as possible."

He looked up from the female, as another of his Shields wrapped her covered body in a plastic sheet in preparation to carrying her back to their base. "So go."

Before he had finished talking, Rowling was shaking his head. "No, I cannot fly as fast as you; no one can. You have to take them. Ash, we only have a small window here. They need specialized help and Sharm, if they are to survive."

Ash grunted agreement as he made ready to shift, issuing

orders to his captains. "Finish up here, take the prisoners back to base, they can play with them there." He grinned when he heard the whimpers from the six humans and shifters who had survived, including the male with the knife in his leg. "Then make your way back to Dragon's Gap. We are off rotation."

A whoop echoed through the hills at his announcement. It had been a long, hard, sad six months since they had been home. He knew his Shields did not blame him or his brothers for keeping them from Dragon's Gap. |He and his brothers appreciated their silence and support, but he had known for a while they had to return and face their past.

There were four Battle brothers. Ace, the eldest, was in seclusion and had been for months. Ash was the second oldest, then Ark, making Axl the youngest. In most dragon families, there were large age gaps between siblings. Not so for the Battle brothers. There were only five years separating each brother; this made for a united brotherhood, whether or not they were together. When they had been dragonets, Axl had given the brothers a family motto. 'We stand together, we kill together.' He felt they needed something to counter the Kingsley brother's motto of. We will kill you.

Either the motto had grown with them, or they had grown into the motto. Ash was never sure which it was. Regardless, dragons everywhere learned to be wary of the name Battle. Ash shook off his thoughts as his brothers moved to where he stood. Ark, who would lead the Shields in his absence, said. "I will make sure we all get home with the wild ones. They seem receptive to returning with us. Fly well brother."

He clapped each of his brothers on their shoulders and growled. "I will stay safe, arrive home in one piece, or our lady will be distraught and I will be in trouble. Then you will pay."

An often quoted warning which made his brothers grin at the mention of Lady Verity, their mother by proxy. Ash gave one last nod to his brothers and let his dragon flow into being.

Rowling waited with both hatchlings he had placed inside the pouch that would go inside what resembled an overly large backpack. Dragons normally used them to transport equipment when in dragon form. The packs were usually tied over the dragon's back. For this flight, that would not be possible.

Ark and Axl hooked the straps over and around Ash's front legs so the pack that held his precious cargo could hang just under his enormous chin. The position would protect the hatchlings and keep them warm. Once the pack was in place, they all stepped back as Ash gave one almighty shake, when nothing loosened. Rowling placed the pouch with the hatchlings inside the pack and fastened them tightly, saying a small prayer that they would survive. Only when Rowling stepped back and gave the signal for the all clear did Ash rise slowly into the air. When he felt the pack would not fall or slip, he turned and headed to Dragon's Gap.

When Rowling had said Ash was the fastest dragon, he meant of all dragons. None could match his battle speed and style in the air. Not even the fire dragons. Ash's dragon was the color of smoke and when in battle, he used clouds to camouflage himself and launch attacks from within. His coloring was not that unusual, the difference was only in his ability to use it for his advantage. Over the years, it had proven to be an effective fighting technique, and more often than not, successful. This was why similar colored dragons wanted to learn from him.

Many years ago, Ace, Ash's older brother, had found evidence that their father had paid someone to tamper with their genetics. At the same time, Ash also found an autopsy report that stated their mother died from side effects caused by genetic manipulation. None of the brothers believed their mother would have willing undertaken these experiments. Therefore, they believed their father was directly responsible for her death. Which was something they had never forgiven him for. So when it had come time to testify against him at his trial for treason against the crown. None of the brothers had turned away from their duty. For them, it was delayed justice.

His dragon asked. *Why are you thinking of that time?*

I do not know. The hatchlings, maybe.

We have more important things to think about. There is a head wind.

Let us do our best.

Ash's dragon poured on the speed as he flew through the morning sky. He could feel the hatchlings sleeping in their pouch. His dragon seemed to be entranced with them, crooning a lullaby as they flew. After an hour, he said to his dragon. *I am worried, it is three days to Dragon's Gap. I know we can shave some time off that, but will it be enough? Rowling has said the hatchlings will survive if we get them to the castle and Sharm within that time. What do you think?*

His dragon snorted his disagreement with the medic's opinion. *He was being optimistic in his time frame. The hatchlings, if they are to survive, need attention quickly. I like hatchlings, they are special.*

Ash let him see his smile as he told him. *All hatchlings are special, otherwise one could not stand all the crying.*

His dragon laughed, but Ash could hear the worry in his voice as he said. *These hatchlings must survive. I feel they are important to us, to all of dragonkind. We must fly, as we have never flown before.*

With that as Ash's only warning, his dragon accelerated above the clouds where the air was thinner. Ash hoped the hatchlings with their little lungs would cope, but he trusted his dragon. If he thought they would be safe, he would believe in him.

They made the three-day trip in twenty-four hours. The fastest recorded time flown by any dragon.

CHAPTER TWO:

T hree months was a long time to avoid capture, especially when you have no money, friends or family to rely on. A person learns not to trust easily. To trust means letting your guard down, and if you do that, you could very well end up betrayed and caged, or worse. Olinda knew this very well as she sat on a bus surrounded by women and children, sipping the first coffee she had tasted in weeks.

She sighed and fought closing her tired eyes while she let her mind wander back over what had brought her here to this point in time. Eighteen months ago, she had given up her job as a head librarian at a prestigious city library after learning her mother had been diagnosed with advanced liver cancer. Because her mother had not been able to work, she had gotten behind on her rent and medical bills. As soon as Olinda learnt of this, she paid them from her savings. This left them with very little money, so Olinda was forced to take on a part-time job as a waitress in the local restaurant to make ends meet.

Sadly, four months ago, she had buried her mother and with grief shadowing her, moved from the rented town-house she'd shared with her mother and into a cheaper apartment. Luckily, Thea, from work who she had known for a year, had been wanting to share an apartment with some-one. She had been a good friend to Olinda throughout most of her mother's illness, helping and supporting her.

After the funeral, it was Thea who advised her to stay in town and keep working at the restaurant while she pro-cessed her grief. That was how her friend, who really was not a friend, explained it. Olinda shook her head as she berated herself for not seeing what was plainly obvious. *Stupid... so stupid!*

Now, thinking back on those days, Olinda saw where she had lost her common sense. Grief was to blame, otherwise she would not have allowed herself to be so easily duped. That was what she constantly told herself or else she had to believe she was a gullible fool, and she so did not want to be a fool. For the following month after her mother's passing, Olinda had taken on more hours at the restaurant. It was a stopgap measure; she had known she would not stay working there forever but for the weeks while her grief was so raw. It had helped get her through each day. And there was a mountain of bills to pay.

Five weeks after her mother's funeral, a man and woman had come to the restaurant for dinner. Her friend and flat mate Thea had introduced them as her brother and his wife. For reasons unknown to her then, Olinda had taken an instant dislike to Thea's brother and his wife, they had just felt wrong. There was no other way to describe the feeling that had come over her when she had been introduced to the couple. At the time, Olinda suspected it was because she felt like there were things not being said in the conversation. Almost like there was another conversation taking place, which she was not privy to. It was as though the three people talking and smiling were acting a part in a play and she was the audience.

Thea finished her shift at eight o'clock after the dinner rush had slowed down, as it usually did on a Tuesday night. Small towns closed early during the week. Thea seemed to be happy her family was visiting; she told Olinda that she would go home with her brother and his wife and they would get a light supper ready, for when Olinda finished her shift. Unable to think of a plausible reason not to agree with her idea, she reluctantly agreed.

Unsure why she was hesitant, Olinda said her goodbyes to Thea and her family and hurriedly went to serve a customer. Coming back with an order a little later, she was relieved to see that Thea and her family had gone. Breathing easier, except for the voice in the back of her mind, advising her to be careful, and that everything was not what it seemed, Olinda still felt better. She had been listening to that soft voice her entire life. Once, when she was around thirteen, she had told her mother about the voice only to have her rage at her for telling lies. When she had tried to talk to her about it a few months later, her mother had refused to discuss it. She even made Olinda promise she would never speak of it again. Needless to say, after that response from the woman who loved her and understood her. Olinda never mentioned the voice that guided her life to anyone again. That had been the only time she had seen her mother angry and frightened. Even when she knew she was going to die, she had not been as scared. There were times throughout her mother's illness when Olinda wanted to ask her about her reaction to the voice. But fear of upsetting her made it hard to ask, so she never mentioned it, and now it was too late.

Olinda's shift usually finished around ten o'clock. Except for that night. An hour after Thea had left, Olinda's manager told her to go home, as they were closing up earlier than normal for maintenance. With her worries over Thea and her family pushed to the back of her mind, while fresh worries crowded her thoughts, she agreed. It was time Olinda knew to make a decision about working at the restaurant; she had to get back to the life she had before her mother became sick. So she spent thirty minutes talking to her manager about handing in her notice. Her manager told Olinda she was sad to see her go, as she was a good worker and the customers liked her. But she understood she had a life beyond their small town. They came to an agreement on when she would leave.

Pleased with the arrangement, Olinda happily changed from her uniform into her habitual jeans, shirt and jacket, and sighed when she slipped her tired feet into her well-worn high tops. She fluffed out her long chestnut hair, after being confined in a bun all night, it felt good to let it hang free. She stared at her reflection in the mirror and saw sad eyes of honey staring back at her from a face with not a lot of roundness to it. Olinda had always been slim, now she was thin, grief had robbed her of her weight and vitality. Deciding to return to her old life was the start of walking out from under the cloud of grief. A tiny spark of relief lit her eyes at finally taking charge of her life. Now she just had to tell Thea that it was time to think of her future. Her mother would not be pleased to know she grieved for too long.

She said her goodbyes to her co-workers and started making plans for the next phase of her life. She and Thea had been lucky to secure an apartment within walking distance of the restaurant. So it was only a matter of minutes until she was standing outside her building in the dark. The voice in her mind started advising her to be cautious and as silent as she could be. Obeying like she always did, Olinda stole quietly up the stairs to the third floor of the building. Forgoing the old noisy lift and stepping carefully to avoid the squeaky steps.

She soon stood on the landing outside her home, listening to the loud voices coming from within her apartment. Olinda knew for a fact the door was reinforced steel, which stopped sound from within leaking out. She and Thea had tested it before they moved in. It was one of the reasons they had taken the apartment, and yet she could hear the conversation taking place behind the door.

"So Thea, you are sure she is a shifter?" A man's voice asked. Probably her brothers, Olinda thought.

"No, I'm not sure of anything. What I know is that she is not fully human."

Olinda stumbled back and grabbed at the wall behind her. Not human? Yes, I am. Then she heard the voice in her mind saying. *True, not fully human, leave now. Run.*

Unable to move, Olinda had stood there, plastered against the wall as those voices reached out to her again. Thea had sighed loudly, then said. "Although, I cannot detect what ani-

19

mal she is."

A woman's voice asked. "Does it matter as long as we identify her as a shifter, we get paid right?"

Then a different man's voice answered. "Right, we have already sent a sample of her DNA to headquarters and by the time our little party here is finished, around eleven, we should have the results.

The woman said again. "If the results come back as shifter or anything other than human, then we drug her and take her tonight."

The same man agreed, then asked. "Thea, your cover is not blown right if she turns out to be just human. Either way, you have a story ready?"

"Yep, all ready. If she's human, we just go on as normal. If it's anything else, we take her and I will tell them her mother's family came by, and she went with them." There was the clink of glasses and then Thea said. "After a week, I'll tell our boss she is not coming back. No one will care. After all, that is the beautiful thing about waitresses. They come and go regularly, people are used to it."

Those last cold words from Thea finally had Olinda fleeing into the night with the clothes she had on and her backpack. In a panic, she accessed her bank and withdrew everything she had in her account. Sadly, it was not much, only a few hundred dollars. Then she just caught the last bus of the night as it was pulling out-of-town, heading south. She traveled all night, fear riding her hard, confusion as to what and who she was keeping her awake. Someone thinking she was a shifter was absurd, regardless of what the voice in her mind said. She was human, her mother would have told her otherwise. These thoughts, along with the fear she was feeling, kept her company over the following months.

Even now, she remembered how shocked she had been by what she had heard. It had been years since the shifters had outed themselves to the world. So no one would care she was a shifter. Olinda was positive her mother, who had sympathized with the discrimination the shifters suffered, would never have lied to her. There would have been no reason to, and yet Olinda wondered, was that why she had been fearful and demanded, she never talk about the voice she heard. Riding the bus that first night, she had tried to remember what she had heard about the shifters being in some kind of danger. Unfortunately, her life had been consumed with her mother, then her grief, and she had paid little attention to the wider world around her.

Over those difficult first days of her escape, she finally pieced together what the danger to shifters was by scouring the libraries. If the town she stopped at had one, she would access the Net and learn all she could. Unfortunately, this led to her almost being captured, so she had to stop. As days turned into weeks, Olinda knew the information she had discovered would not help her, because she still did not know if she was a shifter. There was no one to get in touch with for help, the shifter hot line needed ancestral information and she had none to give.

She finally approached the police in a small town, but that did not go well. The small-town sheriff's department did not care about some woman with a crazy story who did not come from their town. They had politely asked her to leave.

Olinda did not know who to trust, she did not even know why Thea and her family wanted to capture her. All she knew was she was running and continued to run, because the voice told her she would die if she did not. After three weeks of nearly being caught, she realized she was being tracked via the GPS on her phone; she ditched the phone. At the end of the first month, she once more risked some of her precious cash and purchased another set of clothes from a thrift shop. She placed her old clothes in a plastic bag in the hopes she would find somewhere to wash them. So far she had four tee-shirts, two pairs of jeans; and two sports bras. Sadly, she had given up on underwear and socks. Too scared to linger in the town, in case someone would remember her and tell Thea or her family if they came asking. She quickly changed into her new clothes in the public restroom and left.

She traveled by bus as often as she could, usually by finding a ticket someone had lost or thrown away. Sometimes if she could not find a discarded ticket, she would pay for a ride, and hope the driver would be kind and let her ride to the end of his route. Where she would get off and walk until she came to another town.

After one of those bus rides, she arrived at a town that was medium-sized. It had a diner, a restaurant and two motels and a busy main street lined either side with shops. It was a town that was finding prosperity from somewhere; she thought it may have been from the farming community surrounded it. Olinda did not care, she stayed in the town trading cleaning services for a room in the motel. The owner assumed she was on the run from an abusive husband, which suited her; she got to shower and wash her clothes, buy some underwear and eat regularly.

Olinda had been there five days when she eluded capture once more. She had gone to pick up groceries when she had spotted Thea's brother strolling with two men down the street toward the motel. Rushing back to her room, she gathered her clothes and what food she'd stockpiled and run. Luckily, her room was the last in the row and she had shimmied out the bathroom window and slipped around the side of the building. She had stood between two shops on the opposite side of the road and watched as the men turned into the reception area.

Olinda knew she only had minutes at most until they bribed the man in reception, who would give her up in a heartbeat. Especially as she had rebuffed his advances with a knee to his groin. They would then check her room, maybe wait for her to return, or start searching for her right away. Either way, she had run out of time; she ran to the bus stop and climbed on board the next bus and kept on running.

Five times after that she escaped capture, not just from

Thea's brother and his wife, but also from several rough-looking men who were obviously hunting her. And then there was Thea herself. Several days after her near capture by Thea's brother. Olinda had been waiting at another bus stop in some small town when Thea had driven by. It was just an unlucky coincidence that she had seen her seconds before the bus pulled into the stop. Thea had implored Olinda to stay and talk to her. She told her how worried she was for her, she had almost persuaded her she was running from nothing. She was so tired of running, of not being home she desperately wanted to believe her and almost convinced herself that she had misheard Thea that night. Until the voice reminded her she had not, that Thea wanted to sell her, just like she had read about on the Net, and in the newspapers. Did Olinda want to go missing like all those shifters?

Olinda had shaken her head and jumped on the bus as it pulled away, and watched as Thea unsuccessfully tried to make the bus pull over. Olinda escaped that time by pretending to be terrified, which truthfully was not so much of an act. Thankfully, the bus driver believed her when she told him that the woman and men in the following car were city people. Who had targeted her for a sex slave deal they had going on. He had been so incensed he had called the local sheriff, who had stopped Thea's car. The bus driver had done a bit of fast driving, taking a few side streets and back roads. Olinda had thanked him and assured him she would be okay if he let her off at the edge of town. She told him she was going to her people in the mountains where she came from. Apparently, that was acceptable for traveling by herself in that part of America. He gave her directions to a track that would lead her away from the town, and to the next small town where she could catch a bus. Before she left, the driver and passengers wished her well and had pressed money into her hand, telling her she would need it. Then he had slowed the bus to allow her to jump off and with a wave she had run into the surrounding hills.

An hour later, she had found a hollowed out tree and stuffed herself and her bag into it. The money clutched tightly in her hand. The kindness of the driver and passengers had almost broken her. She had spent the rest of the night crying herself to sleep. Sadly, it would be the last time she would shed any tears.

Thankfully, Olinda had read many books on survival and about living off the land. Sadly for her, theory and practice were not the same thing. Unfortunately, she learned that hunting when inexperienced was often unsuccessful. After days of travel, exhausted and needing something to drink that did not come from a stream. She had found her way into another town. Realizing it was still too early for the inhabitants to be up and about for the day. She found a bench at a small park on the outskirts of the town to wait. Unfortunately, she had misjudged how tired she was and had fallen asleep, only to be woken by a man leaning over her. Terror gave her strength to free herself from his grip. It had taken muscle and loads of fear, to knock him away so she could once again run.

With her face, arms and chest bleeding and bruised, Olinda had stayed hidden all day and vowed it would not happen again. That same night before leaving, she broke into the town's pawn shop and stole a knife and gun with ammunition. As she hiked over the hills, she sent thanks to her protective mother for the lessons in self-defence she forced her to take as a teenager. And to her gun instructor for teaching her to use not only a gun but a knife. She realized she had not only been lucky but naïve, to think she would not need either the gun or knife to keep herself safe. Thea and her family were not the only predators in the world.

Olinda learned from that experience and stayed away from towns as much as possible. It was only hunger and clean clothes and the wish to sleep in a bed that drove her to venture into the next town. She planned on waiting for morning before finding a motel. It was near dawn and she had been watching the diner across the street waiting for it to open for early morning breakfast; she had enough money for a large breakfast that should sustain her for the day. She had learned that the most vulnerable time for her was when she was in a shop or diner, where she could be trapped with no escape.

Just as she was thinking it was going to be okay, she felt someone walk up behind her. She was grabbed by the shoulder and spun around. She wrenched herself free and stared at the unknown man. She had never been so thankful for the gun and knife as she was that early morning. Without thinking, she stabbed the man in his shoulder and before he could scream, she pressed the gun under his jaw and in a voice that promised death, she said. "I will kill you where you stand, if you make a sound or move."

His eyes rounded so much she could see the bloodshot whites. The tall male had nodded frantically at the deranged looking woman pressing the gun to his jaw. Olinda had leaned a little on the knife sticking from his shoulder, causing him to whimper, then groan.

She could smell the alcohol on his breath and the urine running down his legs. It was likely he thought she was going to kill him, and unfortunately, he was probably right. Olinda knew at that moment she was on the edge of becoming someone she did not know and feared more. Grabbing his wallet, she had taken the notes, then pushed him further into the alley. With a well-practiced move she kneed him in the groin, dropping him to the ground, he grabbed himself and groaned in pain. Whether from the knife wound or his groin injury, she did not know and worse, she did not care. She retrieved the knife and warned him to not tell anyone. Sadly, Olinda knew at that moment she could have shot him and not cared, instead she did what she did best... She ran.

After that confrontation, she had trekked into the surrounding hillside and made her way to a town she hoped had a bus stop. It had taken three towns before she found one with a bus, which she rode until it came to the end of its line. She eventually ended up in a town where she found a cheap motel. After purchasing some more clothes and taking several showers, she had slept for two days. With nowhere to go and no time to be there. She listlessly left the town, following the voice in her mind, who seemed to be leading her toward something, but refused to say what. Olinda knew if it had not been for that voice, she would have succumbed long ago to the despair and loneliness that lived with her daily.

CHAPTER THREE:

J olted from her musings by the bus going over a pothole, she was brought back to the present. Apparently, they were going to a place called Dragon's Gap. Why the people on the bus were going there, she did not know. She was going because the bus was headed there and she had nowhere else to go.

Olinda had been on the run for almost four months, and she was tired and dispirited. Hunger gnawed at her constantly, and not just for food. Her heart and soul needed more than to feel fear. She had not stopped at any town for over two weeks, ever since the sheriff of the last one had threatened to throw her in jail for vagrancy.

Fearful of being jailed and then released to Thea, she stayed in the countryside, living off what food she carried with her and stretching it to make it last. Walking, always walking in the direction the voice told her to. She had no idea what part of the country she was in; she had been in so many towns and crossed so many state lines she was thoroughly lost. At night she would find somewhere secure to sleep, usually deep within bushes. Sometimes in hollowed out trees which helped to keep her warm and sheltered her from the rain, but more than that, they kept her safe from all kinds of predators.

The last person she had seen was four days ago, and that was from a distance. It was about the same time her food ran out. She had stumbled onto an old disused track that could have at one time been a road, and had been following that for days. This morning, she had wiggled out of her hiding place just after the sun had decided to get up. It was becoming colder now, so walking helped ward off the chill of early morning and as she had no food; walking also helped take her mind off her hunger.

When the bus had driven up the slight incline and passed her, she had thought nothing of it. Other than to wonder why a bus was out on this dirt track to nowhere. Of course, her instinct to run and hide kicked in, but experience had taught her to wait and see if using the energy would be justified. Especially as the bus did not stop when the driver obviously saw her. She kept walking, wariness in every footstep, until she finally made the crest of the hill where she stopped and stared in disbelief. That same bus was now sitting idling in the middle of the road. Wary of a trap, Olinda waited to see what would happen. She reasoned she was far enough away to run if she needed to, but her little voice had not given off any warnings, so she waited.

Finally, the doors of the bus opened, and a woman stepped down and signaled with a wave toward the trees. Suddenly, a bunch of women and children ran to her. Then that same woman turned to Olinda and waved to her. By their own volition, her feet began moving and before she knew it; the woman with bright red hair reached out and took her hand and gently walked with her onto the bus. Then she started telling her and the other women that they only had two more stops before they got to Dragon's Gap. Wherever that was?

She showed Olinda to a seat at the front of the bus and handed her a hot cup of coffee and a sandwich. Telling her she was safe now and to relax, as if Olinda could do that. She looked at the sandwich and coffee; it took a minute for her brain to realize one hand held food, the other coffee. She wanted to cry at the normality of the situation, but the tears lodged in her chest and remained there. Sadly, she was not that woman who could cry or have normal emotions any-more. And as she bit into the sandwich, she wondered if she ever would be again. Maybe shifters like her, if she was ac-tually a shifter were emotionless, it was something to think about. Chewing slowly, she looked out the window and as she had done repeatedly over the last few months. She asked the voice if this was a good idea and got back a resounding. *Yes!*

In-between bites of her sandwich, she sipped her coffee, enjoying the taste. Her memory said it was not the best coffee she had ever had, but it was far from the worse. She watched the red-haired woman named Prudence flutter from one person to another; she seemed to like the children and there were plenty of them. They outnumbered the adults by two to one, most were women, although there were a few males. But they were teenagers or in their early twenties. They looked sad and beaten down by life. She could relate to that.

Olinda pondered who and why they were there as the bus rambled along the dirt track. She had still not come up with an answer by the time as Prudence had promised. The bus stopped for the first of their two more stops.

More women and children got on, and no one got off, it was a puzzle her tired brain could not work out. No one approached Olinda and she could not blame them. She had a good idea of what she looked like; scratched and bruised, with dirty hair. Seriously, she was dirty all over with old bloodstains on her clothes, which probably smelled. Her shirt and jeans were so old they were threadbare in many places. She knew her eyes would be shuttered, and would be enough to give anyone pause unless they had red hair. It seemed Prudence did not see or smell what the others so obviously did. She came to Olinda with another sandwich and another cup of coffee, saying. "One more stop, then home." She sounded so damn joyful about it. Olinda felt her face smile for the first time in so long. It felt strange.

Eventually, the bus joined up with three more buses just like the one she was riding, and together they made their way to Dragon's Gap. Three hours after Olinda had boarded the bus; they drove into a town. One minute they were driving along a dusty road, and the next they were in the middle of a cobblestone street. Climbing a small hill toward a large building that looked like an old town hall. Olinda turned around and looked out the back window at a tunnel made entirely of trees. She knew she had not slept or blinked overly long and was positive they had not driven through that tunnel, yet they were in the town. She knew there was a lie here, but could not work out what the lie was. She gave up thinking about it when there was no warning from her voice. Nor did she have the feeling of fear overwhelming her, as it did when she was heading into trouble. She turned back around and looked out her window again until Prudence came and stood by her seat.

Without thinking, Olinda muttered. "It looks like something from a storybook."

Prudence smiled. "It really does. That is the registration hall." She pointed to the old building. "Every person who comes to town has to register. Then housing and everything else you need will be provided for you."

Olinda turned from her contemplation of the town to face Prudence. "And for all that you want what, exactly?"

Prudence frowned. "Nothing," hesitantly she asked, "why do you think you are here?"

Olinda shrugged. "I had nowhere else to go."

Prudence gasped in what Olinda thought was surprise but could have been horror. But before she could say anything else, two young women who seemed to think Prudence was their information guru called her away. Which worked in Olinda's favor as they kept her busy peppering her with questions, making it impossible for her to return to Olinda. Which she was profoundly happy about. Prudence made her uncomfortable, she had no idea why, she just felt like she was incomplete, like she wasn't completely dressed. As though there should be more to her and the feeling annoyed Olinda.

She tuned the women and Prudence out, along with the rumblings from the other passengers, and when the bus stopped, quickly got off and went into the building. Only to be greeted by an adolescent male named Clint, or at least that was the name on his tag. He seemed like a teenager, but he too looked incomplete, like he was wearing a coat or something. Olinda's annoyance meter almost red lined. Sensing more wrong than right with the people she was encountering, she started to feel like she may have walked into a situation she could not escape from. Reassured by the feel of her weapons in her jacket pockets. She nodded as the teenager handed her a clipboard with a form on it and asked her to fill in the questionnaire. Then he asked her name and wrote it down on a sticky tag, handing it to her and telling her to put it on.

As the room filled with other passengers; he directed her to a small table by a door at the side of the room. Olinda wandered in the direction he indicated as he rushed off to the next woman. She placed the tag on the table along with the clipboard and just looked around at all the people who were now filling the hall. Amazingly, not every accent she heard was American. It seemed like there were English, Canadian, even French people there.

The people who greeted them and offered them assistance were like Prudence and the teenager. They too felt incomplete, like they were wearing human skins. The idea of aliens crossed her mind to be discarded quickly, although to have the notion they were wearing human bodies was just as strange. Everything looked so normal, except when she did a head count, she saw there were far more women than men, and even more children. She tried to understand where she was and who these people were, but her tired brain just would not allow her to.

Curious, she read over the form and apart from her name, age and what city, town or state she grew up in, the rest of the form made no sense. It wanted to know about her parents and ancestors, what shifter they were or if only one was, what were they. With a quick look around the room, she understood her feelings a little better now about people being incomplete. She supposed if they were shifters, then

31

they would give off that feeling. Reading the form again, she asked the voice in her mind. *So what do I write, what kind of shifter am I?*

She still received no reply, just like every other time she asked, and it was still just as frustrating and aggravating. Olinda filled in what she could on the form, which was very little, and then raised her eyes when she felt someone staring at her. After all this time, she knew when she was being hunted or someone had an interest in her. She saw Prudence with the same young man she had talked to on arrival, looking at her and frowning. It didn't take much to know they were discussing her. When they saw she had seen them, they hurriedly turned away, and it was then Olinda realized it was not only the voice missing from her mind. But it was the feeling of the presence that came with the voice, which was absent. She tried prodding it. *Hey, wake up. I could be in trouble. Hey, you in there. Where did you go?* The realization she was alone in her head was a disturbing sensation.

CHAPTER FOUR:

Dispirited, Olinda bent her head over the form until she felt the young couple move off. Thankfully, no one approached her, but the noise from the people in the room seemed to get louder, yet when she looked up, the hall was nearly empty. Realizing one sound rose above the others, she closed her eyes as she had practiced when out in the mountains. Concentrating until she could eliminate one sound at a time, eventually she was able to narrow the noise down to only one. And it was becoming more intense and desperate the longer she concentrated. Turning her head one way and then the other, she was able to locate the direction it was coming from. Something or someone was calling to her, not in words, but in waves of sadness and loneliness.

The sound tugged at her heart and now she understood what was calling to her. Feelings swamped her senses and washed along her nerves. Quickly, she stood from the table and pushed her way through the small crowd of women and children, leaving the building by a side door and following the call. The waves of loneliness led her along a brick pathway running next to the building. Turning a corner, she came to a set of glass doors. Pulling them open, she entered a small foyer belonging to a hospital and another set of glass doors which were between her and the now urgent cries of desperation.

With a cry of her own, she flung the doors open and marched into a long room with cribs and beds lining the walls. It registered on her consciousness that this was a medical ward, but like a steamroller, she kept on moving. Dodging children playing on the floor and people walking or coming to a stop while they watched, what they must have thought was some crazed woman walking through the ward.

They were partially right. Olinda felt like she was a magnet being pulled toward her target, which seemed to be a small crib halfway down the room. Sighing in relief for having found the first source of desperation and loneliness, she looked inside the crib. Unsurprised to find a small baby lying on his side, his cries going unanswered. Someone came toward her and she knocked them back, her senses filled only with the sound of the baby's cries. Tenderly, she picked him up and cuddled him. Instantly he quietened, and her mind felt his joy as her arms cradled him, allowing him to relax for the first time in his short life.

She moved farther down the room to the next feeling of loneliness and to another crib, where an almost identical baby boy cried pitifully. She scooped him into her arms and the sounds disappeared, as with his brother he sighed and his tensed body relaxed. Happiness from both babies filled her mind, and an overflowing rightness filled her heart and soul. Her mind sang with sunlight as the realization that these were her babies, not of her body, but of her soul. Her heart felt full for the first time in her life. The voice in her mind whispered. *Hatchlings!*

Olinda snapped. *Oh, now you speak. Out visiting, were you?*

A sense of amusement assailed her as the voice answered. *In a way.*

With trepidation filling her, Olinda asked. *Am I meant to stay here?*

She sensed humor and anticipation as the voice said. *You are where you are meant to be.*

Olinda sighed. *I'll take that as a yes then.*

She was sure she sensed laughter as she heard the words. *I would dear.*

Then the presence was gone again, and Olinda knew she was once more alone. She looked around until she saw what she wanted, a bay window with a wide seat bathed in sunlight. She laid each baby down in the sun on their backs and stripped them of their clothes. Turning them onto their stomachs, she allowed them to soak up the sun. Her fingers started a movement all of their own, running up and down the baby's spines as she hummed a lullaby. Both infants sighed and closed their eyes. Pleasure like she had never experienced before filled her soul. She did not know or care if it came from the infants or her, she just enjoyed the feeling and not once did she stop the movement of her fingers.

CHAPTER FIVE:

E dith and Ella rushed into the room just after Olinda had knocked a young nurse, Marie, to the floor. Blood poured from her nose and lip. She told them through a cloth she was holding to her face. "I thought she was going to hurt the hatchling. I did not know they were hers."

Edith soothed the female. "It is alright Marie, you did nothing wrong. Are you seriously hurt?"

"No, just a bloody nose. I will be alright. I don't think she is in her right mind, Lady Edith. The lady is unwell."

"I think you are right. Let Ella heal you Marie, then go home. We will manage for the rest of the day and if you feel unwell, call Ella or me, okay?"

"As you say, Lady Edith."

Ella did a quick healing on her, and then, like Edith, she advised her to go home. With a nod Marie left, then Ella moved next to Edith, her fascinated gaze never leaving the female and babies. Without turning away from the female and babies, Edith asked. "What has you so fascinated? You have seen this sort of thing before, minus the violence, of course. That is new."

"No Edee, I have not seen this. No one has. This... This is something different. Something like this is so rare it has only been hinted at in our history books. Who did you call?"

Edith shrugged. "Sharm."

"I wish Keeper was here." Ella whispered. Unfortunately, he was away on the hunt for new books for his library. "He could tell you better what I suspect. What they all will suspect when they see this. You better call them all Edee. Sage, Papa Rene` and Mama Verity." She dragged her eyes from the scene at the window and looked in wonder at Edith, then swept her hand toward the female and twins. "We are witnessing history Edee, we are in the presence of an impossibility, and our world is about to change once more."

Edith swore under her breath; she was trying not to swear as much these days. The little ones kept telling on her. She was determined not to put any more money in the friggin swear jar. Which was such a stupid idea. She should have shot herself when she came up with it. Although Charlie had swollen its contents lately, and she had seen Claire and Reighn sneaking some money in there recently.

Just as she was thinking about calling Sharm again. He arrived, his arm automatically going around her as his lips caressed her forehead. In his other hand, he held a phone to his ear. As she watched him take in the scene, she saw her Shadow become still, just as Ella seemed to do after telling her to call everyone. It was as though a spell had been cast over them, making them and their dragons forget to do anything other than breathe. Suddenly, the hair on Edith's body stood on end. She was unsure if it was because this was the eeriest thing she had ever seen, or there was magic at work. She gently removed the phone from her Shadow's hand and heard his father frantically calling to his son. She stopped him with. "Papa Rene, come quickly. Bring everyone... Hurry!"

Then she disconnected, she did not know what else to do. She could not explain this, it had to be seen to be believed. When she looked around, she noticed Prudence and Clint standing by the doors. They must have entered when she had been on the phone, she waved them over. "Do either of you know what this means?"

Prudence shook her head as Clint moved next to Ella and breathed one word before he too became a statue. "Impossible."

Edith growled. "Yeah, we got that already. Anything else?"

Before they could answer, the room was filled with noise as people raced in. Edith and Prudence watched Rene` and

Verity, Johner and several of his guards with two or three other dragons arrive and just come to a complete stop. Statues had more movement, Edith thought, she asked Prudence. "They are breathing, right?"

"They are Edee; it seems to make no difference if they are male or female. If they are dragons, they all suffer the same result."

"Looks that way to me." Edith agreed. "It appears I as a shifter, and you as a faerie are immune."

Just then, Sage hurried in and rushed to where Edith and Prudence stood. Her eyes traveled over the people, caught in some spell and then to the female and two babies. Her eyes widened as she asked. "So what do we have here?"

Edith gave her a brief rundown on what had happened. Then Prudence told them how she had found the female on the road, she pulled the incomplete form from her pocket and read. "Her name is Olinda Keaton from Wisconsin. She is twenty-eight. Mother's name Lina Keaton, deceased. Father unknown. That is all she filled in."

Sage said. "Well, someone is going to have to talk to her and break the spell these guys are under. Prudence, can you call the Queen?"

She was shaking her head even before Sage finished speaking. "No, my Lady, they are not in residence. They are visiting the High Grove for a week."

Edith asked. "What about Charlie?"

Prudence once again answered. "No, she and Lord Storm and the young ones went as well."

"Damn! Well, what do you suggest? What about you, Prudence?"

Prudence fluttered her wings in agitation. "No Edee, this is not faerie magic. I do not know what it is."

Sage was a witch, but this did not feel like her magic, and it did not feel like dragon magic either. Well, not fully, maybe something more but what that more was, Sage could not define.

Edith asked. "So it's dragon magic, right?"

Prudence and Sage looked at each other, and they both shook their heads. Sage replied. "It does not feel like that."

Prudence agreed. "No, it is different."

Edith asked. "Elemental then?"

Sage did not want to voice what she sensed, but she could not hold back. Prudence must have been thinking along the same lines, or she too sensed what Sage did because she said as Sage did. "Goddess magic."

Edith wanted to scoff at the notion, but the entire time they had been standing there. The dragons had not moved and the female and babies were still in their own space, as though they were not entirely here. "That cannot be, you told us the Goddess had left."

"I know, but that is what it feels like." Sage told her as she shrugged. "That is my best explanation."

Prudence nodded in agreement. "It is what I feel as well Edee."

"Well okay, you would know. So what do we do? I don't think any of us should go near her in case we set her off. I am fairly sure she has weapons in her pockets, and we may hurt the hatchlings?"

"Who do we know that could help?" Sage asked them both. Then all of them looked at each other as though a guiding hand had slapped them upside their heads and they chorused together. "ASH!"

Edith handed Sage the phone. "Speed dial three."

Sage put the phone to her ear and when he answered. "Sharm, what can I do for you?" She had to swallow her instinctive shiver of awareness that his voice always caused.

"Ash, it is Sage. Can you come to the children's ward?"

"Of course, Lady Sage, what is wrong is it the twins?"

"In a way. Ash, we will meet you outside."

"As you wish, I am on my way."

CHAPTER SIX:

A sh said. "Let me get this straight."
He walked back from looking through the glass doors at the immovable dragons and the female who had his twins, for the second time since he had arrived. "She just walked in, hit a nurse, and then took the hatchlings from their cribs. Stripped them and is now sitting in the sun with two naked hatchlings. As some of our family stand doing nothing!"

Edith agreed. "Yep. That about sums it up."

Ash looked at her as she smiled. He enjoyed Edee. She was the Shadow to one of his best friends, and was delightfully irreverent, which amused him immensely. Especially when she turned that wit of hers on the Elder dragons or Reighn. "I see, and where are Reighn, Lars and Stan?"

Sage told him. "All on a mission to see Mama Verity's brother and not due home until the day after tomorrow."

Ash rubbed his neck. "I know Storm and Charlie are still away."

"Yes, with the Queen and King." Prudence supplied helpfully.

He looked at Sage. "What of Keeper? This is right up his alley."

"Away, buying books, due home tonight."

Ash stared at all three of them as he asked. "Right, so what is it you expect me to do. If Rene`, Verity, Sharm and Johner got taken under, so to speak. Then what do you suppose I can do to stop it from happening to me?"

Edith grinned. "No idea, but I think because of your connection to the hatchlings you will be unaffected."

Prudence said. "My Lord Ash, you visit with them every day. If they are causing this spell, we hope the connection you have with them will not harm you."

Sage asked. "What do we have to lose? If we are wrong, you will make a nice statue as well."

"Very droll." He paced once more, returning to where the three females waited. Then shrugged his shoulders as though he was going into battle. "Well, nothing ventured, nothing gained, as they say." With that, he strode purposefully through the doors.

Sage, Edith, and Prudence stared after the handsome dragon. Edith muttered. "Of course it will work, otherwise the bitching from Storm and the others will drive me to drink more."

"Swear jar." Prudence called as she started walking toward the doors Ash had gone through.

Edith groaned. "I really hate that friggin thing."

"Swear jar." Prudence called again.

"Hey, friggin, is not a swear word."

Sage grinned as she told her, much to Edith's consternation. "Yes it is, swear jar."

Edith frowned, and they both knew she was cussing in her head. When they reached the glass doors; the three females held their collective breaths as they watched Ash walk past all the dragons who were still looking like statues. He sat next to the strange female and hatchlings. Edith high-fived the other two and whispered. "Right again, shit I am good."

"Five dollars," Sage told her, "and yes I am telling."

Edith squeezed her lips tightly together. Sage said as she eyed the tight-lipped female. "I can still hear you cussing, you know."

"Oh shut up."

CHAPTER SEVEN:

A sh studied the female, she had to be five-foot-six or seven, and way too thin for his liking, almost emaciated. Her clothes were old, and blood encrusted. He could see no visible wounds. So that was a bonus, and she was filthy, he hated thinking it, but she smelled, or to be accurate, her clothes smelled. She had long dirty hair that could have been chestnut, but was just dirt brown now. Her cheeks were sunk in, he guessed from lack of food. When she flicked her eyes to him, his breath caught in his throat as he glimpsed warm honey. With that one look, they were seared into his soul.

Shadow! Hissed his dragon.

So it would seem my old friend. We have found her at last.

His dragon whispered. *I like eyes of honey, warm and soft.*

Ace agreed, looking past all the dirt, bruises and the numerous scratches covering her face and hands. He could see she was flushed; and had to assume she was running a fever. |Yet even with all that, he felt his body respond to this amazing female.

Shadow. His dragon growled again softly. *Our Shadow and our hatchlings.*

Ash cautioned him. *So it would seem we must tread carefully, my friend.*

His dragon growled. *We must be soft, show our heart, and not be a battle dragon anymore. I wish to be Shadow and Dada, like Storm.*

Surprised by the loneliness he heard in his dragon's voice, Ash asked. *This is what you want my friend, you never said.*

Would it have made a difference? I believed like you; we were bred for war. Now I know we were bred for much more, for Shadow and hatchlings.

Ace could not fault his reasoning. *Alright my friend, it is time to find a new life. To be more than a battle dragon, if this is what you want, then you shall be a Shadow and a father.*

Pleasure enveloped him as his dragon settled into watch the graceful movement of his Shadow's hands as she turned the hatchlings over with careful, gentle movements. The babies were on their backs now, and their eyes were open, staring at her or maybe just at the dust motes dancing in the air.

Olinda knew she should be frightened, or at least amazed by what was happening, but as much as she tried. She could not find the energy to break the spell of peace that had stolen over her. She watched as her scratched and bruised fingers trailed over the skin of the baby's little chests and arms, and was positive where her fingers had been; a golden line blossomed and then disappeared.

"No, you are not imaging it. It really is gold." Said a voice that came from of her deepest darkest desires. A voice that romance writers often tried to convey and never could in novels, a voice that made every hair on her body stand up and wave. *Hello!*

Shyly, she looked at the male from under her lashes and itemized every one of his attributes. From long legs crossed at the ankle in a relaxed pose, and his wide shoulders, which were covered in a black tee-shirt, to his well-defined muscular arms. She sighed in appreciation as she saw the shirt did very little to hide his body's perfection. She could only see his profile, but knew deep in her heart he would be handsome. A fleeting thought made her wonder how it was possible for him to have come so close to her without her knowing. Was he made from magic, which would explain this feeling she was having, or maybe he was like the others? She'd had time to think while sitting here when the tiredness she'd been plagued with had lifted from her mind. It was like she no longer looked at the world from behind a filter and one of those things she could look and think about clearly was the teenager and Prudence, who were not human. Neither was this man, he gave her the same feeling the teenager had. Because logic said no one this handsome was human. "Who are you?"

He smiled a little, really just a quirk of lips, but it was enough for her to become light-headed. "My name is Ash Battle."

"Of course it is. It suits you."

He laughed, and it sounded rusty, as though he did it seldom. "I thank you. I know who you are, or at least I know your name. Olinda Keaton, a delightful name for a delightful lady." He watched, charmed as she blushed and softly asked. "Would you know the babies' names Olinda?"

She raised surprised eyebrows. "Of course, don't you?"

"No, I do not."

"Oh, well this one here." She started dressing the baby, and he handed her a clean diaper. "Thank you. As I was saying, this one is Ion. I think because his hair is what my mother would have called platinum and his eyes are black." She finished dressing him and handed him to Ash, while she dressed and diapered the other baby, telling him. "This little one is called Steel. I think because his hair is jet black and his eyes are platinum."

"Who was it that chose their names?"

Olinda smiled and softly told him. "That would be the Sun Goddess. These are her gifts to the dragons."

Ash's eyebrows rose in shocked surprise. A Sun Goddess had gifted his two hatchlings to the dragon nation. Now the words of the dying female made sense. Olinda cuddled the baby and looked fully into the face of both man and dragon; she did not know how she knew what he was. There was no outward sign that proclaimed him to be a dragon, but there was no mistaking the awareness that filled her. And now she understood the feeling she had about the teenage boy; he too was a dragon. Sighing with delight as her eyes catalogued every inch of his face. She had been right, he was magnificent looking. Green eyes stared at her with a hint of amusement and something else she could not define. He was saved from the title beautiful, because of a slightly crooked nose, although the chiseled jaw helped with that as well. Olinda's mother would have described him as roguishly handsome. He looked strong, confident, and quite capable of achieving whatever he set his mind to. She wanted to reach out and touch his hair, which was so black it appeared as though it was blue. He had braided it into a long rope, and combined with his body and voice, he was everything a woman could wish for. Her voice became faint with a dreamy undertone as she stared at him while she explained. "Did you know they are Sun Dragons? I did not know that dragons existed, now I fear the knowing will change my life forever. Ash, could you take the baby please?"

Just as he slipped his hand under the hatchling, Olinda fell unconscious to the floor. Cursing loudly as Sage, Edith, and Prudence descended on them, Ash cradled both infants in his arms while his dragon worried over their Shadow. And as if the magic had been waiting for that instant in time. All the dragons in the room were released from the spell they had been under, and pandemonium broke out. Sage slid to the floor next to Olinda, while Prudence took one baby from Ash as he handed the other to Edith. With a nod to Sage, he picked up Olinda. "I think we need to leave. Where do you suggest we go, Lady Sage?"

With a quick look at the dragons, who seemed to be getting themselves together, she said. "Your place. I think it would be the safest for her and the hatchlings."

"There is no danger to them here?" He told her with a slight frown.

"Is there not, and yet between the three of them they be-spelled the dragons in this room and perhaps everywhere? So until we can make sense of this, they are to be protected."

He smiled with admiration. "I apologize. I did not take that into consideration, unlike you who would make a great Commander."

Sage grinned. "Well, thank you. I will call your brothers and the Dragon Lord for you."

He looked down into the face of his future. "You know dragonkind well, my Lady."

"Oh please, we are well past the Lady thing; Sage will do."

"Well past." Mumbled Edith.

They both ignored her as Ash inclined his head. "As you will, Sage. I think we will go to the new apartment Lady Verity has placed aside for me. Now, is it permissible for the hatchlings to be taken from medical?"

It had only been two weeks since his crazy long-distance flight to bring them here. Prudence nodded. "Yes, they were released from the incubators this morning. They will be fine as long as we keep them warm." In saying that, she handed Edith and Sage blankets to wrap the babies in. When they thought they were covered enough, Ash led them from the room with Olinda in his arms. His dragon crooning to his Shadow and hatchlings.

CHAPTER EIGHT:

O linda opened her eyes and quickly closed them again, waking in a room she did not know was a disturbing and terrifying experience. Sorting through her fear to her memories was an exercise in self-discipline, especially as she did not want the panic she felt to overwhelm her. The last thing she remembered was a beautiful giant of a man and two baby boys who glowed gold, and they were all dragons. That she remembered very well. In truth, it was probably something she would remember for the rest of her life.

Opening her eyes for the second time, she found herself in a room which had to belong in a medieval castle; it was a bedroom for a princess. She frowned as she tried to make out what was above her, then sighed in pleasure. When her eyes focused and she realized it was a white silken canopy, she almost jumped from the bed. She, Olinda Keaton, was in a bed with a canopy. Her fingers automatically started smoothing over the sheet as she looked around. The walls of the bedroom were a soft rose, and the drapes over the windows were a darker shade of red. The carpet appeared to be gray and the side tables were made from a type of white wood. There were also several doors built from a deep golden wood leading from the room. It was all beautiful, and Olinda could not have felt more out of place if she tried.

She looked at what her fingers were telling her brain about the sheets and blankets, which were luxurious and nothing like she had ever felt before. Then the figure sitting in the chair registered. It was almost like she had not wanted to acknowledge someone was in the room with her until she had no choice. Her hands clenched on the sheet as she croaked out. "Who are you?"

"My name is Charlie Kingsley."

Olinda pushed herself into a sitting position and reached for the glass of water on the side table. She looked at the woman sitting relaxed in a chair by the window. Her legs kicked out in front of her, with her hands in the pockets of the well-worn leather jacket. Olinda would put money on it that the woman had a weapon of some sort in one of those pockets. She had short black hair, and the eyes that stared unrelentingly at her were gray and cold. She reminded Olinda of a photo she had seen of her grandmother and her friends when they had been young in the early forties. Although they had not worn jeans with red tee-shirts under an old leather jacket.

"It is safe to drink." Charlie told her quietly as she studied the female. She and Storm had arrived back just this morning after a stressed Sage called, begging her to return. This slight female had apparently tried to kill Ash and his brothers and had shot at Prudence, who had saved herself by shrinking and hiding. Sharm had been forced to drug her over Ash's objections. Reighn had asked Charlie to evaluate the female to see if she was a gray one or something else. He meant Assassin. Which is why she had sat here with her hand in her pocket on her gun for the last five minutes, watching the female begin the process of waking up. The female was everything Ash described, and in time with care and attention, she would be beautiful. But she was no killer. Those honey-colored eyes held a healthy dose of suspicion as she stared at her over the glass. Which she was entitled to, but there was no memory of killing within her soul.

Olinda had finished the water and licked her lips before she asked. "Where are the babies?"

"Safe."

Olinda was unsure if she meant safe from her, or safe in general. "What happened to the man who spoke to me?"

Charlie quirked her lips in a half smile. "Before or after you tried to kill him?"

Olinda raised her eyebrows. She did not remember that, the last thing she did recall was falling from the seat. "Really, only tried, my aim must have been off."

"Funny, his name is Ash Battle, and he is a Dragon. In case you don't remember, you are at Dragon's Gap. You came here on a bus from somewhere; your name is Olinda..."

"I know what my name is." She growled as she rubbed her hands through her hair and looked shocked when they ran through soft, shiny locks. She looked at her hands; they were unscratched, and all the damage was gone. Quickly she felt her face, which was also healed, and now she thought about it she realized she was clean. Olinda lifted her eyes to see the woman's cold gray eyes on her. A tingle of awareness crawled over her skin as she asked. "What the hell happened to me?"

Charlie answered. "You were bathed by my friends and healed by my friend Edith's Shadow, a healer or doctor called Sharm."

"I am guessing Edith is a woman, and he is a what?"

Charlie bit her lip, then coming to a decision, said. "Listen, I have a feeling you are not going to be happy about what I am going to tell you. So how about you allow me to explain everything I need too, then you can get on with the yelling, kicking and biting thing you do?"

Olinda dropped her head into her hands as she whispered. "Oh, please say it isn't so?"

"I wish I could but I cannot." Charlie answered with a small smile.

"Tell me the one called Ash. Did I bite, kick or yell at him?"

Charlie grinned. "Oh yeah, apparently there was biting as well as a kick to the groin. The poor guy is just starting to walk straight again."

Olinda pulled the pillow over her face and groaned loudly. Charlie grinned as she watched the female with her cheeks bright red groan into the pillow. This female was no killer, a fighter, definitely, but she was too normal, or at one point, she had been normal. Now she was out of her depth and swimming hard, or so it seemed to Charlie. She said now to see her reaction. "His brother..." She shook her head as Olinda lifted the pillow to look at her with sorrowful eyes. Charlie shrugged as she said. "I tell them and tell them, never think a female will not shoot you or use a knife, but did they believe me?" She shook her head. "The answer is no, they did not. Well, they do now. On the whole, the last three days have been hell for them and fun for you."

"So, I have been here for three days?"

"No, you have been here four; three of those were hard on the males."

"Oh, please say I never killed anyone."

"You did not." She watched her put the pillow over her face again and groan.

Definitely not a killer or a liar. Charlie thought she had developed a hardness about her like an armored shield, which would allow her to kill if needed, but the killer instinct was not natural. For Charlie, it was like she was looking at a lie because it was not a true instinct. Other than the shield, Olinda Keaton was just a female that was not quite human, placed in an intolerable situation.

Sighing, Olinda lifted the pillow off her face. "Well, that is something." She frowned as a fleeting image came to her. "The faerie, was she hurt?"

"Nope, she shrunk and flew away."

Olinda breathed out in relief. "Thank goodness. Well, if I am not going to like what you have to tell me. I should get dressed and would there be food and coffee?"

Charlie stood and stretched. "Yep, to both, bathroom is through there." She pointed to a door.

"Umm... Charlie, where am I actually?"

"Oh, this is Ash's place."

"Of course it is."

"Don't worry, he is not here. I kicked him and his brothers out when I got back this morning. Oh, and in case you wanted to know, it is Saturday. Shower and dress, I left you some clothes there." She indicated a chair with jeans, a shirt and underwear on it. "June said they would fit."

When Olinda went to ask who June was, Charlie said. "I promise I will explain when you are showered and dressed."

Olinda expelled a breath of air before she said. "Charlie, thank you, and I am sorry I was not very gracious when I woke."

"Olinda, I have a feeling you have a right to your suspicions, and sometimes they are all that keep us alive. Look, I know this is a big ask, but trust me, you are safe here. On my honor, there is nobody here that will hurt you."

Olinda nodded. "Okay, I will give it a go, for now."

Charlie gave her a serious look. "That is a start. Now I am out of here, I am sure you will find me when you are ready." So saying, she left, closing the door softly behind her.

Olinda looked under the sheet. "Naked, of course. Why not?" She slipped from the bed and walked into the bathroom and swooned. It was delicious, tiled walls in a soft white, with light blue veined marble sinks, and the shower was huge. Three people at least could fit in there. As she counted, her eyes opened wide, twelve shower heads, six on either side plus a rainfall. Who needs that? She wondered. She rubbed her hands over thick, soft towels that were laid on the heated rack as her eyes feasted on the bath. It was a large corner tub that had jets and would fit two. She so wanted to just fill it and soak for hours, but alas, she had somewhere to be and someone waiting for her. She thought about that for a minute; it was such a novel experience to have somewhere to be and someone waiting for her. She sighed, partly in trepidation and partly in anticipation, then looked around at the bathroom. The entire room was one of luxury.

She did a slow circle and halted when she saw the woman staring back at her from the full-length mirror. She had lost so much weight; she almost didn't recognize herself. Her cheeks were hollow and her eyes... her eyes were dark pits of pain, a haunted knowledge of fear and betrayal lived there.

Olinda shook her head. If her mother could see her now... what she wondered, would she be sad, angered, how would her mother really feel? Then she felt the anger that had been festering for months rise and almost swallow her as her heart hurt and her soul screamed. If her mother had just been honest with her, there would be no now, would there? She slapped her hands against the wall as pain exploded in her mind. There would be no one hunting her. She would not be somewhere that made her senses scream in warning.

Suddenly sadness so intense devoured her, and she heard a soothing voice plead with her. *Please, Olinda calm.*

No, leave me alone. I am allowed to feel this way, betrayed, abandoned. You who know so much and will not explain, have no right to tell me how to feel. Leave me to wallow in my pain and anger.

A heartfelt sigh washed through her mind, and then she was alone once more. Olinda hung her head and took several deep breaths, banishing the tears that would not fall along with the anger that seemed to be always present. "First a shower, then dress, then information and food." She said it aloud and her voice filled the room, removing the quietness that was unnerving. It was like the very air waited for her to do something. When she had been alone in the wildness, silence was her friend. Here it seemed wrong as she hurriedly stepped into the shower. "Okay, I can do this."

CHAPTER NINE:

C harlie stepped from the bedroom and strolled the corridor to the enormous lounge. Ash and Storm stood shoulder to shoulder, looking over the view of the lake. They both turned when she entered. Ash asked. "How is she?"

"Awake, sane and showering. She will be out in a few minutes; you cannot be here."

"I am her Shadow." He growled, causing Storm to move his shoulders in a small, uncomfortable shrug.

Charlie moved to his side, and his arm automatically went around her. She softened her instinctive snarl of rebuke as she felt Ash's pain and explained. "Right now, she trusts no one. You have seen that over the last three days, or her shooting Axl and stabbing you, wasn't example enough?"

"She was not in her right mind then. She was sick."

"Agreed, but do you know why she was like that?"

Ash shook his head. "We could not find out. She would just scream when we asked. Finally, Claire told Sage to call for you."

Charlie leaned her head against Storm's arm as she said. "I can tell you, there are only a few reasons a person reacts that way and they all come from some type of abuse. Ash, they called me back for this, so let me handle it."

He was unhappy, but he would do as she asked because he knew she was right. "Reighn said you would understand her the most. He was fearful she would hurt herself."

Charlie smiled as she assured him. "She will not, she is far stronger than that."

Ash sighed and ran his hand through his hair. "I too was frightened for her." He looked toward the bedroom. "To be near her is torture, my dragon and I are finding it hard to cope."

She looked at Storm with all the love she felt for him and told Ash. "I understand. Give me time and give her time. How are the hatchlings?"

He smiled. "They miss their Mama, but at least they do not whimper and cry like they did before."

Storm finally said. "Sun dragons, what do the histories say?"

Ash shrugged. "Keeper is looking through all the written text now."

They heard the bedroom door open and close. Both males moved swiftly from the room. Charlie heard the front door closing behind them just as Olinda entered from the hall. She stood in jeans with a blue tee-shirt and her old high tops on. "He was here?"

Charlie nodded. "With my husband, they left. I asked him to give you some space."

"Did I really stab him?"

"Yes, but he forgives you."

Impressed, Charlie realized Olinda had been listening and to do so, she would have had to be in the hallway. How she wondered had this female accomplished that, without her and two dragons sensing her. Edith was right. There was more to this female than a lost waif.

Olinda shoved her hands into the back pockets of her jeans as she said. "So coffee, food and an explanation, I think you said."

"I did." Charlie moved past her and frowned, wondering what else was wrong, something was missing but she could not place what it was.

Olinda looked at the place Ash had been, she could swear it felt like he was still in the room. She shook her head. *Active imagination perhaps.* Shrugging, she followed Charlie to the kitchen, where she was placing food along with coffee on the table.

"Help yourself."

CHAPTER TEN:

Keeper stood and stretched his back. "Impossible!"

He had been at the history books for the last two days. Researching sun dragons and Ella's origins. So far, he had discovered nothing about Ella that did not lead straight back to her family. As for the hatchlings, he had researched plenty, which was a vast amount of conjecture and very little fact.

He'd read everything he got his hands on from his library and everything the historians had, which was everything he had in his collection. And still he did not believe that apart from a line here and there in one or two books, there was nothing about sun dragons written anywhere. He had found references to reports of oral stories about sun dragons which had been spoken about throughout history. It just seemed that no one thought to write the actual stories down. It was mildly frustrating and, if he was honest; intriguing to the scholar in him.

"You are Keeper Kingsley?" Asked a deep bass voice from behind him.

Keeper sighed, he knew he should have turned the table around to face the door, as Johner had advised weeks before. Turning slowly, his dragon snarled loudly. He too had not heard the male enter. It was disconcerting for them both to know they had let their guard down.

Instantly, Keeper became wary as he watched the male move farther into the room he was using, in what would eventually be the library. "I am."

The male's hands opened and closed; an action Keeper had seen before on former Hunters and Shields. A sword hand his Sire called it, an unconscious act warriors did when they were without their swords. The male looked at the opened books spread over the surface of the large table and overflowing to the floor. "You are Shadow to Ella Field?"

Keeper nodded. "Are you her father?"

The dragon snorted. "No, I will visit the one that calls himself that and his family soon. I am her uncle from her birth parents, on her sire's side."

Keeper raised his eyebrows, the only sign of his surprise. "I see, Ella is my Shadow."

Worriedly, the male asked. "They have not threatened to take her from you?"

Keeper inclined his head. "Yes, they did, however they failed. I will not tolerate Ella to be hurt, nor will my family, and unless you do not realize it, the Dragon Lord is part of my family."

"I did not miss that." The male said. "I am thankful, I worried I would be too late."

"For what?"

He looked at Keeper. "What do you know of your Shadow?"

Keeper eyed the male and saw a hardened warrior and he would hazard a guess, he was an Elite at least as old as Reighn. He had short red hair, close cropped to his skull with hard brown eyes, and sported a well-trimmed mustache and goatee. He spoke with a brogue that denoted his highland origins and once Keeper looked for it, he saw his Ella in the male dragon and smiled. "I would say not enough, and you are proof of that. What line are you?"

"Slorah, from the First Dragons, before the Romans named us Caledoni, known today as Celts. Ella and I are the last of our line. I am Finlay Slorah."

Keeper nodded. "Obviously, you are a royal?"

Suspiciously Fin stated. "My ancestor was a cousin to Kato Kingslayer."

Keeper sighed and pinched the bridge of his nose. "So far back, cousin to our ancestors. I never looked that far into the past. Sad to say, the first historians only considered the First Dragons to be those with a variation of the family name

Kingsley. I have scholars going through all the old texts and reinstating all the names of the original First Dragons. We have not got to your line yet, but now you are here, maybe you would be willing to help with that?"

"I would be pleased to make all the documents I have available to you. So you have been searching?"

"Yes, Ella on our bonding developed a ring of purple, much as you have in your eyes."

Finlay sighed, unsurprised the ring was showing, it only appeared when he was emotionally charged as he was now. "It only shows occasionally, as it was with my brother. Our Sire told us we had it since birth. Ella's father and I were the only ones in our line to breed true. It seems Ella has as well. Is the color permanent?"

"No, it comes and goes. Reighn and Sharm believe it is based on emotion, which makes sense." Keeper seemed to be talking to himself. "Of course, that would explain the physical differences she has to the Fields and their interest in her. I suppose."

"It would. So you know Ella is not from their line?" Finlay asked, relaxing a little.

Keeper nodded. "We only recently suspected. Reighn our Dragon Lord..."

"Asked my brother, Shadow to Ella to research the possibility. Commander Finlay Slorah. I am pleased you are home."

They both spun around to be confronted by Reighn, Lars, and Johner. "My Lord." Fin bowed deeply. He liked and respected Reighn, he had many fond memories of playing with Reighn, Storm, Ash and Ace as a youth. Unfortunately, due to living on separate continents, they had managed to get together only on the rare occasion, but it had always been amusing. "I am pleased to be home as well."

Reighn clasped arms with him. "I see you have met Keeper. These are our brothers, Lars my Prime and Johner my Castle Commander."

He clasped arms with each male. Reighn smiled as he told

the other three. "It has been too many years since we last stood in each other's presence."

Fin smiled. "Far too many years. How are Storm, Ace and Ash?"

"Storm is bonded, Ash is trying to become bonded and Ace will be home soon."

Lars said. "I feel a male's night to catch Finlay up on all the happenings of Dragon's Gap is warranted."

Reighn asked. "Any excuse to drink dragon ale, brother."

"Well, there is that, but at least this is a legitimate reason."

Fin raised an eyebrow. "Even I see that as weak."

They all laughed, then Reighn asked. "So Ella is from your line?"

"That is so."

Reighn nodded with a pleased smile. Keeper asked him. "You suspected?"

"I did. She has the look of him. Fin and his family were known to be dedicated to dragonkind. Fin is the finest swordsman ever trained. Even better than the Battle brothers."

Fin asked. "Who?"

Reighn quietly said. "The Tomas brothers."

"I see." They could see the dragon putting two and two together. "I feel I need to be caught up as Lars has said with Dragon's Gap and my friends?"

Reighn said. "You do and will be. So where have you been?"

"Chasing dragons but not here." He and Reighn smiled at the others surprised reactions as Fin told them. "Dragons fly but not always on Earth."

Keeper grinned. "I have read that."

There was general laughter from his brothers at the often quoted saying, which they all knew was true. Reighn told them. "It has always been that some Shields have gone off world to hunt for the wild ones. It is hopeful those that remained away will come home now."

Fin said. "It was not that we did not like the former Dragon

Lord's rule. It was more that we were not in line with many of our elder's direction on where dragonkind needed to go. Too many fingers in the pies as a friend of mine quotes."

Reighn nodded. "He is right, there were. We have reduced that now. So what called you home?"

"Recently, I was told that our new Dragon Lord has made changes for the better and that my niece was alive and bonded." He nodded to Reighn and then Keeper.

Lars asked. "Who told you such?"

"An Elemental, not two days ago."

"You thought Ella was dead?" Keeper asked, thinking it was the only thing that would have kept this dragon away from her.

Fin replied. "Yes, along with my brother and his Shadow."

Every now and again, Reighn, Storm, or one of the Battle brothers had tried to find Finlay and had always failed. They had not thought to look off world. In the end, they had come to the erroneous conclusion their friend had taken his own life.

Reighn said now. "It seems there are questions to be asked and answered. Prime, take Commander Johner and a unit of castle guards and bring the Field family to court, all the family. No excuses and no reasons given, just have them in court. Also Lars, ask Stan and Jacks to attend, they have been looking into the Fields finances. They should have something by now." As they turned to leave, Reighn said. "Lars I do not care how the Fields arrive or in what condition, as long as they are able to answer questions. And while I remember, make sure the healer, Donald Patten appears. It seems his rehabilitation is not going well. Court will be in session at two o'clock."

Lars said. "Edee will be pleased."

Reighn grimaced as he snarled. "Leave, annoying males."

They saluted, and quickly left, smiles on their faces. Reighn said to Fin. "I expect you there as well. Keeper, you had better find Ella and introduce her to her uncle."

"Yes, my Lord." He pulled his phone out and said. "Edee…"

Reighn sighed and gave Keeper a dirty look as he pulled his own phone from his pocket while he started walking from the room. "Sage, my soul."

Keeper said. "Edith, can you come to our place, please?"

"Why?"

"Edee, it is about Ella."

"I will be there in two. Where are you?"

"At the Library."

"Huh! I am outside." They heard the door open and close, then her footsteps come closer. As Keeper closed his phone, he said to Fin. "The Lady that is coming is Edith, Sharm's Shadow. She is Ella's friend, and you should know she is a Grounder."

Fin's eyebrows went up over his brown eyes. "Really? I did not know they still existed."

Edith rounded the doorway. "They do. So what about Ella?"

Keeper introduced Fin. "Edee, this is Finlay Slorah. Ella's uncle, her true uncle from her birth parents."

Edith said nothing for a minute as she looked the male up and down. Just when Finlay was starting to feel uncomfortable, she hissed out a breath. "Oh thank the Goddess, she is not related to the vipers." Then she fell on the startled male, hugging him and saying. "This is wonderful. I am so happy." She released him with a huge smile on her face and asked Keeper. "Can I tell them, please let me tell them?"

He laughed, firstly; at the male's astounded expression and secondly; at Edith's request. "No, you cannot. Reighn has convened court."

"Ohh!" She pouted. "Not fun."

"You can come to court at two o'clock today, where he has demanded the Fields be present and as a bonus he has demanded Donald attend."

She bounced on her toes. "The twat, now that is what I call a two for one deal."

Keeper grinned at her excitement. "Edee, we are going to our place. Ella needs to be told and introduced to her uncle."

Edith nodded. "She will need Mama Verity, and I need to tell Sharm."

"I will organize them." Keeper said, then asked the dragon. "Where are you staying?"

He shrugged. "I have not thought about it."

Keeper said. "Please stay with us. Ella and you will need time to talk and find out about each other."

He hesitantly asked. "She will not mind?"

Edith asked before Keeper could reply. "Did you leave because you did not care about Ella?"

He looked shocked. "No, I thought she was dead as her Dam and Sire were."

Edith shrugged. "So why would she not like you?" He did not answer, just stared at her. Edith asked. "One question I have for you. How did they get Ella?"

Fin replied. "I cannot answer that as I do not know, but I would very much like to find out."

Keeper said. "Oh, I have no doubt our Lord will be asking that question and several more and will get answers."

"Or I will." Edith muttered under her breath as she turned to leave. "So, Keeper, your mother is visiting Sharm and Ella at work. I will take Commander Finlay to your place."

"Work... Ella works?" Asked a startled Finlay.

Edith looked at Keeper and then Fin again and asked Keeper. "What?"

He hurriedly explained. "Commander Slorah is surprised Ella works. Females that have been raised by females like Ella's mother rarely work, they do not consider working a very ladylike behavior."

"Oh yeah, that archaic drivel."

Keeper agreed. "Correct and we know it is." Hoping to stop any more of Edith's hot words on the subject of the elders, he said to Finlay. "Ella is a healer, a very talented one."

Fin smiled. "My brother was a scientist, a very talented one. Maybe she inherited that from him?"

Edith's face softened as she said. "I bet she did. Keeper, I

61

will take Commander Fin to your place so he can clean up and change clothes. Oh, do you have a change of clothes?"

Fin nodded. "I do. For court, no."

"Do not worry, I will ask June to organize something for you." Keeper told him. "If you would please go with Edee, she will take care of you and explain who June is and a few of the other people in Ella's life."

With a nod to Keeper and a smile to Edith, he left with her. While Keeper was left to tell his Shadow she needed to return home. Keeper looked around and said to his dragon, who had listened closely to what had been said. *So two impossible things in one week, amazing!*

Our Shadow will be pleased.

I hope so. He seems to be an honourable and brave dragon.

His dragon snorted and said. *He better be both. Our Shadow is well loved.*

Let us hope he stays around long enough for Ella to get to know him.

His dragon replied. *Male wants a home.*

Well, don't we all?

CHAPTER ELEVEN:

O linda pushed her plate away. She had eaten more in this one meal than she could remember eating in several days, if not weeks. "That was nice, thank you."

Charlie smiled, the female had eaten less than what Kelsey would for a meal. She passed her a cup of coffee, which she had denied her until Olinda had finished eating, as Sharm ordered.

"Prudence cooked for you. Sharm, the healer I told you about, has said you are to eat every two or three hours or when you are hungry. It will restart your metabolism and stretch your stomach muscles."

"Okay, that makes sense." Olinda sipped her coffee and closed her eyes. Now this was coffee, it tasted like ambrosia. While she had been eating, Charlie had filled her in on where she was, the castle, and the members of the royal family. Also, about the town named Dragon's Gap. Olinda had asked her to explain shifters and the many types of species there were. Charlie had listed the ones she knew and their attributes. There apparently was a Faerie Grove, which Olinda found fascinating. Now, as she sat sipping her coffee, pleasantly full, she sighed. "Such a lot to understand and learn."

Charlie agreed. "Although you seem like you would be up for that."

Olinda gave her a small smile. "Yeah. I enjoy learning or did." She asked. "Who was the other male with Ash when I came in?"

"Oh, that was Storm, my Shadow."

"Okay, a Shadow is what exactly?"

"Shadow, is what dragons call a mate or husband and wife; it is a unisex term. It stands for soul shadow as we shadow each other's souls."

"Wow! That is just so... so sweet. How long have you been together?"

"Not long and it is called bonded instead of married. Now I have a question for you?"

Olinda smiled. "Really, just one, go ahead ask."

Charlie liked Olinda; she was just snarky enough not to be rude or unpleasant. She was positive it was a defense Olinda used to protect herself. Underneath all that bravado, she was fairly sure the female was just holding it together. "Have you always had soft feet?" At her puzzled expression, she smiled, realizing Olinda did not know what she was referring to. "Walking softly. It is an unusual trait unless you have been trained."

"Oh, that?" Olinda sighed. "As long as I have been alive, I could do that. It seems to go along with the voice in my head."

"Huh! Now that is interesting."

"What, the voice?" Olinda looked at her from the corner of her eyes. Expecting her to call her a liar or scoff at her for admitting she had a voice in her head.

"Yeah, look, you are not alone in having a voice in your head. Think about where I told you we are, and who the inhabitants are." Olinda did, and her eyes opened wide. Charlie nodded as she said. "Exactly, but that does not explain you. We know you are not a dragon or shifter or even faerie. So what are you Olinda Keaton?"

Olinda frowned and stated. "Until recently, I assumed I was human. So your guess is as good as mine?"

"What does your voice say?"

"She will not answer, she ignores my questions and believe me, as I have asked plenty of times. Also, we had a disagreement, so she is not here again."

Charlie looked into her coffee cup rather than look at Olinda, in an effort to suppress the laugh at her indignant tone. "So what did you disagree about?"

"We disagreed, because I say I have the right to be pissed

off, and she has no right to tell me I cannot be. If she is unwilling to answer questions or something along those lines."

"That would do it."

Olinda grimaced. "Of course, now she is probably sulking somewhere. So do you have kids?"

"Young, we call them young, and hatchlings if they are a dragon under a year old. I have three, two daughters. One a five-year-old, a two-year-old and a hatchling."

"Are they all, you know, dragon?"

Charlie shook her head. "No, only the baby. The eldest girl is a bob cat. My second daughter is... Well, like you. We have no idea."

"Do you want to know?"

"Sure, then we will know what will happen as she develops and grows. In case you were wondering, we adopted or claimed, as they call it here, all three."

Olinda brushed her hands through her hair. "This feels weird. I have spoken and been in someone's company more since I woke, than I have in months."

Charlie asked. "You feeling closed in?"

"Yep, sort of."

"So maybe it is time you told me about what caused you to run in the first place."

Olinda nodded. "Only seems fair."

One more cup of coffee later, she finally came to the end of her tale. Charlie had taken notes of the town she had lived in with her mother and the names of Thea and her family. She had explained they had Hunters who looked into towns and people who did what Thea and her brother did. Olinda was pleased, and she thought hard to recall as many details as she could of the names of the towns they had almost caught her in. As well as what the people and towns looked like. She mumbled, not so much to Charlie, but more to herself. "I think the worst of it is, I lost all the photos of my life, of my mom. I have my memories but not having the photos hurts and makes all this, funnily enough, even worse."

Charlie understood that; she had one photo of Harper and her mom, which she had carried around since she was young. Scarlett had given her a few more of her mother as a child and teenager, but having none of the mother she knew or her adored sister hurt. "Yeah, I get that. I can have someone go look for you at that address if you write it down for me, and a list of what you want them to find. If they can."

Eagerly, Olinda grabbed the paper and started writing. "I hope they can. There are photo albums and my laptop, which I would love to have back. Seriously, that would be great."

She passed the list to Charlie, who was surprised to see so little on it. "So no clothes or sentimental pieces?"

"No, apart from my photos, there is nothing of that old life I want. I doubt any of my clothes would fit me anyway. Truthfully, I mostly wore what I have on now. Unless I was working. No, leave them, I will have to go shopping, although what I will use for money... yeah, I will have to get a job."

Charlie shook her head. "No, Ash will pay for them."

"The hell he will, I am no man's toy!" Retorted an outraged Olinda.

Charlie laughed at her fiery announcement. "Shit, Olinda, no one who listened to what you have been through, would even dare suggest that. You need to calm your pistols, female."

Olinda settled and shook her head, a bemused smile playing around her mouth as she thought about how quickly she had turned down help. Was she that prideful or was it the name Ash that set her off, she could not tell. Uncomfortable with her outburst, she asked. "So why would he pay for my stuff?"

"Olinda, you know why, he is your Shadow."

"Why... why is he hell bent on me? Surely there is a nice dragon lady, somewhere out there panting, just for him?"

Charlie shrugged while she tried to get that image out of her mind. "Probably!" She was amused to see Olinda frown at her quick agreement. "But life is strange. You may as well ask, why is the grass green or the sky blue?"

Olinda smirked as she said. "I actually have answers for those questions."

A smiling Charlie growled. "Shut the hell up female, it is what it is."

Olinda shook her head. "But paying. I don't know Charlie?"

"Dragons cannot find Shadows among dragons, very few females have been born over the last few hundred years. In fact, until we came into their lives, they were on the brink of extinction."

"Oh well, that sort of..." Olinda thought about that for a moment, then shook her head. "Nah, doesn't help." She ran her hands through her hair again, it had grown. She mused, this was another sign she was starting to feel normal, and she was worried about the length of her hair.

Charlie nodded. "Think of it this way, there is one person in the entire world who will forever have your back. He will never cheat on you or abuse you or any young you are fortunate to have. Dragons have absolutely no concept of divorce, and he will love you forever. It is written into their DNA."

Olinda swallowed hard and whispered. "You sort of cannot argue with that."

Charlie agreed. "So?"

"Well, looks like I am shopping."

Charlie laid a phone on the table. "For you, there are names and numbers programmed in. I am two, June is three and cabs are four."

"Who is first?" asked Olinda, already knowing the answer.

"Ash."

"Of course he is. Did he buy this phone?" Olinda looked at it like it was a snake.

"Yes, it won't bite." Charlie said with a smile.

"If I take it... it means I am accepting everything." Olinda whispered. Her eyes were still haunted, but Charlie was sure she could see a softening in them. "Everything Charlie!"

Charlie sympathized with her as she stated. "The time for

not accepting your new reality has passed my friend."

Olinda sighed in agreement. "I don't have a very good track record with friends."

Charlie grinned. "Got that, although you have never had a friend like me before."

Olinda looked into eyes that she had thought were cold and hard and saw laughter, acceptance and understanding in their depths. "Well, that is true. What can it hurt? I know how to run now, so okay."

Charlie grinned. "This is true."

She did not inform her that there were dragons who could and would find her. No matter where she ran to. Charlie told her with a tone of annoyance in her voice. "One more thing, shifters and dragons find the terms man and woman annoying for some obscure, ridiculous reason. They use female and male."

Olinda nodded, hearing the tone. "Had that argument already. I see."

"Many... many, friggin times." She looked at Olinda and asked. "So what about the hatchlings?"

Rubbing her eyes, she looked panicked and said. "I don't know. Can I leave it for a few days? I mean, they are being looked after right, and there is so much I need to..." She waved her hand around and quickly stood, grabbing the phone. "I need to shop, so how do I get there?"

"There is a cab waiting for you."

"Oh okay... sooo?"

"Turn left and take the lift to the main floor, she will be there."

"Okay, and thanks for this." Olinda held the phone up and waved her other hand around, indicating the food and information.

Charlie started to say, "You are welcome..." but she was talking to an empty room. She sighed instead, thinking, poor Ash, and poor hatchlings, but most of all she felt sorry for Olinda. As she stood, she sighed again, remembering she had not told Olinda that the hatchlings were pining for their mother. She could only hope Olinda would want them soon, before it was too late.

CHAPTER TWELVE:

O linda almost ran from the apartment. Charlie had been right, the walls were closing in on her. It was like there was a stone weight sitting on her chest making breathing hard; she kept running until she made the lift. Once inside, she stood with her head down, her throat closing up with the sadness that leaving the apartment and her babies was causing. She had lied to Charlie when she said she could leave them for a few days; she knew it would be impossible to do so. She just needed a little time to sort out her new reality, to realize where she was and who she was now.

As soon as the lift doors open, she stumbled along the short hallway, seeing nothing of the beautiful architecture or paintings and tapestries that lined the castle walls. Nor did she see Sage, who watched the forlorn female when she stopped on the steps leading from the castle. Sage felt sorry for Olinda, the life she was walking into was going to be so different, and she would be asked to come to terms with it quickly. Her hatchlings and Shadow needed her, but as she looked at the frail female, she wondered if they were asking too much.

Olinda took in several breaths of the crisp air, hoping the pain in her heart would lessen. She closed her eyes and stood for a moment just breathing, letting her heartrate settle. She knew the babies were safe. She could feel their gentle pull on her heart and the sorrowful dragon as he sang for her. She wanted them to stop and pleaded for it all too just go away; it was all too much. Too much sadness, too much wanting. Her heart ached as her arms did for the feel of her sons. Sobs lodged in her chest, adding to the stone that was already there. Then it was like a curtain dropped between them and her: she knew they were there, but the pull from both babies and dragon was gone. She exhaled in relief; she had no idea who or what had given her the peace she sought, but she was grateful. *For a little while, just a little while. Thank you.*

She felt a feeling of contriteness and understanding fill her mind. Suddenly she realised who had helped her; she sent a thank you to the voice. When she opened her eyes, she saw a teenage girl standing by a car.

Charlie heard the front door open and close, the only sign Olinda had left the apartment. So soft-footed. How was that possible? As good as she herself was, she could never walk so softly. She sniffed the air, detecting soap, shampoo, and the conditioner Olinda had used. But no actual scent of the female herself. She let her mind run back over the scents in the bedroom and realized there had been no scent there, either. That was why she had believed something was not right. People always left a trace of themselves behind, unless a spell was used. To have no scent naturally was an aberration that left Charlie mystified. She knew of no creature who could do that. She walked slowly toward the smaller lounge, knowing Storm and Ash had been there listening to their conversation and she bet Olinda had known as well.

Storm kissed her. "You are sad."

"I am, she has not had it easy. They hunted her mercilessly. It would seem they obviously know something we do not about her."

Ash said. "I have called for my brothers they will lead the hunt for these people." He almost spat the word people.

Charlie said. "When they are finished with them. I have a list here of things for your brothers to get for her. If her apartment is still there or her stuff is."

He nodded. "They will see to it." Then he asked hopefully. "The hatchlings?"

She shook her head. "No. She will not deal with that yet, it is not that she does not care. I think she is just so overwhelmed. Ash try to remember, she has been on her own for months. Hiding, running, living in fear. I get the impression she never lived like that before. She is a quick study though, very intelligent. Quick to grasp a situation and make it work for her. This... this situation is just confusing for her. She is thrown back into the world again, and it is not her world or the world she knew. Then, on top of all that, we are asking her to trust all of us. She needs to find her balance, to come to terms with herself. You, the hatchlings, where she is... We are asking a lot from her."

Storm said. "So trust is an issue."

"Among other things. But she is willing to try, at least that is something." She said directly to Ash. "I basically had to beg her to spend your money." He smiled a little as Charlie added. "It was pitiful!"

His smile grew at her tone and he was relieved when she told him. "I got her to take the phone, but I would not expect her to keep it on."

"Thank you Charlie, for everything."

"I hope I helped. I like her; she is my kind of people."

He nodded as he told her. "Claire said you were the only one who would understand her."

Just then, Sage walked in and asked. "How did it go?"

Charlie replied. "Okay, for the most part, she is accepting of Ash, although she is ambivalent about it. Trust issues and you should know she has a voice she hears in her mind that guides her. Apparently it has always been there."

"But Edee said she was not shifter, dragon or faerie. Right?"

"She did." Ash answered.

"What is she?" Sage demanded of the three.

They all shrugged, as none of them had any answers for her. Charlie sighed as she explained. "She does not know, until recently she assumed she was human."

Sage frowned as she asked. "And what of the hatchlings?"

"No, not yet, she barely dealt with everything I threw at her."

"Well, she will have to get over herself, they need her. We will not allow them to die."

They all looked at her; this was not the normal sweet Sage they were all used to. Something had happened, they could feel it. Ash asked. "What has happened Sage, to make you so on edge?"

"The Dragon Lord has convened court for two o'clock."

"Today?!" Storm asked.

"Yes, there are developments with Ella."

Charlie smiled, and it was not a nice one, which made Storm grin. "Her family has finally pissed him off?"

Sage did not smile, but her tone lightened when she said. "Something like that. So this female..."

"Olinda." Ash stated. "Her name is Olinda, and I think you know she is my Shadow."

Sage looked at him with a slight smile on her face. "Huh, well okay." She said nothing for a minute, and they all could see she was conversing with Reighn. When she finished, she looked at Ash and with a softer tone asked. "What do we know about Olinda?"

Charlie told her what she had discovered, and then Ash told her who he was sending to lead the hunt. When they had both finished, she said to Charlie and Ash. "Contact Mitch and his mate, they will help." "Okay, so I will leave you to it. See you all in court at two. I would advise you not to be late, and Charlie, talk to Verity about what you should wear. No reflection on your style, but none of us are used to this court stuff."

"You can say that again and thanks I will." Charlie agreed as she frowned. "I am sure I have something appropriate in my closet."

Storm raised an eyebrow at her words. "I am sure you will find something." Thinking of her closets, which were filled with clothes from her frequent shopping expeditions with Sage, Ella and Claire. He had not realized his Shadow loved to shop when they had first bonded. He secretly thought she had not known it either until she came to Dragon's Gap. Ash asked. "What about Olinda?"

Sage shook her head and said apologetically. "No, it is to be a closed hearing; she is far too new, and as Charlie said, she has enough to deal with."

He bowed, as they all did. "As you wish, Dragon Lady."

Sage grinned as she waved and left. After she had gone, Storm said. "She is growing into the position well."

Ash nodded. "Very well indeed."

CHAPTER THIRTEEN:

Keeper and Ella walked into their apartment, followed by his Dam and Sharm. Ella asked, as she placed her bag on the hall table. "Why is the Dragon Lord holding court on a Saturday, has this ever happened before?"

"No, never that any of us can remember."

Ella asked as he opened the door into the lounge. "So why now?"

A deep voice with a brogue answered her. "That would be because of me, lass."

Ella looked at the male as he stood next to Edith. He was huge and somewhat familiar. "Hello. Do I know you?"

He shook his head. "I am sad to say, you do not."

"Oh, are you a friend of Edee's?"

"Edith." Sharm asked mildly. "Someone you wish to introduce me to?"

Verity stared at the male. He reminded her of someone, but she could not put her finger on who. Edith grinned and asked Keeper. "Want me to tell them?"

He shook his head. "No, thank you Edee. Please, everyone sit and I will explain."

He held Ella's hand as he showed her to her chair as Sharm held a chair out for his Dam. The male held a chair for Edith, who smiled at him, then winked at Sharm, who grinned as his dragon said. *Our Shadow is up to something.*

Sharm asked. *When is she not?*

Keeper said in his thoughtful voice. "My Shadow, I have some news..."

"About my family?" She asked eagerly as she brought her attention back to him.

"In a way, yes. I could find nothing in any of the records."

Ella looked downcast and puzzled. Why was he telling her this now, in front of this male? "Well, I am sure you will." She encouraged him as she looked at the male staring intently at her. She was surprised to find she did not feel uncomfortable, like she normally did when she was stared at. In fact, she felt intrigued.

Keeper said. "No, my bonded, I will not because there will be nothing there."

Her attention went back to Keeper. Sadness wrapped around her as she asked softly. "Why?" She looked at the male dragon, then at Keeper again. "Keeper, why is this male here?"

"Ella, this is Finlay Slorah. He is your uncle on your Sire's side and not the Sire you grew up with."

Ella sat perfectly still and whispered. "You are certain I am not their daughter?"

Keeper smiled as he reassured her. "No, my love you are not."

She turned slowly like a puppet toward the silent male and thought he looked scared... no, not scared, but definitely apprehensive. "What was my Sire's name?"

Finlay took a breath. "Liam... Liam Slorah. Your Dam's name was Morag; I am sorry I cannot remember her surname before bonding. I have tried, but it will not come to memory. Maybe I did not know it? I was only in my fifties when Liam and Morag bonded. It was a very long time ago, many years before you were born."

Keeper said. "I will find it for you Ella."

Ella looked confused. "Thank you, Keeper. I do not understand. I am young, only one hundred and fifty."

Edith sucked in a breath. "One hundred and fifty. What the hell!"

Sharm laughed and said. "One dollar for the swear jar my love, how did you not know?"

"Well, why would I? Seriously one hundred and fifty." She eyed Ella. "You look twenty?"

Ella nodded. "Thank you and long lived, remember?"

Edith frowned as she looked at Verity, who said archly. "Never, you mind Missy."

Edith swallowed what she was going to say and refused to look at Sharm, instead saying. "The vipers, you are the middle sister. It makes no sense?"

Ella said. "What do you not understand? They are young too."

Edith had her doubts and, looking at Keeper and the others, she thought she was not alone. "Females have not been conceived or at least not in the last two hundred or so years, or so we have been led to believe."

Now she had everyone frowning. "That is so." Sharm agreed, he then asked Fin. "How did your brother accomplish Ella's conception?"

"Sharm you don't know." Mocked Edith.

"My soul, your wit astounds me."

"Was he making fun of me?" She asked Verity.

"Of course he was dear."

Fin smiled, as did Ella and Keeper at their banter. Fin rubbed his face and his accent thickened as he told them. "To answer your question, all I can say is I do not know exactly. They had been together for several hundred years, and then Morag was with child. She was confined to bed for the duration. It was most vexing for her, as I remember. I unfortunately was deployed and did not return until ten years later, where I expected to meet my niece or nephew and instead was told they had all perished. Every member of my family." They could still hear, all this time later, the horror and pain in his voice.

"What were you told happened?" Keeper asked him. He could see Ella wanted to know, but knew she would not ask.

"Apparently, there was a fire while Morag was confined. Liam would not leave her; they died together." He shook his head, looking with repentant eyes at Ella. "I see now I should have investigated more. Forgive me, niece."

Ella took his hand in hers. "Of course I do."

Sharm asked. "Who did the investigation?"

Finlay's eyes hardened and they all could see the dangerous warrior within. He looked at Keeper. "How can I reach Lord Reighn?"

"Come this way, I will call him for you."

Fin stood and looked down on Ella's beautiful face. "Niece, I would never have allowed you to be with them. I would have made my home with you. We would have been together as your parents would have wanted. We would have been a family."

Ella stood and threw herself into his arms. "I know... I know... Oh, Uncle Finlay, we have much to talk about, and we are family."

He hugged her back, tears entering his eyes and his voice evidenced by the husky tone of his words. "Yes, lass, we have much to talk about. I will not leave you now."

Ella cried as he held her to him, after a few minutes she pulled away, and he kissed her cheek. "Sweet Ella, so very much your Mama's daughter, but I think with my brother's heart."

"And yours." Ella said huskily.

He nodded. "Maybe... Maybe so."

She sat as Keeper squeezed her hand and smiled up at him. "I am fine my heart, just fine."

He kissed her and whispered. "I know."

Edith said. "Keeper, you should ask Reighn to look into the age of the vipers. I think he will be surprised."

He nodded. "My thinking exactly Edee."

When Keeper and Finlay left, Edith asked. "Ella, are you okay?"

She dabbed at her eyes as Verity hugged her, she had remained silent until now. Saddened at the news of Ella's birth parent's deaths and angry at the Fields for their deception, she said now. "Of course she is. This is wonderful news. Well, not about your parents my dear, but the fact you are not the Field's. Now that is just..."

Ella cut her off. "Wonderful!" She smiled happily. "It is and nerve racking. He seems very nice, don't you think?"

Edith said. "He is real nice and, under all that war stuff, gentle. I like him, as does Keeper."

Ella grinned. "I have an uncle, a real uncle that is all mine." She laughed with the other three. "I am free from them, Mama Verity. I am free."

Verity shared a smile with Edith and Sharm. It was the first time Ella had called her Mama Verity.

"Yes my daughter, you are free."

Sharm asked his mother. "So this is what court is about today?"

"So, your father has told me, he says questions are to be asked. Reighn is not happy, not happy at all. Hence the convening of court on a Saturday, we have two hours to eat lunch and change. Does Commander Finlay have court clothes?"

Edith nodded. "June sent a shield uniform for him. He was pleased she had all his commendations added, and is enthralled with how she knew. Oh, did I tell you, Donald, the twat, will be there."

Sharm groaned, and not just at her description. Edith told him with a glint in her eyes. "I know, but this will be the last time you get to see him."

Suspiciously, he asked. "You know this how?"

Edith shrugged one shoulder. "I just have a feeling, he has annoyed Reighn pass redemption."

Sharm said. "Part of me hopes he is there because he has changed his ways. The other half fears it is because the reports we have received about him are true." He sighed. "Either way, we will find out this afternoon. Ella, I am happy for you. Mama, we will see you later. Please tell Keeper to contact me if he has a need. We will see you all at two o'clock."

Edith and Sharm left, leaving a shaken but happy Ella and a thankful Verity behind. Gently, she said to Ella. "Well, let us get some food ready and do you know what you will wear? It has to be spectacular but sedate."

Ella smiled. "I have the exact dress."

CHAPTER FOURTEEN:

O linda had the cab drop her outside a hairdresser with the name. "Madam Paula's."

She had never been in a place like this before. It really looked to high-end for her. When she had her hair cut in the past, it had always been at a mall salon. The same with her nails, but the driver had assured her she would be taken care of here. She looked up and down the street before straightening her shoulders and venturing into the salon, and was taken aback when she found out Charlie had made her an appointment.

Two and a half hours later she walked out feeling, if not healthier, at least looking better. Her hair was now styled in soft waves and cut to a manageable length. Her face and hands had been steamed, massaged, and moisturized. Her nails were shaped and polished in a cheeky red, which made her smile each time she glimpsed them. She had admitted to the nail technician; it was a color she would never have dared used before. But as she watched the polish go on, she decided this was a new chapter in her life. So new life... new Olinda.

Buoyed by her reception and experience at the salon, she wandered into a designer clothes shop. A place she would never have thought to enter in her previous life, but she reminded herself she was the new edition of Olinda. She braced herself and opened the door and was greeted warmly by a female named Lilly, who appeared to be around her own age and very perky.

Lilly told her an account had been established for her already. Obviously Ash had decided she needed to have new clothes, and when she caught sight of herself in the full-length mirror, she decided he was not wrong. Her borrowed clothing hung on her slender frame. It was a sad fact nothing she wore fit with the stylish haircut or the polished nails.

One look at her by the older sales lady and she was taken under her wing, so to speak. Lady May politely told Lilly to re-stock the shelves. She then quietly told Olinda, Lilly was de-lightful but a little insensitive. Olinda took that to mean Lilly did not understand that Olinda's body was not the only thing delicate about her at the moment. From the sympathetic ex-pression on Lady May's face, she could see the female knew her weight loss was not from a fashion decision.

She thanked her for her consideration and smiled when Lady May said she had seen almost everything that life had to throw at a person. Olinda assumed from that a skinny body like hers would not be of concern for the dragon. She thought that Lady May was about fifty years old, but she remembered Charlie telling her dragons aged slowly. She could have been aged in the hundreds for all Olinda knew.

Once she told Lady May what she had in the way of clothes. She was seated in a soft chair and a few minutes later models walked out from behind a curtain. Lady May had chosen dresses, jeans, trousers and loose tops as well as a few de-signer tee-shirts, jackets, coats and formal clothes for her to inspect. Finally, after consulting with that good lady. Olinda agreed on a few selected outfits she could use for work and a couple of dresses to wear if she was to dine out. She brought a jacket and several pairs of jeans and tops as well, and promised to return for more clothes when she had replaced the weight she had lost. She was a little dismayed when she had seen the number of parcels she would have to carry. Until Lady May assured her they would send all her pur-chases to her residence. She also told her, all the shops would do the same; it was all part of the experience of shopping at Dragon's Gap. Olinda said her goodbyes, promising once more that she would return, and as she walked away, she worried at the thought that Lady May knew where she was living. She supposed everyone knew she was staying at Ash's, and to be honest; she was unsure how she felt about that.

After leaving the clothes shop she went into a lingerie shop where she brought underwear she had only ever dreamed of and nighties that were never intended for sleeping in. Along with some very practical nightwear and robes. She eyed the two styles and decided on the whole; they balanced each other out and if a picture of Ash lingered in her mind as she looked at the sexy items she purchased she could not help that. She smiled and decided not to think too hard about the reason, and hastened to the shoe shop. A shop that had everything she ever wanted, including a magnificent pair of soft leather steel capped boots. After a lengthy debate with herself, she replaced her high tops for new ones. Saying a fond farewell to the old pair, reminding herself again as she let them go. This was a new life and a new Olinda. Her last stop before food was a drugstore where she could buy shampoo, conditioner and other essentials. Five hours had passed, and Olinda was feeling hungry. She stopped at the hamburger place, grabbing the last table outside under a large red umbrella. It was a perfect place to watch people in Dragon's Gap pass by.

Olinda felt the amour she had donned for the last three months start to fall away. She thought about it and came to the conclusion that it began dissolving when she had woken to find the no-nonsense Charlie sitting waiting for her. No, that was not true, she thought it was when she had picked up her babies. Oops! Hatchlings, she smiled to herself; she had to remember that was the Dragon word for dragon babies. She sighed, knowing it was neither of those instances, honesty compelled her to admit it was when Ash had spoken to her. That was when the first piece of shield around her heart had cracked and fallen away.

She shook her head and smiled just before the cheerful teenager arrived and asked her what she wanted to eat. She ordered a burger and fries with salad and a vanilla shake. Then went back to people watching, letting her mind rest and think of nothing, although her habitual wariness remained. When her meal arrived, she was dismayed to see so much food on her plate. But she gave it a valiant effort and ate as much as she could, plowing through a quarter of the burger and eating a few fries. She desperately wanted to eat the salad, it looked so tasty, but there was no room left in her stomach, so she passed on the delicious-looking bowl of greens.

The waitress returned and removed her plate with a frown instead of her cheerful expression. Within minutes the proprietor arrived and ask why she had not eaten the entire meal as other diners did. She explained she had been ill and could not eat everything; he was immediately sympathetic and before she left; he gifted her a container that would keep the new smaller hamburger and fries he made for her warm and the milkshake cold.

He also sent one of his staff to buy her a backpack to place everything in, then refused payment. She was swallowed up with gratitude and touched that he cared enough to be so kind. Before she knew it, another chip of her armor fell away. When she had tried to thank him, he had waved her off, but made her promise to come back so he could feed her properly. She had smiled and promised she would.

Olinda wandered the streets looking at houses and the new construction that was going on around the town. For the first time in months, she had nowhere to run to, no one chasing her and her thoughts were not filled with fear. It was peaceful and yet she felt lost; the feelings were as annoying as the lack of the voice in her head. Finally, her feet carried her to a house that proclaimed to be.

"Grace's Home."

She stood with her hands shoved into the back pockets of her jeans and looked it over. A wide porch wrapped around the entire house, and the blue with white trim made it appear inviting. But not as much as the gardens, which just screamed love and attention. Before she could censor herself, she walked up the steps and around the deck until she came to a swing seat. Taking off her backpack, she slumped down and closed her eyes, allowing the feeling of peace and love to sweep her away.

Grace walked toward the resting female, two glasses of sweet tea in her hands. She placed them on the table and sat in the opposite rocker, knowing she would not have long to wait. Just because the female's eyes were closed did not mean she slept deeply. Someone who had been on the run for over three months and almost captured as many times as this young female had been, did not sleep in unknown territory. Grace knew on some level the female would know she was there and sure enough, seconds after she had taken her seat. Honey-colored eyes flicked open, and she surprised Grace by not leaping to her feet in panic.

Her voice was husky as she said. "Hello, I am sorry to have intruded on your home."

Grace handed her a frosty glass of tea. "My name is Grace and you are most welcome, all are welcome to Grace's home."

Olinda took a sip of tea and said. "Thank you for that and this delicious tea. I am guessing you know who I am?"

Grace smiled. "Olinda Keaton, a recent arrival. I have been expecting you."

"Really?"

"Oh yes, everyone at one time or another will make their way here."

"Why?"

Grace sipped her tea and rocked as she thought about the question. "Some for comfort, some for advice. Some just for the peace my home and gardens offers them and some because they need to talk out the decisions they have already made."

They said nothing for a while, just rocked and listened to the birds sing as they sipped their tea. Olinda broke the silence, her eyes a little wild as she said. "She says he is my Shadow. I have twins waiting for me. I can feel them pining and his dragon singing to me... for me! He is more than I ever dreamed of in a man, sorry, I mean male. In fact, I don't think I could have dreamed someone like him up. They are sun dragons, and he is a dragon. Dragons, for heaven's sake, and that is another thing, all these new terms. Shifters, witches, faeries. What do I know of this world, other than what I have read or been told? Why should I stay to be a wife... damn it, Shadow and mother," she muttered, "how is that even possible?" Olinda looked at her and said. "She said he will never cheat. Never leave me. Love me for eternity. It is totally unbelievably in its simplicity. How does one trust that... trust any of that? Two babies, a male that apparently loves me, even though he knows squat about me." She laughed with a tinge of hysteria in her tones and gulped some more tea when she heard it herself, then sighed and whispered. "And me a librarian. I have no idea how to live in this life? I barely lived in the one I had before. Seriously Grace, I ask you, how is it, I know you are a bear and Charlie is a half-faerie. How did I know they were sun dragons or that he was a dragon? In my place, what would you do?" *There she finally asked it.* Olinda took a breath, then sipped more tea.

Grace rocked and nodded. "It seems like a handful of problems, but you know as well as I do what I am going to tell you." She waited a minute, then said soberly. "Olinda, sweet girl everything you have gone through has brought you here to meet all these challenges. Your strength keeps you balanced, and your tenacity will keep you holding on until you learn what you must to survive here. You are the type of person who will fight to make this work for you and all those who grace your life. Dear girl, never, ever undervalue love, yours or someone else'. It will see you through the good and bad times. Now you Olinda Keaton already know what you are going to do."

Olinda nodded and stopped the motion of the swing. She swallowed the last of her tea and stood, slipping her backpack on. "Yes, I know, and thank you for the drink and the comfort of your porch. Grace, you were right, some do come here to vent and learn they already have the answers."

Grace stood as well, she desperately wanted to reach out and smother the young female in a hug. But knew that would be too much for Olinda right now. As strong as she appeared to be, she was barely hanging on. Instead, she said softly. "You are welcome. Come back anytime. I will see you tomorrow."

Caught up in her thoughts, Olinda nodded, but did not register Grace's words. She gripped the straps of her backpack and hurried away. Grace waited until she made the corner of the street, then picked up the glasses and walked into her kitchen. "You were right, she found her way here."

Sage nodded. "I thought she may." She did not tell Grace that a little help from the dragon lady and witch never hurt. "So, did you help her?"

Grace raised surprised eyebrows as she placed the glasses in the dishwasher. "You did not listen?"

Sage shook her head. "No, I was busy thinking deep thoughts."

"Ahh, well, she already knew her answers. I hope I helped settle her enough to accept them. It must be terrible to have been betrayed as she was, especially by someone you love and cannot get answers from now."

"Yes." Sage sighed, thinking of Ash and his brothers. "Not as bad as when family do it, but still..."

"Oh no, dear one. I meant her mother; she betrayed her."

"Really, not her friend?"

"Well, of course she did, but no, I am talking of her mother. Olinda is not fully human, growing up believing the voice you hear is wrong, told that by your own mother. Who also did not tell you, your father was not human. Her mother had a lot to answer for."

Sage mused. "Maybe her mother did not know?"

Grace sounded angry as she told her. "Oh she knew alright, she very much knew."

Sage looked at the angry She bear' and asked. "How do you know?"

"I, like you, am a mother, would you not know?"

"Yeah, I would, although Charlie and Storm have that problem. They do not know what Cara is."

Grace shook her head in disagreement. "No, they know she is not all human, and they will make sure she knows that as she grows up, they will not hide it from her. Olinda never even had that." Grace sighed. "So very sad, betrayed. At least Ash will help her with that."

Sage agreed. "Yeah, if anyone knows what it's like, he does."

CHAPTER FIFTEEN:

Olinda left Grace's home and continued her walk along the streets of the town. She was unsettled because as she'd talked to Grace, she realized she had just swapped one set of fears for another, and now she did not know what to do. What direction to run in, or how to make this right. And her voice was still not anywhere in evidence.

She wandered aimlessly until she came to what she assumed was an empty building. Why she was compelled to enter this particular building, she did not understand and could not have explained it to anyone if asked. When she tried the handle, the door swung open, whereby she found herself in a place she knew well. The setting was strange and the walls and floors were different, but the scent… that scent was unmistakable. This was a normal slice of her past, and she felt giddy with anticipation in discovering something she could understand. She placed her backpack on the floor by a long table that was scattered with half-opened books. She accidentally kicked several as she made to walk around to go toward what looked like the main library. Bending to pick them up, she saw even more books.

She almost giggled as bubbles of excitement exploded in her chest. *Huh, happiness! I remember what that feels like.*

"So food, drink and then work, although first I should look around." She mumbled out loud and suited action to words, walking through the door to what was going to be a library. Hands on hips, she smiled at the handwritten words on one wall.

'Dragon's Gap library.' On the other wall she saw the same handwriting, but this time the words said. 'Keepers Hoard. Come and Borrow a Book.'

Olinda grinned, someone had a sense of humor. She looked around and saw two lifts tucked into a corner. Next to what looked like restrooms, they were close to a door that was marked. Storage Rooms. The place was enormous, with a mezzanine floor and a wide spiral staircase between floors. This was larger than any library she had ever worked in. Most of the shelves stood empty, but row upon row of books littered the floor and were stacked in piles on the shelves. Someone had made towers of books in front of the other shelving. As she walked between the stacks, she saw a large room with cables coming from the walls and ceiling, she guess it was internet cabling. There were several rooms large enough to be used for conferences or lectures.

Olinda imagined what she would do if she were able to design this library. She would use one of the rooms for a reading room, with large comfortable armchairs and couches. It would be for older people or just people that wanted company or just to sit with others and read. Maybe she would have a coffee and cake counter as well. Then there was a room she would definitely turn into a children's play area where stories could be told, and young ones could select books. It would need restrooms close by for the little ones. Then she would have a room just for school-age children to use for homework or assignments. Jammed packed with reference books and screens for watching lectures. Upstairs would be for the technical division, manuscripts, and preserved documents, as well as aged tomes for all the scholars. She spun in a circle and hugged herself; she could work here and bring the twins with her, immerse them in words right from the start, and give them the love of reading. *Yeah! She could see that.* Olinda sighed, dreams she was just dreaming. Taking her food and sitting with the wall as a backrest. Surrounded by books, she took a bite of the still hot hamburger and dreamed of a future she wished for.

Ash was worried Olinda had not returned by the time he was to be in court. Prudence was looking after the twins, but he had hoped his Shadow would have arrived back by now. He had paced his apartment since his brothers departed for the hunt as he worried about Olinda. His dragon was just as worried. *Our Shadow is frightened. She does not trust us.*

I know old friend; we just have to give her the time Charlie said she needs.

When will she return?

Ash rubbed his head as he told his dragon. *I don't know, soon I hope.*

She may run, she is very good at it.

Ash thought about that and remembered the love on her face for the twins. Remembered the sorrow he had seen when she had stabbed him, the tears she would not let fall. *No, she will not run, she just needs to find her balance.*

His dragon asked hesitantly. *When she has found it. Will she want us?*

Ash could hear the worry in his voice, but had no answer for him. He truly did not know if she would. Such a lot had happened to her in a short space of time. He was concerned she would be unable to get past... Well, her past.

He knew how hard his father's betrayal had been for him and his brothers, as evidenced by Ace, who had taken himself from his family. After returning to the castle, to the Kingsley brothers and to Verity and Rene`. He and his brothers had found comfort and understanding, which had helped them to see why the sins of their father were not their burdens to carry. But their Sires alone, and each of them in their own way, had made peace with their past. Thankfully, he was free now and could help Olinda find that same freedom. But it was hard to help someone, if they were not around, to be helped. His pacing led him to the twin's room where he and his dragon watched the hatchlings sleep.

Prudence slipped in and stood next to him, assuring him. "Commander Ash, I swear I will care and protect them."

"I know you will, Prudence. I was just hoping their mother would have returned by now."

Prudence sighed. "Lady Olinda has much to overcome in a short amount of time. To find she is more than human, a mother and Shadow on top of everything else. It must be confusing."

He nodded. "I am sure you are right. I must leave. Court will not wait for anyone. I will see you when we are finished."

"I will not leave until you are home."

"Thank you Prudence."

CHAPTER SIXTEEN:

Ash strode into court. The cavernous room was reduced by three quarters due to the partitions put in place, making the large courtroom a more reasonable size. He knew this was Sage's idea and as he looked around, he could not find fault with her reasoning.

Edith waved him over to where she was seated. "Hey, how's it going?"

He grimaced. "Olinda did not come back."

"Well, she is shopping. We females tend to get distracted when we are shopping." He nodded but did not seem reassured; Edith took pity on him and said gently. "Listen, if she is not back when we are finished here. I will organize help to look for her."

Ash felt a little better about that. "I thank you Edee."

"Aww, no problem..." Sharm arrived in the room and stopped whatever she was going to say next. They both watched him stalk across the floor with a sour expression on his face.

Edith murmured. "Oh dear, he must have seen the twat."

Confused, Ash asked. "The what?"

"Donald." She whispered as Sharm arrived and threw himself into the chair.

"He is an absolute nightmare. The foolish male thinks he is here to be rewarded for doing his punishment in record time." Edith laughed as Sharm snorted. "Have you ever heard of a prisoner being rewarded? The male is delusional."

Ash argued. "Or he wants you all to think he is."

Sharm looked at him. "Damn it!" He got up and stormed from the room.

Edith asked. "Is damn a cuss word?"

Ash shrugged. "I don't think so, but I am not the authority on cuss words, that would be Keeper."

He was sure he heard her say damn it under her breath, but then Keeper, Ella and Fin arrived and took seats close to them. Ash was happy to see his friend, and they fell immediately to talking over old times and catching up on Ash's brothers and why Fin was here.

Edith asked Ella. "You okay?"

"I am. He is so nice, and he has photos of my parents. Isn't that wonderful?"

Edith agreed it was and asked Keeper, who sat looking around with a contented smile. "You okay?"

He nodded. "Ella is happy, therefore, I am."

"You're a simple kind of dragon, aren't you, brother?"

She had to laugh at his smug expression when he told her. "I truly am."

Charlie and Storm came in with Stanvis and Jacks. Lars escorted Claire and June in. Everyone could see he did not look happy. "Looks like things went bad for him." Edith said softly to Keeper, who nodded.

Claire sat and winked at Edith, murmuring. "He is so pissed off."

Edith nodded in return as Keeper said. "Five dollars for the swear jar."

Claire moaned. "But it is court day."

Keeper shrugged. "No one called for exceptions."

"We can do that?" Edith asked, just before Claire did.

Keeper told them while trying not to smirk. "Not now, now it is too late."

"So mean." Both Claire and Edith told him.

He grinned, then said. "And yet you love me."

Claire said to Edith. "You happy with this swear jar thing?"

"Not now!" Before she could add anymore. Sharm arrived back wearing a satisfied expression.

Ella asked Keeper who the forty males and females that sat away from them were. He looked over at them and whispered. "Nobles, Reighn has allowed to attend. I think they will either bear witness or give testimony."

Ella was going to comment when the door that admitted the Dragon Lord and Lady opened. Sage and Reighn were followed into court by Verity and Rene`, and none of them looked happy.

Sage took her seat and Ella sighed. Sage had such a nice dress style, even when she wore jeans and tee-shirts. Today she wore a knee-length, full-skirt dress in red and gold with a black cloak. She just looked so modern and regal. Her hair was in a coronet, and even her jewelry was simple but sophisticated. Verity was just as regal, she wore a similar outfit to Sage's. Except her hair was in a French roll and her earrings were adorned with purple stones. Although her dress was a more mature style with a less full skirt, she however did not wear a cloak, just a small jacket. They both looked very royal. It was enough to make Ella sigh again. Especially as they were accompanied by the dashing Dragon Lord and Lord Rene`, who wore full dress uniforms.

Sage stared out at her family and friends. She was pleased to see they had all taken Verity's advice on how to dress. It wasn't like court was a normal occasion in any of their lives. Seriously, if she could have avoided today, she would have, and she knew her friends thought the same. Well, maybe not Edith. Sage was sure Edith lived for stuff like this, and by the look of barely suppressed glee on Charlie's face. Maybe her too. She smiled when she saw Ella, who looked beautiful in one of her new purchases. It was the three quarter length long-sleeved dress with a square neckline in shades of blue. And she had on a diamond pendant which Sage remembered Keeper had surprised her with at their bonding party. She looked very chic, her hair, which she had styled in a French twist, showed off her matching diamond earrings. Ella was just so very feminine.

Sage almost swore when she noticed Edith in her sheathed black dress with a charcoal long-sleeved jacket. She'd left her white hair loose to fall down her back. She looked young and happy... no, not happy, content; it was a good look for her. Claire and Charlie must have coordinated, because they both wore dark trousers with pastel colored shirts and three quarter length leather jackets. It was amusing to see they had similar styles. Maybe their previous lives dictated how they dressed. Claire still had the black and white hair thing happening, but Charlie's short black hair looked like it had been blow dried. Amazingly feminine for her, she couldn't wait to tease her about that later. June and Jacks wore pencil style navy blue skirts with buttoned down jackets. They both wore subtle touches of make-up and only a few pieces of jewelry. Her attention was diverted from her friends as the doors opened. *Just as well,* she thought, *I'll be cataloguing and critiquing the males next.*

She watched Johner walk in with a unit of castle guards; he gave Reighn a nod when he rose from his seat, and in his deep voice ordered. "Commander, bring in the people I have asked to attend court."

The Nobles all moved restlessly when Reighn had spoken. Obviously, they were not happy about being here, thought Sage. Well, tough, none of them were, except Edith and Charlie and maybe Ella and then there was Fin. *Oh, shut up, Sage.*

Reighn asked through their bond. *Why are you nervous?*

I don't know... I just feel... I don't know. I wish this was over. There will be no winners here today.

She felt rather than heard him sigh as he told her. *No, my soul there will not. But justice will be done and witnessed. That is a win, is it not?*

She sent him a small smile. *Yes, you are right, and it is for Ella and her uncle.*

Johner called out the names of the people as they entered the court. "Cuthbert and Yestoria Field." The couple walked in for all intents and purposes as two middle-aged people, yet Reighn knew they were both well over the four thousand year mark.

Johner called out next. "Eugenia and Auremia Field."

The sisters followed their parents as they walked down the aisle between the rows of seats. When they got to where Ella sat with Keeper, they glared at her and Keeper with hatred. Ella lifted her chin and stared back contemptuously, causing them to lower their eyes and hurry past her. Especially when Keeper raised an eyebrow and placed his hand on his sword. Not the most attractive females, Reighn had ever seen for dragons. Maybe living a lie made one unattractive, or maybe the ugliness on the inside eventually found its way to the outside.

A sad thought. His dragon commented.

Reighn could see the family looked well rested and well groomed, not a hair out of place on any of them. And yet he knew Lars had removed the walking stick from Yestoria after she had hit two of Johner's guards with the heavy weapon. He was pleased at the guards, and Johner's restraint. They had not punished the family for the abuse. Johner reported Cuthbert had made a deal. If they could enter court without chains, he would not allow his family to misbehave; it looked like it was working. Although he could see Johner was taking no chances, he had guards with stun guns ready.

Reighn asked Cuthbert Field. "Is this all of your family?"

"Yes, my Lord, there are other members of my Shadow's family, but they reside on the other continent and have been estranged for many years."

Reighn knew this was true, well partly true, the family was not estranged or on the other side of the world now. They were actually in custody and in a cell beneath the castle. He had given their interrogation over to his father and his Shields. He now had the full story of what had happened to Fin's brother and Ella's parents. He addressed the court. "You may sit."

Once they had taken their seats, he asked Cuthbert Field. "Do you know why I have requested you to court on a Saturday?"

"No, my Lord."

"I see. Can you tell me then the ages of your daughters?"

"Certainly my Lord. Eugenia is one hundred and sixty. Ella is one hundred and fifty. Auremia is one hundred and ten."

"Would it surprise you to know that I know for a fact, your daughters Eugenia and Auremia are four hundred and forty and thirty, respectively?"

"Told you." Edith whispered to Ella's surprised gasp. Sage noticed several of the Nobles were just as surprised as she was.

"Yes my Lord, it would." Cuthbert Field said as he felt a drip of sweat run down his back. Yestoria tensed beside him. He imagined his daughters doing the same.

Reighn nodded as he softly said. "Yet they are. Maybe you can answer this question instead. Why did you steal Ella and raise her as your own?"

Cuthbert swallowed hard, it took him two tries before he could answer. "I... I... do not know what you mean, my Lord. Ella is our daughter."

Reighn grinned just a movement of his lips, but his eyes remained hard as they stared at the female Yestoria. "Yet your Shadow did not give birth to her. Did you Lady Field?"

Yestoria's face reflected her bitterness as her eyes spat fire and hatred at Reighn, but fear of him when she saw the merciless look in his eyes cooled her words. Without expression, she replied. "I have no knowledge of what you are talking about... my Lord."

It was impossible not to miss the pause she made before addressing him as my Lord. Reighn looked at her and her Shadow with dislike. "Take care Madam; my patience is not infinite. Your lies and yours, Lord Field have almost exhausted any compassion I could have for you. So as you will not grace us with the truth. I will tell you what I know... what my people have learned. Firstly; we will deal with the finances of Lord Field. Second Stanvis, and Lady Jacqueline, please inform the court of what you have found."

Stan and Jacks stood, and together they bowed to Reighn. Stan spoke for them both. "Dragon Lord and esteem court, we have searched the records of the estate of Lord and Lady Field, and my Lord we have come up empty."

"Empty, I am shocked." Reighn exclaimed, although all could hear he was anything but surprised. "Perhaps you could enlighten us how this can be?"

Cuthbert and Yestoria sat stunned as they listened to Stanvis. They had no idea there was an investigation into their finances. Fear snaked along their insides and etch lines on both their faces.

Stan flipped open a folder and said. "It seems my Lord; the Field family live on an income that comes from one source, and that is not from any work Lord Field or his Shadow or daughters do. In fact, my Lord, we could find no other income stream, other than the one deposit that arrives in their bank each month."

Reighn's stare bored into the couple. "I see, so they are destitute?"

Jacks shook her head; her English accent rang throughout the room as she answered him. "No, my Lord, far from it. They own the estate and contents within their home. They have a good-sized investment portfolio, which sadly under performs and their daughters, other than Lady Ella, have a sizable dowry. They are quite able to afford their lifestyle."

Reighn asked Stanvis. "Do you know where the money comes from?"

"Yes, my Lord."

"Thank you both, for your work."

The couple bowed again and retook their seats. Reighn looked at the family, then the Nobles in the room and said. "So, I will tell you what I know." He looked again at Ella and Fin.

Keeper took Ella's hand in his as he saw his brother struggling with what he was about to say. Which meant no one, least of all Ella, was going to like it. Out of the corner of his eye, he saw Shadow's taking all their bonded hands in theirs, for their comfort or their own, it was hard to say. Ella took her uncles in hers as Edith took Ash's, to his surprise, in hers.

Reighn took a breath and released it as he said. "Close to two hundred and forty-eight years ago, a scientist named Liam Slorah discovered a way to give his Shadow the gift she had always wanted, a hatchling. He took his sperm and her eggs and mixed and matched them with different components. Unfortunately, he is not here to ask how he was able to do so and his notes were destroyed. So we can only surmise on how it was done and in truth that does not matter. All that does matter is in one of his experiments he struck gold, so to speak, and he was able to implant a viable embryo into his Morag, his Shadow. Then they held their breaths and waited. It was not the first time this had been done. All over dragon society, experiments were being conducted to increase our population. So you can imagine Liam and Morag's delight when her body did not reject this embryo. Of course, her pregnancy came with challenges. She could not leave her bed to continue her normal life, but for Morag it was all worth it, to have her hatchling." Reighn stopped and looked again at the Field family, then Ella. "A month before, Morag was due to deliver her hatchling. Renata Philsna arrived at the home of Liam and Morag Slorah and demanded her child. It seems she had convinced herself Liam had stolen her embryo and implanted Morag with it. No matter what he or her Shadow or even her sister told her, she would not believe it, or so it appeared. This was the first strike of a campaign she waged against Liam and Morag Slorah. Every day for three weeks she stood outside their home, demanding her hatchling. She went to the police commissioner; he investigated and found nothing untoward. She then went to the medical commissioner; she investigated, but again still nothing was found to be suspicious. As you can imagine, all this took its toll on Morag, the constant harassment when she should have been enjoying the last weeks of her confinement, of her pregnancy. Instead, she was having to see her Shadow defend himself against this supposed crazed female. Sadly, Morag went into early labor. Not totally unexpected, but not ideal.

So on a night, which should have ended in joyful bliss instead ended in murder. How you may ask? Simply put, this was the night Renata took matters into her own hands. What her intentions were, we do not know or truthfully care about now. What we do know is she stole into the home of Liam and Morag and set a fire in the downstairs kitchen. And for reasons of her own, Renata hid in an upstairs hall closet. Unfortunately, what she did not realize was there was a faulty gas valve and the lower house exploded. With Morag in the early stages of labor, Liam, as any Shadow would, panicked and fearful for his Shadow and unborn hatchling rushed from the bedroom, carrying her in his arms. Renata stabbed him at the base of his neck just as he started down the stairs, killing him instantly. He dropped his poor laboring Morag, who tumbled down the stairs dying on impact. We will never know if Renata was insane, perhaps at that moment she was."

Reighn could see several of the forty Nobles nodding their heads; they were inclined to believe that Renata could have been insane.

He shook his head and said. "Although we must consider what she did next, and the insanity plea falls away. Realizing Liam and Morag had died, Renata cut the babe from her mother's dead body and ran."

Gasps and cries of outrage were quickly muffled. Ella was stunned, her face white with grief. Nothing could have prepared her for what she was hearing. Fin lowered his head as his eyes burned with grief and revenge. He felt a small, slim hand take his free one in a warm clasp. He turned his head to the side and saw the lithe she wolf, June, sitting beside him. He squeezed her hand in thanks.

Reighn finished the glass of water Sage handed him and continued. "There was rain that night which prevented the house from completely being destroyed, as Renata had hoped. In truth, she had nothing to worry about. After all, it was her sister's Shadow who would be the lead inspector for the county, and her Shadow was the local magistrate. Between the two males, they managed an excellent cover up."

By now Ella was quietly sobbing into Keeper's chest and June's head was on Fin's shoulder. He had placed an arm around her in comfort. Charlie sat with her hand in Storms, her face like stone which matched Edith's, who was white with fury. Sharm held her in his arms. In fact, all the females were being held, perhaps their Shadows feared they would leap from their chairs and kill the Field's or they needed the comfort. It was unclear.

Reighn cleared his throat as he looked first at a pale, blue-eyed Sage, then his Dam, who sat staring unflinchingly at Yestoria. Returning to his account of the tragedy, he said. "But I digress. Renata left the Slorah home with the babe in her arms and ended up at her sister's home. What could her sister and her sister's Shadow do? I or anyone else as an investigator would have called a healer for help and as her sibling, I would have demanded she tell me what happened. Then I would have called for help, not just for the hatchling, but for the obviously deranged female that was my sister. It would have been obvious the poor female was disturbed, and the hatchling just birthed. But I am forgetting the secret agenda. Yestoria had not wanted the Slorah's dead, or at least not Liam Slorah, but Renata did. Her plan called for Liam to die because she had only one thing on her mind, the hatchling. Renata wanted Morag's babe. What Yestoria wanted was the remedy for the lack of births. As a mid-level scientist, she wished to be the one to have discovered the cure for the population's demise. Imagine, if you will, what that discovery would have done for her reputation and the reputation of her family. Nobility would have come begging to have their own young. She would finally be where she felt she deserved to be, at the top of society. Even back then, social standing was everything to Yestoria and her Shadow. But Renata ruined everything by killing the Slorahs and burning the home down, or at least Liam's laboratory, which was next to the kitchen. There were no notes for Yestoria to steal. Sadly, they had nothing to show for their night's endeavors but a hatchling and the possibility that Liam had passed on his notes to his brother. Because every scientist knew, there were always back up notes and Yestoria knew Liam always made copies of his experiments. After all, he had been her instructor for many years. Yestoria convinced herself that Liam had sent his notes to his brother to safeguard. We have since learned the notes were in his laboratory as he was fine tuning his discovery, so they too were destroyed that night. Regardless, the Fields devised a plan, they would hold the child for a future trade. They covered up the events of the night with Renata and her Shadow, Cebern's help, and they would stay in England. Where they would place Renata in a nice nursing home run by dragons for dragons for a few months. A place for the distraught and unsettled. This was understandable, what with her thoughts about a hatchling being stolen and then the deaths of the Slorah's. Every female at that time understood the strain of not having their own young. It was a feasible excuse. In the meantime, her sister and her Shadow and the hatchling would leave and find another home far, far away at Dragon's Gap. Leaving their own daughters to live with nest families until they called for them. I am at a loss as to the reason for that decision, but it matters not to what happened. Later, when Finlay, Liam Slorah's brother came home and talked to Cuthbert and the magistrate Cebern. You Cuthbert discovered he did not have the notes so desperately sought by Yestoria and had no idea how his brother had produced a viable embryo. In his grief he answered all your questions, never once realizing you were trying to see if you could follow through on your Shadow's plan for a trade. Sadly for him and Ella, it never happened, and eventually he returned to his duties. Before he left, you could have lied once more and told him you saved her from the fire. You could have made any lie up to reunite uncle and niece, but you did not." Scornfully, Reighn stated. "Of course, as you have no honor, it would not have occurred to you to do so." Reighn took a breath and let the anger ease from his soul. He acknowledged Fin by saying. "Here the court wishes to welcome home Commander Finlay Slorah, brother to Liam Slorah and uncle to Ella Kingsley."

The Fields all groaned in dismay when Finlay stood. He bowed to Reighn and Sage. "Thank you, my Lord and my Lady. I am pleased to be home with my niece and friends."

He sat as Ella took his hand. Cuthbert hung his head in despair; he knew now they would be lucky to escape with their lives. Reighn nodded to Fin as he retook his seat, then he addressed the room again.

"Time passed, Ella grew, and the sisters eventually returned to their parents. All was well until Ella became older and every now and again a sign that she was royalty showed. Usually in the form of a ring of purple in her eyes, just as with her uncle and her sire, she had bred true. What to do? The Field's dared not tell her or admit their guilt, and then Ella took all those worries out of your hands. Did she not Cuthbert and Yestoria, she left your home. You could not deny her leaving or object to her discovering her natural talent for healing. You could not complain to Healer Sharm or myself. We would not have understood. Healers are always valued and families consider themselves fortunate to have a child with healing capabilities. We would have wanted to know what objection you could have against her helping dragonkind, especially as her Dam was a scientist in her own right. So you did the next best thing. You kept her under Yestoria's control, but then came along the Grounder. Edith Kingsley it must have come as a shock when she and Ella became friends. What could you do? It would be unlikely you could degrade her in Edith's eyes, as you had done to any friends Ella had made in the past. I am sure you heard of all the good Edith was doing in Dragon's Gap, and you knew there was no way she would abandon Ella. You could not frighten her or warn her off or even threaten her. She is a Shadow to royalty, and she herself is a mystic, where were you to turn. Edith had broken the control you exerted over Ella. You realized you were losing her, so you tried to rein her in by demanding she visit your estate. We can only guess at the pressure you placed her under while there, we do know at some point she threatened to talk to Edith about her relationship with you."

Edith touched Ella on the shoulder, whispering. "You used me to fight them?"

"I did. I am sorry Edee."

"Hush, so proud of you."

Reighn explained. "Ella was now independent, and after that failed visit, she was refusing to return to your estate. You could not make her, not with Edith helping her make friends. Why, even the Dragon Lady became her friend, as did the Queen of the Faeries. Her friends were increasing daily and counted among them were the liaisons. Just those females alone were bonded to powerful males, never mind the others she was becoming friends with. So what to do? It was simple really; you decided to have her bonded to a male of your choosing, but how to accomplish this. It must have seemed so easy, employ witches to make it happen. The shock you must have felt when you heard Ella and Keeper had become bonded. You realized it was only a matter of time until the conspiracy was revealed, panic set in. So you, Cuthbert and Yestoria needed an alternative plan. You contacted Renata and her Shadow Cebern, who told you they could have the bond dissolved. It was a new spell that had been talked about and as a magistrate, Cebern knew all about the spell. Unfortunately for them, they contacted a family of witches in England who contacted the Dragon Lady. You see, unbeknownst to you and your family; the word had gone out. No one was to help the Fields or anyone of their family without her approval. Apparently you Cuthbert and Yestoria did not get that memo."

Reighn spread his hands wide as he said. "So there you have it. Plans were made, witches contacted. Yestoria and her daughters then came to the castle to demand Ella return home with them. Sadly for the Fields, they met with Ella's friend June, our castle liaison. Along with Prime Lars and Commander Johner and ended up banished from the castle and here we are today."

Reighn once again looked at the family that had conspired to keep justice from Fin and Ella, and nodded to Johner who ordered.

"Family Field, you will stand for your judgment."

All four of them slowly stood, they were pale and not a one of them shed tears for what they had done.

Reighn said. "I find you all contemptible and without remorse. Now some may ask, why punish the daughters and to that I say, because they knew. They always knew and did nothing apart from treating Ella like a lesser being, as though she was of no importance." He placed his attention again on the parents as his dragon filled his voice. **"You did not take this child to protect her or keep her safe. You took her to use as a bargaining chip in a long stakes game. You did so to cover your participation in two murders and to protect a murderer."**

Reighn drew in a breath, and his dragon released his voice as he said. "You really are as culpable as Renata and I tell you now, she and her Shadow are in cells. And as I look at you two upstanding citizens of dragonkind. I ask myself why you allowed it to continue, why keep Ella. When you learned there were no notes, you could have sent her away or given her to her uncle. Years later, if you had told Ella what had happened or a version of what had happened. We all know what kind of person she is, she would almost invariably have forgiven you and Renata." He shook his head as he muttered. "Then I realized I do not need answers to these questions, because as my

Shadow advised me when I voiced those same queries to her. Would you tell the truth? I like her, think you would not. The fact is, you did none of these simple things to remedy this tragedy, and for that alone, I find you guilty. With the added charge for both Cuthbert Field and Cebern Philsna of fraud and abusing the trust of their Dragon Lord and the dragon nation, I find you guilty. For the murders of Liam and Morag Slorah and the kidnapping of the hatchling Slorah. I condemn you to the afterlife. You will have company, your sister Renata and her Shadow Cebern Philsna, were also found guilty." Reighn ordered. "Commander, take them away."

Cuthbert cried out. "Wait! We can explain."

"How?"

"She never wanted for anything. She was educated, clothed, what else were we to do?"

"Perhaps not murder her mother and father to start with. Love her and provide her with a genuine family." Said an angry Sage as she rose from her seat and stood next to Reighn.

Both of the Fields shook their heads. The once proud Lady Yestoria, reduced to the bitter female that she was, snarled. "You do not understand, with those notes we would have had standing and wealth far more than we have today and Renata would have had her young. Nobles who were begging for young of their own could have secured their family lines. With that information, I could have taken my own family into nobility where we belonged. If Liam had only shared with me when I asked him to, none of this would have happened. We are not all like her and her sister." She pointed at Verity with a sneer as she spat out. "Her, who sits there in judgment of us lesser ones..."

Verity stood and all could hear her dragon in her voice as she said. "You talk of my sister. You, who have no right to even think her name. She was light to your dark and I remember Anna telling me about you, Yestoria, and that crazy sister of yours. How spoiled you both were, how everything anyone else had you both coveted, and if you couldn't bully it off of them, you stole it. I know Renata never took that hatchling because she was desperate for a child. She was far too selfish to share herself with one. She did it because she was jealous. You both hated Morag, you, because she bonded to a brilliant male who dismissed you when he caught you bullying Morag. Renata took that hatchling to hurt Morag. I am sure it annoyed the hell out of her that Morag died. Renata would have wanted her to live, to prove she was better than her. She would have loved knowing she killed Morag's Shadow and had her child, and there was not a thing Morag could do about it. Especially with Cuthbert and Cebern covering for Renata. I imagine when that fell apart, as everything Renata touched did. The next best thing was the two of you gloating over being here. Knowing Anna and I had no idea about Ella and yet look at you now." Everyone could all see the smirk on Yestoria's face, even now she felt she had out smarted Verity.

Verity straightened her shoulders and said. "You were right to keep the knowledge of who Ella was from me, because if I had known, I would have killed you and Renata without a moment's thought. Just like after today, I will never think of you again and I will ensure your precious name will be wiped from the records. One death is not enough for you or Renata, may someone have mercy on your souls? I will not."

The smirk was wiped from Yestoria as her eyes bled hatred when Verity turned her back on her. She took a step toward Verity, only to be stopped by her Shadow when he held her to his side. Sage smiled and power surrounded her as her eyes turned bright blue and she told Yestoria. "Remain still female, I can make you hurt for days without killing you. By the time I finished with you, they would hear you begging for death on the other side of the world."

Yestoria looked horrified as she stared at the female, who she had thought was no more than a toy for the Dragon Lord.

She felt her heart thump hard in her chest with an emotion she had only recently become acquainted with, fear! Her Shadow secured her to his side with an arm around her waist as together they listened to their daughters turn on them without a thought.

Eugenia and Auremia fell to the floor as they begged Sage. "Please... Please my Lady, we were frightened of them, they made us do it."

Sage stared at the sisters without expression, then looked at their shocked parents. She read disbelief and then confusion in their eyes. She wanted to feel sorry for the shocked couple, but could not find it in her heart. Auremia cried. "We have lived under a tyrannical control. We lived in fear that we would misspeak."

Sage's face filled with scorn as she said. "How dare you? When it was the two of you who ridiculed Ella. You, who called her cinders, not that long ago to my sister June. Clumsy, ugly, pathetic, were those not names you called her as well? Yes, I see how you were scared. Get up, you pathetic, disgusting excuses for dragons and do not think I have forgotten the claws you threatened my sister with. For that alone I should banish you, for everything else, I have no mercy for you."

She stood together with Reighn, Verity and Rene` as Reighn said. "As my Shadow says, for that alone you should be banished, and you will be. Never again will you feel the world beneath your feet. Never again will you feel our sun on your faces. For you who think people are no better than toys for you to play with, I have given your lives over to the Elementals to do with as they choose."

With those words, the two females disappeared as their parents seemed unable to believe what had just happened, or maybe they did not believe their own lives were forfeited. Sage did not know or care anymore. Reighn ordered. "Commander Johner, escort the prisoners to the cells. Judgment will be served by morning."

This time, the older couple said nothing as Johner nodded and a unit of guards surrounded them. Johner looked to Verity who stepped down from the podium and hugged him as she spoke. It was his mother she had talked about, Anna her sister. He returned her hug and then with his guards escorted the prisoners from the court.

CHAPTER SEVENTEEN:

Once they were gone, Reighn nodded, and Lars called for the healer Donald to enter. Sharm groaned softly as the male walked in, or more rightly swaggered in. He looked around and sent Edith a mocking smile. She hissed as she started to stand, but both Sharm and Ash firmly held her in her seat.

The healer moved to the middle of the room and bowed to Reighn. "You wished to see me, my Lord?"

Reighn shook his head as he said. "Not really, Healer Patten. What I wished to do is forget you existed, but you denied me that with your continued subversive behavior. So here we are again, last time, your parents petitioned the court and at the request of your mentor, Chief Healer Kingsley. I sentenced you to administer to the shifters and Hunters under the direction of Commander Kilfer for the duration of two years."

Donald nodded as he said in a tone that bordered on disrespectful. "That is so, my Lord. And I performed my duties with extreme diligence, as I am sure the Commander reported to you."

"It was not a question. Remain silent."

Donald looked a little taken aback at the words and tone of the Dragon Lord, he gulped then nodded. Reighn sighed and pinched the bridge of his nose before saying. "As I was saying, it seems from the reports I have received, you have continued with your rhetoric of a pure nation and your subversive attitude."

Donald could not help himself as he interrupted him to state righteously. "In my off time, not while I was on duty. No matter what that old..."

"SILENCE!" Roared Reighn, his dragon lending power to his voice. **"Enough of this.** You are an idiot and I want rid of you. I have banished you from Earth for the duration of one thousand years. You will be assigned to Commander Slorah's former unit and if, after 500 years, you are still alive. We will reconvene to see if the sentence needs to stand or be renewed. You leave immediately."

He made a sign to Fin as Donald demanded. "Wait, I have no say in this… you cannot do this; I have rights… This is outrageous, what do my parents say… Master, what do you say?"

Sharm stood. "I say nothing, other than do your best to help as many as you can and stay alive."

Edith nodded. "Yeah, you twat. Try not to die too quickly."

Donald snarled. "It is because of her… that bitch you bonded…" He could say no more with Sharm's hand around his throat. The medic had moved so fast, no one had realized what he was doing until he spoke. "Never speak of her again or I will kill you, like the piece of shit you are. My Edith is more dragon than you could ever hope to be. You want to know where your parents are. They declined to come today because you have shamed them and they have told our Lord they disown you. They asked for you to be sent away until you realize what kind of fool you are." Finished speaking, his dragon growled low and menacingly at the cringing male. Then Sharm threw him to the floor, where he curled into a fetal position.

Charlie leaned over and whispered to Edith. "I take it back, no flab."

Edith sniffed. "Told yah, hard in all the right places." Causing several groans to be heard nearby.

Reighn said. "Commander, now please."

Fin opened a portal to the world he had come from and two Shields came through. They saluted Reighn, then Fin, and without a word they picked the cowering dragon up and dragged him back through the portal. They could hear him screaming as it closed.

Reighn sighed and said. "Court is finished for the day. Witnesses, I thank you for your attendance. Family, we will see you later." He and Sage and his parents left the same way they had entered.

June said. "Well, that was traumatic and quick."

Claire agreed, then said. "Look, we are all dressed up, let's go to Lucy's." A restaurant that had been opened for as long as Dragon's Gap had been around. It was a favorite of all the dragons.

Lars told them. "They are expecting us, let's go. We will drink and eat and talk. It will do us good."

Storm asked. "What of the others?"

Lars told them. "They will meet us there, this was Reighn's idea."

Charlie agreed. "I'm in. No young, sounds good."

All the parents agreed with smiles and nods. Ella asked Fin. "Do you want to come?"

He smiled as he answered. "Yes, very much, I was promised dragon ale."

"Yippee!" Edith cheered, she loved the beverage.

Sharm asked. "Ash, will you come?"

He shook his head as he turned his phone off. "I must find Olinda, Prudence said she has not returned."

Keeper told him. "We will help locate her, let's all go into town and look, that was where she was last seen."

Everyone followed him and Ash from the court and when they reached town, they split up and did a street by street search to find the wayward female. Keeper looked in several shops, then called into his library to find a book for Charlie. When he entered, he pulled up short as his dragon sniffed the air. Keeper felt the air against his skin and knew there was a difference to his building. It had nothing to do with the many books placed on the shelves or the clean pathways that had been made. Nor was it the detailed floor plan of the library and the drawings of each designated area, penciled precisely on the wall.

No, it had to do with the slim pale female who lay with books curled around her. Seemingly hugging her body as though they knew she was their protector, or they were hers. Ash entered just behind him and Keeper said. "I feel I should warn you, I will demand she come to work for me."

Ash looked around him even with his untrained eyes he could pick out the order amongst the chaos. "I think there will be no objection; someone who loves like this, should not be denied."

"Thank you, now take your Shadow home."

Ash walked to Olinda, saying. "Thank you my friend." He picked her up, and she instinctively curled into him and sighed.

Ash told her softly. "This is getting to be a habit, my Shadow."

She mumbled. "Ash..."

"Hush, you are safe, my heart."

"Safe... Ash?"

"Yes, with me." He exited from the library as a portal opened and walked through to their apartment.

Keeper shook his head. Impossibilities and a librarian who calls to books and shines the very air with her happiness. He told his dragon. *Dragon's Gap will never be the same again.*

His dragon's reply made him smile. *No, it will be better!*

CHAPTER EIGHTEEN:

W aking again in the same room was as unnerving as it had been the first time. She slowly looked around and found Ash sitting where Charlie had previously sat. "Hello."

He nodded to the side table. "Hello, there is juice for you. Sharm said you would need it."

Olinda shuffled up and leaned back against the pillows; she did a quick look under the covers and heaved a silent sigh. Still clothed, she reached for the juice, keeping her eyes on him. Dear Goddess, he was gorgeous with his long midnight black hair and green eyes. She wondered if males were meant to have eyes like that and were they meant to be that vibrant? He was impossibly handsome. It was like looking at a painting of the ideal male. She was almost too frightened to look beyond the face, to the body, fearing it would not live up to that face or perhaps fearing it would. Her mind buzzed with a sense of wonder and excitement. It was so hard to decide what she wanted, beauty or muscle. Honestly, she was not made of stone. Did the male not realize that flaunting himself in front of a vulnerable woman like her was torture? And she had just woken up. He snagged her attention with his next words, which she was sort of thankful for. If she had accidentally looked at his body, there could have been drooling. So embarrassing.

"We found you, Keeper and myself, in his library." She nodded as she sipped her juice, and he tried again. "Keeper is the youngest of the Kingsley brothers and the new owner of the library. He wants you to work for him. I said you probably would as you looked like you loved it, the books."

She nodded again, seriously his rusty voice just made her blood sing. She had read about lust, but reading and experiencing it was so very different. Ash sighed at her lack of response. He sniffed the air, but she had no scent, so he could not read what she was feeling. He ran his hand through his hair. "I was worried, it is five o'clock."

She nodded again. Wow, it was late, she had been gone for a while. She counted back, yeah, around nine when she had left this morning. No wonder he had been concerned. She finished the juice and asked as she looked at the glass instead of him. "So you are my Shadow and we have two special dragons who are considered myths. In fact, until they arrived here, that's exactly all they were, lines in a book. Now they are real and are to change dragonkind." She looked at him. "I read up, while I was there."

It was Ash's turn to nod. "I see."

Olinda decided to lay it all out for him. She had a lot of time to think while she read about Shadows and Dragon's Gap and the Sun dragons. "I do not know what to do here. I know what is expected of me, I just do not know if I can do it honestly? I don't know you or love you. Although I find it truly amazing you are my Shadow, but I just do not know if I can be that for you."

Ash asked with a slight smile. "What do you think is expected of you?"

Olinda blushed, she could not help it. "We are to bond... you know?" She waved her hand between the two of them.

Ash raised soot black eyebrows. "And you think we have to have love for that?"

Frowning, she asked. "Don't we?"

He smiled gently. "No, we need desire and lust, passion helps, love comes in time. You think every pair that bonded was in love?"

"Well, the books say, yes."

Ash stood as he said. "They lied my Shadow; they lied. It is what they want all females to think. Now tell me, do you find me attractive?"

Olinda snorted. "I'd have to be dead, not too."

Ash grinned. "Good, so would you bed me?"

"You mean have sex with you right, not like sleep with you?" She clarified. It never hurt, she reasoned, to make sure they were on the same page.

Ash's grin grew as his dragon murmured. *So adorable.*

"Yes, I mean join, have sex."

"Well again, I would have to be dead not to want to."

"That is good." He removed his boots, and then his jacket, as he did, he told her. "Because I find you most desirable and I definitely want to have sex with you."

"Please, like this?" She scoffed as she waved her hand over her body.

Ash stopped and looked at her. "Oh yes, there is nothing wrong with you that maybe a little more filling out would not take care of. But that is not what draws my dragon or me."

Wide-eyed, she asked. "What is?"

He smiled as he told her. "I will tell you soon."

Olinda was going to ask why she had to wait, and what did he think he was doing. Then he undid a button on his shirt, and she thought it seemed a redundant question. Instead, her eyes remained glued to the buttons he was undoing, as she cleared her throat and wished her lust filled mind could clear as easily. "Oh well, so we can like, get it on and stuff and you won't like be mad and stuff. Like if I... like, are not in love with you?"

Ash let her see his grin as he slid the shirt off his shoulders and was positive he heard a very feminine whimper. His hands went to his belt as he said. "There were a lot of likes and stuff in that question?"

Olinda grinned as well and almost swallowed her tongue as he slowly let his trousers drop to the floor. "I know, but I am embarrassed. I have never been with a male before and truthfully, books only tell you so much, and never about someone like you." She then said under her breath. "Oh my goddess, his body matches his face. I am lost to lust."

He almost laughed out loud and decided not to tell her just

yet that dragons had excellent hearing. Her observation did not deter him from stalking toward the bed. If anything, it made his decision to bond with his delightful Shadow more imperative.

Olinda watched him as he closed the distance between them and thought there was no other way to describe his advance other than stalking. When he reached the bed, he just kept on moving except on all fours as he crawled up the bed and over her. She shimmied down until she was lying flat on the mattress, and he hovered over her like a big blanket of maleness. She knew she was making sounds, but her mouth and brain were not in sync. One wanted her to shut up; the other was just overcome with hunger for the male, and she didn't even want to think about what her hands wanted to do.

Ash stared into eyes of molten honey and told her in a voice that had roughened with desire. "I will never cheat. I will never leave. I will never stop loving you, and I vow to wait until you love me. If that takes a lifetime, so be it. I will still be here with you."

Olinda moistened her lips with the tip of her tongue and swallowed as his eyes zeroed in on the movement. She could feel how much he was controlling himself, and a sizeable chunk of her armor slipped from her. She murmured huskily. "I do not know how to trust me anymore. My judgment got beat up, you know?"

"I do my soul. I really do."

She nodded, seeing the shaft of pain that entered his eyes. "Okay, so I want to discover that trust with you. So please keep those vows, and I swear I will work on trusting me enough to love you."

He lowered his face to hers, his mouth a hair's breadth away from her waiting lips, and as he expelled dragon's breath he whispered. "Agreed."

Then he kissed her. Olinda did something she had never done in her life before. She let go, released every hold on every part of her heart and body and wrapped her arms around her dragon and learned to fly.

CHAPTER NINETEEN:

V ery early the next morning, after a night, learning about making love with a male that was a dedicated and very thorough teacher. Olinda felt good, almost whole again. Most of the shield she had donned to protect her emotions and enable her to run from the hunters was gone.

She smiled as she snuck out of the bedroom. She was pleasantly sore in all the right places and decided she enjoyed being a student, especially with Ash, who was a patient and considerate instructor. She hoped she had made his night as special as he had made hers. They had talked as much as they had made love, and she thought they had learned a lot about each other. He had told her about his father, and she had told him about her mother and Thea. They also discussed his mother and his brothers; she had heard the deep love he held for them in the memories he shared. He told of his admiration and love for the Kingsley family and what they all meant to him and his brothers.

Apparently, they were all expected for Sunday family day, which started at breakfast around nine o'clock this morning. She looked at the time and saw it was only seven o'clock. She had time to see to the twins and shower and have coffee, which Ash promised he could make. Then she would get ready to meet the family. She walked into the nursery and came to a stop. A male stood between the twins' bassinets.

Instinct had her pulling her gun from the pocket of her robe. Thankfully, she had not given everything up. She had found the gun in the drawer by her bed when she rose. "You have one minute to tell me why I should not shoot you where you stand."

Sharm stilled as he heard her voice, he had not heard her

approach. It appeared Charlie was right; she did walk softly. He sniffed the air and could scent Ash, but as for her own scent, there was none. It was very intriguing. He said quietly, so as not to startle her. "Because I am your healer. My name is Sharm, I am friend to your Shadow, uncle to your hatchlings, and hopefully a friend to you. May I turn around?"

"Sure."

As he turned, she tracked him with the gun. He smiled when he saw her, she looked better since he had seen her last. He kept his hands in the air. It would be no problem to remove the gun from her hand. Dragons were very fast, and he was no exception, but if she felt more secure holding it, who was he to deny her? "Charlie said you had very soft feet and sad to say I did not really believe her."

Ash said casually from behind her. "Olinda, I will make coffee. Sharm, did you all have a nice time yesterday?"

With a smile and a raised eyebrow toward his friend, Sharm nodded. "Yes, we finished early, but it was fun."

Ash said to Olinda, who had still not lowered the gun. "Do not shoot my friend; his Shadow Edith has a decidedly sharp turn of phrase. Also, I really think it would seriously hurt your first impression with the Kingsley family." With that, he reached his long arm over her shoulder, kissed her cheek, and removed the gun from her hand. "Good morning, sweetheart."

"Morning."

"Now why do you have a gun on Sharm?"

"He was in here with the babies. I freaked out."

"Well, he would be. He needs to check them."

"You did not think to tell me that?"

Ash rubbed his cheek with the barrel of the gun. "I should have, I apologize." He grinned at Sharm as he asked. "How are they?"

Sharm dropped his hands. "They are well, they seem more settled this morning."

"Because I am here." Olinda told him as she walked over

and gently touched each baby.

"You can feel their emotions?" He asked her. "And they yours?"

She nodded. "Yes, and Ash's they love his scent. He smells of the winds." She looked at him. "I would like to meet your dragon and fly, may I?"

Ash nodded as he said. "He would like that. They know me?"

"Oh yes, they love their daddy. Really, first impressions?"

"Yes, first impressions."

She looked at Sharm and said. "I am sorry."

Sharm shook his head. "For what, being a Mama and protecting your hatchlings. Never apologize for that. I am sorry for startling you. I was hoping to have a quick check before we go down to family day."

Worriedly, Ash asked. "Will they be able to go?"

"Most definitely. Everyone is eager to meet you and them Olinda."

She nodded. "So Ash told me."

Grinning, he assured her. "It will not be so bad, you already know Ash. Charlie, me and Keeper."

"Who?" she asked Ash.

"I told you of Keeper last night."

"Oh yeah, I forgot."

Sharm nodded solemnly. "See, only a hundred of us left to meet. Easy."

Olinda's face went slack as she squeaked. "A hundred!"

Ash and Sharm burst out laughing at the look on her face. Ash finally managed to say. "No... No, there are not that many."

She scowled at them both. "For that you get to deal with the diapers and bottles, while I shower." And yes, she smirked at the expressions they were now wearing. She backed from the room and ran down the hall, calling back. "Don't forget you promised coffee."

Sharm said. "Ash, my friend, I think we got screwed on

this."

Ash snorted. "What do you mean we?"

Sharm snarled in reply. "I can leave."

Ash eyed his friend and asked. "Which one do you want?"

Thankfully, Edith and June arrived in time to do the diapering. Ash and Sharm took advantage of the ladies presence to decide on how they were going to transport the twins. Olinda greeted both ladies, who she was thrilled to discover were as nice as Ash told her they would be.

It was going to take some time to get used to people wanting to help her, or at least Ash and her. She asked Edith as she watched the two males. "What are they doing?"

Edith sighed, then said. "Arguing the merits of baby slings and carrying the babies in their arms."

Olinda placed the tray she carried with mugs of coffee and several cups of tea down on the table. "I brought you coffee and tea."

Both females said together. "Thanks."

Edith passed a cup of tea to June as Olinda watched the two males. They had got to the trying to figure out how the sling was worn stage. "Should I tell them that a female named Claire called, and she and a male named Lars will be here any minute with carriers?"

Edith looked at her, then at the two males. Ash was trying to tie the sling around Sharm, but it was not going well as Sharm kept twisting around to see what he was doing. June sat with a baby in her arms and a huge smile on her face as she pleaded. "Please don't, I am recording this, it's the funniest thing I have seen for a while." She showed them her phone.

Edith grinned. "I'm with her."

Olinda grinned as well and picked up her baby boy. "Okay, I bow to your wisdom, so Ion, let Mama dress you."

Eventually, Claire and Lars arrived with carriers for the babies, much to June's regret and the relief of Sharm and Ash. Once everything was sorted out and Claire had given Olinda and Ash a quick tutorial on placing hatchlings in carriers. She and Ash went to their very first of many Sunday family days as a family. Where she was slowly introduced to the Kingsley's a few members at a time.

The Kingsleys were very aware they were an overpowering group who could be perceived as intimidating. Within a short amount of time, Olinda felt at home, more than she could remember ever feeling anywhere, and that included her mother's place. It was very easy to see these males and females loved babies, actually young ones of any age. No one seemed to care they were holding in their arms sun dragons that were thought to be myths. To everyone there, they were just hatchlings who needed to be cuddled and adored. Charlie's baby Justice and Claire's Kale came in for a lot of attention. None of the babies found their way into a carrier, they were more often than not held in arms designed especially for that purpose.

She even saw Ash's brothers, who arrived back just after breakfast, carrying a baby or child in their arms as they caught up with members of the family. Eventually, Olinda found herself in a corner with Verity and several females. They watched Ella's Uncle Finlay being included in a male bonding moment. It seemed he knew most of the males there. Fascinated, Olinda stared as they saw shoulders punched, backs thumped, males hugged, she heard several males grunt. "We will meet at training."

Sage said. "I want to say it is like a documentary, you know, like those animal ones you see on TV, but that seems wrong."

"But true." Charlie said with a decisive nod of her head.

Olinda had discovered Stanvis's Shadow Jacks, who was English and seemed to be a quiet, serious type of female, had a wicked sense of humor. She said now. "I know the ones you mean as cubs we used to watch them all the time."

Several of the others nodded, obviously they all had as well, before she censored herself. Olinda asked. "Was it education TV?"

Several sets of eyes turned to her, and she shrugged. "Umm, no offense intended."

"None taken." Jacks said in a voice that held a smile. "And yes, it usually was."

Olinda grinned at Charlie, who was laughing. "What it seemed plausible?"

"True, but I am not sure any here would have asked."

"Oh well, yeah, okay brain and mouth, not always in sync."

Which caused Charlie and most of the others there to howl with laughter. It was contagious and soon Olinda found herself laughing as hard as the others. She just got control of herself when Claire said with a good imitation of the narrator that used to be on the nature channel.

"Join us as we watch the male dragon in their own habitat, watch as they greet another male. Today we will explore the different methods used to rediscover the family connection."

By the time she was finished, they were all laughing again and the undercurrent of tension that new people felt when meeting for the first time was thoroughly gone. Little groups broke off from the larger group to discuss life or families, or to talk about work.

Olinda found herself with Charlie on one side and Verity on the other. Together, they gently quizzed her on how she was coping with Ash and the twins. They cleverly interspersed the questions with catching her up on what had happened in court the day before. And other pertinent information they decided she needed to know about where she was living. An hour later Grace arrived, and Olinda was introduced to Grace's sons and their mates and young ones. One of Grace's sons delivered her tea just before the brothers went to where the males greeted them with more back slapping and laughter.

Olinda had just finished telling them she would like to return to working in the library, when Cara arrived. Olinda knew who she was. Ash had pointed out all the young and who they belonged to when they had first arrived. Without a word, Cara climbed onto her mother's knee and stared at Olinda. Charlie hugged her and said. "Hiya, sweetie, what's up? Did the other girls kick you out?"

Cara shook her head. Charlie explained to Olinda. "Cara is only two and like her daddy, she says little but thinks a lot."

Verity told her. "Storm was always like that, even from a hatchling."

Cara smiled at Olinda and then reached out and touched her hand as she whispered in her sweet baby voice. "Unicon."

Charlie laughed, before Olinda could say anything, she told her. "Cara is fixated on unicorns. We covered her entire room in them. I blame Sage, she introduced the girls to the idea of unicorns."

Olinda missed everything she said. Her entire focus was on the little girl. "Oh... oh, Cara, yeah I get it. Unicorn."

Cara clapped her hands and beamed a smile at her mother and grandmother as she said. "Me unicon!"

Olinda said. "Sanda mlo phojo unicorn somta!"

Cara squealed with delight and yelled. "Mama, unicon. Me is unicon with sista linda."

Olinda touched the little girl's cheek and said. "Olinda. My name is Olinda."

Cara nodded and repeated. "Olinda sista."

With tears blurring her eyes, Olinda said softly. "Yes sweetheart, sister." Then, as though her eyes were waiting for those words, tears streamed down Olinda's face and suddenly Ash was there. She was surrounded by his scent, and still she cried. She was swept into his muscular arms and carried from the now quiet family room, and still she cried. He opened a portal to their bedroom and still she cried. He placed her on their bed and climbed in with her cradled in his arms, and still she cried. He held her as she cried for her mother, for a lost friendship, and for a man she had hurt in a dead-end town. And then she cried for all the times she had run and been so very afraid. She cried for that frightened woman that did not know why she was hunted, and finally she cried for the woman she had been and would never be again. When she eventually cried herself to sleep, Ash held her for a long time with his dragon crooning to her as she slept. Eventually, he covered her with a blanket and sat on the side of their bed with his head in his hands. His dragon murmured. *Shadow had a lot to cry about.*

I think you are right, my friend. Maybe this will help lighten her load.

We will lighten her load, which is why we are her Shadow.

Yes, we are and yes, we will.

She looked peaceful as she slept, and with a gentle kiss to her forehead, he left her to go to his lounge, where he knew his family waited.

"Is she alright?" Charlie asked before he had stepped a foot inside the room.

He nodded. "She is sleeping. What happened?"

She shook her head. "I do not know. Cara called her a unicorn and Olinda seemed to agree. Then she said a sentence in a language I have never heard before and Cara called her sister. Olinda did not seem surprised, and then she started crying."

"How is Cara?"

"Upset, she is with Storm."

Sharm said gently. "Ash, we need to test her."

"Why?"

"Because they seem to think they are related. We need to see if that is true."

"Oh, I see." He looked toward the bedroom and then Sharm. "So what do you need?"

He handed him a square of cloth. "Can you prick her finger and drop blood on this?"

Ash shook his head. "No, I cannot. My dragon will not allow me to. He is on the edge as it is."

Sharm said. "Understandable. Will he allow me too?"

Ash stood still for a moment, then shook his head. "He will not allow any male near her; he says she is too vulnerable."

Ella asked. "Would he allow me?"

"Yes, he can accept that."

Ella smiled as she passed him and slipped into their bed-room. He stood, unable to think of how to help his Shadow, or if he could, and waited as his family waited with him. Claire came from the babies' room with a small bag, a change of clothes within. When Ash looked at her, she smiled and said. "Just in case Mama Verity or Grace have the boys for the night." She dropped it on a chair and asked. "So is it possible that Olinda and Cara could be related, sisters even?"

Rene` said. "Of course it is possible. Dragons have young spaced years apart. Longer than this gap would be."

Ash shrugged. "I, like you Claire, do not know if they are siblings but if they are, we will have to find out how."

"Well, how will we do that? Neither of them have parents to ask?" Charlie growled. No one took offense, they all knew she was worried, and not just about her daughter.

Sharm said. "The DNA will confirm the relationship. Other than that, we will have to use different methods to find out if in fact they are unicorns."

Keeper said. "I am going to go out on a limb here and say Olinda will be able to tell us."

Ash asked him. "Why would you say that?"

Keeper grinned. "She spoke a foreign language and I would hazard a guess, you Charlie, have heard many, many dialects and languages?"

"I have."

"As have we, therefore, we can form a reasonable conjec-ture. It is a language none of us have heard, therefore uni-corn."

Ark said. "Of those who heard it, right?"

"Well, I see what you are saying. Yes, that is true."

Edith said. "Also, she was not dismissive of Cara. In fact, she seemed quite relieved as Cara did."

Reighn asked. "So, any guesses as to what they are?"

Edith said. "Well, I tried again and got nothing, just like

last time. So no help here."

Sage said. "I have been telling you unicorns."

Reighn grinned at her adamant tone and he was not the only one. Charlie looked at her and agreed. "I think you could be right, or at least Cara thinks they are."

Just then, Ella came out and handed Sharm the cloth. He told them. "It is only coming up to midday. I will have an answer by dinner time. Now let us all go and leave Olinda to sleep in peace. Ash, come with us. There is nothing you can do here and you will know when she wakes."

He nodded. "You are probably right. My boys will need me. I will catch you up." He walked into the kitchen and poured himself a glass of water and saw his hands were shaking. He closed them into fists and leaned against the counter, breathing deeply as he reassured his dragon when he asked. *Shadow will not leave us now.*

No, my friend, not now.

He waited until he heard everyone quietly leaving, knowing they were filled with thoughts of unicorns as he was. Axl and Ark remained behind when everyone left. Together, they retrieved what they had stashed earlier in the small lounge. They dropped three albums and a box of photos with a laptop on the dining room table as Ash came from the kitchen.

Ark said. "The female Thea and her brother were still living there. All Olinda's things were in the basement storage of the apartment. We only got what Olinda asked for on the list."

Ash nodded. "It was all she wanted."

Axl told him. "They hoped by holding on to them she would come back."

Ash grunted as he said. "Foolish, she would not have."

Ark agreed. "They did not know her at all."

"Did they tell you why they wanted her so much?"

Axl told him. "At the beginning it was just because they thought she was a shifter, but then something changed and someone ordered them to find her and capture her; they paid them a fortune to do so."

Ark took up the tale. "It was fairly obvious, they were frightened of the one who ordered them to hunt her."

"Do you know who it was?"

They both shook their heads, Axl said. "No, but we have their computers and phones. Our specialists are combing through them to find out."

Ash said. "Okay, thank you brothers, she will be happy she has them back. They are important to her."

Ark said. "Memories. We all need good ones. I am glad it was worth doing."

Axl told him. "They needed culling."

Ash asked. "Did you find all of them?"

Ark replied in disgust. "All but the one we wanted."

Axl placed a flash drive on top of an album. "This will show her everything she needs to know."

Ash grimaced. "Again, I thank you. I am pleased you are home. I feel the Battle brothers will be defending against unicorns."

Axl asked Ash. "Are you going to tell them?"

"Only if it is confirmed that she and the little one are unicorn."

"Storm will not be happy you have kept this from them." Ark reminded him.

"I know, but until we know for sure. I would rather wait. We do not need to go to war with the unicorns or distress our family with explanations none of us wish to tell."

Axl nodded. "Remember, we have felt your Shadow's displeasure, brother." He said as he rubbed his shoulder where Olinda had shot him.

Ash winced. "I understand."

Ark grumbled. "It is not Olinda. It is Sage I am worried about. She will really be unhappy if it turns out they are unicorns and then finds out. You, and by extension us, have kept this from her. Did you both forget she has magic?"

Ash said. "Well, there is that."

Axl warned. "I think brother, you should have given this a little more thought."

Ash was left with nothing more to say. He agreed with them both.

CHAPTER TWENTY:

S torm held Cara as she sobbed into his chest. They were sitting at the bay window of the family room overlooking the meadow below. Usually Cara loved looking at the grass as it moved with the wind and at the dragons that occasionally appeared.

Sobbing, she looked up at him and said. "Sista sad, Dada."

Storm never lied to his young. Edee had said they would know, so he said now. "Yes, she is."

"Me make her sad?"

"No, baby girl, you did not. How could you do that, a sweet little thing like you?"

"Dada, me unicon, sista unicon."

"That does not make Olinda sad, it is wonderful. So you are a unicorn?"

"Yep." She nodded. "Me is."

"Well, I am happy to have a unicorn in our family."

Cara's sobs stopped as Storm wiped her tears away. He was as happy as his dragon to see no more tears appear. Cara looked at him and smiled, not her usual big smile, but Storm was relieved it seemed the crying was over. "Me appy too Dada."

Sharm arrived and said, as he sat next to them on the window seat. "Well, little Cara, how are you?"

"Me not sad. Me unicon, unca Sarm."

"That is very good. Cara, my sweet girl, Uncle Sharm needs to prick your finger with this?" He showed her a small needle and to Storm he said. "We need to test her DNA."

Storm grunted as Cara said. "unca Sarm, no hurt?"

Sharm smiled and caressed her small cheek with his finger. "Oh no. I do not want to hurt you."

Cara nodded and said. "Kay."

"But sweetheart, Uncle Sharm needs some of Cara's blood."

She looked at him and then at her father. "No hurt, Dada?"

Storm shook his head. "No baby girl, now you know Uncle Sharm, he would not want to do this if it was not really important."

Sharm said. "This is for Olinda."

Cara frowned, they could see her thinking. After a minute, she nodded her head. "Kay."

She stuck her little hand out. Sharm smiled and kissed the little palm and then before she knew it, he had pricked her finger and a bead of blood appeared. He dabbed it with the cloth, folded it and slipped it into a little bag. He then took her finger in his hand and placed a pink bandage over the wound. "All done. What a brave girl you were."

Cara looked at her finger with the bandage and showed Storm. "All done Dada, me bave."

Storm kissed the finger. "So I see, and you were a very brave girl."

"Kay." She wiggled down from his knee and ran to her mother when she saw her. They could hear her telling Charlie about the bandage.

"So sisters?" Storm growled. He was unsure how he felt about that and the fact his baby girl may be a unicorn, a species he had no knowledge of.

Sharm shrugged. "Possibly? I do not know and before you ask I have no test to prove they are unicorn nor where we can find one. Keeper is looking through his library now. I thought Cara had seen Papa again?"

"She did, he removed all the memories of her life before she came here, but she still remembers the pain. He cannot find where to remove those memories from or where she has them stored."

"Maybe it is because she is a unicorn. If she is, Olinda may be able to help?"

Storm grunted. "Maybe."

"Anyway, for the moment this test is all we can do."

Storm nodded at the cloth. "How long until you know?"

"We should have an idea by dinner time." Sharm stood as he told him. "I will deliver this and Olinda's sample."

Storm stood as well. "Thank you Sharm, where is Ash?"

"He is on his way."

"Okay."

A few minutes later, Storm watched the three Battle brothers as they arrived and joined his parents.

His dragon asked. *What do you wish to do?*

Beat the shit out of all three of them, but I will not.

His dragon sighed. *It has not been easy for him and his Shadow.*

Storm growled. *No excuse. He needs to tell us now.*

Will he be happy, we listened to his thoughts?

Storm snorted. *Should have better shields, Uncle Andre` taught us all better than that.*

His dragon growled again. *Yes, he did. I remember the lessons well. We could not sit down for many days.*

Storm laughed in agreement as he remembered his uncles' often harsh discipline. *I have a good mind to call him and tell him of the Battle brother's lapse.*

Now it was his dragon's turn to laugh. Reighn looked over at Storm and raised an eyebrow. Then he turned back to his discussion with their father. Storm's dragon laughed. *No need to say anything, brother knows.*

Storm grunted. *We had better add mind-shield classes back on to the training schedule. If these three are slack, the others will be worse.*

What do you think brother will do?

I think we are about to find out. Here comes Keeper, and he looks annoyed.

His dragon chortled with amusement as they went to join the discussion that was going to become heated. *Will you say anything?*

What am I, the Dragon Lord now?

CHAPTER TWENTY-ONE:

O linda woke alone. She felt the bed beside her; it was cold Ash must have left some time ago. For the first time in months, she felt safe and at peace. The hard lump she had carried in her chest since her mother had been diagnosed with cancer was gone. As was the armor she had shielded her emotions and heart with. It was all gone now, the last piece having dissolved with her crying, she assumed.

She looked at her emotions, saw she was balanced and found she was not who she used to be. Smiling, she thought. *I am an updated version of the old Olinda. I am the new and improved Olinda Battle.*

Without thinking about it, she sensed for Ash and the babies and found them. She smiled to herself when she realized what she had done. Perhaps it was a gift come to light, maybe this was because she was the new model of Olinda. *I wonder what else I can do.*

Tentatively she sent her senses out again, trying to locate Cara and found her with her parents, thankfully she seemed okay. Olinda sighed and withdrew back into her mind or body. But instead of finding herself, or at least herself back in her body, she seemed to have landed on an island. She panicked, fear of never returning to herself attacked her fragile nerves.

Suddenly, a tall flame of golden light flared and spoke. *Hush Olinda all is well. You are safe. Calm down and think.*

As she had done for years, Olinda instantly obeyed the command, and once she calmed, she saw a thread that seemed to lead from her to... "Oh look my body."

Yes, I am helping you see what happens when you send your senses out of your body. You will always remain attached.

Olinda, you will never be lost and to answer your next question, we are on an Island. Although it has a different color, as we are on a different plane of existence.

"Huh! So I am not really here?"

Not physically. Your soul or essence of what makes you Olinda is.

"Okay, I sort of get that."

Think astral plane, I know you have heard the term.

"That makes all the difference then."

Still sarcastic?

"Still annoying?"

Ahh! You know who I am.

"I do. Sun Goddess."

You always have been incredibly quick to grasp a situation.

"Thank you. It made running easier. So what can I do for you now?"

You are still angry.

"You are still enigmatic."

I have always been truthful.

"Why am I here?"

The Goddess sighed. *I needed to talk to you and thought this was the right time.*

"You are leaving me?"

Yes, dear one, it is time. You are where you are meant to be with the dragon, who will care for you and the twins. You and they are safe, with a new world opened to you.

Olinda felt the sadness creep over her, as angry as she was or thought she was with the Goddess. To know she would no longer be in her life made her heart ache. "Will you tell me about Cara?"

What is to say, you are sisters?

"And..."

And what? The rest is your journey to discover for yourself.

"So very annoying."

Olinda could hear the smile in the Goddess's voice as she said. *Still so impatient to understand everything at once?*

"Learning is my passion."

Learning is your gift, as is the gift of languages, and there will be more to come. They will be invaluable to you as you travel the road that is before you.

"So, no help with our parentage then?"

What help do you need? Her parents are here, and your grandfather is alive.

"Meaning our father is dead?"

Yes.

One word with a wealth of meaning behind it, thought Olinda. "So we should be thankful he is?" When the Goddess made no comment. Olinda sighed and asked. "Will his father claim us?"

No, he will desire to have you and Cara to produce a male heir for him only. The disapproval the Goddess held for the male was clear in her voice.

Olinda sniffed in disdain. "Well, that won't be happening."

I am sure it will not. He is a very stubborn male with very narrow ideals. He will in time, realize his mistake, but until then he will demand much from you. Take care, dear one.

"I will and thank you for my life."

Goodbye, my sweet girl.

"Goodbye Goddess, it has been an honor knowing you."

Oh dear heart, it was always my pleasure to know you. Raise my gifts well. They will be wonderful brothers to all their sisters.

Shocked out of her sadness, Olinda squeaked. "How many are we talking about?"

Laughter floated to her as she once more found herself in her body, in her bed. She kept her eyes closed as she let the disorientation to her senses settle. When she felt she was as settled as she was going to get, she rose to shower.

CHAPTER TWENTY-TWO:

Fifteen minutes later she walked into the dining room, where she saw the albums and box. Picking up the flash drive, she heard the voice of the Goddess once more. *Do not watch that. What is on there will add nothing to your life. It will only add a burden to your soul. Go into this new life with a healthy heart and soul. Dear one, leave it in the past.*

Olinda did not answer her, nor did she release the drive as she decided to walk around her apartment. So far, she had no idea if she liked it or not, having seen only three rooms. She grabbed a pad and pen from her backpack. Just in case she had ideas for remodeling this room, which appeared to be the formal dining. The walls and floors were made from a blue stone and the long side boards and tall hutch were made from the same wood as the table and chairs. Which, if she was not mistaken, was rosewood. The table would seat at least twelve, made for entertaining, she thought, or a large family. The entire room spoke of wealth and tender care, every piece of furniture looked like it had survived many years of use. For that alone, Olinda loved it.

There was a large rug on the floor, she just stopped herself from stepping off it. She wondered if they would ever actually use the room, still; it was exquisite. But seriously, the rug should be in a museum, as should the chandelier that hung above the table. It was ornate iron which obviously had been switched from candle power to electric; it was stunning.

She entered the kitchen, which amazingly enough was a chef's dream, and made her sigh in delight. All black counters and stainless steel appliances. It even had an old-fashioned Aga stove. Again it had the blue stone walls and floors. The cupboards were painted a light blue and there was a good old-fashioned kitchen table, scarred with age and it too seated twelve. She smiled as she thought that the designers obviously believed families were meant to be large.

Running her hand over the table's surface, she smiled; it was as though it said. Hey... the kitchen may be new, but I am the past and am staying. Olinda loved it, a table with attitude. This was where her family would eat, argue, love, and grow. She could see it all, the years of living with Ash and her boys and apparently girls. Measuring the length of the table, she hoped it would be large enough.

Reluctantly, she left the kitchen and made her way down a hallway to the largest lounge; she already knew there were two smaller ones. One she was going to turn into a play-room for the boys, the other cried out to be an entertainment room for Ash and his brothers. The lounge she entered took her breath away. Especially when her eyes drifted upwards to the vaulted ceiling with its timber beams and three hanging chandeliers similar to the one in the dining room. What made her gasp out loud was the mezzanine floor that looked suspiciously like a library. And appeared to be reached by an old-fashioned iron spiral staircase, proudly taking up space in the room's corner. She itched to get up there and discover how many shelves there were and if there was a sitting area for reading, but she held herself back. This was just a quick look to orientate herself. She had time later to explore everything at her leisure. The lounge itself was beautiful, with large wooden French style doors leading to a wide balcony with loungers and chairs. She turned from the scene of the lake below and the magnificent stone fireplace immediately arrested her attention. "Now, how did I miss you?"

This alone, she thought was totally worthy of a castle. It was large, open, and glorious. She could imagine nights with Ash and the boys playing and loving in front of it. Smiling, she cast her eyes over the floors, which were made of a warm wood instead of stone. There were large leather chairs and couches placed on rugs that were obviously priceless and exquisite, as were the green curtains in heavy brocade. Olinda knew this room was just not going to work as it was. She loved the lounge, but priceless rugs and antiques scattered around did not mix with growing boys. Sighing sadly, she added it to her list to be changed. As beautiful as it all was, it had to go.

Next were the bedrooms, there were four with their own bathrooms, each had a bathtub and a large shower, with loads of storage. Every bedroom had heavy wooden furniture with the same brocade curtains in varying shades of red or green. The floors and walls were the blue stone of the other rooms, and all the rugs were like the ones in the lounge, priceless antiques.

Olinda drew in a breath and whispered. "Oh, my!"

The canopied beds robbed her of speech. Each bed was more elaborate than the next and totally impractical. Children did not need large adult sized beds, or, she corrected herself, dragon sized beds with beautiful canopies. She made notes to have them changed and hoped she did not hurt anyone's feelings.

The room she shared with Ash was her last stop, and as she stood inside the doorway, she looked at it as a male would and snorted her disgust. Seriously, this was such a female's boudoir, there was nothing for a male in here. She wrote furiously for several minutes, then walked around. This room was the only one to have such a massive bathroom. It was still luxurious and still gave her tingles. She so loved her bathroom. Dragging herself from the room, she finally opened the other doors and found what she knew to be dressing rooms. One was for the gentleman of the house, with heavy dark furniture and a wall of shelving, it also had racks for ties. Ash had placed several pairs of his jeans, trousers, and shirts there. A uniform was hanging up in a dry cleaners cover. It looked impressive, with all the ribbons and medals on the jacket. She wondered what it would take to get him to dress in it. Seriously, what female did not love a male in uniform?

She wandered into the next room, which she assumed was hers, and was surprised it appeared someone else had decided this was hers as well. Parcels from her shopping expedition sat on the daybed and shelves. There was a small sitting area surrounded by mirrors, also a revolving shoe rack. Her giddy meter went off the charts as she spun the shoe rack. She quickly changed into some of her new purchases; she felt she was still too skinny, but at least her clothes fit her.

Olinda stepped from the dressing room and stopped in front of her bedside table, turning the flash drive over in her fingers. She dropped it into the drawer with her gun and knife. Someone, Ash probably, had placed them in there earlier. With a determinism she was coming to appreciate, she closed the drawer on that part of her life. Some day she may want to look at what was on the drive and perhaps by then she would find a reason to. But that would not be today. Happier than she had been for many years, she walked from her apartment and into the arms of a male that took her breath away. Her first thought was, he had no right to be that gorgeous, her second was he was all hers.

"Hello my Shadow."

Olinda sighed, realizing she had forgotten the social niceties again.

"Hello, I am sorry about before, it sort of hit me all at once."

"But you are alright now?"

"Yes, I am me again. Maybe a little better and wiser, but I am just me."

"I am happy to hear that."

Olinda wondered how he had known she was awake, but before she could ask the question. His lips met hers and that was the last thought she had for a few minutes as she fell into a kiss that ended all thought.

CHAPTER TWENTY-THREE:

After Ash escorted Olinda back to the family room, where she had been hugged by everyone. And she had hugged and thanked his brothers for her photos and laptop. He had coaxed her into a seat by Grace and Verity, who were holding their hatchlings. Axl had brought her a cup of coffee, and then all hell had broken loose.

The family dining room was not a cheerful place anymore, Olinda thought, as Keeper demanded. "What do you mean? You know how to contact unicorns."

Charlie asked. "Forget that; I want to know how you know about unicorns."

Sage snarled fiercely. "Forget that; I want to know why you never told me?"

Edith asked with glee. "Forget that. Where do they live and can I go there?"

Ash rubbed his hand around the back of his neck as his eyes landed on Reighn. Who had told the room not two minutes ago that Ash knew where unicorns lived and how to contact them? He asked the satisfied looking male, "Are you happy?"

Reighn smiled as he replied. "Immensely, your shields are deplorable. You have become slack. Andre` would slap you around the training yard." Ark and Axl both laughed until he looked at them and asked. "You have something to laugh about?"

They both shook their heads quickly. "No, Reighn."

Storm said. "As Elites, it is deplorable the state of your shields. You are all off rotation until further notice. I think as a punishment for allowing this to happen, you will be tasked with checking all the Shields and Hunters to see what state their defenses are in. It could take months."

"Yes, Commander." The two brothers said, as a punishment, it was the best they could have received, because it meant they got to stay at home.

Reighn said. "As further punishment, I have granted Storm and Papa's requests. For you three to take over the position of Commander and Instructors of the new advanced training school."

All three Battle brothers were stunned. They had put in a request with the Commanders of both the Hunters and Shields. Namely Rene` and Storm for a school to train Shields and Hunters in advanced techniques. Ash wanted to remain at home, especially now, and he liked the idea of leading the training school. To Olinda's ears, they did not sound very penitent. Maybe it was the smiles they tried to hide that gave them away. She asked Ash. "Do you want to run a school?"

"Very much so. I want to stay home with you and our young."

"Well, okay, I am happy, if you are. Truthfully, I like the idea of you being with us at night."

Before he could answer, Axl asked. "And us, of course?"

"Indeed." Olinda answered dryly. Axl grinned as she asked. "What are these shields you are talking about?"

Ash told her. "They are barriers that we have or we placed around our minds to stop our thoughts from being heard or read." Reighn and Storm both snorted in disgust. Ash grimaced at the sounds as he said. "Apparently, my brothers and I have not strengthened ours in a while. Therefore my thoughts, or should I say our thoughts, were easily read and now I am under immense interrogation about unicorns."

He sounded so put out, she almost laughed. "I see. Do I need shields?"

Ash grinned as he said with admiration. "My soul, yours are impregnable."

Surprised, Olinda asked. "How do you know?"

"When you first arrived, we tried reading your mind to find out what was wrong."

Storm said. "We could not, even the Dragon Lord could not."

Reighn nodded. "I did not want to hurt you, so did not press too hard. It is a very impressive shield. I would like to know how that is possible."

Thoughtfully, Olinda asked. "Can anyone read minds?"

Reighn shook his head. "No, there are only a very small number of dragons with that ability."

"Huh, what about others?"

He shrugged. "I am sure there are many shifters and faeries that can and do. That is why we train to keep it from happening."

She looked around. "All of you have had training?"

June answered. "Those that are not like you, who need it, yes."

"Makes sense, I suppose. If I had to guess, I would say the voice who I have since found out is the Sun Goddess, gave them to me."

"The Sun Goddess?" Reighn asked, a little bemused at the simple way she mentioned the Goddess.

"Yes." Olinda nodded. "She came to say goodbye earlier."

Charlie asked. "Did she tell you about Cara and you?"

"Not really. She told me we are sisters but other than that nothing."

Storm asked, and it was easy to hear the doubt in his voice. "Nothing at all?"

Olinda looked at Charlie and Storm and lied. "Not a thing more than we are sisters."

Charlie's eyebrows rose at the lie and grinned. "Nice try. You know I have the gift of knowing and smelling a lie a mile away, right?"

"No, I did not know that. Ash, you need to tell me these things."

He looked totally bewildered as he said. "I did not know

you were going to lie."

"Even so, forewarned is forearmed as they say."

Axl muttered. "Who says this? I have never heard of it." Several males nodded their heads in agreement with his statement.

Grace told them. "It is a saying. Think about it, and you will get the meaning."

Charlie said to Olinda. "Well?"

Olinda thought quickly. "I thought Cara, and I had no scent?"

"You don't, and you do not get to change the subject?"

"But should we not delve into that or at least discuss the reason why?"

Charlie shook her head. "Time for that later, now answer Goddess touched female."

"Oh nice." Sage said, admiringly.

"Wasn't it, though?" Olinda agreed with a smile.

Charlie growled. "Olinda!"

"Oh alright." She grimaced. "It is possible Cara and I share the same grandfather. It is also possible our father is no longer alive and he, the grandfather, will deny us. It is also possible he may not deny us and if he does not, it will be because he wants and needs us for breeding the next male heir."

There was silence as everyone looked at Charlie, Storm, and Ash. Rene` said. "That is a lot of possibilities there."

Olinda sighed. "I know, but she is a Goddess who only ever parted with what she wanted to tell me."

"I will not allow her to be taken from us." Stated Charlie and Olinda saw the hidden assassin within. How she knew that about Charlie she did not know, and maybe never would. But it was as plain as the nose on her face. Charlie killed or did. Now that she found fascinating.

Olinda shook her head as she agreed. "No one will take her. They would have to be lunatics to even try."

Ash said. "I will not allow them to take you." His brothers nodded in brotherly agreement.

She felt safer than she ever had in her entire life. "Thank you. I know you would not."

Storm said. "They die if they try, family or not."

Olinda agreed, what else could she do? As she said, they would have to be lunatics to try. Charlie grinned. "Well, there is that."

"Sista Olinda, me is here." Called Cara as she ran into the room and threw herself into Olinda's arms.

"Hello, sweetheart. I am sorry if I made you sad earlier."

"Me make you cry?"

"No baby girl. Olinda made me cry."

"Oh... Kay, you urt?"

"I was, in my heart." She pointed to her chest.

Cara nodded and leaned closer to her, and told Olinda before she kissed her. "Isa makes it all betta now."

"You did, you made it all better."

Cara smiled at Charlie, who sat holding Justice. She smiled at her daughter, and raised ghost eyes to Olinda, who quietly said in French. "I will not allow anyone to take her from you or use her. Have no fear, she may be of my blood, but she is yours and Storms."

Charlie nodded as Cara looked up at Olinda and said. "Petty words."

"They are very pretty, and if your Mama says it is okay. I will teach you and Kelsey and all the little ones the pretty words."

Cara said. "Kay, Mama says."

"Yep, when your Mama says."

With those simple words Olinda, whether or not she knew it, re-established for not only Cara and her parents but everyone there, whose child she was. Cara, not understanding the undercurrents that were slowly ebbing away, held her finger up and showed Olinda her bandage. "Me have pink owie."

Sharm said as he came in. "We did a blood test on you both."

Olinda cocked an eyebrow up as much to say, really. He told

her. "Ella obtained one from you."

Olinda nodded. "Alright."

Ash asked. "You are not upset?"

"No, you were there, right?"

"Not in the room, but yes."

"So, no need for me to worry."

Ash smiled as his dragon chortled. *She trusts us.*

Yes, she does. Our Shadow is ours, whether or not she loves us.

Charlie asked Olinda. "But you don't need proof, do you?"

Olinda shook her head. "No, we are of the same blood."

Reighn asked. "Do you know if you are a unicorn?"

"Nope, not a clue."

Bemused, he asked. "The Goddess never said?"

"No, she said it was my journey to find out, or some such sh... umm... something like that." There were several laughs at her near curse.

Reighn thoughtfully stated. "Interesting."

Olinda replied, to everyone's amusement. "Or you could just say annoying."

Keeper asked. "You cannot feel if you are?"

The question had her stumbling for a minute about how to go about knowing. Perhaps there was a great big signpost somewhere inside her that said hello you are a unicorn and she just missed it. She looked the dragon in the eye and tried not to smile as she asked seriously. "What would I look for?"

He stared at her, nonplussed. "You know, I have no idea."

"Well, if you get one, tell me and I will try."

With a nod of agreement, he asked. "Would you know the name of your male parent?"

"Not a clue. Another thing she did not supply."

"Sheesh, she was hardly helpful." Edith grumbled.

Olinda agreed sourly. "Tell me about it, and I don't think she is really gone. I'm fairly sure I can still hear her."

"Annoying!"

"Exactly."

"Anyway." Reighn said, halting the moaning, before it

got really started. "Ash, can you contact the unicorns you know?"

Ash frowned and rubbed the back of his neck. "Ahhh…"

"May I make a suggestion?" Ark asked as Ash became more uncomfortable.

Reighn nodded. "Of course."

"We did not leave the unicorns we met very happy with us. It may serve our cause for Sharm to do the contacting as the Chief Healer."

Sharm smiled. "I can do that."

Sage growled. "But not until our questions have been answered."

"Agreed, so start talking, Ash." Demanded Keeper.

Ash grimaced. "Ark, how long?"

"Let me see." Ark pulled on his bottom lip as he thought. "We had just finished scouting Australia and New Guinea and had only been back in England for a half a dozen years. So just on fifty years ago, give or take ten."

All the females looked at him with varying expressions of fascination. Edith had to ask. "Are you sure?"

Ark nodded. "Fairly sure. Yes."

"Okay." She said with a smile. "Let us just say, we the ladies are impressed with your memory."

"It is a gift."

"Thank you."

Ash snarled at his brother, who grinned, and Olinda could see the twinkle of the devil in that smile. With a decided bite to his words, Ash said. "So about fifty years ago, we were in England and came across a horde of wild ones. We stayed with them for a while until they decided to return to Dragon's Gap. Just before we were to return home, Axl was kidnapped."

Verity gasped, as did Grace. Axl stated. "I maintain. I did not allow it to happen. I was taken by surprise.

Ark scoffed. "Of course you were. It had nothing to do with the ale or the sweet, adoring females?"

Which caused a few giggles from the females and a grunt or two from the males. Axl smirked. "Not at all."

Claire said. "I think he protests too much."

Edith agreed. "Way too much."

Axl said. "I say I do not. Ale is ale, I have been drinking ale since I was a teenager."

Reighn asked. "Was it dragon ale?"

"No, we since found out, it was a very potent unicorn ale." A disgusted Ark told them with an equally disgusted look at his younger brother.

June said. "Yet he did not deny the females."

Sage said. "Hush everyone, unicorns, I am growing old here."

Storm mused out loud. "I have drunk with Axl, he can hold his drink. It must have been unicorn ale."

Sage yelled. "Seriously, no one friggin cares about the friggin ale!"

"Swear jar." Said Edith. "Twice female."

Sage growled, whether at Edith or the interruptions, it was hard to say. Ash hurriedly told them as her eyes turned blue. "We eventually found him."

Axl moaned. "Three days, they had me for... oh the horror."

Both Ark and Ash just looked at him with only the kind of disgust a brother can. Grace said. "Oh, my poor Axl." Every male there growled softly as Axl sighed pitifully until she asked. "Did they deflower you, sweetheart?"

Olinda and the other females just lost it. Even Sage couldn't hold her irritation as she too howled with laughter.

The look he turned on Grace was a mix of astonishment and disbelief. "Grace, how could you?"

Which made the males join in with the female's laughter; it took them some time until they could bring themselves under control. Ash grinned as he watched Olinda's face fill with laughter. She looked relaxed and happy. He felt his dragon sigh in relief. Finally, he said. "When we eventually

149

caught up with them, Axl was on his way to being betrothed to the Ri's daughter."

Sage asked. "Who?"

Olinda told her. "It means King. The King's daughter."

"Got it, you are so handy to have around." Olinda grinned at the compliment. Sage asked. "Would you like a job?"

"No, she is mine." Keeper quickly told her. "The library needs her."

Olinda grinned wider. "Thank you Sage, but he is right."

"Oh, okay."

Claire leaned over and whispered to Sage. "She is not the right one. The one who is, will be here soon."

Sage whispered back. "Well, she better hurry."

"As I was saying." Ash said. "To rescue him." He pointed to his brother, who wore a smug smile. "Before the marriage, we traded."

"With what?" Olinda asked, although she had a feeling she knew.

Ash hung his head. "Olinda, my brother Ace, was in Command. It was his idea."

"What was?"

"That I would trade places with Axl."

"Why would you? That would mean you would marry. Oh my Goddess, you are married!" Her voice rose with each word she spoke.

He looked around and saw that she was not the only concerned one. There were a lot of expressions of concern and anger directed his way, except for his idiot brothers. He hurriedly assured her, as well as the others. "No, I swear I am not, it seemed the Ri, was due to leave for a few days. He had no care who his daughter married, she was one of many, and he just wanted one of them gone."

Ark said. "You cannot blame him. I think there were thirteen. I lost count after ten."

"Dear Goddess." Olinda mumbled.

Frowning, Sage asked. "I don't get it, why the swap?"

Ark took over the tale. "Well, Ace told the Ri, Ash was prettier and a better fighter, plus he had only birthed sons. That was a big deal for the Ri, you know with all those daughters?" They all absolutely understood that.

"Okay... wait." Olinda held her hand up. "You guys cannot have young outside a bonding with your Shadow. Right?"

"Oh, we know. They however, did not." Explained a smirking Ark.

"Oh... Oh, I see, got it."

Axl said with a pout. "Also, once his daughter got a look at Ash, she begged."

From all the females came a collective. "Ohhh!"

Ash sighed and looked at Reighn, who laughed back at him. He narrowed his eyes in challenge. Reighn grinned and nodded in acceptance. Ark told them. "So after the Ri left. Ash did the only thing he could."

"He escaped?" Claire asked as Axl shook his head no.

"He killed everyone there?" Edith said with a nod of her head, only to be told no by the three brothers.

"He kidnapped a daughter for trade?" Sage said. "That is what I would have done."

Ark grinned and said. "None of the above. No, he was really clever. He invited all the daughters except the betrothed one to his tent and then..."

Ash hurriedly stated. "Nothing, nothing happened. I swear Olinda. Nothing."

She stared at him and shrugged. "Okay."

Somehow, her easy acceptance of what he was saying didn't relieve him. With his eyes on hers, he hurriedly finished the story. "When they were all there, Ark told the daughter whom I was betrothed to, about her sisters being in my tent. She arrived and then the screaming and punching and hair pulling began. While they were all busy trying to kill each other. I slipped out the back and escaped."

Axl said. "We had to, you know, thump a few guards before we could leave. Well, quite a few, those unicorns are vicious and fast."

Ark said. "So as you can imagine we are not popular with them."

Axl said piously to Olinda. "See sister; I was innocent of all wrongdoing."

Ark stated, "Except you got kidnapped."

Axl eyed his brother as he growled. "It was not a plan."

Olinda looked at Axl and asked, because she really wanted to know. "For what?"

"What?"

"Why did you have to be kidnapped?"

The back of his neck went red as Axl mumbled. "I say again, I did not have to be."

"But you were, so why?"

"It does not matter now, it never worked."

Olinda raised her eyebrows as she said. "I see."

Axl narrowed his eyes as he asked. "Are you mocking me, sister?"

"Hell yes."

Laughing, he hugged her, saying. "So happy you are here."

Which made her smile. Claire eyed him and said. "It was the ale, wasn't it? You wanted the recipe, didn't you?"

Axl sniffed righteously. "I can neither confirm nor deny that."

Ark hit him. "Seriously, we almost died for an ale recipe."

Ash growled. "I almost ended up married for ale, you are an idiot."

"Maybe." Sharm said, bringing the brewing argument to a close. "If you give me their number, I will call tonight and hopefully set up a meeting as soon as possible."

Rene` asked. "Do you know of any other groups of unicorns?"

Ark said. "There is the group in England and there is one in Washington State. I will give you their numbers."

"Why do you have them?" Sage asked him with narrowed eyes. She wasn't over her irritation with the brothers yet.

He grinned as he winked and told her. "Never you, mind."
Again, from the females, there was a collective. "Ohhh!"

CHAPTER TWENTY-FOUR:

The following morning Sharm called Ash to tell him a meeting with the unicorns had been arranged in the library for one o'clock that afternoon.

When Ash and Olinda arrived with Ash's brothers. They were unsurprised to be joined by Reighn and Sage, Sharm and Edith, Charlie and Storm, as well as Keeper and Ella. Sage told them. "There are snacks and drinks, if you want them."

Ash passed Olinda a coffee, as Storm did likewise for Charlie. Everyone sat around a large table, and Olinda asked. "So, who are we meeting?"

Sharm told them. "The English group refused our request for a meeting after we sent a vial of blood from Olinda."

Keeper said. "From that, we have extrapolated that Olinda is not descended from their group."

Sharm agreed. "So we asked the Washington group and they are sending two representatives. The first is a professor Limann. He is a unicorn and a professor of history, he will give us a short history of their species. You should know they asked for an additional two vials of blood from you and Cara. Which I will supply when they come today."

Storm asked. "Why?"

"I do not know. I am sure they will tell us." Just then, his phone rang. He gave it a quick look and said to Reighn. "They are ready."

He opened a portal and a short, round male in a light blue suit stepped through. He was exactly as Charlie thought a professor would be like, with thinning gray hair and glasses. He carried a satchel and as soon as the portal was dismissed, he straightened his tie and the cuffs of his suit jacket while he looked at Sharm. "You are the healer?"

"Yes, you are Professor Limann?"

"Yes. I do not have a lot of time, so shall we get started?"

Sharm's lips tightened at the male's brusque manner. He made the introductions, which the professor more or less ignored while he stared at Olinda. When Sharm finished, Professor Limann demanded. "Where is the young one?"

Charlie replied. "Not here."

He ignored the warning in her tone and said. "I was under the impression she would be present."

"Your impressions were wrong." Growled Storm. "Move it along; you don't have a lot of time, remember?"

The male eyed Storm and snapped his mouth closed while everyone else hid their smiles. He shuffled some papers from his satchel and started to talk. Sharm took his seat beside Edith, and mind sent. *Asshole!*

Swear jar. Edith sent back, which made him smile as he said. *Exceptions were stated.*

To whom?

Keeper before the meeting.

Sucks! I forgot again.

By the time they stopped talking, it was to hear Olinda angrily asking. "A full-blood unicorn, you are serious?"

"Yes."

"So, let me get this straight. I am a full-unicorn, not half a unicorn?"

"That is what I have spent the last five minutes explaining."

"Alright, no need to get snotty. So you are saying two mythical four-legged animals with hooves and horns had sex and produced me, then somehow impregnated my mother all without her knowing." Snarked Olinda.

"Yeah, okay, I see that." Charlie said with a laugh in her tone as she looked at Olinda, who crossed her eyes at her causing Ash to smile.

"Now you are just being obtuse." Stated the Professor.

"I was trying for sarcastic, guess my aim was off." Olinda

155

said in a haughty tone.

The male ignored her statement, although his eyes squinted behind his glasses. "Obviously, a unicorn is a shifter. Therefore, the unicorn in question was wearing a male form when he impregnated your mother. Which resulted in you."

"Seriously, you have tone. Charlie, hand me a gun." Olinda snarled as Ash placed his hand on her shoulder.

"Cool your pistols there, female." Charlie told her, as she looked at the fussy little male who had his nose so far in the air, he was lucky he didn't trip over it and asked. "So if Olinda is a unicorn and the DNA test you and Sharm did, say she and our Cara are related. Then what you are saying is also true for Cara?"

"Well, of course, it is not rocket science, it is simple genetics ..." Storm reached over and slapped the male who dropped to the floor, unconscious. They all looked at him lying on the floor, then at Storm, who said. "Sorry, thought you had finished talking to him."

Axl picked him up as Ark placed his papers back in the satchel and Reighn opened the portal. So Axl and Ark could throw the male and his bag through, which they did. Edith watched as the male landed in a crumpled ball and winced. *That was gonna hurt.* She asked. "Well okay, is there another?"

Sharm said. "Yes, a Lady Jenny Sanders, please do not hit her." He admonished Storm, who grunted in reply while the Battle brothers all smiled and Reighn laughed, which caused Sharm to sigh.

Sage crossed her arms and said. "We will reserve judgment."

Sharm sighed again as Reighn asked Sage. "Why are you unhappy?"

"Because he was an A.S.S."

"Hey, spelling still counts. Swear jar." Edith called to her.

Sage narrowed her eyes and said. "I am upset. He was so not what I thought a unicorn would be like. I thought they were all sweet and lightness and pretty."

"Why?" Charlie asked. "Olinda stabbed and shot Ash and his brothers."

"Hey, I was ill."

"Yeah right." Axl mumbled to Ark. "I think she protests too much."

Ash said. "She was not in her right mind, normally she would not be like that."

"Yeah, what he said." Olinda smiled at Ash, who grinned back and ran his hand down her hair.

Reighn sighed twice, then said. "Enough. We will see what the next one is like. If we get no help from her, I will talk to the Elementals or Charlie can ask Queen Scarlett."

They all agreed, and he opened another portal. This time, a female stepped through. Jenny Sanders was tall, lean and had short golden hair sleeked back from her forehead. Her face was classically French, beautiful and haughty. She wore a white business jacket over a red shirt with a white pencil style skirt, and red high heels. She too, carried a black leather briefcase. She had style polish and was graceful, with slim hands. The word delicate came to mind. Olinda felt uncomfortable. It was as though this female knew something Olinda didn't. Sage sighed with delight and gave Olinda the thumbs up sign. Obviously, this female was more to her liking.

Olinda sat back in her chair and watched the female as she smiled and looked around at the people in the room.

Sharm introduced her. "Lady Jenny Sanders is an emissary sent from the Lochlon Blessing, which is what a family or group made up of unicorn families are called. Allow me to introduce you to everyone, Lady Jenny. This is our Dragon Lord Reighn and Dragon Lady Sage. This is my Shadow Lady Edith, and this is Lady Charlie and her Shadow Commander Storm, they are the parents of Cara, who we told you about. Captain Ark and Captain Axl and Commander Ash, who is bonded to Lady Olinda, who we also told you about. Finally, this is Lord Keeper and his Shadow Healer Ella."

Jenny Sanders nodded and said. "Hello."

Charlie asked. "So that last guy, who was he?"

"One of the most prominent unicorn scientists of our time. Professor Limann was asked to come and collect blood samples to be tested and to answer questions you may have had."

Edith told her. "Well, he was unhelpful, he was more interested in making sure we all understood how brilliant he was."

"I am sorry he did so. I will inform Ri, Caderyn."

Reighn asked. "Ri, Caderyn is who?"

"I apologize. He is the leader or King of our Blessing, and Healer Sharm is only partly right. The Blessing can also be all unicorns in one country or world as it is in Ri. Caderyn's world."

"I see, thank you." Reighn said. The female inclined her head respectfully.

Olinda asked. "Why is it called a Blessing?"

Jenny Sanders smiled as she answered. "Because meeting or seeing a unicorn is a blessing. It has been this way throughout Earth's history. Usually, the unicorn would grant a boon when they happened upon anyone they deemed worthy."

"So the virgin and pure thing?" Sage asked with a frown.

Jenny smiled shyly as she said. "Myth, a delightful story but still a myth that has kept unicorns safe throughout the years."

Keeper wanted to know. "So was it the unicorns themselves that spread that rumor?"

Again, she smiled shyly. "It may have been, who is to say."

Olinda stated simply, her eyes never leaving the females. "Well, not me. My sister and I, which in truth was more than a surprise, do not consider it a blessing or our father a myth. So where is he?"

"I understand how you must feel." Jenny said with a sympathetic sigh.

Which put Olinda's teeth on edge as she said. "I do not think, unless you are Cara or me, you could."

Jenny cleared her throat from the sudden nerves that jumped into her stomach. "Unfortunately, we ran the blood that healer Sharm sent to us and it appears your father has passed through the veil."

Olinda asked Ash. "I am guessing that means he died."

"Yes, that is what it means."

Jenny said. "It is a truly momentous occasion to witness the birth of a new glimmer. What you call a baby or hatchling. It is sad no one was there for you or the glisten Cara." No one in the room thought her sadness was not genuine.

Charlie asked. "The what?"

"I am sorry, Lady Charlie, a glisten is a female baby, and a glint is a male baby, collectively they are called a glimmer. Of course, we only called them that until they become, what you would call a child around five years old. Then they are called a shine, until they reach fifteen, then they are called a blaze.

Olinda nodded. "Uhuh! Well, I am sure for those who do not throw their sperm around like it means nothing, a birth probably is a momentous occasion. It is a shame some of your males don't stick around to see what actually develops, or is that only with human females?"

Jenny disagreed as she finally sat down and pulled a folder from her bag. "No, it is not. Both parents are to be involved always. As decreed by the Ri. it is stated that all possibilities of a glimmer are to be reported so we can monitor and control the glimmer. Not that many of them are conceived. I can assure you, to do all else is against the rules."

Charlie smirked as she asked. "Rules."

"What do you mean, controlled?" Storm asked at the same time.

"So do you know the name of our father?" Olinda asked almost as soon as Storm and Charlie had finished speaking.

Jenny hesitated, causing Charlie to explain. "Please do not

go to the bother of lying, I can tell when you do."

The female looked at her, unsure she was telling the truth. Charlie smiled. "It is a gift."

With a small nod, Jenny addressed Olinda's question first. "Yes, it is known what blood line you and the glisten Cara descend from." She answered Charlie next. "Rules was probably the incorrect word. I should have said guidelines. We have guidelines in raising a glimmer." She turned slightly toward Storm and said, softly. "As for control, we monitor, and if the shine develops an ability, which may or may not happen around five years of age for half-bloods. Of course, for full-bloods, they will develop abilities from birth and will of course have several."

Olinda, her eyes on the female, thoughtfully said. "So let me understand this, that professor guy said I was a full-blood unicorn which is bull as my mother was human."

"He was incorrect. If he had not hurried to be here, he would have seen the full report. You are not quite full-blood." She pulled out a thin folder and handed it to Sharm. "The results from our scientists on the limited tests run."

They waited while Sharm read through four sheets of paper. When he was finished, he told everyone. "It says Olinda is a mix of unicorn and human. Apparently your mother Olinda, may have been half-unicorn, you are closer to full-blood than half."

"I see, so almost full-blood, all the gifts and none of the shift!" She quipped. Several smiles followed her words.

Ash whispered. "I am pleased, I am not sure I like the idea of you shifting to four hoofs."

"Well now, you will never know if you could have caught me?" She whispered back.

"I will always catch you." He whispered. Olinda felt a rush of heat at his words and ducked her head, which made Ash grin.

Sharm said. "As for Cara, she is a unicorn and an elf."

"What?" Charlie yelped, as Storm looked incredulous for a

moment.

Then it was as though something registered in his mind, and he nodded. "I wondered about the structure of her face and ears."

"What about her ears?" Charlie asked him.

He smiled. "Have you never wondered why they are not rounded as Kelsey or ours are?"

"No, it never occurred to me."

"Well wonder no longer." Edith said. "So much fun, now who knows elves?"

She and the others all turned to look at the Battle brothers. They looked at each other, then shrugged as Ash said. "We do not know of any."

Reighn said. "Elves have not been on Earth since magic left."

"Well, apparently that is not true, my Lord. As Cara is half-elf." Charlie grumbled, making Storm smile at his older brother.

Reighn said. "We will deal with that later."

Jenny said. "As it happens, Lady Olinda, you may have gifts or not. I imagine if you did they would have manifested by the age of five." She said this like it was highly unlikely she had any.

Which made Olinda ask. "So, if I was to have gifts or abilities, I would have them already?"

"Yes."

Sharm asked her. "How are they manifested?"

Jenny shrugged delicately. "In many ways, physical or mental. For example, a manipulation of objects, like locks or transporting from one place to another, being able to make oneself disappear. Also things like controlling gambling machines, there is of course a ban on unicorns gambling."

"Of course." Ark said, disbelief clear in his tones. He knew of several unicorns who gambled.

She flicked her eyes toward him and away again as she said. "Also the manipulation of emotions, reading minds, for example."

"Can you tell without tests?" Sharm asked, as he wrote notes in a book.

"Not usually. It is obvious Lady Olinda has none."

"Of course." Olinda said, and it was easy to hear the sarcasm in her tone.

Jenny cleared her throat. The female named Olinda made her uncomfortable, but not as much as the one she was mated to. It was disconcerting, really. She had been prepared to be intimidated and challenged by the Dragon Lord, but this male was unnerving. Jenny knew she was in over her head and wished to be back in her own world. These dragons and others would not be as easy to manipulate as Ri. Caderyn believed. She lowered her eyes from Ash's intense gaze. She felt he could see right through her mask to the unicorn beneath, something she feared would ruin everything if he did so.

Clearing her throat once more, she said. "As for the glisten, Cara. We will have to monitor and test her when she turns five, in three years' time. To see if she develops an ability."

"If she does?" Asked Storm.

Jenny smiled at the male, as scary as he was, he did not make her feel uncomfortable. "Lord Storm, we would have her schooled. We have many respected instructors who may be willing to school a half-blood."

He was seeing what she was alluding to as he narrowed his eyes and mind sent to Ash. *Is she recording this?*

So Ark says.

Reighn mind-sent. *She seems to be quite careful about what she says and only hints at things.*

Sharm said. *I agree.*

Storm said to Jenny. "I understand what you are saying but she could do that here."

Jenny was shaking her head before he had stopped speaking. "Oh no, she would have to come to the Blessing where she would undertake extensive training."

Charlie smiled as she said. "Over our dead bodies. Not going to happen."

"Lady Charlie, I understand your feelings. But the glisten may need specialized training."

"She will get it here."

"It does not work that way." Jenny wrung her hands together. "Ri, Caderyn has set down procedures for all half-breeds."

Storm said. "It does now."

Olinda said. "I advise you to leave that alone. It is three years away, if at all."

Jenny nodded and took a soft breath in and out in relief and said. "As you say, Lady Olinda, well for some general history. Many years ago, when our people did not care about who they impregnated or became pregnant from. Ri, Luthen Lochlon, who has gone beyond the veil, placed a ban on our people and forbade anymore humans to be impregnated."

"Was that to keep your race pure?" Interrupted Edith.

Jenny inclined her head. "In part, but more to keep offspring or glimmers safe because of the gifts that could be passed from their parent. As you can imagine, not all gifts are benign. So a royal decree was issued. It has never been revoked."

"So no glimmers have been conceived since that decree?" Axl asked with a lift of his eyebrow.

"As a rule no."

"Or none that you know about?" Edith stated.

"Or are still alive." Ash drawled. He tempered his statement, he was getting annoyed and was trying hard not to show it.

Jenny kicked her chin up in annoyance. It appeared Ash had struck a nerve, and she told him. "Fortunately, it is not possible for a glimmer to be birthed without the Watchers knowing."

"Excuse me." Olinda laughed, then said with a hard edge to her voice. "My sister and I would put a lie to all of that."

It looked to Reighn as though the female was regretting her impulsive words. Then as he stared into her eyes, he saw she had not misspoken in temper. She had knowingly slipped that bit of information into the conversation, in the hopes whoever was listening, and he knew someone was. Would assume her temper got the better of her. It was a dangerous game she was playing. He hoped she did not pay for it later.

Jenny hesitantly murmured. "So, it would seem."

Olinda looked at Charlie and saw the same knowledge in her eyes that was in hers. They had known someone had known about her and Cara. Casually, Reighn asked. "Who or what are Watchers?"

Jenny almost smiled in relief as she closed her eyes at the question and hoped the Ri, and his people took her expression for regret rather than satisfaction. Quietly, she explained. "They, who monitor planets to see if any unicorns have slipped through to walk your world and to keep them from behaving badly."

Keeper raised an eyebrow as the obvious answer sat in front of them all, but he asked anyway. "So none are allowed?"

Jenny gave a little hesitant laugh. "Oh no, when any unicorns come here on official business, they are to remain in human form. The rules state that quite strictly, and they may not have relations with humans."

"Again, I must point out, Cara and I say otherwise." Muttered Olinda, her annoyance meter reaching the red mark. She said louder and there was a decided snap to her voice. "I think it would be a good idea now to name our father."

"Yes, of course. It was Lindao Lochlon."

"Who was?"

"Ri, Caderyn's son."

"Of course he was." Olinda said with a sigh, and like her, no one there was surprised. On some level, they had all known.

Reighn returned to the previous topic. "These unicorns, called Watchers, are they here on our world, to oversee the visiting unicorns and to watch for any break in the rules?"

Jenny nodded. "Yes, sometimes youths have control issues and slip into their unicorn form or take a lover, not often but it obviously happens."

Sage asked. "And this is where the continued sightings of unicorns come from?"

"Yes."

"Okay." Keeper asked. "You talk of a world and planets, but you came from Washington State?"

"No, I came from a portal opened at offices in Washington State. We actually live on a planet called Uformina and Ri. Caderyn, rules all of Uformina."

"I see." Keeper said with a frown.

Olinda drummed her fingers on the table and said. "This is all very well, but what of our father? It seems he did more than an accidental youthful slip, he actually impregnated not one female but two, years apart."

"Two that we know of." Stated Charlie.

Olinda nodded. "True, so we know he broke your own rules about relating to humans in a carnal way. Where were your Watchers then or since?"

Jenny wrung her hands again. "It is a delicate matter, as we are unsure if indeed you are the family of the one who has gone beyond the veil. You see our difficulty, as you are aware he is no longer here to ask."

Ash said. "Yet earlier you said you knew who they are related to. What game are you playing?"

"I am not Lord Ash." Jenny placed stress on the words I am. Like Reighn, Ash could see she was trying to let them know someone was directing this meeting, and if he had to guess. It would be Olinda's grandfather.

Olinda placed her hand on his tense arm as she said. "Well, Sharm drew blood from us both and we are related. I know our father is no longer alive, and you represent his father. Our grandfather, so you take what he asked for and do your tests and while you are at it, take this back with you." She slid a flash drive over to the startled female. Jenny took it like it held dynamite and swallowed, her eyes traveling over the people there and finally settling on Olinda. "You have the technology to read that I am told, so let the ones who send out your Watchers for our protection read that with our grandfather. Then you tell him his eldest granddaughter said to man up and come and talk to her. Until then, we have no more to say. I am done here." She rose as Ash did and squeezed his arm, then walked out, knowing they all watched her go.

Jenny told them. "I do not think Lady Olinda understands the full import of what it means to be a half-blood unicorn?"

"My Shadow understands, probably more than you do."

"I did not come here intending to disturb and unbalance her or you."

Charlie told her quietly. "She is beyond disturbed, she is angry. Read what she has placed on the drive and you will understand why."

Reighn told her. "The portal is open."

"The folder is for her and you." She told Charlie as she stood and placed the vials of blood that were carefully secured in a container in her briefcase. "It is a simplified version of our history and our planet and language and how Blessings are ruled. There is, of course, an extended version for your scholars. That is, if any are able to understand and read our language."

Reighn said. "We thank you."

Jenny gave one last smile to the room in general, then stepped through the portal.

Charlie went to speak, but Ark made the sign for silence. He closed his eyes, then pointed around the room. Axl, Ash, Storm and Keeper moved to where he pointed and plucked small dots from the walls, floor and from under the table. Also from the folder she had left. They placed them in a bin, and Reighn fried them.

Ark did one more sweep, then said. "We are clear."

Verity entered with Rene` who said. "Highly entertaining."

Surprised, Ella asked. "You were listening?"

Rene` smiled gently at the young dragon and nodded. "Of course, it concerns our grandchild and Ash's Shadow."

"I do not like the fact they think they can use devices to listen to us, that smacks of arrogance." Reighn growled.

Edith asked him. "You knew they were there?"

"Of course."

"The whole time?"

"Yes."

Sage asked him. "Well, why didn't you tell us?"

Reighn laughed. "Oh no, I wanted them to see only some of what they are dealing with."

"Huh! That makes sense. You didn't fry that first one, the professor?" Sage said, disappointed that he had not.

Reighn grinned at her tone. "He was not a bug?"

"Are you sure?" She asked. "Looked like one to me."

Edith asked. "Did Olinda know?"

"Yes, which is why no one is dead." She said as she entered and growled. "Seriously, I am so pissed." She walked into her Shadow's arms and snarled. "No gifts. See what they know."

Ash said. "It is wise they do not. It is never a good idea to show your hand too early."

"Yeah, I understand that."

Edith asked. "Is she allowed to swear?"

"Newbie, so probably." Sage answered sourly.

Olinda grinned at her and Edith. Charlie, now in Storm's arms, asked Olinda. "Can you read that?" She pushed the folders toward her and Keeper, who flicked it open, and they both stared at it. Then looked up smiling and said together. "Yep."

"They assume it will take months, if not years for you to decipher it." Rene` stated. "It is a ploy, while they decide what to do and of course, they can cite things we would have to go away and look up and research. All time wasting exercises."

Olinda grinned. "Tough, Keeper and I will have this read and translated in... What do you think, Keeper?"

"A day, two days at most."

"Yeah, that is what I thought." They could all see the two of them almost quivering with excitement at the prospect of delving into another language and culture.

Charlie said. "All I want to know is, what their rights to Cara are?"

Olinda looked at the couple and said. "They have none."

Storm said. "You said he was her grandparent; there will be rights."

"I did, and he is our grandfather. What Miss Jenny Sanders did not tell you, because she was probably told not to? Is if a glimmer is not claimed within any Blessing before their first birthday, then the Blessings have forfeited all rights to that glimmer. Cara cannot be taken."

"How do you know?" Asked Storm with a touch of hope in his voice.

Olinda's eyes widened as she said. "I don't know how I know. I just do. It is like someone gave me the answer."

"The Goddess, I thought she left?" Edith asked her.

Olinda nodded. "I thought she had, but occasionally I hear a voice. I thought it was her, but now I am unsure. Maybe I am possessed."

Ash laughed gently. "No my soul you are not, the same shield that stops us reading your mind, stops that happening."

"Are you sure?"

"I am positive."

"Well okay." Secretly she wondered at the occasional voice she was hearing. There was a part of her that knew this voice was new.

Ark asked. "So what do we do about the Ri?"

Olinda squirmed. "I don't know, it seems rulers make up their own rules." She looked at Reighn who raised one eyebrow at her statement, grinning she amended that to. "Well, some of them do."

He grinned as he said. "I have heard that."

Keeper said. "We will know by the time we have finished the paperwork she left."

"So that sentence you said yesterday, do you know what it means yet?" Sage asked Olinda.

"Nope, but I will find out."

CHAPTER TWENTY-FIVE:

A sh dragged Olinda away from Keeper after they split the paperwork between them. She and Ash spent the remainder of the day redesigning their home and spending time with the twins. And when they were not being parents, they spent hours learning about each other and what it was going to mean to be a family. After dinner they settled the boys, then she and Ash retired to their bedroom, where Ash took up the mantle of teacher once more, with a very willing Olinda.

Later, after they both fed the twins their last bottle for the night and Olinda was snuggled in Ash's arms once more. She finally told him what the Goddess had prophesied about the girls they were to have. He laughed so hard he'd rolled off the bed, which made her laugh just as hard. It was one of the most enjoyable nights she had experienced for a long time. And by the look of contentment on Ash's face, as he wandered their home with a baby in his arms the following morning. It seemed that the night before had been just as pleasurable for him.

They used the following day to complete the shopping they had both put off. Several times, she was sure she had not purchased clothes that appeared in her closets. On the third day, Olinda slipped out of bed early to give the boys their first bottles of the day and as she rocked both babies. She finally got time to read through the papers given to them by the unicorns. By the time the babies were ready to return to their bassinets, she had a working understanding of the unicorn's language. Walking into the kitchen, she stared blankly at the coffeepot, thinking that she really should learn how to make it. Then she remembered she had to call Keeper.

"Hey Keeper, so have you finished your papers?"

"Good morning, Olinda."

"Oh yeah. Good morning, Keeper."

"Yes, I have read the papers. I assume you have to."

"Yes, do you want to swap?"

"How about Ella and I come over for breakfast and we go through what we have discovered so far?"

"Umm… Well, okay." She was positive there was some cereal left. She could hear the laugh in his voice when he said. "Ella has offered to cook breakfast."

"She has, that would be great. See you soon."

"Goodbye."

"Oh yeah, goodbye."

Ash walked into the kitchen, and she told him. "The coffee pot is broken."

He looked at the counter and saw the intact coffee machine. "It does not look broken."

"There is no coffee, therefore broken. Guess what?"

"Good morning, sweetheart."

"Oh yeah, good morning, guess what?"

He smiled, his Olinda was often forgetful of social norms and she had an obscure sense of humor, which he was learning he actually enjoyed. She amused him and his dragon constantly, she added light to what had been a dull life full of routine. He and his dragon thought she was adorable. "What can I not guess?"

"Keeper and Ella are coming over and bringing food."

"Wonderful, I will make coffee."

"Okay, I will dress." Seeing as she only had a robe on, he thought that was a good idea. As she hurried from the room, he frowned. They were going to have to hire a housekeeper, and quickly, he called June. "Good morning, June."

"Hi Ash, what can I do for you?"

"We need a cook and housekeeper, also we have alterations to the apartment that we would like to discuss with you."

"That is quite a list. What does Olinda say?"

"About the apartment, it was her idea."

"No, I meant about the cook and housekeeper?"

"I have no idea. I have not asked her, should I?"

June laughed softly as she said. "The answer to that is yes, but wait until I get there. I will be up for breakfast; I heard Ella is cooking."

Smiling at her not-so-subtle invite to breakfast, he told her. "She is. I am making coffee."

"Well, make enough for everyone; your brothers have just arrived. I like tea."

"Of course they have, and I am aware you do."

Ash made coffee and tea. Minutes later, June with Ark and Axl arrived. The brothers went straight to the twin's room as they usually did upon arriving at their apartment. Olinda saw them when she came from her bedroom. As she pushed into the kitchen and took the offered cup of coffee from Ash, she asked. "Do your brothers think we do dastardly things to the twins?"

"I do not think so."

"Are you sure? Because as soon as they get here, they rush straight to their room."

"It is because we did not think we would ever have our own young, so they are still amazed by them and protective."

"Oh, I see. June, did you not have food either?"

"Good morning."

"Oh yeah, morning."

"Yes, I have food. Thank you Ash." She said as he passed her a cup of tea. He sat next to Olinda as he told her. "June is here for breakfast and to discuss the renovations."

"Oh great."

"Also, I have asked her to hire a cook and housekeeper for us."

"Oh, thank goodness. I cannot cook and as much as Ash is very good at ordering in, we are desperate. So who will we get?"

June said. "Charlie and Queen Scarlett were just telling me

of two sisters. One likes to cook and the other does house-work."

Olinda asked. "You have to be kidding, why?"

June shrugged. "No idea, I don't get it either."

"So faeries?" Ash asked, bringing them back to the conversation.

June finished her sip of tea, then said. "Yes, Bay likes to cook and her sister Ember will be your housekeeper."

Ash asked. "What does a housekeeper do?"

"She will oversee the cleaners and do light housework, as in tidy rooms, make beds, laundry, vacuum, things like that. Also, she will do all of your ordering, anything you need and organize your schedules if you need her too. Mainly she tends to the house and everything in it. If you wish for nannies, we will find you some that will work well with Bay and Ember. Oh, and you should be aware, they will not live in and must have days off."

"Of course they will. What is normal?" Olinda asked her.

"Weekends usually."

"We will do that." Ash told her as Olinda nodded in agreement.

June smiled. "Okay, so do you want to meet them?"

Ash asked Olinda. "What do you think?"

"Yes, it makes sense. I am not a good housekeeper and we are both going back to work soon, right?"

Ash nodded. "Right."

Olinda smiled and said. "June, please have them come as soon as they can."

"Good." she made a call. "Charlie, yes, send them over. When they are free, please."

Olinda grinned as Ash laughed and asked. "You had them lined up already?"

June grinned. "It is what I do."

Axl and Ark came in, followed by Keeper and Ella. They were followed by Sage and Reighn, who were loaded down with containers of food, which they placed on the counters.

Reighn and Keeper sat as Sage, Axl, Ark and Ella started to set the table and open the food containers. It smelled delicious. Olinda moaned. "I am so hungry."

"Mama sent food as well. She and Papa have the girls for breakfast, so we thought we would come here." Reighn told them as Olinda and Keeper exchanged papers and were instantly engrossed in reading them.

Ash said. "Ignore them. They will be finished shortly. I am pleased you could come. How are things?"

Reighn nodded. "Good, all is good."

As the food was placed on the table and Olinda's coffee cup was refilled, she finished reading. "Interesting."

Keeper finished a few minutes later as he looked at her and agreed. "It is." He looked around at the others and said. "When we have finished breakfast, we will tell you what we found."

Reighn agreed. "I also have news."

Ash said. "I just want to say thank you for the food and company."

Olinda smiled in agreement saying. "Especially for the food."

They laughed and then dug in. Soon plates were full and mouths were busy eating. Olinda was amused to see she actually could eat more than the day before. Her stomach was finally expanding and working again. Within a short time, all the food had been consumed, and they sat around with only coffee or tea as Ark and Axl cleared the table and loaded the dishwasher. Edith, Sharm. Lars and Claire arrived.

Sage asked. "Are your young with the grandparents?"

Lars nodded. "They are. We have come for coffee and news."

Edith grinned. "I am just nosy." She pointed to Sharm and said. "He is here to check the twins."

Sharm nodded. "And for news."

"The more the merrier." Olinda agreed as she moved over a little. Reighn asked Keeper. "So what do you know?"

Keeper said. "The first is what I found out about the Sun dragons, which was pitiful. The best I can come up with is this small quote from an old obscure text written over five thousand years ago in Gaelic. When the Sun Dragons and the Moon Dragons combine to be in the world at the same time. Magic is released on Dragonkind, and a wrong is righted." He then said. "Before you ask, that is all we know. I can make some guesses. It is possible there are another set of twins out there, which are Moon dragons. I looked them up as well and found another quote which said the same thing with Moon dragons instead of Sun dragons. So no help."

Reighn said. "Thank you Keeper, we will treat them as normal hatchlings and see what happens as they grow."

"Because something will happen." Claire stated. "We all can feel that."

"Because we have the Grounder attracting everything and anything to Dragon's Gap. So the possibilities are endless." Sage agreed with a smile directed at Edith.

She sniffed dramatically. "Of course, blame the bear."

Olinda laughed with the others as Sage said. "Who else is there?"

"True."

Storm and Charlie arrived, and Sage asked. "Are your young with the grandparents?"

Storm grinned. "Yes, we left the nannies to help."

Charlie took a seat as Axl handed her a mug of coffee. She gave him a smile. "So what are we up to?"

"Unicorns." Reighn said. "The documents that Lady Jenny gave us?"

Olinda said. "The language was easy once the code was broken, and also the basic history was more or less what we already knew. There is a much more detailed history, but it does not concern us. Cara may be interested when she is older. What was surprising, is how much Cara and I are owed in compensation?"

"Do you want it?" Edith asked.

"What do you think?"

"I think they should give you and Cara everything you are owed and more." She said fiercely. Olinda could see her bear in her darkened eyes as she glared in outrage for her and Cara.

"Maybe you are right. The decision for Cara is her parents to make, as for myself. I will think about it."

"Well, think about your young. Their mother is owed, as they will be." Said Sage.

Ash said. "We will talk about it." Which seemed to satisfy both Sage and Edith.

Storm said. "We will also talk about this. It is not ours to determine alone. We must think of Cara."

"Speaking of Cara, were you able to translate the sentence?" Asked Charlie.

Olinda smiled. "I did. It seems what I said was in a very old language, maybe the first unicorn language ever spoken. As you know, language moderates, and changes over time. In the language of the unicorn, I said. Sanda mlo phojo unicorn somta. Translation; Time to wake precious unicorn from your slumber."

Claire mused softly. "I wonder if that was for you or Cara."

Olinda looked at her. "Maybe both."

Keeper said. "Most of what they gave us were just rules and regulations, nothing earth shattering. They screwed up with Olinda and Cara and are covering as fast as they can."

Reighn looked at Olinda. "Is this Ri, your grandfather?"

"Yes."

"So you will be unsurprised to hear he has requested a meeting this afternoon?"

"Not really. What time?"

"Three o'clock, in my conference room."

Ark asked. "Do you want us there?"

Reighn nodded. "Yes, as well as you, Storm and Charlie."

Charlie growled. "Just try stopping us."

Claire offered. "We will babysit."

CHAPTER TWENTY-SIX:

At three o'clock precisely. Ri. Caderyn Lochlon and his three-person entourage arrived. One of his entourage was Emissary Jenny Sanders. She was with two males that had to be brothers; they were so alike.

Reighn knew the Ri. had to be years older than his people and wondered why he had brought such young advisors with him. He must have older, more experienced females and males to give him counsel. What statement was he trying to make, and to whom?

Jenny bowed and said. "Dragon Lord Reighn, please allow me to introduce Ri. Caderyn Lochlon from the Lochlon Blessing." The two leaders inclined their heads. Then Jenny said. "May I introduce Jordan and Ethan Reading?" They both bowed, and Reighn inclined his head again.

Lars said. "Please allow me to introduce Dragon Lord Reighn Kingsley. I am Prime Lars Axton. If you would take a seat, we are just waiting for the couples to arrive."

Caderyn said. "I expected them to be here. I did say three."

Reighn nodded. "You did, but both have young and young do not care about meetings."

Caderyn did not reply to that as Lars opened the sliding door, displaying a large oval table with chairs, he took his seat and then his people did. Lars stood behind Reighn's chair.

Within minutes, the two couples walked in. Lars directed them to their seats as Ark and Axl arrived and slid into place against the wall behind Olinda and Charlie.

Sitting at the table was a male that had to be Olinda's grandfather. He had long, fine golden hair, and his eyes were the blue of the sky. Ash thought the male's features were delicate, he did not know how else to describe them. As with all unicorns, he was handsome, but something about the male put his dragon on edge.

Olinda stared at the male that was her grandfather and sighed: he was beautiful and she had to assume her father had been as well. She knew the documents had said Caderyn was at least nine hundred years old, but he looked fifty. She thought Sage would have loved to have met the male, he looked exactly how a unicorn should. As she watched the graceful movements of his hands, a part of her was pleased to know who she came from. She could see that she was or would be slim like he was when she regained weight. Even though her hair was brown, not blond, her eyes were the same shape as his. It was sad to see there was not a lot of her mother in her own features.

Charlie watched the male like a bug on a slide. So this was Cara's grandfather. As hard as she tried, she could see none of Cara in him. It seemed her baby took after her birth mother.

Storm sized the male up and found him lacking. His dragon snarled. *He will not take our Cara from us.*

No, my friend, he will not.

The males with him were similar to Jenny, and they were all dressed alike. Even Jenny was dressed, in black pants and jacket with a blue buttoned shirt. Unlike Caderyn, their hair was short and swept back from their foreheads. She wondered if it was a requirement to have their gold hair styled like that. As Olinda took in their appearance, she wondered if Cara's hair would be golden like theirs when it grew. Or perhaps their hair was dyed, so they were uniformed. She found that thought sad and hoped it was not true. The young males were handsome and definitely not delicate like Jenny. They reminded her of bouncers at a night club, both looked hard and had brown eyes that stared at her with intensity. As their eyes lingered on her, Olinda could feel Ash tense beside her. Suddenly, both sets of eyes swung to him, assessing and appraising him. It was unclear if they found him wanting or not. He seemed to find them wanting, if his lack of response to their attention was any sign. Olinda nodded at her grandfather and the three who sat with him.

Reighn said to the couples. "As you can see, we have been visited by Ri. Caderyn Lochlon and his emissary Jenny Sanders who we met a few days ago. These males are Jordan and Ethan Reading. Ri. Lochlon, this is Ash and Olinda Battle and Charlie and Storm Kingsley. I already explained that meeting with Cara was unlikely."

"Why?" asked the male and his voice was like a memory that washed over Olinda's senses. She raised her eyes to his and found him staring at her, then felt a pressure on her mind.

Ash slammed his hand on the table, making Olinda jump. Charlie grabbed her hand under the table and held it as Ash growled. "Do not, social politeness says I cannot kill you. That does not mean I will not. You will not break my Shadows shield; it is a gift from a Goddess." The pressure on Olinda's shields instantly vanished.

With a slight smile, Caderyn apologized. "I apologize, it was reflex only." His smirk said otherwise.

Ash remained tense as his eyes narrowed, then the two unicorns shifted in their seats. Ash nodded as he said. "Do not, it would not be your Ri' life that would be forfeited."

Caderyn watched the two half-bloods subside, and barely concealed his sneer, cowards, all of them, not like this dragon. What he could do with a warrior like him.

Reighn said. "Please refrain from anymore reflexes. You are here as a courtesy only to Olinda." Reminding Caderyn, he was the power here, not him.

Caderyn inclined his head in acknowledgment. The smirk remained in place, but the tightening of the skin around his eyes told of his displeasure. The young unicorns all looked at Reighn, then at Ash with shuttered eyes. Caderyn turned his amazing eyes on Olinda as he asked. "You say you are my granddaughter?"

"No, I do not. How would I know that? What I know is I am

Cara's sister. Whether we are related to you, we do not know."

Ash said, and his voice held his dragon. "He knows you are. That is why he wants to meet Cara. You cannot have either one."

Caderyn just kept the growl from his voice as he calmly stated. "They are of my blood."

Olinda asked. "What is going on?"

Ash explained. "He wishes to take you and Cara with him today."

Olinda shook her head as she felt Charlie and Storm tense. "No, that will not happen."

Caderyn banged the table with a fist. Fortunately, this time Olinda did not react. "He was my son, my only child, his mother died giving birth to him. My son was a strong, brave male. He had a spine of tempered steel, which he got from me. His mother gave him her beauty."

"Oh, I see. So you are implying, not all unicorns are beautiful?" Olinda asked.

He gave her a quizzical look as he answered. "We are, all full-blood unicorns are exquisite."

By the expressions of the three half-bloods with him, he had said this often. Olinda thought maybe it was said so often the insult slid right off them. Unfortunately, it did not slide off her, and on behalf of sweet, beautiful Cara, she felt her temper rise.

He looked Olinda over almost as one would look stock over and told her. "Klister was exceptional, you have the look of her." He looked pained and Olinda wanted to believe it was because he had loved his mate and missed her, but she could not. She felt it had more to do with the fact she did not quite measure up to his expectations.

She murmured without emotion. "I am sorry for your loss."

He tipped his head to the side as he told her. "I know you have suffered. I read the information about you and Cara. I am sorry you were left alone, it was unintentional."

"Really!" Charlie scoffed. "Twenty- six years apart. I think that ship has sailed, your precious son left them both, and you allowed it. Not once, but twice, we know you did." She held her hand up as anger slipped into her voice. "My Cara suffered horrendously, and your Watchers did nothing. On your orders."

He looked pissed off, as Storm said. "There are only two reasons for that."

Ash agreed. "They, and by they... I mean, you and your son hoped either Cara or Olinda would die or be killed. You gave orders for your Watchers to do nothing, and that is what they did, nothing. When neither of your granddaughters died, you waited and had them watched to see how they developed. When Cara went beyond your reach, you turned your attention toward my Shadow." He looked at Olinda, pain for what he was about to say in his eyes. "You had her hunted, to see what strengths and abilities she had, to see if she could be harnessed for breeding." Reighn hissed out a breath, along with the others, all except Olinda, who sat immobile. Ash said quietly. "For that alone you should be held accountable."

"You believe this?" Caderyn asked Olinda. "I am your grandfather; you are of my blood, you knew my voice when you heard it."

"I did and yes I believe my Shadow. I know he would not lie. I believe you hoped in the beginning we would both die. Then your son died, and you turned your thoughts to preserving your line. We were told, no half-bloods are permitted, but you have allowed half-bloods to exist, probably encouraged their births. Our father was not the only one to have children, it is obvious these three here are all half-bloods. You have Watchers to not oversee and protect humanity or unicorns. It is to monitor the children to see what gifts develop, so you can claim them. You knew who I was, and instead of helping me, you hunted me. I, unlike my Shadow, do not believe you had no one watching Cara. I think you left her to her abusers on purpose and were hoping to see what she would do as a half- elf. I believe you were hoping her abilities would develop early." She leaned a little toward him as she softly told him. "I hope I am wrong. In fact, I pray very hard I am because if I ever find out for a fact, you did exactly that. I will ask her uncle, the Lord of all dragons, to wipe you from existence." She leaned back in her chair and drew in a breath of air. "You think to claim both Cara and myself, you cannot. We were unclaimed, therefore you lost all rights to her and me. You waste your time trying to convince her family or me otherwise."

Caderyn drew himself up in his chair. "You think to dictate Uformina law. My law to me?"

"Sure, I studied it. I also know Cara and I are owed an inheritance from not only our father but also our grand-mother. And because of the neglect we both suffered and Cara's two years of hell, you personally owe her and you owe me for having me hunted. Quote: No one of royal birth shall be left unguarded. Unquote. Your words I believe. We are en-titled to compensation and we demand compensation. We deserve at least that and if we do not receive it. I am sure I can persuade my Lord to disseminate the information we have discovered. About your habit of allowing your grand-children to be abused and hunted." She shook her head as she looked at him. "I am ashamed to be related to you. I will do everything in my power to make sure my sister never meets you. And I will work to help and protect all the half-bloods you have bred and if I can get them away from your Blessing, I will. Because for them I think it is no blessing at all, only servitude."

Caderyn quickly stood, causing everyone else to stand. Anger bled off him in waves as his hands clenched and un-clenched, showing his loss of control. Olinda was in no doubt if he could have reached across the table and throttled her, he would have. He hissed as his eyes went stormy gray. "En-titled... You dare?"

"Yes, I dare. You left us and gave orders for us to be ignored, and then you had me hunted. You allowed Cara to be abused. My mother struggled. I struggled. I know he told her who he was, she loved him desperately, and called his name at the end of her life."

He raged. "You lie."

"You want what I say to be a lie, so it will soothe your conscience. Lindao is an unusual name, Olinda is just as strange." She flipped her hand at him. "Please, as if I would not remember him. I saw him until I was five-years-old, then never again, and Cara's mother is an elf. I am betting she died giving birth to her daughter. There is no other reason Cara would have been placed into the system. He never even bothered to check to see if she needed help and neither did you after his death. Shame on you, we are your granddaughters, our grandmother, your mate would be ashamed of you for what you allowed him to do, for what you did, as am I."

"He was my son, my only child!"

Ash's features were hewn from stone and with his dragon in his voice, he stated. "You could have had two granddaughters to remember him and your mate by. You threw them away like trash."

Olinda said. "I have no more to say to you. Make sure Cara and I receive what we are owed."

Storm said. "You have no rights to our daughter."

Charlie said carefully and slowly. "She is ours, we claimed her, do not make my Shadow and I have to enforce this, because we will."

"You threaten me. I am Ri. of Uformina."

Reighn said, and the power of the Dragon Lord was in his voice. "We are well aware of who you are, and I declare you have no rights to either Olinda Battle or Cara Kingsley. Do not test me on this Ri. Do not test the dragon nation. We will go to war for our own."

Ash said slowly, and no one could mistake the anger he held in check. "Your mission here should have been honest. Charlie knows when you lie, even in your heart. And what she and I know is you never wanted Olinda once you found out she had no abilities you could capitalize on? You hoped by winning Olinda over you would have access to her sister."

Olinda laughed bitterly. "Well, that seems plausible. I bet you understood that I would have no reason to leave my home from our meeting with your Emissary. So, as my Shadow said. You thought to take Cara. You want to breed her with some male of your choosing in the hopes you will have another son to raise."

Storm's dragon stared out from his eyes as his skin turned to scales. Charlie's eyes turned ghost gray as the male snarled. "You think you know what I want?"

Reighn said. "If she does not, he does." He nodded to the figure behind him. Caderyn and his people turned swiftly, only to be confronted by an Elemental with swirling universes in his eyes.

What you purposed to do here today was unwise. The one known as Olinda is Goddess touched. If you would open your senses, son of Lethem Lochlon, you would see this is so.

They all looked at Olinda, Caderyn's eyes widened as he said. "Goddess touched, which Goddess?"

"Why would that concern you?" Asked Ash.

The Elemental said. *The glimmer known as Cara is not of your blood alone. Her place in this world is by your son's design. Which you forfeited by not claiming her. Look elsewhere for your heir. Your child's daughters are not yours for the taking. We will not permit it.*

Caderyn slumped in his chair as the Elemental vanished. "I thought I could have him back or a piece of my Klister. I see I was wrong." He looked up at Olinda. "You will not be contacted again, all that is owed to you and Cara will be forwarded."

Olinda could not bring herself to call him grandfather, instead she said. "Goodbye Ri. Caderyn." She then bowed to Reighn. "With your permission, my Lord?"

He nodded, and she turned with Ash as he guided her from

the room, followed by Charlie and Storm, with Axl and Ark walking behind them. Reighn said. "A portal is open for you. Please do not make me regret any more than I already do, this meeting."

Caderyn nodded. "I will forward the amount owed. She is very much like my son, but has my Klister's softness. He and I were always missing that. I think years ago I made a mistake and again just now."

Reighn said nothing, he agreed with him and still did not trust the male. "Goodbye Ri."

"Goodbye Dragon Lord."

"Remember your history, the last time our races met in battle. Unicorns barely survived."

Caderyn nodded, he was unsure if Reighn spoke the truth but he would find out, he had a sneaky suspicion the Dragon Lord was correct. He left through the portal with a heavy heart. Jenny and the brothers followed him through the glowing doorway, with thoughts of a future racing through their minds.

Ark walked back into the room with Axl after seeing the two couples to the lift. Lars and Reighn waited while Ark closed his eyes and slowly turned in a circle, searching for devices left by the unicorns. When he found nothing, he said. "We are clear."

"Thank you, Ark." Reighn said wearily as the brothers departed.

"He is an asshole," Stated Lars as soon as they were gone. Reighn smiled at his Prime. "Agreed, our people did well, though."

"Yes. No one died, that I say, was a good meeting."

Reighn nodded in agreement. "Considering who was here. Yes, I agree."

CHAPTER TWENTY-SEVEN:

By mutual agreement, the two couples went back to Olinda's and Ash's apartment and ended up in one of the small lounges. Claire and Sage entered after them. Claire told her. "The boys are asleep."

"How did it go?" Sage asked as she and Claire sat on one of the couches. Before they could answer, Sage said. "Reighn and Keeper were studying the histories right up until the meeting. Did you know the dragons warred with the unicorn's way back when?"

Everyone said no, they had not known that. Storm asked. "Who won?"

Sage grinned. "We did, of course."

Charlie said. "He was an asshole." Then held her hand up as she said. "I will pay the swear jar, but it is hard to see Olinda or Cara as his granddaughters."

Storm said. "I did not like the male, he was sly. It was he who had Olinda hunted."

Sage and Claire gasped. "The pig!" said an outraged Sage.

Claire shook her head. "No good will come of that decision for him."

Ash looked at Olinda. "What did you think?"

"You know what I think, he is no family to me. Before we went in there, I was unwilling to take anything from him. Now I believe we should have everything we are owed. Regardless of what I choose to do with it, he will pay."

"Karma is a bitch." Storm grinned at the laughter that followed his statement.

Olinda grinned as well, then sobered as she said. "He has ruled for too long and expects everyone to bow and concede to him. Even when he was here, he believed we would all fall into line with his wants."

"Wrong place for that." Sage said from her comfortable position on the deep-cushioned couch. "Hey, if you don't want this couch. I will take it."

Olinda shook her head. "Nope, Ash and I love it."

Ash said. "It is good for..." Olinda placed her hand hurriedly over his mouth, saying. "Yes, well... we all do not need to know that."

They all laughed at her pink face and Ash's laughing eyes. Sage and Claire both jumped up and said. "Eww!"

"Seriously." Olinda yelped. "Not that!"

"Not yet." Mumbled Ash, causing them to all laugh again as Sage and Claire once again sat down. The laughter released the pent up tension they had from the meeting.

"Why did he bring those young males and Jenny with him?" Asked Olinda. "It seems illogical. They would not be good advisors. I mean, they never even spoke, they just stared at Ash the whole time. Older people would have made more sense."

Storm shrugged. "He wanted you to see the studs you could breed with."

Again, Sage and Claire said. "Eww!" This time, Charlie and Olinda joined them.

Ash looked at Storm, who grinned at him. Ash was positive he felt a twitch above his left eye as he said. "I think he wanted to show you how valued half-bloods are."

Charlie said. "But he doesn't value them, his entire attitude is for pure bloodlines."

Ash replied. "That was the impression I received."

Olinda frowned. "I feel sorry for them?"

Claire asked. "Who?"

"The three with him."

"Why?" Storm asked. "They seemed healthy."

She smiled at him. "Just because they look healthy does not mean they are. To me they looked sad and hungry for acceptance."

Charlie disagreed. "When did you see that? I didn't. To me, they seemed like trained killers."

Olinda shrugged. "Well, yeah, they were that too. It was just a feeling."

Claire said. "Well, enough of that for now. Your cook and housekeeper arrived and they are delightful."

Just then, two females entered the lounge. Claire smiled and said. "This is Bay; she is your new chef."

The female was about five foot six or seven, slim and beautiful. She had spiked blue hair, which suited her small, round face. She had a delightful smile, and her eyes twinkled with humor as though the world amused her.

Olinda, although she had agreed with the plan for both housekeeper and cook, was hesitant. She trusted Ash and Charlie and was coming to trust the others, but she worried about having other people in her home. Seeing the spunky female standing in front of her, she took all those concerns back and threw them away, she just felt instantly comfortable with the faerie. Whether it was the blue hair or the amber eyes that made her relax or the jeans and long-sleeved shirt. She didn't know, but when she looked at her sister, she felt the same. So guessed it was just the females themselves.

Ember was almost identical to Bay, except she had long purple hair. Her brown eyes also held humor in their depths, and she was dressed in almost identical clothes to her sister. She smiled sweetly at Olinda and Ash.

Charlie said. "Ladies, you know this is your last chance, if you cannot make this work, it is back to the High Queens Grove for you."

They both sighed together as the one named Bay said. "We understand, Lady Charlie."

Olinda grinned at the exasperated tone. Obviously, they had this talk already. "Why is it your last chance?" Asked Ash, who was unsure if he wanted faeries that were deemed unworthy near his family.

Charlie answered. "The sisters have a slight problem with

authority. They were both in the High Queens guard and found that too restrictive."

Storm asked. "Who did you punch?"

Ember tried not to smile as she said. "Our commanding officer."

"Both of you?" Asked a startled Ash.

Bay stated. "He had no appreciation of style."

"He deserved it." Ember agreed.

Storm looked at their hair and the clothes they both wore, which comprised dark colors and jeans. So very different to what most faeries wore, and grinned. "I see."

Ember shrugged and looked at Olinda and Ash. "We have a hard time fitting into Grove life."

Olinda said. "I can imagine it would annoy you, especially if they have rules like dress codes?"

They both beamed a smile at her as Bay told her. "It did. We don't mind rules that make sense, but seriously, some of them are just so old-fashioned, it is time they realized what century we live in."

"Yes, well, I am trying." Charlie sighed. "I can only do so much, you know?"

"Oh, we know you are Lady Charlie." Ember told her.

As Olinda looked around the room, which she knew Ash and she had left in a mess, she saw it was tidy and clean. Just then, a heavenly scent wafted in from the kitchen.

"Bay is making cookies." June said as she entered.

Olinda said. "You are hired, both of you."

"Thank you." said Ember. "We really like the hatchlings and think we will all get along."

"Welcome to our home. Ash hon, are you okay with that?" She asked him.

"If you are happy, I am. Welcome ladies."

June told Olinda and Ash. "The castle pays their wages. I have spoken to the sisters about their pay and time off."

Worriedly, Olinda told them. "Oh, good and food we have not shopped."

Bay said. "I have ordered all the supplies needed, they were delivered while you were at your meeting. If it pleases you, may we sit later and go over what type of meals you and Lord Ash require."

Ember said. "At the same time, we can discuss what duties you wish of us both."

"Good idea." With that settled, Ash led them all into the kitchen, telling Bay and Ember. "We eat mostly in here. The formal dining room, is I suppose for formal dinners." He scratched his cheek as he said it.

Storm said. "Seems reasonable to me. I think we have one of those as well."

"So, I am right."

Olinda and the others hid their laughter when they realized they were serious. Several minutes later, seated at their kitchen table, Bay and Ember served coffee and tea with freshly baked cookies.

Charlie sipped her coffee, then asked. "You think he meant it, about leaving them alone?"

Ash asked. "Did he lie?"

"No."

"Then he meant it."

Sage murmured. "Sad for him."

"His own fault, he left that sweet baby to be hurt. He owes her." Stated Olinda.

"All because she was not a male." Growled Charlie.

"Really?" Asked Claire.

Olinda told them quietly. "Yes, if either Cara or I had been a male, he would have snatched us up minutes after we were born or if we had developed abilities."

"Sexist asshole." June mumbled.

Storm said. "No, he is a purest."

Ash nodded. "Not just for bloodlines, abilities as well. Even you, my soul, said you saw your father until you turned five, when they say your gifts should have appeared."

"That is true, after I turned five I never saw him again."

Sage asked. "Do you have gifts? I did not know that."

"She is also Goddess touched. I should imagine a Goddess could mask any gifts." Storm said, with a glint in his eyes.

Olinda laughed. "Yes, I do, and I bet the Goddess did exactly that. I believe it was to make sure I arrived here for Ash and the boys."

"But why... I mean, why you?" Asked June.

Sage asked. "Obviously, your father makes you royalty, but what about your mother?"

Olinda shrugged. "She was human. I don't recall her telling me she was anything different. Look at my father, she never said anything about what he was."

Ash gently reminded her. "You are forgetting you are three quarters unicorn, so she must have been half herself."

"Oh, I had forgotten that. I wonder why she never told me. It seems wrong that she kept that secret. Although she may have not wanted to admit it."

Sage said. "Maybe she was frightened for you?"

"Do you think he knew and chose her because she was half-unicorn?" Asked June.

"Makes a kind of logical sense." Keeper said as he and Ella arrived.

Olinda asked. "Why not impregnate a full-blood then?"

Ella said slowly. "Was he angered at his parent and from that anger sought your mother to cross his father?"

"Maybe that could be true, but does not explain Cara?" Storm said.

Olinda said. "I wish to think it was for love. He and her mother fell in love, maybe mine as well."

Charlie said. "I like that version too, so when she asks, we will tell her that."

"Yes we will." Olinda agreed. Even though they all knew it was a lie. He mated an elf for the abilities they hoped the child would develop. He was, after all, his father's only son.

"So maybe, that is why you have gifts and the Goddess liked you?" Claire grinned at Olinda.

"Because I am three quarters unicorn? Why not?"

"It is one reason I like you." Ash said as he wiggled his brows up and down. She laughed, as did the other females, to the groans of the two brothers.

"Or it could be she has the ideal temperament and gifts to raise two special dragons." Mused Claire.

"Well yeah, maybe." Sage agreed.

June asked. "So, you are saying the Goddess hid all Olinda's abilities from her father."

"Yes." Ash answered.

Olinda thought about that, then said. "Well, that would explain a lot, actually."

Sage asked. "What about Cara?"

"Her gifts, if she has any, will develop around five." Charlie told them.

Claire said thoughtfully. "So, he died around the same time Cara was born, otherwise he would have had contact with her like he did with Olinda."

Sage asked Olinda. "Do you know how your father died?"

"Yes, he was an enforcer for his father and was killed in the line of duty. That was all it said in the report."

"Will he really send you money?" Axl asked as he and Ark walked in from the babies' room.

Olinda thought about it. "I don't know?"

Reighn said as he entered the kitchen. "He will send it, as King, he cannot be seen, not too. You are my family. He understood that when he left, I will not stand by as you and Cara are forgotten or ignored. He will pay." He kissed Sage and took a seat next to her, as Lars did likewise to Claire. Bay and Ember came with more cookies and drinks. Reighn said. "Ladies, I hear you are to work for Lady Olinda and Lord Ash?"

"We are, my Lord." Ember replied respectfully.

He looked them over and smiled. "I like a person with style. You should fit in well at the castle. You know who their hatchlings are."

Smiling at the compliment, and slightly relieved he was not going to make them leave. Bay answered for them both. "We do, my Lord, Lady June and Lady Charlie explained it."

"You feel capable of defending them?"

"Oh yes my Lord." Their serious faces showed they meant it.

He nodded. "Good."

Ash said. "Ladies, join us. You will need to know what we are to discuss here today."

They nodded and grabbed a cup of tea, each sitting on bar stools at the breakfast bar. Olinda asked as she stared at the bar. "Was that there this morning?"

Ash grinned as he told her. "No, it is an addition."

"Oh okay, did I want that?"

He eyed his Shadow and said. "No, I did."

"Excellent choice. I like it; the builders are very quick."

"Magic." He stated simply.

Olinda opened and closed her mouth, then said faintly. "Oh okay."

Sage asked. "So getting back to the Ri. who will know if he doesn't pay?"

"People will know, it always gets out." Reighn assured her as he placed two cookies in his mouth.

Charlie asked. "So Olinda, is Cara safe?"

"Yes, how can she not be? She has the whole dragon nation in front of her as well as her family and me, then there is her deadly mother and father. Your daughter is safe, but do not be surprised if he tries reaching out again."

Charlie sighed and rubbed her face. "We will deal with that when it happens.

Storm asked Olinda. "What do we do for Cara now?"

"As I have gifts given by our father, even though they will not admit it. It is possible she will too, but we have the added complication of her being half-elf."

"We have three years to search and find out about the elves." Said Reighn. "My niece is safe for now and will remain so. If we cannot find the elves, we will ask the Elementals to find them. Seeing as they saw fit to come today, they must know something."

"We have time for Olinda and I, to learn all there is about unicorns. I swear we will find out everything we can about them and elves." Keeper assured everyone there.

Charlie hugged Olinda as she said. "I know you will, Keeper. I would prefer not to go to war with the unicorns. It will really upset Sage and Cara, they still like them. So learn all you can."

Olinda laughed. "Got it and I am unicorn too."

"There will be no war." Reighn stated. "The Elementals will not allow it."

"Oh yeah, forgot about them." Charlie told the room.

They spent a leisurely hour filling the faeries in on what they knew about unicorns and the sun dragons and discussing the meeting with the Ri. When the babies whimpered, the impromptu meeting broke up, as parents needed to see to their young and others needed to go back to work. Keeper asked Olinda before they left if she felt well enough to start work in two days.

She told Ash, after Keeper had left, that she was excited about the prospect of being back in the library. They sat with Bay and Ember as they fed the twins and discussed how they were to work together. It was easy for Ash to see that Olinda liked the faeries, and for that, he was happy. If he had to leave home for any length of time, she would be surrounded by people she enjoyed and who would protect her.

CHAPTER TWENTY-EIGHT:

F inlay Slorah known by his friends as Fin, walked the hallways of the castle. He had been told Lady Edith had her studio on this level. He strolled the corridors unhurriedly as he looked at the tapestries and paintings. There was nowhere he needed to be, and no one had work for him at the moment. Although he did have a few concerns for him and his dragon to think about.

Ella and Keeper were at a meeting, and if he was honest with himself, he was bored and feeling useless. Idleness did not sit well with him, he could not remember a time he had felt like this. So he decided to do something about his situation. In his short time here, he had observed the dynamics of the family his Ella found herself related to and by extension himself. He had thought about each person and what they were like, what attributes they had that could help him. After careful consideration, he had discarded all but three, maybe four people. He could talk to the Dragon Lord or his Prime, which was in truth talking to Reighn. He could talk to the delightful Grace: she was a wise female and very charming, but not really helpful for a former Shield. The same could be said for Rene` and Storm. He knew their advice would be to return to service, but he did not wish to do so any longer. Those days he felt were over. Fin had discarded all the other options and was left with the Grounder. He felt Lady Edith was his best choice, she would know what he needed; he hoped.

He wanted to retire at Dragon's Gap and hopefully court a certain female wolf when he had settled his immediate future. His dragon, unlike some he had seen and heard of, was a long-time campaigner of wars and a very wise battle strategist. He knew the value of planning for the future, which would help when he went into battle to secure his Shadow.

As he came to the room that housed his quarries studio, he crossed his fingers and prayed he had chosen correctly. Looking into the room he saw easels with paintings placed in differing positions. He could not see the reason why the paintings were there, but they obviously needed work. He eyed the female as she sat on a stepladder in front of a large painting. "Good afternoon Lady Edith."

Edith grinned. She had known he was there, her bear had warned her of his approach. "And to you, Commander Fin. Come in please."

She started her descent down the ladder. Fin closed his hands, stopping them from reaching for the female and hauling her onto her feet, which he was fairly sure she would not appreciate at all.

"May we dispense with the title?"

"I will if you will." She responded with a smile.

He followed her to the patio and took a seat after her, she offered. "Tea or coffee?"

"Coffee please."

"Are you settling in well?"

He sighed. "I am but I am not."

Edith wiped her hands as she sat, then poured their coffee from her heated urn. She took a sip of hers before asking. "So tell me."

"I do not do well with being idle."

"Oh me either, I like being useful."

"I have commanded Shields for many years. More than you have been alive. Probably more than anyone but dragons."

Edith grinned. "Probably, so you need work?"

"Yes."

"Be a Shield."

"No, I do not fit that life anymore. I have not for a long time and especially now I have Ella and…"

She said when he stopped talking. "Oh please. I do not

talk out of turn. I can keep a secret. Have you found your Shadow?" She quipped with a smile, not thinking he had, so was surprised when he nodded and whispered. "I have."

"And you are not compelled to claim her?"

"I am, but I need to settle my life first. My dragon agrees."

"You must have a very well-adjusted dragon."

Fin smiled and nodded. "We are. So my problem is twofold. I wish to work and have my own home. Keeper and Ella are newly bonded. I feel I am encroaching, even though they go out of their way to make me feel included." He smiled as he said. "I think if it was me and I was so new to bonding, the last thing I would want is my uncle living with me. Also, I believe my Shadow will demand her own space."

"Well, we do like that." She agreed with a smile, which he returned.

"I have heard that as well."

Edith thought for a moment, then said. "I am sure I know of both a job and a place to live."

"I do not want to leave Ella."

"Oh no, it would be here at Dragon's Gap."

"What is it?"

"One moment." She pulled her phone from her pocket and hit speed dial five and then touched speaker. "Lars, it is Fin and me."

"Hello, to you both."

Fin was going to tell Edith he had not gone to Lars because he did not think he could help, but remained silent and sighed quietly instead. Lars asked. "What can I do for you Edee?"

"Have you already hired someone for your weapons museum?"

"That is a horrible name."

"What are you calling it?"

"We haven't decided yet and no we have not."

"Lars, I have Fin here. What does that tell you?"

"I see. Wait one moment please."

They could hear two sets of boots approaching. Edith closed her phone, saying to Fin. "Lars and Storm have weapons. No, that is wrong, they hoard weapons, which they have decided can no longer be housed in their homes because of their young ones."

"Ahh, I see, so they have placed them on display?"

"Well, yes and no. Hi guys." Edith said as Lars and Storm arrived.

Storm asked Fin. "You wish to work?"

"I cannot remain idle."

"Also, he needs to move out of Ella and Keeper's place."

"Of course he does." Claire agreed as she walked in.

Lars kissed her cheek as Edith asked. "Meeting over?"

"Yes, all sorted."

"Why are you here?" Asked Lars.

"I was ordered to appear and update a certain nosy bear on what took place." Edith grinned as they all looked her way. Claire told them. "While I am here, I can help Commander Fin find his new home. I have the ideal place."

Surprised, he asked. "You do."

"I do, now tell me Com…"

"Please," He interrupted her, "just call me Fin."

Claire smiled. "Fin, I feel that you would not be happy living alone?"

"I have always lived with others. I think I am too old to start living by myself."

"I think then to ease you into living by yourself, you should have a place here at the castle for the time being. So I am suggesting Storm's old apartment. What do you think?"

Storm said. "It is ideal, and already furnished for a male. I will take you there to see it."

Fin looked a little disconcerted. "I do not know what to say. I am not a royal to live at the castle."

"I disagree, unless that purple ring in your eyes is lying." Storm said, with a grin.

"Also, are you not our Ella's only relative? Do you really

think we will let you go now?" Asked Edith.

"You are family, once in. You never get out." Said Claire, making Edith laugh and leaving the males confused as to why she found that funny.

Edith flapped her hands. "Well good, the place Claire has for you is better than the one I was going to suggest. So you all have this, I have work to do. Now go get him a place to live and explain the weapons thing you have going on, which has no name." She turned to Fin and said. "Fin, visit anytime. I am usually here or at the Gallery. We females enjoy talking to people who have not always lived here at Dragon's Gap. So do not be a stranger. Oh, and Claire do not forget to tell him about the party next weekend for Ash and Olinda."

Claire asked. "Have you told Olinda and Ash?"

"Why would I do that?"

Storm said. "She told Sage."

Now that, the males understood and found funny. They all said their goodbyes and left Edith to get on with her work and as she hummed a cheery tune under her breath, her bear growled. *You know June is his mate.*

Oh please, it is as plain as the nose on my face.

That big a sign.

Wow! You are snarly this afternoon, annoyed you did not get to eat a unicorn?

I like Olinda and baby Cara.

Low blow.

Snickering her Bear told her. *Claire left without giving us her update.*

Edith swore several times, much to her bears delight.

CHAPTER TWENTY-NINE:

K eeper stood next to the table and looked at two baby carriers with two hatchlings sleeping peacefully inside. His heart melted as he watched them, they really were adorable. It was so hard to see them as anything other than hatchlings. He looked around at the shelves, which looked newly stocked; it appeared Olinda had started work.

"Oh, I thought I would get an early start. Sorry about the hatchlings. Ash had to see Storm this morning and apparently the brothers were organizing classes for mind control. So the hatchlings had to come with me."

"Good morning, Olinda."

She blinked a few times, and he could see her mind catching up to what was actually happening in present time. It was not that she was rude or did not know the niceties of social behavior. Keeper had discovered by observing her, it was that her mind was usually somewhere else. On books or on what she was doing, or Ash or the hatchlings. In fact, he bet if you asked her at any given time, she would give you a list of what she was thinking, which would make a person's eyes bleed. He thought that for Olinda, being on the run must have been an exercise in discipline and control. She would have had to teach herself to remain focused and vigilant. He was honest enough to say he broke out in cold sweats, when he thought about her out there running from evil and never getting caught. Just as well she had the Goddess with her, or Olinda may have never made it to Dragon's Gap. At least he was not alone in his thoughts, he knew Ash and his brothers said the same, and he knew Reighn thought so as well.

"Good morning, Keeper."

"Are you saying this will be the only time my nephews will

be here?"

Olinda stopped and looked at him. "Are they really nephews? Ash is not related to you."

"Oh, Olinda, do not let our mother or father hear you say so. The Battle brothers are as much their young as we are. Their mother was our Dam's best friend until her death. Mama has known each of the brothers from the time they were birthed and loved them for that long."

"Oh, I did not know that, I stand corrected."

"Yet you live in the castle, in a family apartment?"

Olinda shrugged. "Well, yes, we do. I assumed that was because of the boys."

"Yes and no, but mainly it is because of Ash."

She smiled. "That is good. He needs that security of family, they all do. It is probably why the brothers hold so tightly to Ash and their older brother."

"I think you are right. Thankfully, they have you and the boys now to help soften their hard edges. They were well on the way to becoming hard, unforgiving males."

Olinda sighed and changed the topic. "As for the twins, well, we have builders and decorators in today, doing building and decorating things. June and Ember have organized them. I just gave them the lists Ash and I compiled. Do you think that was okay?"

"Yes, it is what they do. You would have only gotten in the way."

"Yeah, Ash said that. So I thought one day having them here would not hurt and we are just setting up."

Keeper lifted one eyebrow. "Really? The only day because the quiet room for infants that is on the floor design shows it will not be?"

"The... what now?" Asked a startled Olinda.

He turned and walked away. Olinda looked at the twins, then to where Keeper was heading, shrugged and trailed behind him. He stopped and pointed to the wall, where there was a large floor plan of both levels of the library. It was in

Olinda's hand-writing. "Oh!"

Then he moved his finger over the plan and she could see, clearly, a room that held two sketches that looked very much like cribs.

"I see. So what do you think?"

Keeper studied the plan again, as he had done for the last few days. "I stood in this room and apart from the shelving, I had absolutely no idea how to go forward. It has been over a month since I decided to share my hoard, and nothing had been done. In one day you found our library's voice."

Olinda smiled. "Thank you, it called to me. So what do you not like about the plan?"

They spent the next hour discussing and transferring her design onto their laptops. Together they added and subtracted rooms and played with other ideas, and when they had the design fixed to both their liking. Keeper said he would call the builders and decorators. Grace's sons would decorate the library after the dragons had finished the building work. This they would complete overnight, using magic.

Several minutes later, Charlie arrived with a faerie. "Hello Olinda, Keeper."

Together, they said. "Hi."

"I have brought Sunny; she will do your art work."

They both called out hello to the faerie as she walked around the room. She waved as she looked at the words written on the wall.

Olinda said to Keeper. "I did not know you were getting art like that."

"You dislike the faerie art?" Keeper asked her. He thought everyone loved their work.

Olinda shrugged. "What I have seen is beautiful. They are to do the boys' rooms and the playroom at home, but it is not my library. So not my call."

Keeper told her. "As to that, you are wrong, you have half ownership of this library."

Shocked, she gasped. "I what?"

"You own a building that has books in it." Charlie said helpfully.

Keeper asked her. "How is that helping?"

She grinned as she asked him. "Oh, was I meant to?"

Olinda asked Keeper, ignoring the conversation between him and Charlie. "How is that possible, and are you happy about this? These are your treasures."

"One; I am immensely proud of my collection and to share it with people who love books as much as I do is enthralling. And two; these books, this building loves you Olinda, they sing when you are here. The very air shines with your smile, so yes. Ash gave you the gift of the library, although I would have anyway."

She was almost too scared to ask. "How much did he pay for it?"

"A dollar, a fair price. I thought."

"Are you saying I own a building full of books for a dollar?"

"Yes… Yes, I am. Now the art, what do you think?"

Olinda took in a breath and let it out slowly, then another. When she felt she could talk without squeaking in shock, she said. "Fine, I think you need old masters from the castle or the museum for where the academics will be. They will find comfort in them."

Keeper agreed. "I see the sense of that. We will ask Edith for advice on which ones."

She pointed to the scrawled writing on the walls that Edith had done in jest. "You need to keep those."

"They were a joke by Edith about my hoard."

Charlie said. "But they are true, both statements."

He shrugged, it was true, but he felt embarrassed.

"And it is funny." Olinda told him. "Which is good because libraries should be a place of fun and magic."

Keeper looked at the three females. "True, I have always found books to be magical."

Sunny said. "Me too."

Charlie said. "There you go then, we are in agreement."

Keeper nodded as if he came to a decision and said to Sunny. "We will need the two statements. I would also like to have peaceful, relaxing murals in here. And for the young ones area, we will need light and cheerful colors." He and Sunny walked off into what would become the play and reading area for the children.

Charlie looked around and stated. "You need help."

Olinda did the same. "We do, I know."

"Ask Claire, she is the liaison for Dragon's Gap. She will know of people who need part-time jobs, and she will also know of other librarians or at least people who have worked in one." She looked at Olinda. "They are really excited about its opening."

Keeper heard the last of what she said as he came back to them, minus Sunny. "Really, I am amazed."

Charlie smiled. "What are you amazed about?"

"That people still read or just read."

"Are you?" She tipped her head to the side as she studied him. "Like you, people love the idea of having a place to go to and be surrounded by books. Most dragons and shifters remember when that was all there was."

Olinda said. "They love the familiarity of old friends, which is what some books and libraries are to some people. Safe places to read and be with like-minded people. A place to go and not be judged on what you read or think. To just take a break from life." She smiled. "Well, for me that was always my experience."

"Yes exactly." Charlie agreed as she said. "My experience as well. This is a good thing you two are doing and saying that. I have come to take your hatchlings with me. Verity and Grace wish to spend time with their grandsons."

Confused, Olinda asked. "Grandmothers, Grace and Verity?"

"Do you want to say they are not their grandmothers?" Asked Charlie pointedly.

"Hell no, not me. I am not brave enough for that."

"Good call." Keeper said, which made them both laugh.

Charlie took both hatchlings with her when she left a few minutes later. Olinda watched them go and sighed, she would miss them as funny as that was. She had them for only a short time, and yet they were such a big part of her life now.

Sunny and Keeper went over some more ideas he had come up with about the hatchling's quiet room before they finalized the deal. With nothing to do downstairs, Olinda raced upstairs to start shelving books and old documents she had prepared earlier. She had been there for a while and happiness was radiating off of her in ever-increasing circles. She loved the feel of the books, even the dust on some of them, which made her sneeze, could not halt the pleasure she was feeling. She hummed as she placed books lovingly on shelves and did not see the two figures appear at the end of an aisle. A deep voice said. "Excuse me Prin…"

Olinda dropped the books in her hands and froze. Her legs would not move and her brain stopped thinking as her heart thumped hard, wanting to escape her chest. She opened her mouth and a loud, horrendous scream erupted. Within seconds, Keeper stood in front of her. She grabbed his shirt with hands that shook so much she could not feel them. Her heart was racing so fast it was hard to catch her breath, and her fight-or-flight instinct was trying hard to kick into gear. She could not focus and was positive she had gone blind.

Roars sounded from outside the library vibrating the building. The two figures moved back against the wall. Keeper, without removing his gaze from the males, calmly told her. "That will be Ash; he will be here in a second, you are safe. Olinda. I am here."

She held tighter to his shirt. "I… I… I know but my body does not, so… so… sorry."

"Hush, sweet one, all is well."

Then, within a blink of an eye, a glowing doorway opened and Ash and his brothers strode through holding swords. Immediately following them were Reighn, Storm, Lars and

Stanvis.

Ash wrapped his arms around Olinda and peeled her hands from Keeper's shirt. She sobbed with relief when she felt his arms surround her. "Hush my soul, your heart is racing too fast. Calm, I am here."

"So... so... sorry. Scared... so scared."

"I know... I know, Olinda calm please, you will cause yourself harm."

Reighn flicked his fingers, and another portal opened. "Take her to Sharm, she will not settle with them here. Go Ash."

He nodded and lifted a shaking Olinda into his arms, sending a warning glare at the males standing by the wall before carrying her through the shining portal. Sharm directed him to a bed as soon as Ash appeared. Olinda clung to him, afraid to release him, and begged. "Do not leave me."

He leaned down so his face was near hers. "Never my heart, never."

Olinda whispered. "Okay... so... sorry."

"Do not be. You have a right to be frightened. Calm now."

She pleaded. "Okay, no drugs please."

Sharm assured her. "Dear one, we are healers, we do not use drugs." He slipped an oxygen mask on her face, saying. "Just breathe deep breaths, you will be fine, Olinda. You are safe. We are here."

She nodded, but kept her eyes on Ash.

CHAPTER THIRTY:

Once they were gone. Reighn asked Keeper. "The twins?"
Without looking away from the intruders he replied.
"Charlie took them with her."

Reighn nodded, then roared at the two males. **"Who dares enter my realm without my knowledge?"**

The two males moved closer, as one said. "Dragon Lord, we apologize. We meant no harm. We opened a tracer to Princess Olinda and arrived here. I am Jordan Reading and this is my brother Ethan Reading. We accompanied Ri. Caderyn, to the meeting with Princess Olinda."

"I remember." Stated Reighn.

"We have come to ask the Dragon Lord if we can form a Blessing under the rule of Princess Olinda."

"Why would you want to?"

Jordan told him. "We are all half-bloods like Princess Olinda, without her parentage, obviously."

Ethan said. "Our mothers are human. She said she would protect us."

Reighn agreed. "She did say that."

Jordan told him. "We were taken to live on Uformina by fathers who have no time or care for us. As half-breeds, we are very low in the Blessings ranking."

Lars asked. "How many of you are there?"

Ethan answered. "At last count, we number over one thousand males and three hundred females."

Reighn asked. "What of your mothers?"

Jordan came forward a little more. "Some of our mothers still survive. Some have since passed away."

Stanvis asked. "Are any of you in contact with them?"

Ethan nodded slowly. "We have spoken twice to our

mother. Some others have spoken more to theirs, some less. It is not encouraged."

Storm asked. "Do they have other children?"

"No, none do."

Reighn asked Jordan. "Do they know they have young?"

"All know, my Lord."

"Will they come here?"

Both males smiled. "Dragon Lord, yes they would."

"What of Ri. Caderyn?"

Their shoulders straightened. "We have defected."

Keeper said. "No, you are asking for sanctuary."

"Oh." The one named Jordan said with a nod to Keeper. "Correction, Dragon Lord, we are asking for sanctuary."

"Sanctuary is granted for all unicorn full and half-bloods who wish to come to Dragon's Gap. To live here with or without their mothers." Reighn intoned a variation of the age old vow. He looked at Lars. "Take them to the center." He asked Jordan. "I am assuming the tracer is what you used to open a portal?"

"It is not a portal, my Lord, like you do." He explained. "It is more a transference of energy from one place to another, which manifests in a type of shade that stands before you."

"So you are not really here?" Asked Stanvis.

"It is a metaphysical question." Ethan told them, which made Keeper grin.

Reighn shrugged. "Regardless, you will need a portal to bring you and your people here?"

"Yes my Lord."

Ark asked. "Who is the tracer?"

Ethan replied. "Jordan is the tracer; he locates the target."

Reighn eyed the shades. "Ri. Caderyn will not be happy to lose that talent?"

Jordan nodded. "Agreed, if he knew of it."

"I see." And Reighn did. They had hidden their abilities from the Blessing and Caderyn. Olinda was right, they were not treated well. "When are the others ready to come?"

"As soon as we call for them, my Lord."

"Then do so."

Jordan said. "My Lord about Princess Olinda."

"I will see to her and explain to her and her Shadow why you appeared. Preferably before he kills you."

Ethan pleaded. "Could you tell them both we did not mean to scare her? We did not think she would be so frightened. She was not at the meeting with Ri. Caderyn."

"Olinda, unfortunately, has not had an easy time lately. As you know, before she came here, she was hunted. Unless you have had a similar experience, it would be hard to understand her fear."

Jordan agreed. "It would be. Have the ones who did this been found?"

Ark said. "Yes, my brother and I saw to the hunters."

Ethan inclined his head in respect. "We unicorns, thank you. We would have done so if we had known." He asked Reighn. "May we speak to Princess Olinda?"

"Yes, but get your people here first. Then you will talk to her."

"Thank you." They both bowed as Reighn nodded, and then he turned to Storm. "You and Lars see to this for me, have the Matron's help. Contact Mama and Grace, ask Sage to call out the troops. I am off to see how our unicorn princess is coping."

CHAPTER THIRTY-ONE:

By the time Reighn made it to Ash and Olinda's place, she was home and sitting on the balcony. Ash was with the hatchlings in the nursery. "Ash." he said as he entered the bedroom.

"Reighn."

"How is she?" He asked as he took a hatchling from Ash and sat in the rocker with a bottle and baby in his arms.

Ash sat with the other baby and started to feed the waiting baby, as Reighn did the same. "She is angry at herself for being what she calls a wimp. I looked it up, it means spineless coward."

"Olinda?" Reighn asked, surprised. "A coward... really?"

"I know, I explained that someone who had done what she had over the last four months should not feel that way."

"What did she say?"

"That she cannot help feeling like she does."

"I will talk to her." Reighn told him as he rubbed the baby's back.

Ash shrugged as he said, with a glimmer of amusement in his eyes. "She is not a Shield, Reighn. You cannot yell at her and tell her to toughen up."

Reighn burped the baby and then placed him in his bassinet and stood looking down at him. "I am well aware of that. I have daughters and a Shadow, they dislike yelling."

Hiding his grin, Ash said. "I see."

Reighn asked with an edge to his voice that Ash could not miss. "Do you doubt my abilities to soothe Olinda?"

"It just seems unnatural, that is all."

Reighn stood straighter, and Ash was sure he heard his dragon in his tones when he said. "You are more like your brother than I thought possible." He turned and strode from the room.

Ash let him get to the door before he said. "I will take that as a compliment."

"It was unintended, you ass!"

Ash looked into Steel's sweet face and said. "Your uncle owes the swear jar double for swearing in front of you and your brother. Auntie Sage will be cross."

He burst out laughing when he heard Reighn's whispered yell. "Screw the swear jar."

Lighter of heart from crossing words with Ash, Reighn found Olinda wrapped up in a colorful blanket. He wondered why these extraordinary females found such peace with the balconies. As far as he knew, they all used them for solace. He took the seat opposite her. She looked at him without saying anything; she was so sad it almost broke his heart.

"Olinda, I am sorry, I cannot take the fear away from you but you are intelligent enough to know who can."

She nodded and sucked back a sob. "I thought I was okay, you know. I did the loads of crying thing, saw my grandfather and got angry but seemed okay. Then this happened today. I was like a clinging fool hanging onto Ash like a limpet."

Reighn smiled at her description. "And you believe he will think less of you because of that?"

"Well, yeah. I am not a silly, weak female. I was strong, capable. I survived my mother's death. The months of hiding and running. All of that and then one thing happens and I fall apart. What must he and all of you think of me?"

"That you are a beautiful, intelligent, strong and capable female who endured much and survived. We are proud to have you in our family."

Olinda let go a sob and threw herself into his arms. He rocked her as his dragon crooned a soft lullaby. Sage leaned her head against Ash's arm and whispered. "See, I told you he knew how to do it. She will be okay but call Rene`. It is time she saw him."

Ash watched as his Shadow cried and Reighn, his friend, his brother, his Dragon Lord, held and crooned to her and murmured. "I think you are right, it is time for her to have some peace."

"She loves you Ash."

"Does she?" He asked sadly as he looked down at her. "I think not yet."

"Oh, I know she does. No female worries that much about her Shadow, if she does not love him."

"I hope you are right."

CHAPTER THIRTY-TWO:

Much later that day, Rene` stepped into the apartment of Ash and Olinda, with Verity by his side. "Good afternoon Olinda and Ash. I hear you, Olinda would like to talk to me?"

"Reighn said it would be a good idea and Ash said you are the most trustworthy person he knows."

Rene` smiled at Ash as he said. "I thank both of them."

Olinda asked. "Can you help me?"

"It is what I do. Let us go into the little lounge that my Verity has told me about. She says you are making changes."

"We are." She asked Verity. "Edee told me you designed all the apartments?"

"I did, dear one."

"Are you upset at the changes we are making?"

"Oh no, never. It is what is supposed to happen. You and Ash are making it a home for your family. This…" She swept her hand around. "Was just a base for you two to build on?"

Relieved, Olinda smiled. "Thank goodness, I was so worried you would feel slighted."

Verity hugged her. "Do not worry, now go talk to Rene` he will make it all clear for you."

"Thank you." Olinda looked up at Ash. "I am sorry."

"For what my soul."

"Maybe I didn't try hard enough?"

"Maybe you tried too hard."

"Oh, I never thought of that. I love you. I never thought I would, but you make my heart whole. Never think you don't."

"As I love you, my heart. I will be here."

She looked into his beautiful green eyes and reached up and kissed him. "I know." She whispered. "Mine forever, thank you my Shadow."

Ash's heart filled, and he felt his dragon sigh. She was finally theirs.

CHAPTER THIRTY-THREE:

A day later, Ash sat on the balcony off of his bedroom, it was nine in the morning. Olinda was sleeping. He had finally worn her out around five this morning. They had made love almost constantly since she woke yesterday, after three hours of sleep which she had indulged in after an intense session with Rene`.

It was like having a complete Olinda, where he had seen glimpses of who she was before. Now it was like all the pieces had come together. It was as though the help Rene` gave her and admitting she loved him opened floodgates to her emotions. He loved every minute of being with her and would be in bed with her now, except Reighn had summoned them to his office. He did not know why, and Lars had been less than forthcoming.

His dragon told him. *You are whining like a little girl. Our Dragon Lord commands us.*

Ash growled back. *He knows I am with our Shadow; he has decided to be annoying.*

His dragon laughed as he said. *I do not think the Dragon Lord is that petty?*

Olinda joined the conversation as she yawned and stretched. *Huh! See what you know. I put nothing past that male.*

Ash turned around and stared at Olinda. *My Shadow you can mind-send along the bond?*

She smiled at him. *Yes, I guess it is strong enough now. Hello, my dragon.*

Hello, my Shadow, we need to fly soon.

Yes, we do.

CHAPTER THIRTY-FOUR:

R eighn asked with a delighted look. "Prince and Princess, guess what you are doing?"

Ash and Olinda had spent the last fifteen minutes in Reighn's office being brought up to date about the unicorns and what, why, and who was here. "No, I am a librarian."

"And I am a Commander."

"And now you are unicorn wranglers." Said Reighn with a touch of delight.

They looked at each other, and Olinda shrugged as Ash crossed his arms and stared at Reighn with narrowed eyes. Reighn told them. "Lars and Stan will help, as will your brothers. Stan has contacted Mama, she and Grace as well as the Matrons are going to help with their mothers. Now come with me and meet your Blessing."

Goddess. You are so lucky you are not here. Olinda growled, and she was positive she heard laughter.

They walked with Reighn into the room used for court and saw nearly two thousand males and females standing around.

Olinda said. "Ri. Caderyn is so going to notice this many of his people are missing."

Reighn agreed. "I know, but as you said, we are fore-warned, therefore forearmed. Also, I have it from a very reliable source that says he will think long and hard about whether it is worth making an issue of this."

Ash said. "We had better be prepared."

"That is why you are here, Prince Ash."

Ash growled at the title, making Reighn smile as he addressed the silent room. "For you who do not know, this is Olinda and Ash Battle." Instantly everyone bowed, Olinda and Ash returned the salute. Reighn asked. "Now as half-bloods, we have been told you breed true. Is this so?"

Jenny stepped forward, making Olinda gasp and ask. "Jenny, you are a half-blood?"

"I am Princess. Dragon Lord, only half-blood males breed true. Most females from unicorn fathers have gifts like Princess Olinda."

Startled, Olinda said. "Oh, you know?"

Jenny answered with a smile. "Yes, we, Ethan and Jordan, decided not to say anything. It was, we believed, safer for you and us."

Ash asked. "How did Ri. Caderyn not know."

She smiled bitterly. "He does not lower himself to look and relies on others, like his advisors, who tell him it is not possible for half-blood females to have gifts. He believes that to this day."

Olinda murmured. "Well, that is just bull-headed."

Reighn asked Jenny. "What do you need?"

Ethan answered. "We have places to stay, courtesy of the Matrons and liaisons, and we have been told our mothers will be here within days. What we would like is work and, if possible, most of us can shift. Would we have permission to do so?"

Reighn bit back words about assholes that hurt the ones they were responsible for. It was unhealthy Sharm had told him on more than one occasion to stop shifters changing skins. It was their right to shift. He would hate it if his dragon could not wear his own skin, as the kits called it. He said now. "Shifters should shift, that is your right. If you want to shift, do so."

Ash said quietly. "The meadows that we can see from Storm's apartment and the one from the family's day room, Cara, looks out on. What do we call that room?"

Reighn told him. "Sage, calls it the Sunday family room."

"So, the Sunday family room, those meadows should work."

Reighn looked at him, then Storm, who nodded and smiled. Reighn said just as quietly. "For Cara the world, if that will make her smile, then do so."

Olinda pulled Jenny aside. "Jenny, I have a problem that I hope you can help me with?"

"Princess, anything."

"Do you know what a Keeper is?"

"Yes, Healer Ella told us."

"As you know Cara was hurt, she was seen by her grandfather, who is a Keeper."

"Can I guess? She has a memory."

Surprised, Olinda nodded. "Yes... pain."

Jenny sighed. "It is what we call a hidden memory. It is rare, but I have read of gifted unicorns who have the ability. Some might say, the unfortunate ability of being able to compartmentalize their minds or information in their minds."

Olinda asked. "You think she has this?"

"I would put money on it."

"Could you talk to her father about that?"

"Of course, she is young, she has many years before she has to cope with pain."

"Storm!" Olinda called. He came to her immediately. She smiled and said. "Storm, Jenny will tell you about Cara and her brain."

"There is a problem?"

"Not one your father cannot fix now."

"Good." He kissed Olinda's cheek. "Thank you, sister dear."

She ducked her head and hurried back to stand beside Ash as he addressed the gathering. "Behind the castle is a meadow, or should I say several large meadows, we will make it into one complete one, if you tell us what you would like there..."

"Excuse me Prince Ash." A small silver haired female with black eyes interrupted him as she stood surrounded by four females who had to be her sisters.

"Yes, Lady..."

"Oh Kim." She told him as she bowed.

"Well, Lady Kim, how can I help you?"

She smiled. "I was just going to say my sisters, and I can shape the meadows, if that is permissible. We will use our gifts and place what would be acceptable for the Blessing there."

Reighn said. "Most acceptable. Please go with my second Stan and his Shadow. They will show you where the meadows are." They hurried to where Jacks and Stanvis stood and left. The males, realizing they could shift, let out whoops of delight that replaced their worried frowns.

Claire said to Jenny as they walked to where Olinda stood. "Do not be surprised if your females end up shifting as well."

Jenny got a look of hope in her eyes. "We will hope for that to happen."

Claire smiled. "Stranger things have happened. This is, after all, Dragon's Gap."

June and several teenagers arrived. Claire said to all the unicorns present. "We will find you work, but first you need to fill in these forms, so we can match you with the proper positions and yes. If you wish to be Castle guards, you are most welcome to apply and you can also try out for the Hunters and Shields."

"Healers are always wanted." Said Ella as she and Keeper, Sharm and Edith arrived.

Keeper said. "I need people for the library."

Edith said. "Please anyone with artistic talent that would like to use it, see me."

June called out. "If there are any teachers and anyone with musical talent, please see me."

Sage said. "Anyone who has gifts out of control or wishes to learn to use what you have better, see me."

Claire handed out clipboards as she passed one to Olinda, she said. "Start writing Princess."

Olinda squealed. "Oh my goodness. You aren't going to call me that, are you?"

Sage passed her on her way to a group of females, saying. "What do you think, Princess?"

"Ash is a Prince you know?" She called to them both.

They grinned, and Claire said. "We know, but he is bigger than you."

EPILOGUE:

Very early the next morning, Storm picked Cara up from her bed as Charlie picked up Kelsey. Together, they carried the girls to the balcony overlooking the meadow.

Storm asked Cara. "Baby girl, can you see your surprise?"

Cara rubbed her eyes as she woke completely. "Me have supise Dada?"

"Yes, for you and Kelsey." He looked to where Kelsey was in her mother's arms, staring about her with huge eyes.

Charlie pointed toward the meadow. "Look girls."

They looked down and saw the ground was covered in a silver mist. It rose to enfold the meadow in a mystical blanket.

Cara whispered. "Isa don't see nofing Dada."

Kelsey whispered. "I don't see anything, Mama."

Charlie said. "Wait, my babies… wait."

Then slowly a gray shadow moved, then another and then another. Cara was almost bouncing from Storm's arms and he clamped her to him as she screamed. "Dada, Mama, Kelsey, unicons. Dada me see unicons!"

"Yes, sweet girl, unicorns."

As they watched, more arrived. Mystical silver and white horses with horns stood in the mist of the newly formed unicorn meadow and looked up toward the family and bowed.

"Dada, they are bowing." Said an awed Kelsey.

"Yes." Storm agreed. "They are saying hello."

Cara leaned over and yelled. "Ello unicons. I see you. Me unicon too."

Charlie, Storm, and Kelsey laughed at the adorable toddler as they watched a female with honey-colored eyes and a tall male with green eyes walk from the mists surrounded by silver unicorns.

Cara yelled out. "Sista Olinda, me see you wif unicons."

"We see you, Cara. We see you, Kelsey." Ash's voice rang out. Accompanied by the sound of trumpeting unicorns. As the sound died away, they heard the sweet voice of Olinda call out through the early morning mists. "We wish to introduce you to the Blessing of Dragon's Gap."

ACE & HARPER'S STORY

CHAPTER ONE:

Harper Easton was in the middle of a crisis. A dark cloud of gloom shrouded every thought with its taint of despair.

"Cheer up girl, it may never happen." Her friend Frankie advised as she placed her berry shake, *it was always a berry shake.* On the table while sliding her tall slim body, some might say athletic, not Harper. She just called her *Anorexic.* Onto the bench seat opposite her.

"Unfortunately, it has already happened." Harper mumbled into her coffee, *and yes, it was always coffee for her.*

Frankie eyed her despondent friend and sighed deeply and loudly. Causing Harper to raise her granite colored eyes, fringed with thick lashes from her cup to stare at Frankie. And when those eyes zeroed in on her like twin lazers Frankie sighed quieter this time and asked herself for the millionth time. How did her best friend not see what the world saw when they looked at her? A beautiful, admittedly short woman, Harper was only five- foot-three in her socks, because Frankie was positive Harper didn't own stockings. What she did own was the classic hour-glass figure of a woman from the forties. Harper was what Frankie thought of as the quintessential woman of that time. With long auburn hair, which usually had a soft wave, surrounding a face any woman would be thrilled to have.

Unfortunately, Frankie saw once again, Harper had ruthlessly tied her hair back with... was that... yes, dear Goddess... a piece of string, not even a colored piece of string. The horror of it made Frankie close her eyes for a full minute. Time and again, she had addressed Harper's total lack of dress sense. For example, today she had worn jeans and a black tee-shirt and boots, for goodness' sake. Boots!

Obviously, it was time to reintroduce the topic again, about how clothes projected the right image. With a quick glance down at her own person, she nodded in satisfaction. She was dressed in a long-sleeved pale green button-down shirt, with white cuffs that matched her white slacks and green shoes with a slight heel. With this look, she was projecting success.

Frankie knew she was taller than the average woman, at five- foot- ten inches, and slim, not skinny, which she had heard her figure referred to occasionally. She possessed nice boobs, not too much but not flat-chested either, which she thought was just right for her slim figure. She knew her face was pleasant to look at, not too long or too round, and when she'd looked again this morning. As she did each morning, she saw her skin was still clear of wrinkles. Her best feature she knew without a doubt were her eyes, which were divine with long lashes, not thick like Harper's but with mascara they made her eyes pop. Of course, her eyes were a soft brown, which helped. A boyfriend once commented that she had eyes like a cow. She knew a compliment when she heard one and was surprised he had noticed the soft, dreamy look in her eyes. Not many did. Her hair was a nice chestnut color that emphasized her cheekbones. At present, it was styled into a short bob. *Why?* Because she inadvertently got it caught in one of Harper's creations and ended up cutting off over half the length to release herself. Sad as that was, she made the best of her shortened locks and refused to accept defeat. Unlike her friend, she would not wallow in despair, she would grow her hair out again, but until then, she would rock this bob cut. *Stupid metal statue.*

Harper eyed her friend and read every thought that crossed her mind, Frankie Spring, and once again, Harper thought it was a ridiculous name for her friend. Should never ever play poker. She was just not devious enough, unlike Harper, who carried with her secrets inside secrets; like the one she had now. She had never told Frankie why she was in this town or that she had a sister called Charlie. Admittedly, until a month ago, maybe two, she might stretch that to three months... no more... well, maybe. She was almost sure three months... Yeah, that would be the maximum time that had passed since she discovered her sister was probably not dead. Still, she should have told Frankie. She gave a mental shrug. Too late now. Today she was leaving, and it hurt more than it should.

She found as she sat looking at her only friend, a friend who was special in more ways than any normal human should be. That leaving her was going to be a hard thing to do. Frankie was otherworldly and not a shifter. She was like Harper born on earth, but not to human or shifter parents and Frankie was the only person in recent years to have slipped into Harper's guarded heart. As she watched her friend bounce to a song she could only hear, her heart cracked a little more. In her twenty- eight- years of life, she had only ever loved three people. One was dead, and it seemed like the other one was probably alive and now Frankie. So before she changed her mind, she blurted out. "I am leaving today. Do you want to come with me?"

Frankie, mid-bounce, stopped and listened to her friend. Frankie had the ability to listen with more than her ears and she did so now. What she heard surprised and pleased her; she drank her milkshake almost to the bottom and raised her head, saying with her habitual smile. "Okay, when do you want to go?"

Harper released the air from her lungs in a gust of wind. "I have to go today, I have put it off too long already."

Frankie pursed her lips in what Harper had come to call her thinking face, then she drawled. "Allrriighty then... I am going to need an hour, maybe two tops, to get my place closed up."

Harper said nothing, just sat watching her from eyes that went ghost gray. Frankie slurped some more of her shake and stared at her friend, then murmured. "Oh, I see."

Harper sighed. "Yeah, it's okay Frankie; it was just a thought. I will miss you, though. You are just weird enough to be interesting."

"I choose to take that as a compliment." Frankie stated as she did the lip thing again, which meant she was thinking.

Frankie could not think without making her lips screw up into a twisted pout, it generally made her look crazy or constipated. Harper accepted it as another fascinating quirk of her friend, and she had many. She truly did not want to leave Frankie, if she was honest, she was fearful of leaving her. Goddess knew what danger the woman would get into without her. The fact Frankie had lived alone without her, until five years ago, made Harper break out in a cold sweat when she thought about it.

It had been fate or some kind of divine intervention that had made Harper stop in this town to resupply for her cross-country trip. Five years later and it was still a mystery how it happened, but within minutes of meeting Frankie, she found herself in a barn creating art. All because of a wounded soul calling to her, and that soul was Frankie. She had been standing in front of a vegetable stand at the street market, and Harper stopped because she thought she was hurt or in distress. She was honest enough to admit that her stopping was out of character for her. Just noticing Frankie was odd, but to stop and ask if she was alright was just plain weird. And, of course, that was when the waves of loneliness emanating from Frankie drew Harper in.

Some called what she had a gift. Harper knew it for what it was. An annoying ability to find out shit about people, which she never wanted to know in the first place. It was why she kept to herself, well that and her ability to kill people if they annoyed her too much. It turned out when she talked to Frankie it was to discover she was trying to decide between carrots or potatoes, which is why she was making the thinking face. After that first meeting, it only took three weeks for her to become a fixture in Harper's life, and a mutual benefit came from the friendship. Which Harper will probably never acknowledge, she eased the loneliness that filled Frankie's soul. And Frankie unknowingly kept the darkness in Harper's soul from overtaking her. To this day, Harper was unsure how Frankie had slipped past her guard and succeeded where others failed by becoming important to her. But for better or worse, they were friends. An aberration for Harper and a novelty for Frankie. She was a person who danced to her own beat, as she often explained to anyone who would listen. For most people, she was just too weird, amusingly her weirdness, just amused Harper.

Now, though, Frankie was not happy. Her friend, her only friend was leaving. And she was not coming back and expected that she, her best friend, was not leaving with her. *Well!* Frankie thought she could just think again. If Harper left without her, who would she have? Also, she had promise that guy she would leave with Harper when the time was right. It seemed like the time was right.

Frankie drank the last of her shake, sighed at the wonderful taste and wondered if she should mention the guy. She had been meaning to tell Harper about him for a year now, but something always seemed to come up and she invariably forgot. But as she looked at her small deadly friend, she thought maybe now was not the right time either. Harper looked like she had a lot on her mind, and there would be time to explain later. Satisfied with her reasoning, she said. "I am going to definitely need the two hours, so I better get going."

This is what made Frankie lovable Harper thought. She asked no questions and did not demand a blow by blow account for having to leave town. She just decided she would go with her. Of course, this was also why Harper feared to leave her alone. Because she did not ask questions. In truth, this innocence was what made Harper fearful. Thinking of her alone in the world, vulnerable to any unscrupulous person, with a sob story that pulled at Frankie's soft heart. It was not like it hadn't happened to her in the past, or so she told Harper, not exactly like that, but Harper could read between the lines.

Frankie made to get up, and Harper placed her hand on hers to halt her progress. "Frankie, you know what I am saying. I will not be coming back."

"We," corrected Frankie softly. "We will not be coming back, and all I can say to that is. Thank goodness, I feel it is time we went on a road trip. So let me go, I have shit to do. Did you pack already?"

Harper nodded. "I did."

What she did not say was magic helped her place everything she owned from her barn back in her storage unit in New York. Being a half-blood faerie had its advantages. Harper lifted her hand from Frankie's, and for the first time in thirteen hours, since deciding the time was now to leave, she felt lighter. She smiled, whether it was at the sight of Frankie dressed as she was in a green shirt and white trousers with her new haircut. Which looked ridiculously cute on the tall, skinny woman. She could not say, or maybe it was the prospect of yelling at her sister. *Yeah! That could be it.* Either way, for the first time in hours, Harper felt as though the gloom over her thoughts had lifted.

"Okay then, see you at your place."

Frankie squealed with delight and smiled as she bounced her way out of the diner. Someone of Frankie's build should not bounce, Harper thought *she looked like a pogo stick.* But as usual, her thoughts remained hidden behind her impassive face.

CHAPTER TWO:

Harper and Frankie had been at Dragon's Gap for two days. Five days of travel to get here, and Harper was unsure if the trip had been too short or too long. Either way, Frankie had made it enjoyable with her observations along the way, and her total lack of worry over where they were going. When they finally arrived, Harper had been a little surprised that Frankie had not been surprised.

She had smiled at Harper and asked. "Don't you think this is just a wonderful place?"

When she'd asked. "Do you know where we are?"

Frankie just laughed and bounced to her own song and replied. "You are so funny, Harper. We are at Dragon's Gap, the only place to be."

Harper had shaken her head and muttered too low for Frankie to hear, but she bet Harper was cussing, which had made her smile. That was two days ago, now the morning of their third day at Dragon's Gap. Harper decided they would visit the castle. Not wanting to go through the squealing and sighing and loving looks directed at her from soft brown eyes, which she knew Frankie would do. And she definitely did not want to listen to her repeatedly saying. "Oh my Goddess, Harper, it's a castle." Which would just get on her last nerve, so she decided to not mention the visit before they finished eating breakfast. It wasn't like she didn't have cause. The first day here, Frankie had said the word castle at least a thousand times, to the point she heard it in her freaking sleep. She eyed Frankie again as she sat opposite her in the diner where they were eating breakfast. Today she was dressed in a flowing white dress that displayed huge colorful flowers. She had topped it with a short yellow bolero jacket and tan shoes. Harper refrained from telling her she looked like a walking garden. Which she could have easily done, especially after Frankie had literally screamed at her to change her hockey sweater. Which was absolutely decent, it didn't even have holes in it. When the screaming and nagging eventually got on her nerves, she changed into a black tee-shirt and leather jacket. It was really to save Frankie's life, her nagging could have resulted in her untimely demise. It had been a very close call. But when she had emerged from her room to see Frankie frowning heavily in disapproval at her jeans. That was when Harper accidentally, on purpose, let her see the knives she was stashing around her body. Thankfully, Frankie decided to forgo the nagging and just sniff loudly in disdain, Harper knew that sniff. Her step-mother had been real good at it. She had growled with exasperation and slammed from the hotel room with Frankie yelling after her. "Childishness will not win you friends, Harper." Which made Harper growl even more.

Now forty minutes later, they stood across from the castle, and Harper groaned softly as Frankie squealed. "Oh my Goddess, it's a stone building."

Ever since she had threatened her with mayhem if she said the word castle. Frankie found every word one could imagine to describe the friggin castle. Seriously, how much could a woman take? "It's a castle, call it like it is."

"Are you sure? I don't want to upset your feelings or anything. I know how…"

"Last nerve Frankie… last nerve!"

"Yippee. Castle… Castle… Castle."

Harper's lips twitched with humor as she agreed with a sigh.

"Yep, looks like one."

"Please say we are going in?"

"Yep, looks that way."

"Yippee!"

Harper started the trek across the wooden drawbridge, listening to happy Frankie sounds. "It's a drawbridge, Harper." Frankie said, as she walked a little behind her so she could look around.

"Yep, looks like it."

"Oh my Goddess, was that a unicorn?" Frankie nearly screamed in her excitement. "Harper, there are unicorns."

Harper hung her head. "Yep, there are, and no we have to go in."

"But later, right?"

"Yep, later."

Frankie was in her own private heaven as she hugged herself. Unicorns and an honest to goodness stone castle, right out of the pages of one of her favorite novels. Could this day get any better? He would be here, her one true love she just knew it. Okay, she didn't really, but if this was a book, he would be. Frankie felt the bubbles of glee bounce around her blood system as she walked across the wooden drawbridge. Okay, she really skipped across the drawbridge to the castle.

They had spent the last two days looking around, getting a feel for the place, which is what Harper told her they were doing. Then this morning after breakfast, Harper said they were going for a walk to see what else was here. As though she had not seen they were heading to the freaking castle that just sang to every one of her senses and had since they arrived. Just because Harper had given her one of her ghost stares, which she reserved for people who asked stupid questions. When she had innocently pointed out the enormous castle a few times, or maybe a hundred times on their first day. That in no way should have been a reason for Harper to demand that she never, ever say the word castle again. Frankie stared at her as Harper's eyes catalogued everything, constantly searching for danger. Because Harper knew that something other than human lived in that castle. When she felt Frankie's eyes on her, she asked. "What?"

Gleefully Frankie said, no, she really sang. "Harper, we just crossed a moat."

Harper pretended she didn't hear her because they had just crossed over a moat. *A friggin moat.* That ran under a drawbridge. *A friggin drawbridge. How the hell did I end up here?* She had not believed her eyes when they had arrived and seen the castle. *A castle in this day and age, really?*

She had hoped it was a movie set, which was one of Frankie's ideas. One of the many, many ideas she came up with on their first day here. Much to Harper's disappointment, Frankie had discovered it was not a movie set. For her peace of mind, it would have been so much easier if it had been, because where there was a castle, there were guards, usually armed and dangerous.

Harper growled silently and grimaced. *Friggin Charlie. Only she would live in a damn castle just to make my life harder.*

When they finally got to the end of the drawbridge, they both looked up... way up to the top of huge wooden doors. Frankie whispered. "Castle doors, so cool."

"Those things have to be at least fifty or sixty feet tall." Harper muttered, not expecting an answer from Frankie which showed how this monstrosity had confused her thinking.

"Oh, not that tall."

Harper turned her eyes on her and raised dark eyebrows as she asked. "Are you sure?"

"Oh positive. It is because you are short, from my height. I would say twenty or thirty feet, no more."

"Well, thanks." Harper shot back. "When did we start comparing heights?" *And yes, she was slightly sensitive about her height.*

"So what do we do?" Frankie asked, ignoring Harper's words even more so when Harper sarcastically replied. "I don't know? Knock, ring a bell. What do you suggest?" Frankie did the lip thing. "Oh my Goddess, you are thinking about it?"

Frankie smiled. "Ah-hah, knock. That is what they are for?" She pointed to a big brass door knocker in the shape of a dragon that lay on the door by its companion. Harper had been studying them as she waited for Frankie to finish thinking. She had just come to the conclusion that together they would weigh a ton, maybe more.

"They could weigh a ton. Can you even lift it to bang it?"

Frankie grabbed its tail and slammed it down repeatedly. "Yep, looks like it."

BANG... BANG!

She again used the knocker to thump on the wooden door. Each bang sounded like cannon shots to Harper, *and yes, she had heard cannon fire, damn Charlie.*

BANG... BANG!

Harper looked up again and saw nothing. Disappointed, Frankie asked. "What now?"

Harper almost did the lip thing. Quickly, she pulled her lips straight and slammed her hands on her hips and said in a really loud voice. **"THE ONLY THING WE CAN, GET THE DYNAMITE!"**

Frankie stood still, with her eyes wide as saucers, as she screeched at Harper. **"WE HAVE DYNAMITE!"**

Harper winked at her, Frankie asked in a softer voice. "What is wrong with your eye?" Harper sighed and shook her head. Frankie quickly consoled her. "It's okay Harper, I'll go get the dynamite. Is it in the pickup?"

Harper was about to explain there was no dynamite when they heard a voice yell down to them. "What do you want?"

Frankie said. "That was rude."

"Yep." They both looked up to the top of the castle. "Battlements." Harper said when Frankie opened her mouth to ask.

She changed her question and cupped her mouth and yelled. "We want to come in."

A male's voice asked. "Why?"

Frankie replied. "Because."

"Because why?"

"We need to."

"Who do you wish to see?"

Before Harper could tell her. Frankie yelled back. "We are on a quest for the King and Queen. So open the damn door or I'll have your head." Silence ensued as he disappeared from sight. Frankie gave Harper a wide smile as she stared at her until she asked. "What? I thought that went well."

"Did you? Quest, king and queen. Really, Frankie?" Harper shook her head slowly from side to side.

Frankie huffed. "Yes I did. In books there is always a quest and a king and queen."

"Yet, we are still outside." Harper muttered, and this time she knew Frankie heard her.

"But not with arrows sticking out of us, so that's a good thing." Frankie returned cheerfully.

Harper decided not to discuss it with her anymore. A short while later, Frankie murmured. "He seemed nice, though."

Harper eyed her lanky friend and wondered how deep the moat was, and if piranhas swam in there. She thought about tossing her in but that may attract too much attention, so she decided to ignore her instead; it wasn't like she had friends to spare. They silently stood watching the door; at least Harper did. Frankie bounced and looked around herself.

Eventually, a door magically appeared from the large doors and opened. Warriors wearing black shirts with red and gold embroidered vests, carrying large swords strapped to their backs, lined up on either side of the opening. One guard motioned for them to enter. Harper moved first, with Frankie walking behind her. "There are twenty, ten on each side."

Harper stopped mid-way and looked up at her friend. "Why?"

"In case you wanted to know."

Harper sighed and walked on again. Coming to the end of the guards, she stopped and again looked up at Frankie. And knowing she should not ask, but curiosity sadly got the better of her, she asked again. "Why?"

Frankie smiled. "In case you wanted to..." She flapped her hands around. "You know... With your knives and stuff."

Instantly, more males poured from what looked like hallways. Harper eyed her friend. "Really!"

Frankie shrugged. "Touchy."

Harper put her hands up and nudged Frankie. "Hands."

Frankie put her hands in the air but couldn't take her eyes from the males coming toward them. They were all huge and dressed as the first guards were. Frankie asked, not bothering to lower her voice. "They are all really tall and did I say huge already? I mean their muscles must have muscles. Do you see the way they fill out their shirts? I wonder if they have them specially made."

Harper watched the males watch them and saw the smirks and a couple of chests get puffed out. There was a lot of flexing of muscles under Frankie's impressed gaze. She really wanted to laugh at her friends' observations and the male's posturing but did neither. One; she didn't want to hurt Frankie's feelings and two; some males, even well-trained ones like these, were touchy when you laughed at them. Especially when they were armed.

"Yep, I saw."

CHAPTER THREE:

F rankie looked around at what was obviously an entrance or greeting foyer. She never remembered what it was called. It could have been the grand hall. She thought about that for a minute. No, she was sure it was an entrance or foyer, anyway it was fantastic. All large stone walls and floors, like a proper castle, should be. With a huge medieval fireplace dominating one entire wall, the other stone walls held delicious looking tapestries. There were so many they almost covered all the stone. Two large sweeping staircases on either side of the fireplace rose to the upper level and there were suits of armour guarding each staircase. Several corridors led away from where they were, which was where the males had come from. The floors were a piece of art in themselves, with beautiful large stone tiles that looked almost like two entwined dragons. One red and one gold. They seemed to be embedded in the stone; it was amazing, and the stones just reeked of legends and age. What a wonderful place. Seriously, it was enough to have her swooning.

Harper watched everything around her and felt a hum coming from the stones beneath her feet; it was like a small vibration that had her toes curling inside her boots. The hum was soothing, almost like a lullaby that sang a greeting to her. She sent her senses out and was only a little surprised to encounter something in return.

Hello.
Welcome home.
This is not my home.
It has always been your home.
Do I know you?
We have waited a long time for you.

Who are you?

In time, you will learn of us.

Then the presence disappeared, leaving Harper feeling disconcerted. She hated this mystical stuff, but unfortunately being half- faerie, she had no way of stopping it. And worse, she did not know if she really wanted to. After all, it was her last link, other than Charlie to her mother.

Well, color me a mystery. She thought as she looked at Frankie and the guards. Nope, none of them seem to have heard the voices. *Okay, just me.* Harper grinned, talking to invisible people... what next dragons.

The males had come to a stop in a half circle around them. While Frankie gleefully grinned, she finally sighed and said. "This is nice for a castle, don't you think, Harper?"

"Yep, I do."

"Do you think they will let us look around?"

"Yep, I do."

Several of the guards were having trouble holding it together, and several others wore confused expressions, which Harper discounted that was normal around Frankie. The ones that worried her were the two that were dressed similar to the other guards. Except there was no fancy vest for these two and their swords looked like they had seen more use than the others. They were yet to look away from her and Frankie. Also, there had not been any checking them out, as the others were doing.

Did she say hot! Which meant one of two things, they were gay and she really hoped they weren't or they were badasses, which she really hoped they weren't. It just made things harder, not impossible, just harder. Frankie was doing the lip thing when the males parted like the red sea, and the tallest male they had seen so far walked up to them. Frankie's mouth dropped open, and she squeaked. "Harper, do you see him?"

"Yep, I do" Then Harper looked up and then up some more and asked a Frankie question. "How the hell do you breathe up there?"

He raised just one blond brow and smirked. Frankie told her with attitude. "See, it is a height thing."

Harper groused back. "Really, it is not, he is just absurdly tall."

"Oh, he really is not. It is just you are so sh..."

Harper turned her granite eyes on Frankie, whose voice died away when Harper asked with a decided edge to her tone. "You were saying?"

"Nothing." Before Frankie could say anything more. The giant male said. "Ladies please?"

Frankie shivered, she was positive the little bubbles in her blood which had died down since they had become sur-rounded by all the guards came back to life. The sound of his voice shot right into her blood, and she was sure those bubbles were starting to pop with excitement. She shut her lips tight so her thoughts would not spill out. *O.M.G! Did I say O.M.G gorgeous?* Finally, she managed to croak out. "Please what?"

"Please stop talking."

"Oh, okay." Frankie frowned at the tall male and looked at Harper. One thing this male would have to learn, she, Frankie Spring, abhorred rudeness. And his order, as far as she was concerned, was rude. She said so now to Harper. "Slightly rude."

Harper replied. "Yep, it was."

The male frowned at them both until Frankie did the lip thing. Harper thought she heard a growl come from him, but when she looked up, he looked calm. *Huh! Must have been mistaken.*

"Thank you ladies; I am Commander Johner Kingsley, of the castle guards. These males are the castle guards. Now if you would come with us, we will escort you to see the Prime. He would like to have a little chat about why you are here?"

Harper asked. "What or who is a Prime?"

"He would be the second to the Lord of the Castle." Johner

explained while his Dragon roared. **SHADOW!**

What... Who... Where?

There in front of us, are you blind?

No, of course not.

And yet you did not recognize our Shadow?

I was not looking for her, was I? She is very cute.

Johner could hear the thread of suspicion in his dragon's voice when he said. *We are talking about the tall female, our Shadow.*

Johner snorted. *I do not know who you were talking about, but that was who I was talking about.*

We take our Shadow.

What has come over you? We don't act like that, we will court her.

I want Shadow NOW!

Too bad we are a Kingsley; we behave accordingly.

NOW! His dragon demanded again.

Johner told him quietly. *Remember what happened with Sharm and Edee.*

He could tell his dragon was thinking about what he'd said because he stated. *We will court our Shadow.*

Johner waved his hand for the females to precede him. Harper put her hands down, shrugged, and walked past him and several other males, including the two who did not look like castle guards. Frankie scowled at him, put her hands down as well and sniffed loudly as she walked past him, causing Johner to smile.

Two guards walked in front, others fanned out around them, as more followed. Harper could feel the male's eyes on them, making sure they did nothing stupid. Which made her smile, knowing something they did not. Harper Easton did not do stupid, Frankie... well, stupid followed her sometimes.

Frankie walked ahead of the male with the golden blond hair and could feel his eyes on her. She bet he was hoping she would do something outrageous so he could pounce on her. *Ooh, pounce. Now that had possibilities. No bad Frankie.* Johner Kingsley may be heaven to look at, tall with muscles and cute with that straight nose and those blue eyes and his long, straight hair. Which she would like to run her fingers through. *Grrrr, no bad Frankie.* He also may have a body that was mouth-watering, enticing, but he'd gone and pissed her off. There would have to be groveling now. Harper found herself totally entertained. Especially when she thought about them trying to get Frankie to talk and make sense. *Hahaha!*

When they walked down a set of stairs and along several underground tunnels and past every office in the castle, at least twice. Frankie's annoyance waned. The guards in the lead finally came to a halt. As they parted, Harper could see they had arrived in front of two doors. Harper, like Frankie, knew what lay behind those innocent looking doors, bare rooms commonly known as interrogation rooms.

Johner cleared his throat, the first sound from him since before they had started walking. "Ladies, please take a room each."

The two lead guards opened the doors, showing exactly what Harper suspected. Frankie refused to look at Johner, she opened her mouth, then snapped her lips together and instead gave Harper the thumbs up and a smile. Harper winked in reply, before they each entered the interview rooms, they were just like one would see at any police or sheriff's station. The only difference was these were cleaner and smelled of lemon. Unfortunately, both Harper and Frankie had seen the inside of police interview rooms enough to critique one.

Entering, Harper looked around and spotted the camera in the corner; with a shrug, she sat at the table to wait. Frankie, finding herself alone, paced. She did not like closed-in spaces, and as much as she hated to admit it, even to herself, she was scared without Harper.

Johner felt sweat roll down his back as he watched the females enter their rooms, and when they were safely inside, he dismissed the guards. Something itched at him, a fleeting impression that he could not make any sense of, especially with his dragon grumbling at him. He sent someone for the female's vehicle and to find out where they had been staying and retrieve their possessions, which along with their vehicle, would need to be searched. He was sure there were no explosives, but the female had many knives concealed around her person. So it was better to be safe than annoyed later.

CHAPTER FOUR:

Johner, Ark and Axl walked into the command room that held the live feed from the interrogation rooms. Right now both females were on screen. Johner's dragon roared. *SHADOW!*

He pleaded with him. *I know... I know. Just give me a minute, please.*

We left her.

Yes, but she is safe. I swear.

He collapsed into a chair; they were to wait for Lars, Prime to the Dragon Lord. Johner looked up when his father walked in. Rene` had been a father to Johner since he was two years old, he was as much his son as any of his birth sons. Concerned at Johner's look, he asked. "Son?"

"Shadow." was all Johner could get out over the roaring of his dragon and the struggle he was having to contain him.

Rene` looked at the two females and then to Ark and Axl. He gave a nod to the screens, and they both shook their heads.

Ark told him. "No idea."

Rene` mused. "She's a little thing."

Johner finally got control of his dragon with a promise they would be with their Shadow shortly. He straightened in his chair as he squinted at the screen that held Frankie pacing in her room. "Do you think so?"

Rene` looked again at Harper. "Yes, quite tiny."

Johner looked to where his father was looking and laughed. "No, not her, the other one."

Rene` turned his attention to Frankie and smiled. "Well, she is delightful."

Johner smiled with pride. "She is, and she says the most

adorable things."

Ark and Axl snorted at his description. Johner asked. "What?"

Ark stated. "You have not seen the recording yet?"

"No."

Axl loaded it up, and they spent the next few minutes watching and listening to Johner's Shadow and the other female as they entered the castle grounds. Rene` laughed with the three young males. Ark asked as he pointed to Harper. "Doesn't she remind you of someone?"

Rene` agreed, sounding as puzzled as the others. "She does?"

"Yeah, like someone we know, but who?" Johner asked.

Ark and Axl shook their heads. Ark mumbled. "No idea, but someone."

Rene` pulled on his bottom lip as he studied her and then said. "Well, never mind, Lars is unable to attend. So I will take his place. Let us go Johner, and question your Shadow and see what we can find out. Something is niggling at me, and I want to know what it is?"

Johner stood, saying. "I had the same feeling. Papa, do you think that's a good idea; you know with her being my Shadow?"

Rene` was by his side in a second, his arm around his shoulders. "Can you honestly say you and your dragon would be fine with one of the boys and me talking to her without you?"

Johner ducked his head and sighed. "No. I really want to say I would, but sadly, it would be a lie. I am fairly sure there would be blood. Lots of blood."

Axl said to Ark. "Meaning ours."

Ark grunted, then said. "I think it was just your blood he was talking about."

Axl sucked in air between his teeth then said. "Remember, I can run faster than you."

"Bastard."

Rene` shook his head at the two and, with his arm around his son drew him out of the room, away from the fools. "That is what I thought son, a dragon can only be pushed so far. So let us go get this done."

"I don't think I can go in that room by myself, my dragon..."

Rene` nodded. "I understand. We will interview them together. It will make it easier for you."

Johner seemed to be having words with his dragon, so Rene` waited. Sometimes a compromise had to be reached and that could take some time. Finally, after a few intense minutes, Johner relaxed. "He is unhappy, but is willing to go along with it."

Rene` clapped him on the shoulder. "That is all we can ask of him. Let us go see what has brought your Shadow here to our door."

Ark called out. "Remember, the small one has weapons."

Rene` smiled. "I do."

They walked to the interview rooms. Johner opened the door to Harper's room. His dragon made his voice sound gruffer than normal as he said. "Come with me." Something about the female set his teeth on edge. He couldn't say why, she was so little, yet she seemed to fill the room with her presence.

Ark and Axl sat down, turned up the sound, and relaxed in the chairs. "This is going to be fun." Axl said with glee.

Ark grunted his agreement as they settled into watch.

Harper stood without a word and walked behind the older male, with Johner following. They entered the room that held a very agitated Frankie. When she saw Harper, she grabbed her in a hug, asking. "Did they hurt you?" Not waiting for an answer, she glared at the two males. "Did they use rubber hoses and a phone book, or did they go right to the electric shocker?" Harper allowed her to pet her face and back, then run her hands down her arms. She almost burst out laughing when she twirled her from front to back to front again, asking. "Where are the marks?"

Rene` and Johner stood just inside the door with stunned expressions on both their faces as Frankie questioned Harper. Who stood in her embrace and tried desperately not to laugh at her ridiculous questions, and the look on the males faces. *Could someone say affronted?*

"Female." Johner snarled with his dragon in his voice. "We do not torture females."

Rene` placed a hand on Johner's arm when the sound of wounded pride from his dragon entered his voice. Johner tipped his head back and Harper, who had escaped Frankie's embrace, but not the hand on her arm which gripped her. Saw him take in several deep breaths to help center himself. She wanted to tell him it would not work with them, but *Blah!* They had locked Frankie in a windowless room. She dismissed the tall male called Johner. He was dangerous she was sure. But he did not set her internal alarm off, not the way the older male did. He was the power, the one to stay wary of. She knew he was older than he appeared. It was a feeling of age that surrounded him and that smile... that smile said. I am older and wiser tread carefully, but the twinkle in his eyes. Oh... that twinkle said, let me see what you can do? It was just enough of a challenge for Harper to throw caution to the wind, almost. Frankie stared at Johner and asked Harper. "Why is he doing that?"

Harper swallowed her snicker and said. "He is thinking."

Frankie eyed her and then Johner but refrained from commenting further. Her question seemed to break the tension in the room. Rene` moved to the table and waited while Johner, now calmer, brought over two more chairs. He placed one beside the one Harper pushed Frankie into and took the other to Rene`. Both males sat after the females did. Frankie smiled in appreciation. Gentlemen, *how nice.*

Rene` said. "Thank you Johner. We will begin with the interview now."

"Yes, my Lord." Johner said, then nodded to the small camera in the room's corner. "Start recording please Axl."

Frankie asked Harper. "What is he doing?"

"Talking to someone called Axl, who is monitoring the camera."

Frankie looked around as she asked. "Camera?"

"Yep."

"Where?"

Harper turned Frankie's head and tipped it up and pointed to the corner where the wall met the ceiling and showed her the small camera. Frankie did the lip thing and then she jumped up and bounced as she waved. Again Harper thought, *pogo stick.*

Frankie called out. "Hey, hey, Axl. How you doing?"

Harper watched the males watch Frankie and hid her grin at their amazed expressions.

Axl said to Ark. "That one is a little loose in the head. I think Johner has his work cut out for him."

Ark sighed. "For your age and experience, you know nothing about females. She is not loose in the head, which is a terrible term, and you had better not let Edee hear you say it. Seriously Axl, you should try harder to recognize when someone is something other."

"What other, like a faerie?"

"I am not sure. Now the short one, her you need to watch."

"Really, she is small and quiet."

"Did you learn nothing from Olinda?"

"She does not look like Olinda."

"Brother, you make me weary. Do not let her size fool you, this one is a killer."

Axl grinned. "Her, I understand, the other one is the problem, unpredictable."

"What you know about females is pitiful."

"Yet, if I remember, I got more dates last month than you."

"Brother, shut up."

Frankie returned to her seat and asked. "Was he one of the nice dragons that brought us here?"

They both noticed the looks on the male's faces. "What...

You thought we didn't know, seriously?" Frankie frowned as she looked at Harper and asked. "Was it meant to be a secret?"

Harper shrugged. "I doubt it; they are everywhere."

"See, that is what I thought, but they act like we did not know."

"Maybe they think we are unobservant."

Frankie thought about that for a minute as she did the lip thing again and said. "I suppose that could be a possibility."

Harper nodded. "I would say so."

Concerned, Frankie asked. "Oh, should I have said nothing?"

"Too late now and Frankie, I think they know about the dragons."

Frankie shrugged and said. "Yeah, I guess they do."

Rene` could see where this was heading and cut them off. "Ladies, we would like to ask you a few questions."

"They are so polite." Frankie whispered to Harper.

She whispered back. "Yep, they are."

Frankie said, "You are so polite."

"We thank you." Johner said with a wide smile.

Rene's brows lifted, and his voice was a little sterner when he said again. "Ladies, my name is Rene` Kingsley." When Frankie opened her mouth, he said quickly. "Yes, Johner is my son." She subsided and ducked her head. "They," He nodded toward the camera, "are two of the guards that brought you here."

Harper asked. "The two without vests?"

Rene` raised his eyebrows but answered her. "Yes, they are Shields what you would know as commandos. I think the term is, their names are Ark and Axl Battle."

"Cool names." Frankie mumbled, and they heard a short growl quickly cut off. Johner tipped his head to the ceiling as his father looked at him. Rene` sighed twice before continuing. "As you already know, Johner is the Commander of the castle guards. Prime Lars was meant to interview you, but he has been detained. I have been asked to come and interview you instead. I am Commander of the Hunters, what you may know as soldiers." Harper wanted to ask by whom, but thought the answer may upset Frankie, so she kept quiet. Rene` asked. "Now could you tell us who you are?"

Harper answered before Frankie could. "My name is Harper, and this is my friend Frankie."

"Best friend." Frankie said out the side of her mouth.

Harper dutifully said. "Best friend."

Rene` said. "Now we are getting somewhere. Why are you here?"

"Because you brought us here." Frankie answered, while she looked at Johner.

He smiled at her like she was so sweet and shook his head, and said slowly and distinctly. "No, my father meant. Why. Are. You. Here?"

Frankie leaned a little over the table and said. "Because. You. Brought. Us. Here!"

Both males stared at her as she stared back. Harper waited, then Johner rubbed the back of his neck and swallowed the quick words on his tongue and instead asked. "Okay, let us try this. How did you get here?"

Harper waited as Frankie gave him a puzzled look. "We walked here with you and your guards."

"Yes... yes, you did, but before that. How did you get here?"

"Oh, I see. In a pickup." Frankie answered as though it was obvious, and she could not understand why he was asking.

"Good... Good, so why?"

Bewildered, she answered. "Because it was a long way to walk. I do not know why you need to know that?"

Harper waited, Rene` leaned back in his chair and watched his son and the two females while his dragon churned over who Harper reminded them of? Neither he nor his dragon missed the fact she conveniently left off their last names. That, they knew, was no accident. Johner hitched his chair closer to the table and eyed his Shadow as he asked. "So if it was a long way to walk. Why come?"

Frankie copied Johner with her chair and almost swooned as she caught his scent, saying. "Because we needed to."

"It is not an easy place to find?"

Frankie did the lip thing, Harper waited as Frankie looked at her, then the silent male and finally Johner. "We found it really easy. Are you sure it is hard to find?"

"Yes, I am sure."

"I am shocked. We just drove on through the tunnel of trees and presto, we were here. Right Harper?"

"Yep, that's right."

Johner tried once more. "So, I ask again, why are you here?"

Frankie stared at him for a few seconds, then said. "Because you brought us here."

Johner sighed loudly, flicked his eyes to Harper, who stared back at him with an expressionless face and shuttered eyes, then back to Frankie. "Alright, what decided you to travel here to the castle?"

"Harper brought me."

"But why? You must have some idea?"

"Oh, I do."

They went back to the staring. Rene` sighed loudly twice again. Harper waited, a half smile on her face. *See!* His Dragon said, looking at Harper. That *expression seems like...*

Rene` turned his head from side to side as he asked his dragon. *What is that noise?*

His dragon whispered so softly, it was more a feeling than words as he answered. *The Ancients are singing.*

Why can I hear them?

We were Dragon Lord.

So Reighn will hear this?

If he is in the castle, yes.

Why are they singing?

I do not know.

Rene` mentally shook his head as he dropped his chair back onto the floor with a thump and asked sternly. "Alright Harper, why are you here?" He held his hand up when Frankie went to speak, causing her to snap her lips together.

Harper told him. "Looking for someone?"

"Could you give me more details?"

"I could?" She replied. "If I was so inclined."

Reneˋ smiled. Harper wasn't sure if it was a friendly smile or not, as he asked. "What would help you become inclined?"

"Eww! I know... I know!" Frankie said as she held her hand up and wiggled in her chair. They all looked at her. "What I do know?"

Rene's brows went up again as Johner said, not quite under his breath. "This should be good."

Harper waited as Reneˋ asked with a calmness that was belied by the annoyance shining in his eyes. "Please tell us?"

Frankie gave them one of her best smiles, wide with teeth showing. Harper never had the heart to tell her it made her look demented. But as she witnessed the male's reactions to her friend's manic smile, she thought she might just have to. Frankie rushed out. "She needs coffee, and I need a berry shake. We missed morning tea, right Harper?"

"Yep."

Johner dropped his head onto the table as he groaned. Reneˋ sighed. As fun as this was, Harper needed to get out of the room, so as not to hurt Frankie's feelings, she said. "While Frankie is right. I would be inclined to tell you why we are here, if you could tell me why you're filling the town with folks?"

"How long have you been here?" Reneˋ asked sharply.

Frankie replied innocently. "Since you brought us in."

Annoyed, Reneˋ said. "Seriously, I will not entertain you as your Shadow will, so cease this nonsense now."

Frankie straightened in her seat and demanded of Reneˋ. "Someone is being rude. And what is a Shadow, and why are you annoyed you were not put in jail?"

Reneˋ lifted an eyebrow and his dragon looked out at Frankie and Harper. "Maybe a little time in the cells beneath the castle will encourage you to talk."

Frankie's hand grabbed Harper's arm and squeezed as her face paled. She sucked in a scared breath, causing Harper to snarl a warning.

"Enough! I will allow you to scare her like that only once. Consider yourself warned dragon." Her eyes turned ghost gray as her anger vibrated throughout the room. Johner felt the hair stand up on his arms and Rene` was sure he saw a small blue flame in the depths of her eyes. What fascinated him was he felt and saw her anger swirl in the air between them and was almost positive he could reach out and touch it.

His dragon rose to the surface, reacting according to the perceived threat, causing Rene` to stand abruptly and accidentally kick his chair into the wall behind him. At the actions of his father. Johner stood just as hurriedly, looking for the threat. Which caused Frankie to jump from her chair with a startled yelp and scramble behind Harper, who had also stood.

An instant later, in Harper's capable hands, knives appeared where none were before. Suddenly, the door crashed open, and one of the Shields from earlier and a powerfully built male with enhanced, almost magical energy surrounding him stood in the doorway. He was so spectacular, he literally took Harper's breath away.

Reighn took in the tense situation and felt Ark's dragon still beside him, with both dragon's attention solely on the small female with knives, he asked his father calmly. "Sire, are you alright?"

Rene` heaved in a deep breath and felt his dragon recede as he answered absently. "Yes, thank you my son." How he wondered he had lost control of the situation causing his dragon to rise. There was no intent of danger here, power yes, but nothing that would make his reaction so volatile. He and his dragon were far too old to lose control like that. Then they all heard Frankie ask. "Do you see the size of him, Harper, he has got to be the biggest one yet, dontcha think?"

"Yep, I do." Harper responded, and once again Frankie's innocent question broke the tension that held them captive.

Reighn walked farther into the room, releasing the hold he'd placed on Ark and Johner, who went immediately to Frankie and stood near her. She did the lips thing again as she looked up at the male.

Finally, Ark asked Harper as Axl entered the room. "Why does she do that? Is she alright?"

Harper didn't bother looking away from the powerful male stalking into the room. "She is thinking."

"Put up your knives, female." Reighn growled as he stood next to his father, and to Johner he said. "You allowed our father in here while she remained armed?"

"Dude!" Harper growled back. "No one allowed anything, he's a grown man, hardly senile. Frankie, what do you think?" She asked as she sheathed both knives under her jacket, while the room seemed to hold its breath. Ignoring the sudden atmosphere Harper's words invoked, Frankie answered. "Nah, not senile."

Reighn looked at his father, then the others in the room, and together they all said. **"Dude!"**

CHAPTER FIVE:

T hings moved swiftly after the males all repeated the word dude. Harper and Frankie were introduced to Reighn, and then found themselves following him, Rene` and Johner from the interview room.

Frankie asked question after question of Johner about the castle. Who he was, what his job was like, what was a Shadow. Did he have a family? Was there a King and Queen anywhere? Then more questions about what he meant when he said she was his Shadow?

He patiently answered every question, even the one about her being his Shadow. Harper would have slapped a gag over her mouth long ago, like... after question two. After they had walked up a flight of wide stone stairs, Harper asked Reighn. "So, you are some big honcho here, then?"

Reighn nodded. "I am the current Dragon Lord, my Sire." He indicated Rene`. "Was the former Dragon Lord."

Harper asked. "And that means what exactly?"

"Ohh, I know... I know."

They stopped as Frankie bounced in place. Harper reached out to grab the bouncing Frankie. *Really Pogo stick.* When Johner growled, she slapped her hand instead to his chest. The males all tensed as Reighn did a quick scan for knives, because the female was incredibly fast with them. Harper moved in close, pushing between Frankie and Johner and placing herself in front of Frankie, therefore missing the worried look she gave Johner. "Listen here dragon, I haven't decided about you all yet. So it would be prudent of you to withhold anymore of your growls." She stepped in more and Johner felt the hand of trepidation squeeze his lungs; an unnatural occurrence for a dragon.

"You should be aware at this time, there are only two people I will kill without a thought for. One of them is my girl, Frankie. So regardless of what you think she is to you, remember I already know who and what she is to me."

Silence met her words as Johner dipped his head and opened his mouth to apologize, but Frankie sniffed loudly, saying. "Aww! Harper, you love me?"

Harper moved back from Johner, her gray eyes never leaving his, and the tension eased as she said. "Yep, it seems that way."

"Knew it." Frankie said as she took hold of Johner's arm and moved him along, passing rapidly by Harper as she stated. "So Harper, the Dragon Lord runs Dragon's Gap and basically the entire world, so watch your manners with how you talk to him."

"How do you know shit like this?" Harper asked, partly amazed and partly amused.

Frankie grinned, then sighed. "We talked to people in town and then listened to their answers, or at least I did."

Harper grumbled. "Seriously, I never heard anyone say stuff like that?"

"Because you don't listen, you are too busy looking for who knows what."

All the others knew what she had been looking for, danger, armed attackers, and assassins. Harper just shrugged and moved on, saying. "To be honest, people like to talk to you. When you aren't being weird."

Frankie giggled. "Well yeah." She whispered to Johner. "She likes you, she just you know..."

Johner gave her hand a squeeze and whispered back. "I do, and will apologize when we are alone. So she will know that I meant no harm."

"Yeaaah! That is probably a good idea." Frankie said, worrying her bottom lip. "Just you know... be careful."

They arrived at another flight of stairs as they walked up them. Rene` slipped along the mental pathway to Reighn.

Your thoughts, son?

I like them both. I like Harper.

Frankie is adorable and well suited for Johner. She will lighten his life.

That she will, and give him a merry dance along the way. My brother deserves her joy. But you are wary of Harper.

Yes, there is something about her; she gives my dragon an itch.

Is it because she is nothing like our Charlie?

Maybe that is it. Charlie's heart was opened when she arrived here, and her heart softened more because of Storm and the young ones and our family. I am not sure this one's heart is even cracked. I fear she could hurt Charlie.

You think that after her display just now. No Papa, her heart is hurt, broken even. But she loves and in that she is more like Charlie than you can imagine.

Rene` thought about what Reighn said, then replied. *I do not see it; she has a hardness, an emptiness to her.*

I think Papa, you are reading her wrong, she is all heart. She is wounded and you are mistaking that for emptiness. Look again and not with just your mind. Look beyond the surface she shows the world. Go deeper with all of your senses and see what I have seen, and when you do, tell me your thoughts are the same. She is a wounded, frightened soul, very frightened. You talk of emptiness. She is not empty she is overflowing with feelings. All boxed up and hidden from herself. Whoever did this to her is dead when I find them.

CHAPTER SIX:

Charlie and Harper stood a room apart, neither moved nor spoke. Storm shifted to stand next to his father and Reighn, so he could see his Shadow's face. Frankie sat munching on a handful of nuts Johner had found for her when she mentioned she was hungry. He was now on the phone ordering her a berry shake; she sighed, half in love already; the male was a dream come true.

When they had finally arrived at Johner's brother's apartment, Storm opened the door and Reighn quickly informed him who they all were. But Frankie had the idea they already knew and were prepared for her and Harper. Something given strength too, when from the kitchen emerged two females who were introduced as Rene's Shadow Verity, and Reighn's Shadow Sage. Then again, Reighn was quick to explain who Harper and Frankie were, and again Frankie had the feeling they already knew. Both of the ladies seemed very nice. It was, Frankie thought in their eyes; they possessed an energy that emanated from each of them, making her feel instantly comfortable. Which she would admit was something only Harper had so far been able to do. Although Charlie gave her the same feeling, she was so much like Harper, and yet so different. Frankie liked them all. It was hard to say if Harper did. Right now she was in a staring contest with her sister, who Frankie was amazed to see held Harper's gaze. There were few that could.

As she ate her nuts, she catalogued the differences between the sisters; it was obvious Charlie was older, and she had hair which was really black and straight and way shorter than Harper's long, wavy auburn tresses. Although their eyes were identical, and they were almost the same height.

Frankie sighed. They were so obviously related, evidenced by the fact they both had the same body shape and dress sense. Seriously, it was a shame no one taught these females to dress. It looked like she would have to have the dressing to impress lecture with Charlie as she did with Harper. "How your males could not see they were related puzzles me?" Frankie said to Verity and Sage when they joined her on the beautiful dining table.

Sage replied. "No surprise to me."

"Males never look for the obvious." Verity assured them both. "It is a failing I have noticed often over the years.

Sage explained. "It is not their fault; they are just not wired to see the little things."

Frankie stated. "That is true but still obvious."

"Agreed." The ladies said together.

"Do you mind we are right here?" Rene` told the three of them, with annoyance. Because as he looked at the sisters, he could not understand how he had not realized who Harper was. He was inclined to blame Frankie and her unusual mind. She threw his powers of deduction off. All three women laughed at him and his sons, who wore disgruntled expressions.

Frankie called out to Harper. "Hey, Harper, you have a sister called Charlie. How come you never told me?"

"Thought she was dead."

"Oh. I see, well that is kind of cool, you know, because she is not."

"Yep, I suppose." Harper looked at Charlie. "So not dead then?"

"Nope, and you suppose?"

"Yep, not sure it's really you?"

Charlie raised a brow and smirked. *Harper! Her Harper was here. Goddess, she had missed her so much.* Her heart had dropped into her shoes when Harper walked through the door, even though Storm had prepared her. It was still so shocking, all the yearning and grief, the anger gone in an instant. And now, after all that, Harper had the audacity to say she did not believe it was her. Charlie narrowed her eyes, she knew their bond as weak as it was, had snapped into place as soon as Harper arrived at Dragon's Gap.

Two nights ago she had woken from sleep with a racing heart and pounding awareness, something had changed. At first she had thought there was danger. She had instantly sent her senses out like Scarlett was teaching her to do, and on the edge of her awareness, she thought she felt Harper. But thinking she was mistaken, and it had only been another dream, she rolled over and snuggled into Storm's arms, going back to sleep. Now she realized she had been wrong. "You know it is me, Harper, so stop the drama." Charlie cocked her head to the side and let her eyes run over her sister. She was older, thinner and harder... her heart hurt for that. Harper always had attitude, now it looked like it had solidified into coldness. But as she looked into eyes exactly like hers, she saw she was wrong. There was pain, anger, and hope all mixed up in the shadows. *Ahh! Not so cold, little sister.* Casually, she asked. "So not crazy then?"

Harper kicked her top lip up in not quite a sneer, which used to drive Charlie nuts as teenagers. "Nope."

Charlie's eyes narrowed again as she hissed out. "Well, that is good."

"If you say so." Harper shrugged and turned to go, looked at the startled people in the room, and glared as she snarled. "What... you coming Frankie?"

"Umm... Yeah, I guess." Frankie said as she jumped from the table.

Johner slapped his phone in his hand as he asked. "Frankie?"

She smiled sadly. "It was cool while it lasted."

Harper moved to open the door. The rest of the people in the room just stared between her and Charlie, which amused her. But the expression on Charlie's face had her almost laughing. As she reached out to open the door, Charlie snapped out. "You are an auntie."

Harper raised an eyebrow, turned, and looked at her sister. *Thank the Goddess!* She breathed out a sigh and said. "Is that a lie?"

Charlie demanded. "Why the hell would I lie about that?"

Harper snapped back. "Why ask me that? How would I know? You are a stranger to me. I can't be knowing what is going on in your brain, can I?"

"Stranger... I am not a stranger. I am your sister. I am no different than I always was." Charlie snarled right back at her.

Harper let go with a skeptical laugh as she said. "You are so not the same."

"How am I not?" demanded an outraged Charlie.

Harper shrugged. "Shadow and kids, that is how."

"Oh yeah, there is that." Charlie said a little sheepishly as she realized Harper was right; she was different, they both were.

Harper, looking a little smug, knowing she had scored against Charlie, said. "Told yah. So you have a boy?"

Charlie answered. "More."

"Like pulling teeth." Harper stated as she looked toward the ceiling, missing the gleam in Charlie's eyes, then with exaggerated patience, she asked. "Do you have two children?"

"No, three, two girls and a boy."

Frankie slid back onto the table, saying in a loud whisper. "It's like watching tennis, huh?"

Verity nodded. "Better."

Reighn whispered. "Wish I had popcorn."

Storm rumbled. "Do you mind?"

Frankie did the lips thing, then said. "Not really, it is kind of cute to see Harper like this, better than watching her slice and dice people."

Slowly, they all turned to her, except Charlie and Harper. Rene` asked. "Slice and dice?"

Frankie chewed on her nuts, swallowed fast, and said. "Yep, she is really good with those knives. Not so good with guns."

Harper admonished. "Frankie."

Frankie grinned, then stated. "So true Harper, don't be saying it isn't. You know I have seen you at the shooting range."

"Yep, I know, but still." Quickly changing the subject from her not that impressive target shooting, Harper asked Charlie. "So kids, huh?"

"Yep, still can't shoot, huh?"

Now it was Harper's turn to narrow her eyes at Charlie as she smirked. "Your point, cut yourself lately?"

Charlie snarled silently, damn Harper, she knew she had no aptitude for knives. Almost as much as Harper did for guns. Deciding to forgo that topic, she asked. "Would you like to meet my young?"

"Not so much."

"Seriously, I tell you, you are an aunt and you do not want to visit with my children?"

"That is about right."

Charlie stepped forward, fists clenched, as she remembered how annoying Harper could be. *Now that I never missed.*

Storm said. "My soul, maybe..."

Both females turned eyes of granite in his direction. Storm, Commander of the Hunters, leader in rogue kills, quelled before that look and just stopped himself from ducking behind his Sire. He swallowed the rest of his words as Frankie sucked in her breath, whispering. "Man, why did you do that?"

He mumbled in return. "I was just trying to help."

Frankie gave his shoulder a pat in comfort. "Yeah, I know, but seriously, sisters."

Charlie's eyes turned speculative as they returned to Harper, who sighed loudly, then asked. "I suppose they have names?"

"Of course they have names. Why would they not?"

"I am waiting." Harper said as she scratched her cheek.

Charlie's eyes narrowed once more as she told her. "We

have Kelsey, who is five. Cara who is two and baby Justice, who is almost three months old."

"Nice. What else you got?"

Charlie eased back and crossed her arms, but before she could speak, the door behind her opened. Tansy, one of Charlie's nannies and a faerie, entered. Only to stop with a scream, when a knife flew past her face and stuck in the wall. Instantly, she became tiny and flew to hide behind Storm, who yelled. "What the hell!" He started advancing on Harper, only to come up short when her hands filled with knives and she lowered into a defensive crouch.

Charlie also yelled. "What the hell?"

Reighn roared. "Female, put up your knives, there is no danger here."

Harper stood, and her knives magically disappeared. Charlie got up close to Harper, standing almost nose to nose with her, which gave Storm's heart a jolt. Charlie, her heart beating a fast tattoo, yelled in Harper's face. "What. The. Hell!"

Harper said softly. "Back off sister, before I make you."

Charlie took one look at her and sneered. "I so would like to see you try?"

They both heard the groans from Storm and his family, as well as Tansy's tearful cry. Frankie brushed her hands together, dusting off the salt and wiggled off the table. As she looked over at the very worried Verity and Sage, who had a blue globe forming in her hands. She said to Sage as her globe disappeared. "Very nice."

Startled, she looked at Frankie and asked. "How did you do that?"

Frankie winked at her and Verity and hopped down from the table and before anyone realized what she was doing, she had shimmied between the two females. Making space by pushing her elbow into Harper's chest and moving her back. She knew, as everyone else did, Harper moved because she wanted to. Frankie held out her hand to Charlie. "Hi, I am Frankie Spring, Harper's best friend. She would kill for me, she said so. You can ask Johner or Reighn or Rene ` they heard her."

Charlie took her hand, gave it a shake and quickly dropped it as though the contact stung her. She looked at Frankie with eyes so much like Harpers, it was like staring at her twin. Except these eyes had the same confused, laced with amazement and a healthy dash of speculation expression most people got when they encountered her for the first time. Harper never looked at her like that. In all the time Frankie had known her. She only looked at her with understanding and amusement, even when she was annoyed with her. It was the same way she was looking at her now.

Charlie's eyes traveled over the tall, skinny female and knew she was in the presence of something other. Something more than what she showed the world. Before she could stop herself, she whispered. "What are you?"

Frankie grinned and replied for all to hear. "I have been told, I am an improbability."

Sage said to Reighn. "Another one, coincidence. I think not."

He took her hand and kissed her palm. "Nor I. It is truly a new age we are moving into."

Johner cleared his throat. "Fra…" Which was all he could say before three sets of eyes turned to him, and a tingle of awareness skated over his skin. Making him actually duck behind Rene `, they heard him say. "Yes, well, carry on."

Which caused them all to smile, and it lightened the tense atmosphere. Frankie said. "I see the trouble. Being sisters, you are alike, and that can cause friction, so I am told. I would not know as I have no sisters or brothers or mother or father or grandparents, aunts, uncles or cousins." She stopped and blinked, then said. "That I know of."

Everyone looked at her, and when she still said nothing more, they continued to wait. Frankie blinked several more times, then she did the lip thing. Charlie's eyes widened as Harper waited and was surprised it was not Frankie that broke the stare off. It was Charlie who finally flicked her eyes to Storm and back. Then she smiled, transforming her face from annoyed to amused. Her expression softened and made the beauty of the adult Charlie shine as she asked Frankie. "You're a touch weird, aren't you, sweetie?"

Frankie nodded slowly and leaned nearer as she said. "I have been told, just weird enough to be interesting, right Harper?"

"Yep, that's true."

Charlie tipped her head to the side as she told her. "It's okay now Frankie." She was the only one to see the filter lift, and the worry in the soft brown eyes. In that moment, she realized Harper had brought someone special to Dragon's Gap. She knew Harper, whether or not she realized it, had come here, not only to find her, but for Frankie, and in her own way she was keeping Frankie safe. Harper took a deep breath and let it out slowly, and waited until Frankie moved back to the table. She looked at Charlie, who had stepped back a foot, and asked. "So Faeries?"

Charlie nodded. "Yes a Grove."

Harper searched her memory for the meaning of the word and nodded. "They welcome you?"

"Yes, of course. I am the liaison between Dragon's Gap and the Grove."

"Of course you are."

"What does that mean?"

"Exactly what I said."

"You make it sound like I am their bitch."

"Just saying it like I see it. You cannot fault me for that?"

"Sure I can. You know nothing."

Harper smirked as she told her. "I know what I know."

It was Charlie's turn to say with exaggerated patience. "They call us gray ones; you are one too." She raised her eyebrows when Harper made no comment. "I imagine you already knew that."

"Yep, I know, Juna told me."

"Well, of course she did. Why tell me. I didn't need to know?"

Harper almost grinned at the long ago Charlie bitch about what she should have been told by Juna. The fact she would scoff at just about anything their mother told her or spend most of the time arguing logistics and probabilities with her. Charlie always conveniently forgot, and it seemed she still did. Juna, their mother, had ended up telling Harper because she, one; believed what her mother told her and two; she knew the information would keep her and Charlie alive. Which it had done on many occasions. Another faerie emerged from the other room with two girls and carrying a baby. They called to Charlie when they saw her. "Mama?"

This time Harper did not react, and the first faerie, Tansy, moved to Charlie's side and grew as Charlie scooped up the little girl. She looked at Harper as she told her. "These are our daughters Kelsey and Cara and our son Justice."

Harper nodded. "Well okay." She stared at the girls, then smiled at Cara and said. "Hello little unicorn."

Cara said. "ello."

Kelsey smiled when Harper said. "Hello little cougar."

"Hello." She then walked over to Harper and looked up at her. "You are like Mama."

Harper shrugged. "Maybe?"

"You are the same but different, you have a big hole inside. It is all dark."

"Maybe." Harper repeated softly, then asked. "You can see that?"

"Yes, I don't think we can fix dark holes?"

"That's okay, I will fix it, and Kelsey, it is not your job to fix holes."

"Oh, but we fix holes, that is what Grandmama and Grandpa say."

"Did they also say sometimes holes cannot be fixed?"

Kelsey answered seriously. "No, why do you have a hole?"

Harper looked up at Charlie and replied. "You should ask

your Mama that, she put it there."

Charlie breathed deeply, keeping her temper leashed as she narrowed her eyes on her sister. "Kelsey honey, can you go with Rose and Tansy please?" She passed Cara to Tansy all the while she kept her eyes on Harper, who stared back at her, challenging her to deny her statement. She told the girls. "I need to talk to Auntie Harper for a minute."

"Okay, Mama." Kelsey smiled as Cara waved at Storm. They left with their nannies after being introduced to Frankie. Who made them giggle and promised to visit later.

CHAPTER SEVEN:

As soon as the door closed behind the children. Charlie yelled at Harper. "What is the fucking matter with you?"

"Me? What did I say?"

"You blame me for the hole in you?"

Harper slammed her hands on her hips and scowled at Charlie. "You bet I do; you left me Charlie, just walked away. Then believed I was dead."

Charlie grabbed Harper's collar with both hands and pulled her toward her, snarling into her face again, much to everyone's surprise.

"Now you listen to me, you little pain in my ass. I left because I won a scholarship and it was safer for me to go. Remember sister, it was you who damn well told me that? So do not get all snotty now because you have decided it does not sit right in your memory."

Harper's eyes blazed, and she grabbed Charlie's hands and thought about squeezing them hard. Then rethought that when she realized she had actually forgotten that it was at her urging, Charlie had left. *Damn it!* Harper let her hands go and grumbled. "That explains the dead thing huh, not likely."

Charlie said as she once more stepped away from her. "I came back, and you were gone. Our bond was gone. When I finally found her, she said you were dead." Charlie almost begged her to understand what she was saying. "There was no bond, Harper. I could not feel you."

Harper shrugged as sadness choked her, making speech impossible. Charlie, unfortunately, took the gesture as uncaring, and her voice hardened as she hissed. "How about I spell that out for you, seeing as it is not getting through?

D.E.A.D. I cannot make it any plainer than that."

Harper growled, angry all over again at her sister. "Unbelievable. She says I am dead, and you go boohoo and fucking shut the door on us. You believed her because she always told the truth."

"I didn't go boohoo, who does that?"

"Not you apparently." Harper snarked back.

"I thought you died. They told me you had died. I could not feel our bond anymore." Charlie said with a calmness she did not feel.

Harper stood eyeing her sister with her arms crossed again while her toe started tapping. Both females totally forgetting they had an audience. Harper felt a little guilty. She had slammed the bond closed before she killed their father. Not wanting Charlie to have to feel any of what was going to happen and what came later. By the time she tried to re-open the connection to Charlie, she could not. She believed her step-mother's family had killed her. Leaving her no option other than to leave earth for the gray zone where she remained for a long time grieving for her beloved sister. And while there, she had realized she was a true gray one with a terrible gift. Killing for her was far too easy. When she finally emerged from the zone. She moved to the town of Bethany, hoping the slower pace of life, away from the bigger cities, would help her control her dark side. It was there she met Frankie and found something better than a slow way of living. Harper found someone to help her fight the compulsion to re-enter the dark place that turned her from a reasonable human to a wanton killing machine. She had found Frankie, who in her innocence held the compulsion at bay without even knowing she did. That was why she sent Charlie away all those years ago, or she should say she had sent her away before the dark Harper emerged fully. She had been so frightened she would hurt Charlie. Making her leave kept her not only safe from their father and step-mother but from her. At least the dark side of herself, which had been growing and taking over her life. Her biggest fear was that Charlie would find out what she had been left with after they fought the shades in the gray mist. It had taken Harper years to return to the person she was now.

Charlie sighed as she too remembered she had closed the door on those emotions when their bond was severed. Her heart had opened with her love for Storm and their children and the family who belonged to her now. She admitted she felt guilty as she stood in front of Harper. She wondered now if Harper had been living without hope, without a reason to be alive. Had she just gone through the motions of her life? She at least had lived with a purpose to see justice done.

Harper asked now with loads of attitude, which grudgingly Charlie supposed she was entitled to. "Did you see a body? Any... body. Did you see my corpse? No, because I wasn't damn well dead."

Charlie frowned and tried not to grimace, Harper was right, but still... "Well, yeah, it seems you aren't."

"Did you at least shoot the bitch?"

"What do you think?" Shrugged Charlie with an eye roll, not admitting to how many she had killed in revenge for Harper's death.

Harper growled. "That you better have."

"Where have you been Harper, where were you?"

Harper shrugged, unable to tell her, unable to put voice to those years in the gray zone. Charlie asked. "I am guessing you thought I was dead as well until recently and then when you felt our connection again, you came here?"

Harper shrugged one shoulder this time as she said. "Who said I thought you were dead?"

"I assumed you did because this is the first time you have come looking for me."

"Maybe it was just that I was so pissed at you. I never tried. How about that, huh?"

Charlie stilled, Frankie stilled, and everyone around her heard her whisper. "Uh-oh! That did it."

Charlie slammed both hands on her hips and glared at Harper, asking. "If I believed you were dead, and you knew I wasn't, where have you been?"

Frankie whispered. "And she's sunk."

Harper stared and said nothing. Charlie's voice notched up an octave. "Harper Elliot Easton, you answer me right now, you hear?"

"Yep. I do."

Charlie's foot began tapping now, and the room got tense again. Reighn stopped chewing on the nuts Frankie had given him. "This is not good."

"How do you know?" Sage asked as Frankie shook some nuts into her hand.

Storm whispered. "It is never good when they use all three of your names."

Harper stared at Charlie, whose foot tapped quicker and harder. Everyone agreed with Verity when she said. "This is so tense."

Harper said. "Nope, not going to go there. You closed our bond, you have no right to be pissed."

"That is a lie. I searched for the bond. It was already closed, you did that first. So you tell me why and tell me now, Harper!"

Frankie jumped up and ducked in front of Harper again. "She was with me in the town we were living in. Well, at least for the last five years, before that she will not say and I have asked."

"Repeatedly." Harper grumbled.

"Well, you should have just said then." Frankie told her with attitude.

Before Harper and Frankie could get into it. Charlie asked. "Is that right Harper?"

"I guess." Harper then told Frankie. "Go sit down Frankie, we are okay."

Frankie skipped back to her seat and whispered. "Phew, tragedy avoided."

"You're a cheerful little thing, aren't you?" Reighn murmured.

Frankie grinned. "I think so, Harper am I cheerful?"

"So much, it is sickening."

Frankie laughed, as did the others. Charlie asked. "Well Harper, you want to explain?"

"What about you? Why is it always me?"

"I THOUGHT YOU WERE DEAD!"

Harper grunted. "Well sure, bring that up."

"Enough!" Reighn said, and they both turned to where he stood from leaning against the table. "Apparently someone, somewhere, told you both that each of you had died for their own pleasure or you both assumed for whatever reason, you were both dead. Obviously we can see that is untrue." Frankie went to speak, but Reighn raised a brow at her. She did the lip thing instead, secretly Reighn scared her a little or maybe a lot. "So as a family, we will work on re-establishing and fixing the broken relationship and finding the truth of the situation. Now Charlie, I am guessing you are the elder sister."

Harper grunted, causing Charlie's eyes to narrow. "Yes Reighn."

He smiled as he asked. "Good, so what do you wish to happen here?"

"Hey, why don't I get a say?" Asked an annoyed Harper.

"Quiet younger sibling." Reighn told her. They stared at each other for a minute or two, then Harper scowled and looked away.

Reighn's dragon grinned. *She is a worthy female.*

Reighn agreed. *I agree, but she is hurt.*

His dragon asserted. *We will mend her as we did our brothers, Shadow.*

I think this is not something we can do alone. I believe it is just as well we have asked Uncle Patrycc to come home.

Maybe so.

Before Reighn could explain what was to happen, Charlie turned to Harper, pointed a finger at her, and snarled. "You will stay here, Harper, in this town, and you will like it. Did you hear me, Harper?"

Harper eyed her sister; she had grown and changed, not just aged, her whole personality had changed, and there was only a glimpse of the sister from her past. She wondered if Charlie thought that of her. She would almost have to really, she supposed it is what happened when time passed away from each other. She was unsure whether she was sad or happy about that. She felt Charlie's tenderness, her immense sorrow and her deep joy that she was here and alive. She also felt her fear that she would leave. It was very similar to Frankie's fear. Sighing inwardly at the love and regret she felt coming from her sister and basking in the joy. That after all these years Charlie was here, in her life, and not just her dreams. She shrugged nonchalantly. "Fine, but don't think you can go all bossy on me, Charlie."

"Harper, don't be ridiculous, of course I will." Was Charlie's laughing reply, then her voice changed, and she said sharply. "I mean it, Harper, I will not let you go, now I have found you."

She snarled at her sister. "I am not deaf Charlie, I said okay. Damn it and I found you, not the other way around."

"So you say."

"Damn Faerie."

"Did you just call me a Faerie?"

"What is it with all the damn questions? Now where do we sleep and someone better get my truck." A smiling Charlie placed her arms around Harper, who almost screeched as she struggled within the bands of steel wrapped around her. "Oh my Goddess, what are you doing?"

"It is called hugging," Charlie snapped. "Now shut the hell up and enjoy it."

Harper moaned. "This is not happening."

Frankie leaned on Johner as she wiped at her eyes. "Aww, they are hugging."

Before Harper knew it, they were all hugging her, she

begged. "Please, kill me now."

Verity said. "Hush female, we are hugger's. You will accept the salute and enjoy it or I will be wroth with thee. Do I make myself clear?"

"Yes Ma'am, clear as glass." She replied with a deep sigh.

"Isn't it crystal?" Storm asked her.

Both Charlie and Harper asked together. "Why?"

Then Harper said. "Crystal is not clear, glass is clear." They looked at each other and grinned at the saying they had often quoted as youngsters. Harper sighed and felt a flame of happiness flare to life in her heart. Damn, it was good to be here, even if the lot of them were crazy and friggin huggers.

"While I am talking about family." Verity said as they all pulled away from Harper.

Frankie asked Harper. "Was she?"

"Yep, I would say she was."

Verity gave them the look she reserved for her sons when they were trying her patience, which had both girls cringing inwardly. Once she was sure her message was received and understood, she said.

"On Sunday we have family day. Which means we spend the day together doing family things, starting with breakfast and ending after dinner. I expect you two to be there to become acquainted with our ever growing family."

Harper sucked in her bottom lip as she wondered, *was this really what her life had come to, family day.* "You know Frankie, and I are not really family."

Several gasps and smothered coughs occurred when she voiced her opinion. Verity asked with arched eyebrows. "I am sorry, did you take that as an invitation for your presence?"

"Ahh yes." Harper said with what she felt was politeness, until Charlie smacked her arm, so it seemed it wasn't.

Frankie shook her head and mouthed *Rude.*

Verity said. "I see, so now you know you were wrong. You will attend Sunday?"

"Yes Ma'am, we will be there." Frankie said with what

Harper could only call glee.

"Oh, I know you will." Verity stated.

Harper refrained from commenting as she eyed the female dragon and started making plans to be gone. Ignoring Frankie's bouncing up and down and her comment. "So cool."

Verity almost laughed as she watched the young female. She could almost see her mind trying to find a way out of family day. "Please do not make me send my boys to find you, it irritates them."

Sage told her with a glint of laughter in her eyes. "The only excuse acceptable is work."

Charlie said casually, not wanting Harper to know she desperately wanted her there. "We are all happy to attend with our young ones and as their aunt you will of course want to come and get to know them." She smiled at Harper, who smirked back at her.

Rene` said quietly. "You both will attend, and Harper, if you have problems with the Faeries of the Grove. I suggest you work them out as Queen Scarlett and her light King Elijah usually come for part of the day."

Harper stood looking at the crowd of people as Charlie secretly applauded Rene`. *Thanks Papa, she will not like it.*

I know sweet one, but your sister has to come to terms with this. They will live in proximity to each other.

I wish it was that simple.

All expression was wiped from Harper's face as she asked. "You are serious?"

Rene` replied. "Deadly."

Harper growled low, raising the hair on everyone as she snarled out one word. "No."

Rene` growled in return. "Yes, there is no choice for you, Harper. Your sister and her Shadow have a rapport with the Grove's faeries as her family, you too..."

"No!" Harper snarled, cutting him off. Anger and danger in every line of her body. Her eyes bled to mist and her hands balled into fists. "Just no... I will not be made to have anything to do with Faeries. In fact, if that is a condition, I am out of here."

Charlie held her breath as Rene's face hardened and his eyes elongated when his dragon rose. Reighn slowly walked between the two combatants, exerting the power which made him the Dragon Lord, and softly said. "No Harper, it is not a condition; no one will make you associate with anyone you do not wish too. This is to become your home and home is a place to feel safe and welcomed in." Turning to his father, he asked. "Papa, do you not want Harper here?"

Rene's eyes widened as he heard his son's words and shame coated his mind as his dragon subsided saying. *I am sorry.*

As am I. Rene` softly said. "My dragon and I are sorry. Harper, please forgive us. We seem to be on the defensive where you are concerned. I do not know why. Please know that I wish you to make your home here as much as everyone else."

Harper thought maybe he was not telling the complete truth, but he seemed to be contrite, and she nodded her head, taking the pinched look from Charlie's face. "Okay."

CHAPTER EIGHT:

F rankie said to break the tension between Harper and Rene` "If we are staying."

"You are." Reighn and Charlie said together.

"We will need some things then."

Johner asked. "Like what?"

"I need work as does Harper, and she needs a barn for her art."

"You are an artist?" Storm asked, and Harper read shock in his voice. Charlie was stunned. *Oh, my dearest Harper.*

Harper frowned at him. "Why do you say it like that?"

Which made Storm smile his slow smile before saying. "It was not a slight, more a comment on the temperamental artist."

Harper gave him a hard stare. "I am so... not temperamental."

Frankie choked on her shake, Johner patted her on her back, wheezing she said. "Harper, you should not lie like that."

"Frankie, how can you say that I am?"

"Am I or am I not allowed in your workspace?"

"Not discussing it." Then she looked at Storm and growled. "Why are you smirking?"

Storm, who was smirking and not even trying to hide it, raised an eyebrow as Reighn asked. "What kind?" Interrupting Storm's next comment before his brother had a knife buried in his chest. Charlie must have thought the same, as she shifted to stand in front of her Shadow. Frankie said. "Famous."

Harper sighed. "Frankie."

Frankie's look became mulish when she said. "What... it is

true? You have your art in galleries all over the world. Harper is a sculptor and a painter." She told them. "At the moment her medium is marble." She flipped open her phone and showed them pictures of Harper's work. "See."

Photo after photo of large beautiful pieces appeared, bears, lions, wolves, couples entwined, a mare with her foal, stallions, unicorns, people. Not all were in metal, some were in marble and bronze. Frankie pointed to a few photos and said. "Harper calls these her whimsies." They were paintings so beautiful they made the breath stop in their bodies. Then she showed them the half-finished work of what was obviously a faerie in flight.

Rene` looked at the pictures of the beautiful works of art and then the small female standing looking uncomfortable in his son's apartment. Her heart was dented he realized, not dead. One could not have a dead heart or soul and create such magnificent art.

Reighn inclined his head in respect and softly told her. "The barn will be up in three to four days. We will provide you a place to live, both you and Frankie. Mama, what apartment?"

She looked at them both and smiled. "The bronze will do nicely."

Just then several whirlwinds flew into the room, the Faeries had arrived. Queen Scarlett and King Elijah grew, as did their guards, and bowed to Reighn and the others. "Forgive our intrusion, Dragon Lord. Niece, we felt a new gray one arrive?"

Charlie nodded. "Yes, it is my sister Harper who I thought was dead and her friend Frankie." She asked her. "I am sorry. What is your surname?"

Frankie smiled. "Spring."

"No, not happening." Harper snarled once more as she made for the door.

Reighn stepped in front of her. "No, you stay."

"Why the hell should I?"

"They are your aunt and uncle, that is why, and they are very nice people. Your sister has a relationship with them."

Harper shook her head. "See, that is where you don't get it. I am not my sister, never was, never will be." She leaned closer to him and whispered. "For that I am sorry." Louder, she told him. "These people are nothing to me. They left us, we were abused, left alone in the clutches of an evil asshole and his bitch, who rejoiced in our mother's death and punished us for breathing. If they could have killed us, they would have. Our mother called for help with her dying breath. Do not lie and call it any different Charlie, you know she did." Harper reminded her when she saw she was going to talk. Charlie snapped her mouth closed and just nodded, knowing now was not the time to debate Harper on that memory. Harper carried on. "They did not come, and we were abandoned, alone. I killed to keep us safe. I made my sister fight shades. We fought demons and things I never want to think about again." She mind-sent to Reighn. *After that night, I was changed. It left me marked with something inside me, and darkness haunts my life now.* His eyes opened wide, but he only nodded, not letting anyone else know she had talked to him on a mental pathway. Her eyes held anger and fear with a touch of deep despair as she said to him. "You have no idea. Charlie may forgive them. That is her business, I cannot. Now step out of my way. I like you Reighn, but this is not your concern."

Gently he said. "That is where you are wrong; you are my concern."

Startled, she asked. "What the hell... why?"

He leaned down, his forehead almost touching hers, and whispered. "Because you are family."

"Oh Reighn, that is just not right."

"But it is what it is."

"Harper, you have to speak to them." Charlie pleaded with her.

Without looking at her, Harper said. "See, that is where

you are wrong. I don't have to."

"Yeah, you do, she is Juna's sister."

Scarlett placed her hand on Charlie's arm as the shattered look in Harper's eyes hurt her heart in return. "Cease niece; the time is not right, we did not come to cause hurt or disagreement."

Frankie asked. "Then why are you here?"

Scarlett and Elijah both bowed to Frankie. "To offer our friendship and an invitation."

"From whom?"

"The High Queen, she will wish to speak to Harper."

Harper asked without looking at them or Charlie. "Now why would she wish to do that?"

Scarlett said. "You have the ability to quebliss and fight in the gray mist."

Harper raised her eyes to Charlie, who read betrayal as she asked of no one in particular. "Now, how do you suppose she learned of that?"

Charlie spread her hands wide and hunched her shoulders defensively. "What? I thought you were dead."

At Harper's look of disbelief. Charlie growled. "Do not have an attitude with me. I believed you were dead, and it would not make any difference. How did I know you would magically appear again?"

"You always were a chatterbox." Snarked Harper.

"Really?" Storm asked. "Chatterbox."

Sage and Verity smothered their laughs at the sour look on Charlie's face as she said. "When I was young. I learned to stay quiet as I got older."

Harper sniped. "Apparently not."

Frankie said to forestall another round of arguments. "Well, that is all very nice, but I think this is not the right time. Please ask the High Queen to wait until Harper is ready, however long that takes." She grinned at Harper as her look turned mutinous. Frankie said to the Faerie Queen and King. "Maybe wait until we have settled in more?"

Elijah inclined his head and said. "As you wish." Instantly they reduced size and left.

Everyone stared at Frankie. "Who are you that you can make the Queen and King leave?" Sage asked, with a speculative look on her face.

Harper said quietly. "She is special and also tired. Frankie, we leave."

Charlie called softly. "Harper please."

She hung her head. "I heard you Charlie, sister of my blood. I am broken, not everything can be fixed in a day. I will not go back on my word."

"Harper, I am sorry."

"Another day, please."

"As you wish, they are family though Harper."

"No, yes, maybe. You and Frankie, your children, all these people apparently are family. It is to be determined if they are, please leave it for now."

Storm placed his arm around Charlie and squeezed, causing her to stop what she was going to say, and with a quick look up into his face. She relented and said instead. "Okay, another day."

Reighn nodded his agreement. "Let us take you to your new home."

"Thank you." Harper said with relief. He held the door open for her and Sage to leave through, leaving Storm, Charlie, and his parents alone.

Frankie walked with Johner as they followed the others. Softly, Frankie told him. "So I will stay with Harper, and you will court me."

"How long must we court you for?"

"I am thinking." She screwed her lips up again as she thought. "At least two weeks."

"My dragon will not cope, three days."

"Oh, that will not do, ten days."

"I wish I could say that would work, five days."

"Oh... Oh, okay, five days. Harper, Johner is going to court me for five days."

"Great. I am happy for you." Harper called back as she smiled.

Sage, walking next to her, asked. "You are happy about that?"

Harper grinned wider. "You have met Frankie right?"

Confused, Sage looked back at the happy couple and remembered the nulling of her blue globe and said. "Yes."

"Now she is your brother's problem."

"Oh I see, but she is so sweet and innocent, her nature shines like sunlight."

"Very sweet, a little crazy and very talkative and just plain happy all the friggin time!"

"Annoying." Reighn said from behind them.

"See." Harper pointed her thumb over her shoulder. "He gets it."

They made it to their new apartment on the floor below Charlies. When Sage opened the doors to the apartment, she was overwhelmed at its beauty. The entire place was decorated in shades of bronze and cream. Frankie said. "I love it."

"Yeah." Harper spoke softly as she gazed around at what was to become her new home. June, who came in behind them, was introduced, and she began the tour. "You have three bedrooms with bathrooms, large walk-in closets, and balconies. A kitchen, lounge, and a half bath for guests and two offices."

Once the tour was over, they talked for a few minutes longer. Then Sage, June and Reighn said their goodbyes, leaving Harper to wander around her new home. Johner trailed around after Frankie, noting what she liked and did not. Harper found herself on the balcony of her lounge watching dragons flying and she could just glimpse the faeries as they flitted through the skies and her heart ached.

Johner moved next to her. "Frankie is marking her territory." At Harper's confused look, he said with a shrug. "I assume the rolling around on the bed is what she is doing."

Harper smiled. "Sounds about right."

He brushed a hand through his hair as he said. "I apologize for my conduct earlier."

Harper sighed. "As do I, she is dear to me."

"I understand. I will keep her safe. I swear."

"I know you will, she is fragile, her heart has been stepped on and beaten. She thinks I do not know, but she was abused as a child by people that cared nothing for her. Her young life was fraught with fear and pain, and she was often locked in dark cupboards for days at a time. Most of what happened to her she has suppressed, but it is there and what she remembers is barely worth remembering. You will need to have your brother Keeper, or your father, remove those memories soon." She warned him. "She needs patience and love, loads of love. You should know, she does not think like we do. Something got wired wrong either before her birth or because of her childhood."

Johner nodded as he thought about what she told him. "How do you know what my father and brother can do?"

Harper looked at him and decided to be honest for Frankie and herself. Also, these people were to be her family, so they deserved honesty at least. "I am what you would call a Seeker. I can find anything, anywhere."

"Is that why Charlie is upset, because you did not look for her?"

"I could not. I was not on Earth for many years."

Johner sighed. "I see. These are matters for you and your sister. Just know I am always available to talk with. Now as for my future Shadow, the way she thinks is what I like the most about her, she is unique."

Harper laughed, then said. "She is that alright, you know as well as me that Frankie is not all human, right?"

"I do. I assume you have not been able to discover what she is?"

"No, something stops me. Either it is her or me. All I know is the answer to Frankie is not for me to discover or at least not yet."

"You believe you will find out?"

"I believe we eventually will. I also believe you will make an excellent mate for her. She needs someone like you who is strong and calm. You probably guessed she is afraid of closed-in spaces."

"Well, that explains your reaction to my father's threat."

Harper gave a lopsided grin. "Yeah, an overreaction on my part."

Johner grinned as well. "Maybe."

"Listen, you should know, some people will try to use her, and you will have to guard against that if I am not around."

"Do not worry, the Kingsleys are very good at watching out for our loved ones." Together they listened and smiled at the joyful sounds coming from a bedroom. Johner said under his breath, "Five days, I can do five days."

Harper grinned, knowing for him, five days was going to be an excruciating long time.

CHAPTER NINE:

The next day, Johner arrived early with coffee for Harper and a berry shake for Frankie. When Harper let him in, he said as he passed out the drinks. "I thought I would take you on a tour of the castle."

Frankie was excited. "Harper, isn't that exciting?"

"No, I can think of nothing worse than to be stuck with you two." She crossed her eyes at them as Johner grinned. "Seriously, it is the last thing I wish to do, playing third wheel to you two. So not happening. Go with my blessing."

"Oh Harper, it is the castle." Frankie told her, all starry-eyed, as she looked at Johner.

Harper placed her hands under her chin and fluttered her eyelashes. "Oh Frankie, I know." Making Johner laugh and Frankie pout, she dropped her hands and swung her bag over her shoulder. "Nope, I have places to go and people to see."

"Where and who?" Frankie asked suspiciously.

"Never, you mind."

Frankie demanded. "There will be no killing, right?"

Harper grinned at her and Johner, whose expression was a cross between amused and worried. She sniffed dramatically, then said. "I swear, I cannot swear to that."

"See?" Frankie grumbled to Johner. "This is why we have to leave towns."

"So dramatic, I am off. See you later for dinner. Frankie, remember you are cooking steaks, salad, and chips."

Johner asked Frankie. "You can cook?"

Frankie sighed. "Only steaks, salad and chips."

"Oh, I see."

They waved as Harper left, then Frankie said when she was sure Harper was gone. "I cannot really cook. I buy dinner and have it delivered. Harper doesn't know."

Johner thought maybe Harper did, but allowed her to believe otherwise. Frankie looped her arm through his as they left the apartment. "Do you know of a place that will deliver dinner?"

"Yes, but I will cook for you and Harper."

"Oh, how wonderful, are you sure? We have no groceries."

"I will have them delivered today. Do not worry, I will take care of everything."

"Thank you, Johner, so where will we go first?"

While Johner and Frankie discussed where in the castle, their tour would begin. Harper was making her way to the front steps, but it was slow going, as there were so many tapestries and paintings to look at and study.

She finally made the steps leading from the castle and breathed in a breath of fresh air. Looking right, then left, she closed her eyes and smiled when she felt the pull from her right. So it was to be exploring the town today. Happy with the decision, she set off to discover her new home.

CHAPTER TEN:

Harper stood on the sidewalk in front of a single red door, which was in the middle of a stone wall that went on for an entire block. There were several more doors, but this one was the only red door. At first she thought it may have been a hole in the wall pub like they have in England. But she changed her mind when she stepped back and read the large sign screwed in place above the door.

"Broadsword Stronghold, sounds like my kind of place. Must be a weapons shop." Pushing the wooden door open, she entered a wonderland of weapons. Large, small, old and new, wherever she looked, there were weapons of all styles and periods of history.

Lars watched the small female enter and grinned as he murmured to Fin. "That is Charlie's sister, newly arrived at the Gap."

Fin eyed the small female. She had the look of Storm's Charlie about her as Lars said, but the hair was different. Reddish brown and longer, and when she looked at him, he saw her eyes were a darker gray than Charlie's. They held that same something he had seen in the eyes of some of his Shields, after they returned from a hunt off world. Sadly, they had been unable to talk about what they had experienced. Eventually he was forced to send them to Master Patrycc or Lord Rene` for help. Unfortunately, if he did not get to them fast enough, most never made it back home. Looking at the female while she stared at swords, he felt sad knowing she had faced something so horrendous it left a mark within her. He asked Lars, "I see, and is she as feisty as Lady Charlie?"

Lars grinned as he whispered. "I am told, worse."

"Truly!" Fin said and looked her over again, from her boots

to the top of her head. He would wager she knew he was doing so. With a nod to Lars, he slipped from around the counter as Lars returned on his journey to the gun range while he spoke into his phone. Which is where he had been going when the door suddenly opened and she walked in. Fin bet he was calling Storm to report Lady Harper's movements. His dragon found that amusing.

Harper kept track of the two dragons from the corner of her eye as she walked around the large shop. It was an amazing place. There were weapons of all kinds and age on the walls, some in display cases and others just showcased on shelves. As she looked them over, she realized her mistake: this was no shop; this was a place to show off weapons, a museum.

Suddenly, she came to a stop. "Oh, you are beautiful, just beautiful." She crooned to the sword that was on its own stand. It was just sitting there proudly in the open, as though it had every right to do so. She would wager all she owned it was not a replica. It looked well used and well cared for. She would have loved to have been able to lift it from its cradle, but knew it would be too heavy. *Ooh, it was divine.* She had always hoped to see one. Even a replica would have satisfied her, but to see an original was beyond her wildest dreams. She ran her finger along the flat side of the blade in a caress of wonder and delight.

Fin asked when he approached her. "Do you know what it is, lassie?"

Harper had been aware he had been walking slowly toward her for the last two minutes and appreciated his consideration in allowing her time to know he was coming. "Oh yes." She breathed out in awe. "It is an Ulfberht. Goddess, it is gorgeous. I always dreamed of seeing an original. Although I would have happily settled for a replica, but this... this is just beautiful."

"Thank you. It was commissioned many years ago, so long that I am unsure of the date now. As with all Ulfberht blades, it was made for my hand alone."

Harper wheezed out a breath. "Give me strength, for your hand."

Fin grinned at her tone as he took it down and turned it over. So she could see his name was etched in the steel, *Finlay Slorah.*

Awe coated her voice as Harper said. "I read that Ulfberht liked to do that, and I always wondered if it was true."

"Now you know it is."

"Yes, I do."

"You know blades?"

"I have a few, none like this. I run more to Katanas."

"I have a few of those. They have not arrived yet. They should be here by the end of next week. We are still gathering our collections." He explained, as he replaced the sword.

Harper dragged her eyes away from the blade and was immediately seized by the broadsword that stood upright on the wall. She walked to it and ran her fingers down its blade. "Oh, who is we?"

"Myself, I am as you saw Fin Slorah, your sister's Shadow Storm, and Lars, who is Storm's nest brother and Prime to the Dragon Lord."

"Oh I see, you guys are combining your hoards and are showcasing them?" She looked at him to find his eyes on her.

"Yes, we allow people to train with some weapons and we teach."

"That is so cool. So where do you do that?"

"Underneath we have a shooting range and several rooms for sword and martial arts."

"So can anyone use them?"

"Of course, do you wish to train lass?"

"Yes, I do, but not today. I am just looking around, but it would be great to have a place I can train with my knives and swords."

"Please feel free to come back anytime. We are open twenty- four-hours, seven days a week. If I am not here, one of our assistants will be or Lars or Storm."

"Thank you, Lord..."

"No, it is just Fin."

"I think you are not just anything Fin." She smiled and said. "My name is Harper, not Lady Harper, just Harper. I will see you soon. Good-day."

Fin inclined his head as he said. "Good-day to you Harper."

She left Broadswords happier than she had been before she entered. She now knew of a place to train and had realized one of her dreams. More importantly, she could see the sword at any time. Harper walked down the main street, where there were people everywhere walking, talking, laughing, or sitting at an outside cafe having coffee at a place that looked busy. There was a place called Tessa's, which seemed to be an old-fashioned tea house. It too looked busy for ten o'clock in the morning.

Harper had not really looked around last time she was here. She had been more interested in finding out information from people. And well, Frankie had been with her, and that alone was a distraction. She would admit she was feeling exceedingly relaxed as she admired the displays in the shops. Then, in a reflection from the dress shop window, she saw it sitting there, taking up over half a block of the main street. The Dragon's Gap Library.

It was truly her lucky day, a promise of a steak dinner and a sword she never thought she would see, let alone touch. And now a library it was a day of gifts. She had no idea the Gap had a library. How, she wondered, had she missed this the last time she was here? Quickly she crossed the cobblestone street, deciding she liked this town; it had a good feel to it. Perhaps it was all the magic floating around or all the different species of shifters. Whatever it was, it was a good place to live and bring up young ones. On that thought, she pushed open the glass door and entered a place that brought back instant memories. Of a time she and Charlie escaped to their local library to hide from their father and his wife.

"Hey." A slim female with long brown hair tied back in a ponytail greeted her. She looked like she had been ill but was on the road to recovery. Harper would not call her exactly frail, more like someone to be careful with. She thought Frankie would call her fragile. That was until you looked into eyes of honey, which was where the fragility ended. This female was tempered steel. Harper liked her instantly, probably because she reminded her of Frankie.

"Hi, I am Harper Easton."

"I am Olinda Battle."

Harper stared at the female as she tried imagining which of the Battle brothers she was bonded to. Olinda asked with a smile hovering on her lips. "Are you trying to guess which brother I am with?"

"Yep."

"That would be Ash."

"Okay, I have not met him. I know Axl and Ark, so are there any more?"

"Yes, altogether there are four, the oldest Ace and then my Ash and their brothers Ark and Axl."

Harper frowned. "Why do their names all start with an, A?"

Olinda shrugged. "I think their father, who was an asshole, had designs on making them the Elite Shields or something. So short names starting with A for Alpha."

"Well, he succeeded as they are… Well, the ones I have met are very Alpha."

"I know, right. So are you new to town?"

"I am, this is a wonderful place. I like libraries, they give you peace and refuge."

"Thank you. Keeper and I, have you met him?"

"No, he is another brother of Reighn's, right?"

"Yes, Keeper is bonded to Ella; she is a healer; her uncle is Fin."

"Oh, I just came from Broadswords, which is another amazing place."

Olinda nodded. "I think so too. I go there to train with guns and do knife work, as Ash calls it. What do you do?"

"I use anything with a blade. To be honest, I don't like guns much. I can use them but prefer my blades." Harper told her as she looked around and spied a coffee bar. *In the library so cool.*

Olinda's eyes widened as she listened to Harper talk, and when her silence impinged on Harper, she swung her eyes back to her. "Oh, you didn't mean that?"

Olinda shook her head. "Well, not really, but good to know. So do you want a tour?"

"Sure, can we get coffee first?"

"Now, that is no problem." Olinda turned and started talking about the library and how it came about as they walked into the large sitting room with a coffee counter. "Wow, this is like someone's lounge, it's fabulous."

Olinda looked pleased. "Thank you. We wanted somewhere people could come to sit and read, talk and meet friends. I know there are cafe's and places like Tessa's, but they run on profits. We run on comfort, if someone nods off for a nap, no one wakes them and ushers them from the building."

Harper looked at her as she asked. "This was your idea, right?"

Olinda grinned. "Libraries were my refuge when I was young, and yes... before you ask... we have a place for kids to do the same here. The difference is we have Keeper who will counsel them. You know what he does."

"I do, yes."

"Good, saves explaining. We also have other staff that are trained to help young people."

"I am impressed and awed."

Olinda beamed at the compliment, recognizing the female who looked so much like Charlie did not talk for the sake of talking, and said what she meant. "Thank you again, we work real hard at it. So Harper, do you know Charlie Kingsley?"

"She is my sister."

"I thought so, apart from the hair you are almost identical."

"I am going to take that as a compliment because I can hear you like her."

Olinda grinned. "I really do. She was my first friend here."

Harper nodded. "Even I can see that would be no hardship; I have a friend, her name is Frankie. She is like you, sweet with a rod of steel underlying all that delicate stuff, and she is not a unicorn. So don't go thinking, it is because you are one that makes you like that." Harper told her when she could almost see the thought forming.

"How do you know I am a unicorn, and I don't really think that?"

"Yes, you do, and you are wrong. You are just a strong person, always were, always will be and as for knowing you are a unicorn. I know the same way I know Cara is. I am what is known as a Seeker, so my gift is I can find the truth of things and people."

"That must be so disconcerting. I mean, you don't even have to search for the information. It is always there."

Harper raised surprised eyebrows at her comment and saw why she and Charlie were friends. She gave Olinda her first relaxed smile.

"It is, but like all gifts, I can close it down for a while to give me relief."

"You can do that?"

"Yes, it just takes training."

Olinda sighed, and Harper found herself offering to train her. "I will train you if you like?"

"How did you know?"

"I am a Seeker, Olinda."

"Oh yeah, normally I would have to think about your offer, but I really need your help. Some of these new things I can do are disturbing, so that would be wonderful. Thank you."

Not only did Olinda's face light up with pleasure, her entire body glowed. Harper nodded and said. "So you know my friend Frankie I spoke about."

"Yes."

"If she comes in, and I am sure she will with Johner, who is courting her."

"Johner is courting... Oh my, I bet Verity is ecstatic."

"Probably." Harper said dryly. By now, they had reached the coffee counter. Harper placed her order with the young female unicorn, who asked Olinda. "Do you want your usual Princess?"

Olinda sighed. "Yes, thanks Lory." She looked at Harper and was going to apologize.

Harper said before she could say anything as they moved to a table. "That was for my benefit, so I know whose company I am in, not to out you."

Olinda brushed her hair off her face. "It is just so hard, getting used to them all calling me that, and it is embarrassing."

Harper shrugged as she looked around the room, noticing the ten or so people huddled down with cups of tea or coffee and books or newspapers. "So order them to stop. You can or make your Ash do it, he can as well."

Olinda grimaced, thinking of Ash demanding that the unicorns refrain from calling her princess, and the blood that would be spilled; when they scorned the idea, which they would. "I don't want to come off all bitchy."

"Well then, don't ask Charlie to do it." They both smiled, thinking of Charlie's idea of politely asking them to stop. "Seriously, though, if you want it to stop, don't dither. Hurt feelings are easily overcome. Finding yourself not wanting to mix with them will be more hurtful, for the unicorns and eventually for you as you become more isolated from them. Don't push them away because you are uncomfortable with your feelings." *Dammit! That was some excellent advice. Maybe I should heed it myself.*

Olinda nodded. "You are right. Thank you for that. I will

sort it out."

Harper asked. "Now, my new friend, could you tell me who the little kitten following us is?"

Olinda looked behind her and smiled. "Can you not tell?"

Harper winked at Olinda, almost making her spit her coffee out as she answered. "Well no, she is in disguise."

"I see, well that would be your niece Kelsey. She is in her cougar skin today, as they call it. Apparently she does not want to change back."

"Do you know why?"

"If I had to guess. I would say she is sad her daddy took her sister Cara to visit the unicorns."

"Oh, I see, and Kelsey came to story time?"

"Yes."

"Okay." Harper turned around and spied the kitten under a table. She was adorable, a sweet gray and white fluff ball with dark tufted ears and the cutest little bob tail. Harper pointed to the kitten, then her shoulder. Instantly, the kitten ran and jumped onto her, then wrapped herself around Harper's neck and shoulders as she asked her. "So you are a little bob tail?" The kitten butted her head against her cheek. Harper reached up and scratched her behind her ear, and she purred. It was like a having a little motor vibrating against her neck.

"Wow, did you know she could do that?" Asked an amazed Olinda.

Harper shrugged. "Sure, why not? She is a cat."

Olinda grinned at the simple statement. "Sure."

Harper sipped her coffee, then said to Olinda. "Now, as I was saying, Frankie will be in here eventually. Do not tell her I am training you. If you do, I will be training everyone she meets or whoever she feels will benefit from my help."

"Oh, she is a stray finder. I knew someone like that when I was growing up. She used to bring home stray puppies and kittens all the time."

"In Frankie's case, it is people who she thinks need help."

Olinda grinned as she asked. "Does Johner know this?"

"Huh! You think I should warn him?"

"Ahh, yeah."

"No need to get snippy. I will tell him tonight."

Olinda laughed, not at all offended by Harper. "So we should get started on this tour."

CHAPTER ELEVEN:

A pleasant, relaxing hour and a half later Harper had seen the library, been introduced to Claire who was holding story time, and met and fallen for Keeper. Claire and Keeper had taken one look at the kitten wrapped around Harper and smiled.

When they came back to where they started from. Harper thanked Olinda and asked Kelsey. "So kitten, I am going to visit your Mama." Harper had done a lot of thinking while they had toured the library. She realized she needed something to bridge the divide between her and Charlie. It was a first step in becoming friends and sisters with her again. "So, do you want to come with me or stay here?" The kitten settled more on her shoulder and purred louder. Harper looked at Olinda, saying. "I am taking that as she is coming with me. Can you call Charlie for me?"

"Why don't you?"

"My phone won't work here."

"You need a Gap phone. We have our own network. None of your electronics will work unless you buy new or get it changed, which I had to do." She laughed, then told her. "June said Edith threw hers into a wall. Edith is a bear and some-times short-tempered."

"That must have really piss... annoyed her?" Harper re-membered just in time not to swear as she had a kitten with big ears on her shoulder.

Olinda could not help the smile spreading over her face at Harper's hastily revised words, thinking of Edee's swear jar. "You are right."

Edith, Harper knew was Sharm's Shadow, another brother to Reighn. The couple were away on a vacation at some beach for another few days. Harper wanted to meet her as she owned the art gallery that was getting ready to open. She was hoping Edith would show her work.

Harper said. "Okay, so we will go to the phone shop first, then to Kelsey's home."

"Or you could meet Kelsey's mom at a certain kitten's favorite hamburger place, just past the phone shop." Olinda said, at this the kitten pricked her little ears.

Harper nodded. "That sounds good. If you could ask Charlie to meet us there, if not we will go to her place after lunch."

"No problem, I will get Kelsey's bag for you."

Kittens did not shift with clothes on as older shifters did, so having extra clothes with them always helped. Harper looked around her as she petted the kitten. When Olinda came back with a red back pack, she said to Olinda. "You need a changing room with spare clothes for all the young ones."

Olinda stared around her. "Why?"

"For the kits and cubs as well as the other young ones that shift."

Olinda frowned as she said. "Not that many young shift, most are half-breeds like me."

Harper smiled as Keeper joined them again. "Olinda, is everything okay?"

"Harper said we should have a changing room and clothes for the kits and cubs. I was just explaining not that many shift."

Keeper eyed the small female that was so much like Charlie and asked. "You think we will need it?"

Harper leaned nearer. "I think what was not possible once, is probable now."

He looked thoughtful for a few minutes, then said. "We will make sure we have a room set aside. I will have Mama and Grace see about clothing."

Harper nodded and said. "We are off. If you could make that call please Olinda, and thanks for the tour. I will call you with a time for lessons."

"Okay, bye." Olinda and Keeper waved as they watched her and Kelsey leave

Keeper asked. "Does she unnerve you?"

"No, does she you?"

He smiled. "No, I like her."

"Me too, she is insightful and is going to help me learn control."

"And what will Ash say about that?"

"What, after he investigates her."

"Yes, after that." He said with a laugh in his voice.

"Umm, okay."

Olinda called Charlie as Harper and the kitten Kelsey went into the electronic shop. She found a phone she liked, as well as a laptop and tablet. Then the sales assistant, a nice female lion sold her a music app for her phone and loaded it with music that Harper liked. She then showed her how to get more. No one seemed to bat an eye at the kitten on her shoulder, maybe it was normal for Dragon's Gap.

As they left, Harper told Kelsey it was an enjoyable shopping experience. The kitten butted her head against her cheek in agreement. Harper assumed she enjoyed it as well, or it could have been the idea of food that prompted the action. They found the hamburger place easily, spotting the large umbrellas over wooden outside tables in a beautiful tranquil courtyard.

It was delightful, just the setting alone made you want to stop, relax and eat. Harper snagged the only empty outside table and lowered the kitten on to the wooden surface, she asked the kitten as she sat looking up at her. "Apparently this is your favorite place to eat, so you have to decide will you eat as human or kitten?"

Within seconds a shower of sparkles tingled over Harper's skin as Kelsey shifted back to human. "Hello Auntie Harper." Greeted a subdued Kelsey.

"Hello niece, so would you like to dress, then we can order when your mom gets here."

She nodded and stared glumly at Harper as she helped her dress in jeans and a tee-shirt. "So your mom will be here soon, want to tell me why you are sad?"

Kelsey sighed. "Cara gets everything now she is a unicorn. Dada never takes me flying anymore. He is all about unicorns now. I am just a cat."

Harper nodded and said. "I see, what about Mama?"

"She has Justice, he is cute, but a hatchling and Mama is working with Auntie Scarlett and Auntie Sage. And there is no one my age to play with!" She burst out, which seemed to be the biggest problem.

Harper sighed when Kelsey did, then said. "Well kitten, those are a lot of things to make you unhappy. So what do you think we should do about them?"

"I don't know, Auntie Harper, what can we do?"

"We could talk to your Mama and then you and she could talk to your dad."

Kelsey looked at her and her eyes were tragic as she sighed deeply again. "But Auntie Harper, what can they do, they cannot play with me all the time and they cannot stop Cara from being a unicorn or Justice being cute. No, I am doomed." Kelsey shook her head as she had seen her Grandma Verity do. "I am sad to say, it is a lost cause." That was her Uncle Johner's favorite saying when playing games and losing to her Dada.

Such a drama kitty. Harper thought as she silently laughed at Charlie, who rolled her eyes as she pulled out a chair and said. "I do not know where she gets this from."

Harper grinned. "Cats... all drama queens."

Kelsey smiled at her mother, who tweaked her hair. "Hi, my Kelsey."

Kelsey sighed loudly. "Hi, Mama."

Charlie grinned as she said. "What Miss Kitty, is not telling you, Auntie Harper, is she starts kindergarten on Monday?"

"But Mama, Monday is a long time away." Kelsey moaned as she looked pitifully at her mother.

"Monday is four days away. We will discuss this at home.

Maybe we can find something for you to do for the next few days."

"Maybe Dada will take me flying?" Kelsey asked hopefully.

"Well, I am sure he would love to." Charlie did not tell her he already planned to do something with Kelsey on Saturday when he could get another day off.

Harper said. "Maybe, Miss Kitty, might like to come to my place tomorrow morning and we can go visit my new barn. See how much they have done."

"I am sure she would love that. What do you think Kelsey?" Charlie asked.

"Mama, can I? That would be amazing." Kelsey looked at Harper with eyes that held a large dose of hero worship.

When the waitress came over, they ordered burgers and fries with shakes while Justice slept peacefully in his carrier and Kelsey told her mother about her morning.

When she had finished, Charlie asked Harper. "Why did you want to meet me apart from giving my daughter back?" She smiled letting Harper know she had not worried about her having Kelsey.

"I have something for you." She reached inside the shopping bag she had beside her chair and pulled out a photo album and flash drive. She passed both to Charlie.

Kelsey's eyes widened. She knew there were no albums in the bag when the lady at the phone shop handed the bag to Auntie Harper. She looked at Harper, who grinned and whispered. "Magic."

"Oh." Kelsey whispered back. She then looked at her Mama who was flipping pages with photos on them in the book.

Harper told her. "There are more on the drive. I had them copied to save them. They were all loose photos in a box. If you want I can get the originals?"

"Thank you, these are great." Charlie stopped when she came to a photo of their mom and the two of them laughing at the camera. They were at a park, it looked like they were on a picnic. "Oh Harper, I don't know what to say."

Harper shrugged. "We are sisters, this is my... I am sorry for being a pain, regardless of what has happened. I missed you peacemaker."

Charlie looked up from the photo and into gray eyes so much like her own, except within Harper's was a darkness she never saw in hers. "I missed you too. Frankie made you do this right?"

Harper shrugged, a smile playing around her mouth. "She mentioned it."

Charlie grinned. "She's a nagger, huh?"

Harper blew out a breath. "So much, and always with a friggin smile."

"Must be annoying."

"You have no idea?"

"I like Frankie." Kelsey stated as she sipped her shake.

"As we all do." Harper agreed with her.

"Oh my goodness. I cannot believe this!" Charlie said as she quickly flicked through pages of the album.

Kelsey asked. "Can I see Mama?"

"When we are home, I will show you all the photos. Oh look one of your grandmother and grandfather." She had found a photo of her father and her mother laughing. She flipped it around so Kelsey and Harper could see it. "You could see they were in love."

Harper nodded. "You have got to wonder what happen to them."

"He became an a.s.s.h.o.l.e." Charlie spelt out for the sake of Kelsey, as she closed the album reverently.

"Well yeah that he did."

"I cannot believe you have all these."

"Hid them for years, so she never found them." Harper told her simply.

Charlie asked. "Are you going to tell me what happened?"

Harper smiled at the waitress as she delivered their food, and then took a bite of her burger. Ignoring the question, she moaned as she chewed. "Dear Goddess, this is one great burger."

They all applied themselves to their food and in between bites discussed the library, Broadswords and the gallery. Kelsey told her about the school she was starting and her new teacher, Miss Amelia Gill, who was apparently a puma. When they had finished and Harper ordered coffee for both her and Charlie, Kelsey decided to play in the newly installed playground. Harper finally answered Charlie's earlier question she looked at her over her cup and said. "To answer your question, no. Charlie. I really don't want to tell you what happened. Can we just mark it down as done with? Will it change who we are, for you to know?"

Charlie looked back at her. "No, I suppose it won't. Just answer me one question. Was it necessary?"

"Yeah, he was going to hurt a lot of people, maybe even kill them. I did not want to do it. But truthfully, I have not had a sleepless night since doing so. He had totally gone crazy, he always had a touch of it after Juna died, but he really lost it after you left home."

Charlie looked off to where Kelsey was playing, then back to her. "She said he hurt you, and you killed him."

Harper raised her eyebrows. "If by hurt, she meant he wounded my heart for being like he was, yeah, but physically no. There were kids Charlie, Kelsey's age and younger. He was going to do it for money; he was desperate, things were not good between them, so he sought a way to get the income Juna used to bring into the home by hurting others. I could not let that happen. Her and her family were all involved, in case you were wondering?"

Charlie nodded. "Okay, enough said, they all deserved it, justice was served."

"Yeah, that's how I feel about it."

"Good, so your barn is almost up?" And just like that the topic was done with. Several deaths justified as far as the Easton sisters were concerned. And as Charlie looked at Harper, she knew they would never think or talk of it again.

It was well and truly in the past. The future is what they had to concentrate on now.

"Yeah, it is almost complete." Harper smiled. "So happy, I cannot wait to get back to work."

They spent another half-hour talking about Charlie's family and Harper's work. Then when Justice started making baby noises, they called it a day. Harper kissed Kelsey good-bye and looked at Charlie with longing. Charlie hugged her quickly, unable to bear that look, not knowing the same one was in hers. She was pleased Harper had taken the step of seeking to reunite with the photos. They did more than touch her heart. They showed Harper was still in many ways the same sister she had always been. Charlie held Kelsey's hand as they walked to the castle. "Mama, is Auntie Harper gonna stay with us?"

"Yes baby girl, she is."

"Good, I love her heaps."

Smiling, Charlie told her. "Yeah me too."

CHAPTER TWELVE:

O ver the following days, Harper and Frankie familiarized themselves with the royal family and the people of the castle. Much to Frankie's delight, Johner, true to his word, courted her relentlessly, which was also to Frankie's delight as she basked daily in his attentions.

As promised, he asked Keeper to visit with her and explain what he could do to help with her issues. Frankie decided to have the unwanted and unknown memories removed. On Friday, Keeper arrived early in the morning and assured Johner and Harper it would not take long to help Frankie. Two hours does not seem like a very long time, unless a dragon is pacing one's lounge. Then it is considered an eternity. When he returned to Johner and Harper, Keeper explained Frankie would sleep for the rest of the day, maybe longer. Johner made it clear he would stay with her, so Harper made herself scarce. Two heart pounding hours in the dragon's company was enough for her.

Before she left, she asked Johner when Edith would return. He assured her she was home. No one missed the Sunday family day unless on a mission or dead. As Edith and Sharm were not on a mission or dead, they were home. And if Edith was home, she would be in her studio or gallery. Harper thought she would try the studio first and followed Johner's directions, and found Edith exactly where he said she would be. In a room converted to a studio on the castle's main level. It appeared as though she was in the middle of restoring a large painting.

Edith looked over at the female as she stood in the doorway. She had known she was coming, but what she did not know was how much like Charlie she would be. "Wow, you are like twins, huh?"

Harper didn't even pretend she did not know what she meant. "So we have been told, she is older."

Edith grinned as she asked. "I bet she loves you telling everyone that?"

Harper grinned back. "Not so much."

Edith laughed, then said. "Well, I am ready for coffee. Would you like some?"

"Yes please."

Edith eyed her as she asked. "So Keeper is with your friend?"

It did not surprise Harper she knew what was happening. It seemed Johner was right, gossip in the castle traveled fast.

"Her name is Frankie, and no, he is done. Johner finished pacing the carpet off my lounge floor and is with her now, so..."

"Yeah, I get that." Edith climbed down from the ladder as she motioned for Harper to enter and was pleased she had waited. Not many realized as a bear, her studio was like her den.

Her bear told her. *I like her even with darkness.*

True and her art, oh my!

You are excited?

I am hoping she will showcase her work at the gallery.

The cougar told you she was coming.

No, Claire told us, someone with gifts was coming.

You quibble.

Whatever.

As Edith moved to her outside table where her urn of coffee was, she watched Harper walk around, looking at the paintings. Finally, she asked. "What do you think?"

"Masters."

"Oh definitely, mostly unsigned but great works of art."

"Yes," Harper sighed. "They truly are."

She walked over and took the cup of coffee as Edith asked. "So what can I do for you?"

"You own the gallery?"

"I do."

"Want to show my work?"

Edith almost vibrated off her chair with excitement. "Yes, most desperately."

"Oh… oh, well okay." A little startled, Harper kept one eye on Edith and pulled her phone from her pocket, saying. "These are available."

Edith nodded without touching the phone or looking at the photos. "I will take them all."

"Umm, you haven't looked at them yet."

"Do not care, just get them here. Do you need help?"

"Ahh no, when do you want them?" Harper asked and wished Frankie was with her; she would have gotten a kick out of this conversation.

"ASAP. I can devote the whole gallery to them. They just finished decorating it."

"Okay, so there are twenty-five sculptures and forty paintings."

"Excellent. So when can you have them here?"

"When do you want them?"

Edith grinned. "Now, would work."

"Done, let's go."

"How?" Edith asked, then she gasped. "Friggin' hell, are they here at the castle?" Imagining crates all throughout the castle. Edith hurried to her washroom to clean her hands as Harper stood and stretched, saying. "In a manner of speaking."

Edith turned from the sink and stared at Harper, who grinned. "It's called a kind of magic."

Edith grinned, remembering the movie. "Fabulous, give me a minute to clean my hands and then we can go to the gallery and decide where to place everything."

Harper nodded as she sipped the rest of her coffee and walked around looking at the art waiting to be cleaned or in the process of being restored. "You do great work."

"Thank you." Edith said when she joined her, "I know I need a bigger space. I am taking on students as well."

Harper said casually. "You can borrow some space in my barn, if you want."

"That would be great." Edith almost clapped her hands as Molly did when she was happy. Scoring space for her students with Harper would be a dream come true. She could only hope she could get her to teach, casually she asked. "Are you interested in teaching?"

"Well… Frankie's always on my ass about sharing my knowledge, so… maybe?"

Edith closed her door as they left, saying. "If you decide to do so, let me know. I can help with that."

Her only answer was a grunt, so Edith was not any the wiser if she would teach or not. Normally, she would not take that as an answer, but she also knew the value of stalking her quarry. For this hunt, she listened to her bear, who advised her how to catch her artist.

Once they got to the gallery, Harper called her art to her, using her magic. Edith was amazed, she had never seen this type of magic up close and personal before. As piece after piece appeared, the display of magic entranced her bear as she stared out at the materializing art. When it was all at the gallery, they spent time moving the sculptures and paintings into the right position, again using Harper's magic. Which, she explained was based on affinity. She loved her work, and her art possessed a bit of her essence until she let it go. So when she called it to come to her, it was eager too. Much as a puppy would run to someone who held a treat for them.

Edith stood and watched her place a sculpture of a unicorn with a foal and could literally see the love within the piece. It was a humbling experience and an insight into what made Harper who she was. She was all about love and family. Edith could not help but admire her, as she ran a loving hand over a bronze statue of a woman that stood about thirty-six inches tall. The sculpture was of a faerie in a flowing gown with wings that encased two young girls. The look of love on the faerie's eternally beautiful face was startlingly similar to Scarlett's.

"Oh my Goddess, this is beautiful, it looks like Scarlett."

Harper smiled. "Our mother was her sister."

"I don't know what to say, it is simply beautiful and I think very personal."

"It is. I only made two of these, one for me and one for Charlie. This is mine, it is not for sale."

Edith grinned as she murmured. "As if I would. So..." She grabbed her tablet, and they went through the art, with Harper naming what Edith could sell and what she could display only.

Edith was thrilled, having Harper's pieces validated her belief that Dragon's Gap was ready for the beauty of art. She hoped it would encourage others to show and sell their work. Edith called Verity to come and see what they had done. Within a few minutes Verity was in the gallery, enthralled at what she saw and exclaiming over and over. "Oh my... Oh my!" She stopped in front of a portrait of a male with a much lived-in face. It was easy to see it had been done with layers of love and compassion in each brush stroke. Harper stood with her as Verity asked. "Is this for sale?"

She shook her head. "No, he was one of my instructors and friends."

"Yes, I can believe that. You are very good Harper."

"Thank you, I appreciate you saying so."

Verity looked around for a little longer, but she already had an idea of what she wanted, and she would put that plan into action at a later date. She decided they needed lunch, so took them to Grace's home and introduced Harper to the older bear.

Harper enjoyed meeting the feisty females, who never once asked her about her past or brought up Charlie. It was an amazingly relaxing afternoon. She felt really happy as she wandered back to the castle, just in time to shower and greet

Frankie as she woke.

Frankie was happy and seemed much more centered and quieter whether that would last remained to be seen. She admitted to Harper she was still never going to like closed-in spaces, but at least the crippling fear of them she had lived with was gone. Later that night, the three of them lingered over another dinner perfectly prepared by Johner. Harper told them of her day and listened to Johner explain her barn was almost finished. When she mentioned how far ahead they seemed to be, he told her they would be completed by morning, as the dragons were to place the roof on overnight.

After dinner, Frankie and Johner went for a walk. Frankie was to stay at Johner's place again, leaving Harper alone with a beer for company. She sat on her balcony watching dragons lower the huge barn roof into place. As Johner promised, it would be finished by morning. She sipped her beer while she watched what seemed like hundreds of people, male and female, scurry over the building. When she tired of watching them do stuff, she had no idea about, she turned in for the night. More settled than she had been for many years.

CHAPTER THIRTEEN:

O n Saturday Frankie kept Harper so busy shopping for a new phone and computer, as well as visiting Madam Tessa's tea shop. Then having lunch with Charlie's family and listening to an excited Kelsey, who had been flying with her father. There was no time to visit her barn.

Harper suffered through the hugs when she, at Frankie's nagging, gave Charlie the statue of their mother and them as children. Harper was positive she saw tears in her sister's eyes. It was unnerving, which she made sure Frankie knew and that it was her fault she had become unnerved. Apparently Frankie did not see the problem with tears, she was all about the love of sisters or something.

Harper tuned her out and tuned into Storm, whom she loved talking to; he was so blunt it was funny. She also enjoyed it when she, Storm, and Johner played a virtual fighting game. And he became like every other person who hated to lose and loved beating the hell out of his opponent. Their father's enthusiasm for the game and his language, which was so different from the normal calm male they were used to. Fascinated Kelsey and Cara, whose attention was divided between their father and Frankie.

Cara and Frankie had instantly bonded with each other in the first few seconds of Frankie entering the apartment. Secretly Harper thought it was like meeting like, and when Charlie became annoying with the sniffing back of tears, each time she looked at the statue.

Harper felt it was her duty to tell Charlie of her suspicions. And then watch with amusement as Charlie tried to be diplomatic when asking Frankie about the way she looked at life. The horror in Charlie's eyes as Frankie started to explain her philosophy of life amused Harper enormously.

They left the family late in the afternoon and by then Frankie was in the talking mood. So they spent the rest of the day while Johner worked, discussing plans for each of them to find work. Johner finally collected a happy contented Frankie after dinner, leaving a just as contented Harper to herself. She slept well again that night, secure in the knowledge her world was better than it had been for a long time.

The following morning, she rolled from bed and looked out the window at her completed barn and could actually feel the excitement bubbling up. She hoped to have time today to explore it and set it to rights. She sighed as she walked into the shower. *Sunday family day!* Whoever heard of such a thing? And yet she knew she would attend, because Frankie, Charlie and now Edith would expect her too.

And to prove her point. Frankie arrived with Johner to go with her to the dining room. Harper couldn't get over the idea that they thought she would have ducked out of the coming day, which was absurd: couldn't they tell Verity Kingsley terrified her? Defying her would take more guts than Harper possessed.

Together, the friends were greeted with friendship and a gentle love that neither of them were used to. Thankfully, the spotlight was taken off them during breakfast when Reighn announced Sage was pregnant. What seemed to astound the dragons more was that they were to have twins. Those that were not dragon grinned and shrugged much as Sage did. To them, it was not unheard of for shifters to have twins or more. For the dragons the miracle of her being with child was in and of itself magical, but for them to be having twins just sent them into raptures.

By lunch time, Harper was positive she had spoken to everyone there, if not once at least twice or more. It was the young ones who really dominated her time. Kelsey and Cara decided as she was their aunt, she was their toy to be dragged from one end of the room to the other to witness everything.

Toys, games, unicorns and, when they were not hanging around her with Kammy, Molly and Ava. The adults were no better, filling her arms with babies at every opportunity, although she did sort of like that, the little ones amused her, especially with their unasked for observations. The babies just made her heart hurt with some unknown emotion.

As the clock moved closer to lunch. She decided it was a good time to give herself a minute or two or half an hour maybe, to visit her barn. She needed to ease the pain her heart was feeling. So when she felt she would not be missed, she slid out of the room, hoping no one noticed. Unfortunately, in that she was mistaken, Charlie watched her walk from the room as Reighn nudged her shoulder. "She left."

"Yep, she did."

Frankie said, as she joined them. "She needs a minute or three; this is a lot for her."

Charlie asked. "Not for you, though?"

"Nah, I'm just loving the atmosphere." She smiled broadly and looked around at all the family.

Reighn told her. "Again, I say you are an inordinately cheerful person."

Frankie nodded as she sipped her shake. "A rainbow of delights, Johner calls me."

Which made him and Charlie laugh. Kelsey ran over, followed by Molly and Kammy. "Frankie, where is Auntie Harper?"

"She went to her barn sweetie." At her downcast expression, Frankie told her. "She will be back soon."

Charlie said. "I will go get her later if she doesn't return."

"Okay." Kelsey sighed. No one could miss the tragic face she blessed them with or the fact Kammy was trying to copy her.

Reighn asked. "So, little one, are you ready for school tomorrow?"

Kelsey smiled. "I am Uncle Reighn."

Kelsey had come in for a lot of attention and not just

from Reighn and Verity, because she was going to school for the first time the following day. It was very exciting for all her family. Although Storm was not pleased as he once again voiced his objections when he came and swung her and Kammy into his arms. "Why can she not be schooled at home, how am I to keep her safe if she is not home?"

Charlie said again and if her tone had a hint of exasperation in it, no one blamed her for it. "As I have said many times. She needs to go to school to learn and make friends."

A sentiment Storm glowered at and then with a grunt he carried a giggling Kelsey and Kammy to his brothers. While Charlie watched her daughter giggle with delight. Frankie said quietly to Reighn. "She will be alright, for Harper, this is a big deal. She needs more to do, if she is idle for too long, she gets lost in her head."

Charlie said. "So, I need to find work for her?"

Frankie asked. "Don't you already have the ideal job lined up for her?"

"You are a little scary."

Frankie laughed. "Only a little, I am slipping."

She strolled away as Charlie looked at Reighn, who stared after the laughing Frankie and said. "So okay then."

She nodded. "Yep."

Harper had been in her barn long enough to have marked out the wall where it could be cut and expanded to include a classroom for Edith's students. She decided to use a small room for a paint/play room for the little ones. Then walked up the stairs to the loft and found a one-bedroom apartment and sighed in pleasure. As she looked around at the open planned kitchen, dining and lounge space, she decided she could live here. Frankie had more or less moved in with Johner. So she happily spent time calling furniture to the apartment from her storage in New York. She even took the bedroom set from the apartment she was staying in because she adored the enormous bed she was currently sleeping in.

When Harper had not returned and Verity called out, there

was only fifteen minutes until lunch, Charlie as promised, left to get her. Harper was on the main floor of her barn and using her magic again to call her equipment to her. Charlie stood in stunned silence as she looked around her: she had imagined an empty wooden shell, like barns she had seen in the past, not this elaborate building. The floors were warm and made from wood with red and gold tones and she bet they had a preservation spell on them courtesy of Sage. The walls were all lined in wood panels painted a soft white. There were iron hanging chandeliers, which were turned off at the moment as the dozen skylights allowed the light to flood in. It was surely an artist's dream studio. She watched as tool boxes and large covered things, which she assumed were machines of some kind, appeared.

"You seem to have a good understanding of your magic." She told Harper as she moved further into the barn with Justice in her arms.

Harper nodded and turned toward her. "More so recently, I assume it has to do with the Elementals or it is just all the magic flying around here."

Charlie grinned as she stopped next to her. The place was larger than she had first thought. She could see a small kitchen and a small lounge area toward the back of the barn with what looked like large glassed in offices. "There is an entire apartment up there." Harper told her as she pointed at the loft.

"Are you going to live here?"

"Yeah, Frankie has more or less moved in with Johner."

"That makes sense, it is beautiful."

Harper swung around in a circle with her arms spread wide. "I know. Not what we would call a barn."

"No, it is what dragons would, though."

"Yep." As Harper came to a stop, she looked at a wall lined with shelves and instantly tools of all descriptions filled them. On the other side were even more shelves that were suddenly filled with different size boxes and underneath was a counter with a stool on wheels.

Charlie assumed it was a work area. Suddenly, in the middle of the floor, a large oblong stone that almost reached the rafters appeared.

"Wow! That is huge. What will you make out of it?"

"I have no idea." Harper said as she caressed the marble. "Whatever speaks to me, I guess."

"That is how your art works?"

"Yes, I will seek what it wants to tell me, then shape it to that."

"I see."

"Well, after all, that is what my talent is, seeking. Has yours increased?"

"My talent for justice, more so since I arrived here."

Harper looked at her. "I heard about the faerie. You did right, in case you were wondering if I agreed or not."

"Honestly, the gossips. I knew when I did it you would have agreed. I suppose that is another reason for you to dislike the faeries."

Harper sighed. "Give me time Charlie; big things are happening here. I am coping as well as I can."

"Okay, I get that."

Harper took the baby from her and cuddled him. She looked down into the face of sweetness with purple eyes. "He is royal?"

Charlie was not surprised she already knew the workings of the dragon nobility. "Yes, from what line we do not know."

"Does it matter?"

"To us no, to some yes." Charlie looked at the picture she made with her son. She was so much like her and yet so different. "I was never as brave as you."

"Brave." Harper looked at Charlie. "Or foolhardy?"

"No, you were never that, rash but not a fool."

Harper shrugged and walked around her barn with the baby in her arms as she told Charlie. "I thought you were alive. I thought I saw you once in a town about six years ago.

You looked normal, laughing, talking to people." She heard Charlie draw in a breath and blurted. "I don't know if it really was you, but I was not making good choices back then. I got angry. I have a darkness within me. It fills that hole your Kelsey talked about." She whispered as she admitted. "It took me years to master it, to control my reactions to it. When I thought I saw you that day, and now I see you. I believe it was not you, but it was someone who looked enough like you. It sent me spiralling out of control. It was a bad time for me." She flicked her eyes toward Charlie and saw her staring at her, but could not read what she was thinking. She sucked in her bottom lip for a second or two, then said. "I spent months fighting it, fighting the battle to kill. It is a terrible compulsion that comes over me." She shook her head and looked once more into the baby's face and sighed as she said. "Then I met Frankie." Harper closed her eyes. "For not walking up and finding out if it was you that day, I am sorry. It was childish and hurtful of me. I have no excuse." She looked at Charlie from the corner of her eye and saw she was staring up at the sky.

Anger pulsed from Charlie as she thought about what Harper had revealed she dismissed the sighting she spoke of. It may or may not have been her, who cared. What she was angry about was Harper keeping her condition a secret from her. She demanded to know. "Was it from that night?"

Harper nodded as she closed her eyes for a minute. "Yeah, demons and shades, they left a mark."

Charlie asked, knowing the answer already but needing confirmation. "I do not have that in me?"

"No Charlie, not in you."

Anger swallowed Charlie whole, it had not been long after that night of terror that Harper made her leave home. Storm asked through their bond. *My soul, do you need me?*

No my love, I am alright.

I am but a thought away.

Thank you.

She knew he monitored her and would wait for her to call him. She wanted to scream, then scream some more, and then tear into Harper, shred her to bits. How dare she? How could she do that to her, the heartache, the fear she had lived with? She remembered how loneliness followed in her footsteps for years. She turned to demand answers. To release the anger building within her and stopped cold as she looked at her sister standing there waiting for her scorn, for her rage. Charlie could see that Harper believed she deserved it and suddenly the anger just vanished, everything just fell away. In that instant of clarity, she saw the truth of the situation and realized they had all been victims, and some still were. Harper carried such a heavy burden. What could she say that she had not already said to herself? All she could say was that she loved her.

"Harper, who the hell cares, it was so long ago, we are different. I am not angry, I cannot be. It is a waste of energy and I refuse to be that person. You are here with me in my life. I just don't want to care about the past anymore. It won't change what happened, what I did, what you did, or what they did. All I want is here. I love you, have done forever, and will do so forever. So screw the rest."

Harper walked over and passed the baby back to his mother, and placed her hand over Charlie's heart. "You were always smarter than me and wiser. Give me time. I am getting there. I swear I will work hard to be what you want. What I want to be, I love you, have done forever, and will do so forever."

Charlie asked her. "What do you want to be?"

"A whole person, loved, and to find peace."

"Okay Harper, you are loved. The other two we will work on together."

"Yeah, we can do that. So is it lunchtime?"

"Yes, we came to remind you." Together, they looked down at the sleeping baby.

Harper murmured. "He is a sweet little dragon."

"We think so."

Charlie wondered as they walked to the castle what the conversation revealed. Harper had issues and not the easy to fix ones, but she was in her life and staying. Again, Harper had reached out to her. In some respects, she was so much braver than Charlie, and sometimes so much dumber. At least she was willing to work and hopefully rid herself of this darkness. She hoped once they cleared that problem up, things would get easier. Frankie said Harper needed to be busy, that she got into all sorts of trouble when she was idle. *Okay, she did not say that exactly, but it was implied.* Charlie worried as she imagined the terrible trouble Harper could reap on Dragon's Gap. She hoped the job she was going to offer her would help.

Together, they entered the family room for lunch, just as Frankie said to Sage and June. "We need to work. Both Harper and I are not used to doing nothing. What work can we find to do?"

Sage asked. "Doesn't her art qualify?"

Frankie grinned. "Nope, she can only do so much of that until she wants to bludgeon someone to death with a pick or saw. So work?"

They all looked at Harper, who shrugged. "True."

Charlie looked at her sister. "I could use Harper if she wants to use her other skills."

"What do you do?"

Sage said. "Charlie and I run, or more Charlie now actually runs rescues. We retrieve those that need rescuing and bring them here to Dragon's Gap, to keep them safe." In a few sentences, Sage explained the procedure and why they did it.

Harper nodded. "I'm in."

They all moved toward the balcony overlooking the unicorn meadow. Reighn asked as he joined them, handing around drinks. "What is it you do, Frankie?"

She grinned. "I am an organizing fiend. It is in my blood."

June asked. "What blood would that be?"

"I am half brownie; my mother was brownie, and my father was something else."

June gasped. "I don't understand, aren't brownies like three inches tall or something?"

"That she worries about, not the other thing?" Edith said to Harper, who grinned as she sipped her beer.

Frankie laughed. "No, that is a fable; they were or are normal sized."

Sage said. "Is that why you could dissolve my magic?"

Frankie shrugged. "Maybe what I am is non-magical, I am a.... What did the guy call me?" She tapped her chin. "Oh yes, a null... Yes, a null. See, I can cancel magic. Apparently it is a magic all of its own."

"I do not think I have ever heard of a null person before." Said a mystified Sage as she looked at Frankie.

Edith said. "What am I then?"

June answered before anyone else could. "A bear that cannot shift."

Reighn told them. "A Grounder is something entirely different."

Edith stated. "Exactly, a null."

Sage told her. "No, it is so not the same."

Edith scratched her neck. "How is it not?"

Sage explained. "She is a possible witch."

"Half-witch maybe." Frankie butted in.

Sage shrugged. "Maybe half-witch, you Edee are all bear."

"Still can't shift... a null."

"Shut up."

"So rude." Edith said to Harper.

She grinned and replied. "Yep."

"It is a specialized magic." Rene` explained as he joined them. "Few survive until adulthood."

"What guy?" Harper asked suspiciously.

No, they do not, but then we were not on Earth then. Said an Elemental, who appeared next to Reighn.

Frankie grinned and said. "That guy. He's an Elemental

Harper."

"Yeah, I see."

"Hello, how are you?" Frankie asked with a smile.

We are well, Lady Frankie. And pleased you have arrived.

Frankie nodded. "Aww, I said I'd get here."

We were concerned.

"I am sorry, but I needed to wait for Harper to be ready."

We understand.

Harper looked at her friend. "You did, did you?"

"Well, yeah, I wasn't coming without you. Although I did not know you had family here."

She smiled at Harper, who asked. "Why are you here?"

She is here to help Lord Reighn with the magical beings who will come to Dragon's Gap.

Reighn said. "It is a large endeavor."

We understand. The Elemental stated. *Although a serene being such as Lady Frankie will manage well, and her talent will only be occasionally used, until then she is as she is.* He disappeared with that pronouncement.

Johner appeared as if by magic. "My love, are you alright?"

Frankie sighed and smiled at him, saying. "I am now you are here." He took her hand in his and squeezed it encouragingly. To the others staring at her, she said. "Well... So yeah, that is me."

Charlie asked, slightly stunned. "When did they contact you?"

"Oh, about a year ago, they told me what my talent was and how I could help Dragon's Gap and the Dragon Lord. I told them I would, but not until Harper was ready to come here."

"So they orchestrated all this?" Harper asked Frankie, who screwed her lips up in thought. "Yeah, probably, almost definitely."

"Well, we all know the Elementals provide." Reighn stated in his Dragon Lord voice.

"Or interfere." Edith mumbled.

Harper mumbled back. "Agreed, sneaky bas..."

"Yes well." Charlie interrupted her.

Harper glared at Frankie, who opened her eyes wide and asked her. "What?"

"You never thought to tell me?"

"Nah! Not really, seemed pointless."

Harper looked at her friend and then Johner, who looked just as dumbfounded as everyone else. Then she looked at Frankie again and realized to Frankie's way of thinking it really had seemed pointless. She sighed and said. "Yep, it probably was."

Johner said. "My love, please tell me things like this. I do need to know."

"Oh okay, just as well you told me." He kept the relieved sigh to himself. Frankie said to June. "So work?"

Sage asked. "Can you really organize?"

"Like a fiend."

"Well, I need help, so do you want to be my Personal Assistant?"

"What do you do?" Frankie almost squealed with glee at the thought of working.

Together with Johner, they walked to the other side of the room and sat on a couple of couches. Sage and June talked while Frankie listened. Every now and again Frankie would nod at something Sage or June said. Her eyes became more excited the longer they talked and the happier she became, the more she moved to her own song.

"She will be working with Sage before dinner is finished." Claire told the others who watched them.

Harper asked. "Seer?"

"I am."

"Did you see Frankie coming?"

Claire smiled at the abrupt question. "No, I saw someone who would mesh well with Sage, June and Reighn."

"That is definitely Frankie. What will she do?"

"Organize and help run the castle and become a buffer for Sage as the Dragon Lady. A lot of power goes with the position."

"It will suit her talents, all of them. She is as honest as the sky is blue, plus Johner will like that she will stay here?"

Rene` answered her observation. "He will, his dragon will not chaff at thinking she will leave him." He watched Harper watch her friend. They had over the last few days come to a truce. It would take time for her to accept him, but he was patient. He understood it was more the lack of trust she had in fathers rather than she did not like him. So he knew it would happen. He listened now as Reighn asked. "Harper, what will you do other than your art?"

"Become a retriever. No training necessary, just point me in the right direction and let me go."

Charlie nodded. "Fine, I will have my secretary get in touch." She left to go to her children and Storm as they entered with the nannies after cleaning up for lunch.

Harper looked after her as Reighn said. "You will have to address that soon."

"I am working on it; we already started, she is amazing. I wish I was not so damaged. Oh, thank you for my barn, it is perfect." She smiled up at him.

He inclined his head as he said. "You are welcome. I have someone coming that will help you. Will you see him?"

She looked at Claire. "Did you see me coming?"

"Oh yes, and the one who is to be your Shadow. I told him of you."

Harper sucked in a breath. *Oh hell a mate.* "But not my name?"

"No, that is for you to do."

"I am damaged." She confessed.

Reighn shrugged and told her softly. "Anyone can be damaged. It is how we cope with the damage that shows our true character."

"Okay Reighn, I don't want to be like this. I will take all the help I can get. Hope he is as cute as yah all!" Harper grinned at him and his father as she sauntered away.

He sighed as his father was wont to do and understood why he did so now. He looked after Harper and Claire as she laughed and followed Harper. Rene` clapped him on his shoulder. "It gets easier, I promise."

Reighn grunted in response, not amused or believing him.

CHAPTER FOURTEEN:

While Harper, and the rest of the family were sitting down to a family lunch. Ace, the eldest Battle brother, was packing to leave Dragon's Citadel. His sanctuary since his Sire's trial.

He was one of only two fire dragons, the Dragon Lord being the other. Together, they held the ethics of the dragon horde within their dragon souls. When a transgression against dragonkind was known or believed to be happening, Reighn or Ace investigated and then solved the problem permanently, whatever form that may take.

For Ace not to have known his father led a rebellion that if it had succeeded, would have removed the entire royal family. Felled his belief in his intelligence and crippled his dragon's belief in himself. Ace, like his brothers, always knew their father desired more in life and felt he had always been short-changed of his position within dragon nobility. He and his brothers had no idea of the depth of his depravity or of the genetic manipulation he subjected them to. Reports discovered on how and why their beloved mother died, were only some of the revelations unearthed of his father's corrupt nature.

When Ace began to view the world and people around him through a soul gone dark and a heart filled with pain. It resulted in his own ethics and judgement being compromised, and when his dragon withdrew, his counsel. Ace was filled with doubt, second guessing every decision he made, which caused him to become dangerous. Worried he would overreact to a situation or worse, not act at all. He knew it was time to seek help, before he could follow through on the impulses he was plagued with, to raze the world.

Reighn had made it possible for him to go to Master Patrycc Maythom, the Redeemer. The only dragon that was capable of counseling and keeping an ethical dragon from succumbing to his despair. Ace had taken months to come back from the killing edge. Master Patrycc also spent months showing him and his dragon that, from the rubble of their lives, there was much to be redeemed. Over the last months, Ace and his dragon had taken time to relearn who and what they were now. It had been, at times, discouraging and humbling for them both. But Ace knew they had come out the other side more ethical and a far better person and dragon.

"So you are leaving?"

Ace looked up from his packing to the young male that leaned his long, wiry body against the door frame. Dressed much as he was, in black jeans, shirt and boots, his long blond hair in a warrior's top knot above a handsome face. Ace was positive the male with the golden eyes would always have a touch of arrogance about him as all males had in their youth. In Hayden, it was not a bad thing. His confidence had taken a hard knock. To learn you and your dragon were vulnerable when you have been led to believe your entire life you were indestructible... was tough.

Ace knew that feeling well, so if he was arrogant, Ace did not begrudge him that. It seemed to serve him well by giving him the confidence to understand who he was now, and not enough to make him unlikable. He grinned at the male, who had obviously just come from training; he looked fit and healthy. A change from the dragon who arrived carried on a sling between two dragons. His wings and body so badly damaged from fire it was hard to believe he would survive, let alone ever be able to fly again. Thankfully, he was almost healed. A few scars remained. No one battled dragon's fire and came out unscathed. Although the mental and emotional damage was taking time to heal. Privately, Ace believed Hayden needed a Shadow, someone more than his young brother, to fight for. Maybe knowing he had someone out there would help him. It helped Ace, knowing some-one, somewhere, was for him and his dragon. Hayden looked around the sparsely furnished bedroom as all the rooms in the Citadel were. And realized he was going to miss the taci-turn male, who he considered a friend.

Ace told him now. "I have been told I am needed at home."

"That was why the Dragon Lord and his Prime were here?"

"Yes, they came to tell me the Seer said it was time for me to return." He did not tell Hayden it was because his Shadow would be at Dragon's Gap.

Hayden walked in and stood looking out over the moun-tains. The Citadel was somewhere in what the humans called the Himalayans. It was positioned on the very edge of a cliff, or more precisely, was built into the cliff side and hidden by dragon magic. It was the domain of Patrycc Maythom, redeemer of bodies, souls and hearts and, in Hayden's case, his mind. Master Patrycc was brother to Lady Verity, former Dragon Lady and mother of the present Dragon Lord. Hay-den thought the Dragon Lord looked like Lady Verity, except where she had a soft face and shy eyes, the Dragon Lord was hard and worldly. His eyes held secrets and mysteries Hay-den never wanted to find out about. He sighed longingly. He missed his brother, and he missed his home, but most of all, he missed his dragon talking to him more than all the other things combined. "I want to return home." He said before he thought too much about what he was saying.

Ace nodded and quietly said. "It cannot be long now, my friend."

"I hope not, I miss living."

Ace understood that, while being here, it was like living half a life, with days filled with meditation and training. Every minute of every day was filled with a form of rehabili-tation and many hours with Master Patrycc delving into you and your dragon's hearts, minds and souls. All the time for-cing you to search out what hindered your abilities. What it was that wanted to hurt you and caused in his case, his soul to turn black. "Take each day as a blessing and find your balance, then you will be home." Ace told him it was the same advice the Master had given him many times over the last few months.

"Ace is correct, it will not be long now Hayden, but to get there you are required in meditation."

Hayden bowed. "Yes Master, goodbye my friend. If you see Clint, please tell him I miss him and will be with him soon."

They clasped arms in goodbye. "I will and Hayden thank you."

"For what?"

"For helping me through the last months without your assurance, I would make it. I would not be here."

Hayden smiled, a lightening of his dark features. "I am glad I could help." He walked out a happier male than the one that had walked in.

"That was nicely done. He is almost where you were a month or two ago, he will be home soon." Patrycc clasped his arm and then pulled Ace into a hug. "I am pleased you are leaving."

"I am sorry I was such a trial." Ace dryly stated.

"Ahh humor... interesting." Patrycc grinned at Ace's raised eyebrow. "Tell my sister I will come home with Hayden. I am in need of her tender care."

Ace asked. "I can hardly wait. Are you sure that is all you are going home for?"

Now it was Patrycc's turn to say. "I am sure my visit is to my sister, not to meet my Shadow."

Ace sighed. "I only hope she will accept my help."

"Of course she will. You are, if nothing else, charming."

Ace cocked an eyebrow at the Master. "Charming, Master?"

"Definitely or so my Verity tells me." He grinned again, "She is, of course biased, or so my nephew Reighn says."

"He has always been jealous of me." Stated Ace as he closed his pack.

Patrycc Maythom, the Redeemer for dragonkind, grinned

but did not reply. He just touched Ace's shoulder before he walked toward the open door and said seriously. "You have all the tools to remain healthy and help your Shadow, but if you need me, call. I will be there in a moment. Are you flying or using a portal?"

Ace shook out his shoulders in preparation for his flight. "Thank you Master; I am flying. My dragon and I need the time and the flight to settle back into who we are now."

"Good choice. Goodbye, my friend."

Ace picked his pack up and turned to the male that started out as Master and ended up a friend. "And to you, my friend, do not make it too long until we meet again."

"I will not. I need to meet the female who is Shadow to the Elite Shield, Ace Battle."

"As do I."

CHAPTER FIFTEEN:

Harper and Frankie had been living and working at Dragon's Gap for three weeks. Harper spent most of that time on assignments away from home. Frankie walked into her job like she had been born to it. Sage and June had no idea how they ever managed without her.

It was Monday, the day after another family day. Harper had spent the entire Saturday working on her large block of marble, chipping away at the stone. What was emerging, she thought, was probably going to be a masterpiece. Amazingly enough, she was finding family day fun and highly entertaining. Especially when the little ones ganged up on either Axl or Ark. They seemed to place themselves in the firing line, along with Clint, who had missed being there yesterday due to work.

This morning, when Harper finally rolled out of bed and looked at her messages, it seemed she had received another assignment. Dressing slowly, her mind full of her new sculpture, she ate a scant breakfast and presented herself at Charlie's office just after seven o'clock. A brief rundown on where she was to go, from Charlie's secretary, a female cougar named Betty, which was standard before a retrieval. She was once more issued with a phone and again offered weapons and ammunition, these she declined. She picked up her keys for a new vehicle. They rotated vehicles often, so no one got used to the same car being in the same area more than once or twice.

Harper was headed to a notorious section of England. She just loved portals they made traveling faster and helped the rescued get to Dragon's Gap safer. This area of England was known for harboring shifters, predominately females, and their young. In the three weeks since joining the team, Harper had taken out three large holdings of this particular cartel. Two in Europe and one in Australia. She and her team had rescued over two hundred females and young from each location. Where she was headed today was apparently their main compound. Unfortunately, many of the captives were held by shifters and humans that were unwilling to release them. Time and again, they seemed to think their prior claim was more important than Harper's or the females themselves. So she often found herself defending not only herself but those she rescued. Harper lost count of the injuries she had received over the last three weeks. She was never more pleased for healers and her quick healing abilities than she was since starting this job.

Betty told her they only received this information late the previous night. It seemed the cartel was gearing up for a big trade, so Harper and her team would rescue who they could and kill the rest. That was not quite what Charlie ordered when she had taken her first assignment. But Harper felt that was the sentiment of her. "Go get those assholes."

She nodded to Betty and snagged another cup of coffee from the reception area before wandering to the rear of the castle to find her vehicle. Harper made the steps and drank the last of her coffee, and then took several early morning breaths of crisp, fresh air.

When she felt satisfied with how things were going, meaning she had missed Frankie. Which was good, because she would only yell at her for leaving again so soon after being back for just two days. She had also missed the disapproving Reighn, who would give her the Dragon Lord frown, because she was off again. She was positive he stood in front of a mirror and practiced that frown or he had just perfected it since her arrival. Regardless, she had avoided both.

Smiling to herself, she sauntered down the steps to the parking lot and came to a halt as she looked up, then up some more. If anyone had told her at any time in her past.

She would sometime in her lifetime be standing toe to snout with a fire breathing, crimson, green-eyed, seventy foot dragon. With only knives to defend herself with, she would have laughed herself silly. But here she was standing, not two feet from said dragon. Knives raised and a glint in her eye that read death or nothing.

Suddenly, males arrived from everywhere. Rene`, Ark and Axl ran from inside the Castle. Lars and Johner flew in from town, changing as they approached. Reighn, Storm and Keeper arrived from the training grounds, transforming with a thought to human as they touched down. All to protect the dragon from her. *Amazing.*

"Seriously dude. I wouldn't have hurt him too much." Harper stated as Reighn sighed deeply, which he seemed to always do around her. "Sheathe your knives, female."

Now that he said frequently, all the dragons were in their human forms, except for the dragon Harper had been facing off against. She placed her knives away and watched as the Dragon Lord called to the dragon. "Welcome home Ace, it has been too long. I am sorry about your reception, Harper is a little quick with her knives."

"Oh, right|! It is all my fault. Nothing said about the great big ball of flame shooting in the sky... Typical."

Reighn crossed his arms and gave her the Lord's stare and asked. "Finished?"

Harper mimicked his stance. "Seriously, you are going to cop attitude?"

Reighn stared some more. Harper's eyes narrowed, her lips tightened as her hands moved quicker than eyes could follow even a dragons'. Instantly six small knives evenly spaced appeared, dug into the stones, in a semi-circle around Reighn's feet, who still didn't bat an eye. Harper growled, worthy of a dragon, so mad she could snort flame herself and snarled. "I am so out of here. See you when I return." She spun around and vanished in a puff of air.

"She's become quite dramatic ever since she remembered

how to do that." Commented Keeper.

Storm added. "And faster with those knives."

Johner said. "But she is talking more."

"Especially to Reighn." Rene` agreed.

Reighn pulled out the knives, and as he straightened, he felt the huge dragon shift. A male the same size as him stood clothed in a black tee-shirt and black stone-washed jeans with black boots and a well-worn leather long coat. Apart from the short military haircut, he looked like all the Battle brothers, with the carved from stone good looks and green eyes. Except where they had a softness around the eyes and mouth, he did not. Before Reighn could embrace him, the knives disappeared from his hands, returning to Harper.

At his request, Sage had spelled all her knives, ensuring they always found their way back to her. It made Reighn feel better knowing she always had their protection. He enfolded the big male in a hug, brother to brother, friend to friend. Lord to dragon and felt him return the hug and the feelings. He finally released him to his brothers.

Ace stood quietly in his family's arms, the first physical contact with them he had in just under a year. The love and relief from his family and friends swamped him and made him pleased he had returned home. Through Rene` and Patrycc, he had been kept up to date on the goings on at Dragon's Gap. He knew of all the new bondings and hatchlings but as he reveled in the warmth of being with his brothers. He knew learning things second-hand was not the same as being with his family. He had come full circle since his father and other relations betrayed the realm, he was finally home.

Rene` hugged him and said. "You took your time getting here. I was thinking of sending out a search party."

"Sorry, my dragon and I needed time to settle and come to terms with our new... friendship, I suppose."

Yes, that is a good word. Stated his dragon.

Rene` said. "I understand, if you need to talk. I am always

here for you."

"Thank you. Where is Ash?"

Ark told him. "Hatchlings do not care that older brothers are returning home."

Ace grinned, he could not wait to see Ash and his amazing Shadow and the sun dragons, his nephews. "Well, uncles and brothers can afford to wait awhile."

Rene` led him inside, an arm around his shoulders as Reighn said. "So home five minutes and already pissing off one of the deadliest people here."

They all laughed as Storm said. "Truth though, that is fairly easily done."

All but Rene` and Reighn agreed. Ace raised a soot black eyebrow, his voice slightly rusty from disuse as he asked. "That would have been?"

Axl answered. "Harper the knife."

Rene` growled at him. "Do not call her that."

Ark assured him. "Everyone calls her that."

Johner sighed. "Frankie coined the term, and it has stuck, sorry Papa."

Reighn said. "Fine, but if I find out, it upsets her. Then I will not be pleased."

"As you say my Lord." They all chorused except Rene` and Ace.

Reighn heard Keeper say quietly to the others. "If she does not like the name, he would not have to say anything."

"True." Axl agreed. "There would be nothing left of us to be displeased with."

Ace asked Rene`. "Who is this female?"

Rene` grunted. "Later." Because just then Verity rushed toward Ace. Within seconds, he found himself in the arms of the female he and his brothers had secretly called mother for more years than he could remember. "Ace James Battle."

Ark said. "Wow, he is in so much trouble, all three names."

"Nah." Johner told him. "That is her. You have been naughty, but not that much. I have to send you to your room voice."

Storm agreed. "Yep, he is golden."

"Heard it a lot, did you?" Ark asked all the Kingsley males. They all nodded their heads in agreement, even Rene`.

"Storm more than any of us." Reighn smirked at his brother.

Storm shrugged smugly as he said. "I liked to test the boundaries."

Keeper muttered. "And Mama's patience."

Ace turned a little with Verity still in his arms and grinned. The first natural one in months, Verity said. "Do not listen to them. I am quite wroth with thee, Ace Battle." It showed how emotional she was when she slipped back into the speech of her youth. "You have been gone far too long." She pulled away a little to look into his face, a face she had known from a hatchling. A face she'd loved for that long and a face she had missed every day since he left. She told him with all the love a mother had for her child. "You have been greatly missed, and not just by me. Do not leave again, you are most assuredly needed here."

He squeezed her tighter, and she felt his body give one deep sigh and settle. "I will not."

Verity smiled as her dragon said. *Finally, our boy is home.* "There is no one here that can keep these ones in order. Rene` is just running amuck since he decided he can stay here and command the Hunters. And Storm has decided the same for the Shields and do not get me started on Reighn. Then there is Keeper, who has resigned his commission and Johner with the castle guards, plus the Shadows and hatch-lings."

Ace grinned at the grunts and the annoyed whispers. "How did we become the ones in trouble here?"

"Is she talking about us?"

Verity, with an arm still around him, moved into the castle, leaving the others to follow. Ace grinned as his thoughts strayed to the feisty little female. His dragon told him. *She is ours.*

Yes, we will court her.

Our Shadow.

Yes, my friend, our Shadow.

His dragon sighed deeply. He had missed his brothers and family. *I am happy we are home. I will think on how to capture our Shadow.*

We will talk to Reighn; he is her protector.

His dragon growled in return. *We are her protector; she is ours.*

Yes, my friend, he told his dragon patiently, *but he has claimed her, you can see that as well as I can.*

I see it. We will talk to the Dragon Lord.

Yes, we will.

CHAPTER SIXTEEN:

The following Sunday, Frankie, who had settled in her new apartment with Johner and in her new position as personal assistant to the Dragon Lady. Smiled when one of her favorite people entered the family dining room.

Clint Sorren was a teenager, or at least he appeared to be a teenager. He was a fabulous young male, who was always willing to help anyone, and was loved by all the females. Even Harper liked the young dragon. Frankie sighed as she thought of Harper, who was still not home. And from their conversation yesterday, she would not be back for another week. Her smile morphed into a sad frown, she missed her friend. Even though her own life was busy and full, it was not the same without her best friend around to talk to.

Sighing again wishfully, she would talk to Reighn. He and Harper seemed to have connected. Maybe he could make her stay home. She needed to make friends with her family. Harper had made enormous progress with Charlie; it was the Faerie Queen and King she needed to form a relationship with, and as her best friend, Frankie could only do so much. Seriously, that female is a pain in my ass, as Charlie would say. Harper needed to stop running. Frankie had said as much to her when they talked last night. She had not replied, but Frankie was sure she heard her.

Amused, she watched Clint slide around the room until he came to a stop in the shadowed corner by the windows. With his eyes locked on the new fire dragon, Ace Battle. Clint was always quick with a smile and never found her annoying, and not just because, like some people, he was afraid of Harper or Sage. She wondered why he was so interested in Ace. What did he have that made the teenager look at him with expressions ranging from terror to hope? It hurt her heart to see him so troubled; she made her way slowly toward Ace. She had not spoken to him since his spectacular arrival, but had been entertained when Sage relayed what happened when he met Harper before she left.

Now, looking at the huge male, she saw someone with scars on his soul and heart. This was a dragon that needed this large, wacky family to make him whole. Just look at what they were doing for Harper, admittedly slowly, and that was because she would not stay home, but it was working, *damn it.* Frankie smiled as she thought of what they had done for her, and not just because she was bonded to Johner. How they accepted and treated her just like a normal person. Not once since she and Harper had arrived did she feel alienated, so when Ace moved away from his brothers and stared out the windows overlooking the unicorn meadows. She sidled up next to him and quietly said. "So hi, my name is Frankie."

Ace looked down at the female and smiled, which he was doing more of since arriving home. Coming home had been the right move, although he knew he had needed the help from Master Patrycc. It seemed being home with his family was helping his dragon to come to terms with what he considered his failures. Together, they felt more centered, more alive than they had for months.

"I know. You are Johner's Shadow."

"Yep, that is me. So you met my girl Harper, before she left."

"I did."

Frankie's entire being stilled as she felt and listened to the words spoken. "Oh!" She sighed gently. "So she is your Shadow?"

He nodded in reply, then took another look at her. "Ahh, I see. You can read people. That is an amazing ability."

"I think so, although until I came here it seemed weird."

"I am sure it did. You must have felt out of place in the larger world?"

"Yep, that I did, until Harper arrived in my life."

Gently, he said. "I am sure she was a relief for someone as sensitive as you."

Frankie looked up at him and smiled, letting him see the being beneath the shell she wore. "Few people would understand that. Harper buffered the world for me. I don't think I did too much to return the favor for her."

"I doubt that; I feel you, Frankie, are far more a friend than you believe."

Frankie looked over at Reighn and Charlie. "You know who claims her."

He followed her eyes. "I do, I have spoken to Reighn."

"And Charlie?"

"No, I have not done so yet. Do you advise me too?"

"She will know. That female knows everything."

"I bow to your wisdom."

"Yeah... just, you know, watch for guns. Apparently, she is dynamite with them, like Harper, is with her knives."

"I have seen that and will take your warning to heart."

She grinned at him, then whispered. "So Ace, do you know the teenager who has finally decided to come talk to you?"

"Who?" He asked just as softly.

But before she could answer him, he heard a youthful male voice say. "Excuse me sir."

Ace looked behind him as Frankie said. "Ace, this is Clint."

Ace frowned. "Clint, are you Hayden's brother?"

The boy nodded and ducked his head. "Yeah, I am."

Frankie stepped back as Clint moved forward to take her place. He asked softly. "Do you know if he is alright?"

Ace placed his big hand on the boy's shoulder, tipping his head up so he could look into his eyes. Clint surprised himself by meeting the green eyes of one of the fiercest dragons in the world. "He is doing well. His consultations with Master Patrycc will be completed shortly and he will be home soon. Clint, he misses you very much. Now why did you not come and see me when I first arrived back?"

Clint shook his head. "You were busy and I…"

"Clint, I would have spoken to you before now. If I had known you were here. Where are you staying?"

"In the singles male's dorm."

"I dislike the sound of that. Frankie?"

"Yes, Ace."

"I would appreciate it, if you could find someone to supervise him moving into my place, whether or not he knows it, he is family."

Charlie came over just as he finished speaking. She eyed the enormous dragon suspiciously. "Clint, are you okay?"

"Charlie, I am to move into Commander Battle's apartment."

Charlie's face tightened as she demanded. "Why?"

"He is family and living in the single males' quarters." Ace mildly stated with a tinge of amusement.

Annoyed, Charlie asked. "Why didn't I know you could have moved in with us?"

Clint and Frankie laughed at her. "What?" She asked with more annoyance coloring her tone. "I do not understand the humor."

Frankie told her. "We just wondered where you would have put him."

"Well, there is that." Charlie agreed with a scowl.

Frankie told him. "Come on Clint, let's get you moved, we have time before lunch."

Clint beamed a smile that almost broke his face. "Umm sir?"

"It is Ace, you call me Ace." He told him. "Clint, there are no thanks needed. You and your brother are family. That is all there is to it.

A relieved Clint nodded as Frankie dragged him from Ace, leaving him alone with Charlie. Ace raised a soot colored eyebrow over amazing green eyes. Involuntarily, a shiver of awareness tingled down Charlie's back. "So I was told you met my sister."

"I did, yes. I am guessing you know who she is to me."

"I could tell from what Reighn said and how Frankie acted, that female cannot fabricate to save herself."

"She advised me you already knew. Her words were, you know everything."

"That is true. So, were you going to mention it today with the family here? A sort of tell the older sister, so she will not kill me in front of them thing."

He laughed, and a rusty, unused sound emerged from the male that had Charlie's ire softening. "I have been told you are a master with guns and to be wary. I figured you would not risk a stray bullet."

She told him seriously. "I never have stray bullets."

Ace inclined his head in acknowledgment of her statement. "Or maybe it could have been that I saw an intelligent, understanding and loving sister and thought to myself. I wonder will she help me win her sister, because I swear I will love and protect her for a lifetime and longer." He stated in his deep toe curling voice.

She had thought the other Battle brothers were handsome and charming. They were nothing on this one, and she knew Harper was done for. Charlie nodded as she cleared the emotion from her throat. "Okay, Harper and I have just reconnected, but I will help you all I can. She is not like most females, she is more sensitive..."

There was a choked off snort from behind them as Storm arrived, his arm automatically going around her. Charlie harrumphed and asked her Shadow. "You wanted to say something?"

Grinning, he told her. "She was threatening him with knives at their first meeting and he was in dragon form."

Charlie hid her grin and dismay as she answered. "Seriously, that does not mean she is not sensitive."

Sage said as she joined them. "I think it does and slightly crazy."

Claire said. "She is not crazy, just wounded." She looked at

Ace. "So you found her, then?"

He respectively inclined his head to Claire, who so long ago had told him his Shadow would come to him. "I did, and thank you. Your prophecy in my darkest of times gave me hope."

Claire smiled, and she too inclined her head. "Good, I hoped it would."

Reighn eyed Ace and Charlie, but before he could comment, Edith said from behind them where she was standing with Sharm.

"I like her, she is all soul. Ace, you should look at her work before you decide on what type of person she is. Art shows everything about the artist and, in my opinion, it is the purest expression of truth. Harper is all about truth in her emotions. I believe like Charlie does, Harper is very sensitive."

"Do you have any of her works on display?" He asked, knowing Edith owned the gallery.

She grinned with glee. "Yes, Harper placed some for show and sale. Come in tomorrow and explore the wonderful world of Harper Easton." Before she turned to greet the young ones, she said to Charlie. "You should come and see what your sister shows of herself, you may be surprised."

Charlie looked at Ace. "Well?"

"Tomorrow at nine."

"Okay."

Reighn said. "Well, seeing as we are all in agreement with Ace being Harper's Shadow, who tells Harper?"

CHAPTER SEVENTEEN:

Ace wrestled with his thoughts as he wandered around the outside of the castle. A week had passed since he and Charlie spoke together about Harper being his Shadow, and since Clint had made his home with him. They often shared meals together and Ace discovered he liked the youth. He was different from his brother Hayden. Clint was quieter, more introspective, he would make a great healer. Ace's dragon agreed with him.

Having spent the last two weeks training and reconnecting with his brothers, Ace knew Ash was pleased he was back. Especially when he thrust a hatchling into his arms and taught him how to give him his bottle. Ace knew it was Ash's way of telling him he was loved. He had met and become entranced with Olinda, who was a soft, sweet female with a rod of steel for a spine. He had listened closely when Ash told him of Olinda's life before Dragon's Gap and had been amazed that she survived the experience. He laughed when he found out Ash was now a prince to the local Blessing. Ash had been unamused at his mirth. They ended up wrestling on the lounge floor, much to Olinda's amusement; it had felt like old times. Every day, he and his dragon were pleased to be home.

When he and his brothers met up with the Kingsley's brothers for a night of drinking and renewing their bonds over games of pool. Ash told him he was not content to leave Dragon's Gap or his family anymore. He was happy with the position he had been offered. It did not take much for Ace to see that his brothers were all happy where they were now.

Apparently, Sharm had conducted extensive testing on his brothers and concluded his father's meddling in their genetics had done nothing more than strengthen their bodies.

And given them abilities to heal quicker than other dragons. It also seemed that the brothers were highly intelligent. But Sharm was quick to point out that it was impossible to say whether the manipulation of their genes contributed to this or they were naturally intelligent. What was unknown, Sharm told him, was the effect on the next generation? Only time would tell.

Sunday was family day, a new reality for him but one he found enjoyable. Apparently, the concept started when Edith arrived at the castle. As a Grounder, she possessed the knack or gift for causing life to change around her. Either because she urged people to look at problems from a different perspective or because she was a catalyst for change. When he had asked Edith which one it was, she had smiled and said. "Call me Edee, and who the hell knows, does it really matter?"

Ace thought it did not. He could see this family day made Lady Verity happy, and that was all that mattered as far as he was concerned. It amused his dragon that it involved every member of the royal family, or anyone considered family. Everyone was encouraged gently by Lady Verity, or ordered by Lord Rene` to attend. He had enjoyed the family days and relished the contact with his growing family. Today marked two weeks since the meeting with his Shadow and Ace was feeling restless. Breakfast had finished about thirty minutes ago, which is why he was outside walking the well-worn path around the castle. He knew he was being observed by several unicorn stallions whom he supposed came to keep an eye on the male predator near their meadow. They had nothing to fear from him, his dragon was quiet today because as they had left the family room, Charlie mentioned Harper was returning today. Which made him content knowing she would be with him soon. The last few weeks had been an exercise in restraint that tested the renewed bonds between him and his dragon. It was just as well the long journey to return home, and the time spent alone united them once again as a team. Or else his dragon would have flown to be with Harper. Although he and his dragon were in a bit of a quandary on how to approach the feisty faerie. His dragon felt they should employ guile. Ace felt a direct approach would be better. So far, they had not reached an agreement.

As well as considering his approach to Harper, he also needed to decide on work. He, like his brothers, did not wish to return to scouting or leading a unit of Shields, those days he hoped were over. Rene` and Reighn said he could decide what position he wished to hold at home and as he laid awake again last night. He finally realized like Ash, he wanted to remain home to find a place here with his Shadow, of course, that depended now on her staying home. He sighed as he told his Dragon. *I did not know it was this complicated having a Shadow.*

His dragon snorted, then said. *No more than being in a battle. We plan for all contingencies and attack when she is not looking.*

I think that may not be the wisest thing to do with a Shadow. Especially one who is as handy as she is with knives.

His dragon huffed a breath. *I forgot about that.*

Ace let him see his grin. *I thought you had.*

He laughed now silently as he passed the last of the unicorn's meadow and out of the stallion's range. He walked along the side of the castle where there used to be stables and saw what everyone had told him was Harper's barn. He stopped to admire the building; it was impressive, someone had planted gardens around it. He would bet that was Mama Verity and Grace. It also looked like a new walkway to the doors had been laid. He remembered the art he'd seen when he went to the gallery. The only words he could think of to say about her pieces were inadequate to describe them, even to himself. In truth, he had been as stunned as Charlie. What he had seen humbled him for the talent she possessed. It was truly an insight to the female he was going to join the rest of his and his dragon's long life too. He knew Charlie had not left the gallery unscathed, either. In the two hours they were there, she learned a lot about her sister, more he thought than she really wanted to know.

CHAPTER EIGHTEEN:

His musings were interrupted by a sharp, demanding voice sneering. "What do you mean, you do not know? This is what you do, is it not?"

"No." A quavering voice replied, which if Ace was not wrong, seemed to belong to a young girl. He started making his way to where the voices were coming from when he heard the male say. "Really, you are my assistant and a shifter, and you cannot locate a few willing females to entertain me."

"I am not that kind of assistant."

"You are not any kind. Well, if I cannot have any shifter females. You will have to do."

"What?!" squealed the girl, and Ace's anger spiked at the fear he could hear in her voice. Why she was alone with this male, he did not understand. Surely she must have a family somewhere who should be protecting her, and he damn well would find out where they were. After he saw to this fool of a male.

The male's voice was more aggressive now as he snarled. "Come here, you little slut. I want what I was promised."

Just as Ace made the corner of the castle, he heard Clint ask. "What are you doing with Joy?"

"Be gone, you worthless scum, this does not concern you."

"Clint." cried the frightened girl.

"Shut up, slut."

Clint's dragon growled as he snarled. "Let her go, she does not belong to you."

"I will do what I like. I purchased her to service me and she damn well will."

Then, as Ace was ready to pummel the insolent male, he heard the familiar drawl of Johner's voice. "And what kind of service did you have in mind for our young Joy here? I know for a fact she was assigned to fetch and carry. I believe for you, while at Dragon's Gap, or so my Shadow told me. Was she lying Prince Tarin? Were you thinking of compromising one of our adolescent females? One who is hardly in her teen years?" His voice had become harder as he had spoken, and moved closer to the trio.

"He was." Snarled Clint, his dragon still not receding completely. "He wanted her to find him females to bed and then when she would not, he wanted her to do it." Proving, he had been close enough to hear everything that had been said. Before any of them could react, the Prince punched Clint on the side of his head, knocking him out. Joy screamed as Clint dropped to the ground in a crumpled heap and wrenched her arm free from the male's hold and fell to her knees beside the prone boy.

Ace had the male by his throat before the Prince knew he was there. His dragon rose to the surface as Ace's eyes elongated and crimson scales dusted his skin. His voice deepened, and when he spoke, the Prince swore he saw flames in his eyes. "You dare to touch my claim. I should kill you where you stand." Fear wafted from the Prince, as Ace squeezed his throat and to his surprise the male passed out.

"I think he pissed himself." Johner said as he rose from where he had been tending to Clint.

Ace grunted in disgust.

"Asshole faerie." Johner pulled his phone from his pocket to call Sharm and tell him what had happened, and ask him to call June.

Ace, with a flick of his hand, threw the male away from him. He and Johner watched the Prince as his body skidded across the dirt and his stomach caught on an exposed root. Finally, coming to rest in a tangle of limbs. Ace shrugged as Johner raised his eyebrows at him.

"Sorry, forgot my own strength. Is Clint alright?"

Johner nodded. "He better be. The females will kill that

ass, if he isn't." He indicated the Prince lying groaning on the ground.

Ace looked at the young girl. She was lucky if she was out of her teens. She had long, sable hair and a narrow face that housed bright blue eyes. As with all young wolves, she had long limbs that gave her a coltish look. But unlike other young wolves, her clothes hung on her thin frame and he could almost taste her hunger. Anger boiled within him, and he quickly soothed his dragon. *Calm down, we will care for her.*

His dragon growled. *She is young and frightened. She is hungry.*

I know we will feed her.

With Ace's assurances, his dragon's anger faded thankfully, he did not want to frighten her. The young girl was barely hanging on as it was. In fact, if it wasn't for Clint lying on the ground, Ace was sure she would have bolted by now. He called his brother. "Axl, find me and bring two of your sandwiches and a protein shake. Thanks, and make it fast." He grinned when he heard his brother cussing as he closed his phone. He turned his green eyes on the young wolf and asked. "Now who are you?"

She brushed the hair from Clint's face before she answered. "I am Joy... Joy Danners. Clint's friend, why do you need food?"

Ace looked down at her. "I do not, you do. I can feel your hunger from here."

She made a face and blushed, it was true she was starving; she had not eaten yesterday or today. She was going to meet Clint and get some food with him later.

Ace smiled and said. "Also, you have not had a sandwich like my brothers. Do not tell him I said so, but his sandwiches are to die for, as my brother's Shadow, Olinda would say."

She smiled as she mumbled. "I like Olinda."

"Who does not?" He crouched down next to her and asked. "Where are your parents?"

She shrugged. "I do not know." She looked at him from the

side of her eyes as she whispered. "My mother never came with me. She made me leave. She was very sick, I think she is dead."

"Who has been looking after you?" She shrugged again and mumbled. "Clint and me."

Ace raised her face with a finger under her chin. "And have you been living alone in the dorms, like Clint?"

She shook her head no. "I have been living with some others."

"I see, and how do you know Clint?"

She smiled. "We met at the center last week. He helped me get a job."

"This job?" Ace could see he needed to have words with Clint. The boy may have thought he was helping the girl, and he was, but it would have been better to tell him about her.

"Other jobs like this, he said it was easy."

"What age are you, little wolf?"

She sat up straight and lifted her chin, looked him in the eyes and lied. "Fifteen."

Ace nodded and said. "I give you an A, for effort. Now the truth."

Her shoulders slumped and her chin lowered as she mumbled. "Twelve."

"Okay, now the ones who gave you this job. Do they know how old you are?"

She nodded with a frown. "Clint would have told them. I was just meant to show that guy around. You know, fetch stuff; that was all. I swear."

Ace smoothed a hand down her hair as he calmed her. "I know, young one. I understand. Do you know who hired you?" She shook her head. Ace asked. "So you have been living rough for how long?"

She ducked her head. "A long time, even before I came here, my mother was not good at keeping a job. When the tiger came through the town where we were, she made him take me. I was hoping I would find someone I knew from before, but there is no one here."

Ace knew she meant from her pack. Johner asked softly. "So where have you been staying?"

"I was living with the others."

"What others?" Johner asked.

She sighed and rubbed her eyes and whispered. "We sleep all over the place."

"Here at Dragon's Gap?" Johner asked, stunned that this was going on and he did not know or that Conor or Claire did not. Things were slipping if this young wolf was falling through the cracks.

She nodded as she bit her lip. "Yes, my Lord."

Saddened, Johner shook his head. "This is not right... Not right at all."

Just then, Ace saw Axl loping over to where they were. He stood and moved a few feet away to meet him. Axl stilled when his eyes met Joy's, then he seemed to shake all over like a wolf.

She watched as the brothers talked. It was easy to see they were brothers. They looked so much alike and she could tell they liked each other. She felt a wave of loneliness swamp her, which was instantly superseded by comfort. It was as though a blanket was wrapped around her, making her feel safe and warm. Then everything went from her mind as the delicious aroma of food moved closer.

Ace walked back after talking quietly to Axl, who had grinned and loped off again. He handed the food to the young girl after she jumped to her feet and her hand was inside the bag before he had passed her the shake. Then she moaned in appreciation, her eyes lighting up after she had taken the first bite.

Ace grinned as he said. "I know, remember not a word."

She giggled around her mouthful and nodded as he pointed to the ground, away from Clint. She nodded and sat, crossing her legs as she plowed through the first sandwich. Axle had given her two sandwiches and several of his cookies, or the cookies that Bay had made for him, as well as the protein shake. Johner watched her with a worried frown on his face until they heard voices coming closer. He spun around as Sage, June and Reighn, accompanied by Sharm, and several of his healers, arrived.

Sharm raced to Clint as Reighn demanded. "Sage, slow down. You will hurt yourself and my young."

Sage ignored him as she came to a halt and swore. "Hell's bells, I thought he would behave himself with a female to assist him."

June asked. "Where is she, the assistant?"

Ace pointed to Joy. Sage paled, as did June, who groaned. "Oh no."

Sage shook her head as her eyes took in the skinny young girl eating, if she was not mistaken, an Axl sandwich, she mumbled. "Oh, that looks so good."

June growled. "Sage, keep your mind on business, not food. We have a disaster here."

"Yes... Yes, of course, Frankie is going to be so angry with me." She looked around at all the people there, and her shoulders slumped. "There is just no way I can stop her from finding out."

June agreed. "You are in so much trouble, she told you, and Johner, the ass would not behave himself, regardless of who you gave him. She is going to be so pissed."

Mournfully, Sage looked at Johner. "I know, Johner, what do we do?"

He spread his hands. "Hope Frankie and Harper do not find out."

"Oh my Goddess, Harper!" Sage screeched. "She will absolutely kill me." She pointed at the adolescent female still eating and demanded to know. "Is that a cookie... that looks good, too?"

June hissed at her. "Sage, keep your mind on what is happening."

"But I am hungry." She wailed. "Please tell me she is sixteen… eighteen?"

Ace almost laughed at her hopeful look. "Sorry, she is not even thirteen."

June asked. "Wolf."

Ace told them. "Without a pack."

"Fuck." Both females cursed together, looking at each other.

Ace nodded. "Exactly, I will take her with Clint. She will be safe with me."

"Alright." June nodded. Young wolves needed to belong to a pack, or they chose badly. June had first-hand knowledge of what happened to pack-less young girls.

Sage whispered to June. "She will be okay with Ace at least Frankie cannot be mad about that."

June whispered back. "Do not count on it."

Reighn sighed loudly as he surveyed the battered body of the faerie prince. "Damn it Ace, really?"

"He told her to service him." Ace replied.

Several sets of eyes looked from a fearful Joy, who had finished eating and had hurriedly stepped behind Ace.

"And he still lives. I admire your restraint." Reighn said as he picked his Shadow up and carried her away, amongst her squealed complaints and June's laughter.

"So my problem then? You know if my Frankie blames me, you are naming one of your hatchlings after me." Johner yelled to Reighn's back. Only to be answered by male laughter and squeals from Sage.

He grinned at Ace and walked to meet Conor and Claire, who had arrived and were now talking to June. Johner was going to need all the help he could get. This was a problem for the Gap and the castle. No young person, no one at all, should be without a home.

Ace could see June, Conor and Claire's shoulders tense and their spines straighten as Johner spoke. He figured they would handle that problem. His problem was this sweet young female that was standing behind him, watching

Sharm treat Clint while she devoured the protein shake. He moved her aside as Sharm and several males picked Clint up and placed him on a stretcher. He turned and saw another three males doing the same for the Prince. Sharm asked both Ace and Joy a few questions about what happened? How long had both males been unconscious? When he was satisfied with their answers, he gave the girl a smile, then told her to come and see Clint later. Nodded to Ace with a knowing smile and followed the stretchers.

Frankie arrived just as they were being carried away. She placed her hands on her slim hips and demanded in tones no one had ever heard her use before. "What the hell happened?"

Ace almost laughed as he saw Johner's shoulders hitch around his neck. "Frankie, my heart..."

"So not... you... you..." She pointed a finger at Joy, then Ace, and then Johner and growled loudly. Stamped her foot and swiveled around, yelling over her shoulder. "Fix this Johner or no loving time for you."

Joy stood wide-eyed as she watched Johner slowly turn red and Frankie storm away. "Oh wow!"

Ace agreed with her, Frankie, in a temper, was impressive. "So I have a spare room." Before she could speak, he said. "You know Clint lives with me. My Shadow and I will enjoy having you live with us. Now when Clint is healed, together you will collect your things and go with him to my place and make sure he does nothing else to get himself knocked out."

Joy giggled and said. "Oh, you mean stupid?"

"Yes that too."

"He is gentle and sweet." She said. "He wants to be a healer."

Ace could hear the concern in her voice, and to waylay any more worries, he told her. "He is one of the finest males I know. Who will be a healer? Now what do you wish to do?"

She ducked her head and toed the dirt. Softly, with a slight hesitation in her voice, she told him. "I want to go to school. I enjoy learning."

Ace smiled. "I as well enjoy learning. You young lady have joined the right pack. We all love a good book. You do like books?"

She giggled again. "Yep, I love the library."

Ace nodded. "Good, off you go." He held out some money. "Get more food, do not..." He looked at her seriously. "Go hungry again. If you run out of money, find me or my brothers or Olinda. They will give you more, also find something nice to wear. You and Clint will be required at the family dinner tonight."

"Oh but..."

He held his hand up to stop her words. "Lady Verity is not to be trifled with. She will know, she like Lady Charlie, knows everything."

Joy giggled again, showing her youth once more. "Okay, so I should buy something..."

Claire came over. "It's okay Ace; I will sort it out."

"Thank you Claire." She looked at Joy and then at Ace. "No thank you, she will thrive as your claim."

Ace smiled. "It is all I can ask for."

Joy looked at the hundred dollar note he held out to her and then at his face, then back at the money. "That is a lot of money."

Ace opened her hand and placed the note in it. "Good. It will be enough to feed you and find you something to wear. If not, Claire will pay, and I will pay her back. Do not worry Joy; you are not alone anymore."

Tears flowed down her face and before he realized what she was going to do. She was in his arms, sobbing her relief and fear away. With a look of wonder and sympathy shared with Claire, Ace's arms hugged the young wolf, as hers gripped him. After a few minutes she sniffed, then wheezed out. "Okay, thank you, Ace."

"It is my pleasure. Welcome to my family, little wolf."

She released him and went with Claire, who smiled and

told him. "She will be okay."

He sighed as his dragon said. *We claimed her.*

Of course we did.

His dragon smiled. *Hope our Shadow likes teenagers.*

Ace hoped so as well. He looked to where the others had been and realized he was the only one left. As he was about to continue on with his journey, he felt someone at his back. Turning, he came face to face with two hard-faced, unyielding faerie warriors. Both were dressed in black leathers, with swords sheathed on their backs. The only difference between the two was one was taller than the other, otherwise they were almost identical, with long brown hair, weathered faces and dark eyes. Ace knew these faeries were from the Forest Dwellers Grove, reputed to be the most vicious of fighters. Ace felt his dragon shift to watch them. "Warriors."

The one on the left greeted him. "Commander Battle."

"Do I know you?"

The one on the left smiled. "I do not think we have been introduced. I am Daru. This is Mercca."

"What can I do for you?"

"We are looking for Prince Tarin. We have been assigned as his guards."

"I see. Would he be about this high?" He raised his hand to the height of his nose. "With long brown hair that needs a wash. Rumpled clothes, blood coming from his ears with several bruises around his throat, in the shape of a hand print."

Daru nodded. "Yes, that would just about describe him, minus the blood and bruises."

Ace nodded. "Last I saw of him, he was on his way to medical."

Mercca said. "We thank you for your help Commander Battle."

Daru casually asked. "Would you know what caused all those bruises and blood you spoke of?"

Ace nodded. "A guardian of a young female wolf aged twelve."

Daru frowned, anger pulsed from him and the other warrior. Their eyes darkened as he said. "It seems the guardian had no choice."

"Female pup. No choice at all." Mercca agreed.

"That is so. Now gentlemen, please call me Ace. I am unsure if you a familiar with my brothers?"

Daru nodded. "We have not met, but we know of the Battle brothers."

Ace bet they did. As warriors and guards, they would have felt it was their duty to know everyone who could be a danger to the Grove or their charge. "I and my brothers are starting a weekly poker game with the Kingsley's brothers and a few of the lions. Do you play?"

They both grinned and nodded. "We do."

"Next Friday at Ark's place."

"We will be there." Said Daru. They saluted Ace, then shrunk and flew toward the medical center. Ace grinned and shoved his hands into his pockets and continued his stroll. He was no closer to any answers.

His dragon told him. *But we were entertained and have another claim to look after.*

Ace agreed. *That we were my friend. Life is looking good.*

CHAPTER NINETEEN:

While the family was gathering for dinner. Ace was again explaining what had taken place earlier in the day, and when Clint and Joy arrived, the family immediately embraced them.

Not just as Ace's claims, but because what happened horrified them all. With Claire's help, Joy had shopped, and she was positive she spent far more than the hundred dollars Ace had given her. But Claire kept telling her it was okay and that Ace would be fine with what she spent. So she just brought items Claire told her she needed. She had picked out a dress in green and a nice pair of bronze shoes with a little heel to wear to dinner. And for the first time in weeks, if not months, she felt clean.

Claire had taken her to a hair salon where she had her hair professionally washed and cut and her nails manicured and a pretty pink polish applied. She felt like a million dollars. Joy was amazed at the welcome she received, even though Clint had told her it would be like this, she was a little overwhelmed. She stared shyly around her as Axl and Clint guided her through the introductions. They seemed to have appointed themselves her guards, which amused Ace. Clint, being a teenager, took all the adulation as his due for being a hero.

"You did good." Edith murmured as she stopped next to him. "Mama Verity is in love, and Papa Rene` has her enrolled in school already."

Ace smiled. "She likes school."

"She is delightful. Sage and I will take her shopping tomorrow and get her more clothes and school clothes."

"Thank you Edee."

She grinned. "She likes art. You may want to remember that."

"I will."

CHAPTER TWENTY:

Harper drove through the tunnel of trees and chuckled to herself, remembering how she left weeks earlier and wondered what became of the dragon she had encountered. She also wondered if Reighn had cooled off in the time she had been gone.

In the weeks she had been away, she'd traveled to England with the Retrievers and Hunters. Where they took down a cartel of humans and shifters while rescuing several hundred males, females, and children. She then went on four more rescues and joined with teams who were involved in breaking up several traffickers.

She personally sent at least fifteen males and females who thought it was a good idea to sell young female shifters to the afterlife. Then she worked two more jobs until she felt the darkness living inside her try to break free. It was a sign to call it quits for a while and return to the people who loved her and center herself once more. She needed home. She had done one last pick up and returned to the Gap.

The night was dark, no moon showed through the clouds as she drove her car full of physically and emotionally battered and bruised females to the medical center. The Retrievers had rescued thirty shifters from some depraved humans who thought they ruled their small corner of the world. And believed they were within their rights to hold shifters against their will. Usually the Commander of the mission would call in the Hunters, after those that needed rescuing had been driven away. When that happened, dragons would come and take over the town, establishing law and order if they could. This time the Commander had called in the flaming dragon unit to administer the Dragon

Lord's Justice. Harper had seen the flames for miles as she drove her carload of people from the town.

Putting all that to the back of her mind, she sighed as she looked out the window, seeing the tunnel coming to its end. She loved the way the trees formed the tunnel and even loved the barrier of Dragon magic she passed through. She was happy to be home, smiling, she finally admitted to herself this was home. She may as well get used to the idea, ever since she and Frankie had come to Dragon's Gap, to confront, or some might say yell, at her sister, Charlie. She knew there was no other place she wanted to live. She sighed again, but this time it was a sigh of happiness. She and Charlie were well on their way to fixing their relationship. Her love for Charlie was a more mature one now. She adored Charlie's kids, who actually loved her in return, and as for Storm; she thought he was the most honest male she had ever met. Blunt and straight forward, there was no hidden agenda within him. He was what he was, a male that adored his young and loved his Shadow to her bones and found Harper amusing. It made her happy to know Charlie got it right.

Her relationship with the Queen and King of the Faerie Grove was more complicated, and she knew it was of her own making. She'd thought long and hard during her absence and decided it was time to repair what she had broken. She knew she needed to talk to Scarlett, needed to explain her anger. It was going to be hard to confront, and not just for her. Dragging up all that happened in the past may not be wise but she told herself, needs must. And she would fix it this time while she was home. Frankie was right, not much good came from hiding in her work; be that her barn where her art was or out on the road. Even if she really liked what she did.

Clearing the tunnel, something heavy lifted from her shoulders and music filled her mind. Stirring her blood and making her think of long ago places and flying dragons returning home from battle. It was a song to a warrior of welcome. Then a softer, more enticing tune over shadowed the other, it sang of longing and a promise for a future. The feeling of it almost made her heart stop and tears fill her eyes. She had never heard either song before, but every time she returned, something new was happening at the Gap. *So music yeah! She could live with that.*

As the songs faded, she let herself relax. This was home where people knew and cared about her, loved her. A place that wanted and adored her so much it sang to her. As her passengers started to wake from their exhausted sleep, she drove toward the building where people waited to see to all their needs. To welcome them home.

Harper was hurting, her body had taken a beating from the weeks of wrestling females like these from the people who had them hidden away. The thought of the people who held females captive made her teeth ache, along with a rib or two. Which she assumed were probably broken, and she thought she had bruised kidneys as well. Some males thought hitting a female was a good choice. Unfortunately for them, Harper was not one to allow such behavior to go unpunished. They would hit no more females or children ever again. She looked at the wide-eyed fearful females as they murmured tearfully and said. "Calm, we are at Dragon's Gap. A haven for your kind."

The female next to her, who was maybe in her forties, said. "We thank you for your kindness; you mean our kind, right?"

Harper grinned, which was becoming easier to do, another thing that amused her. "Close enough. I am taking you to the center where people will help you and answer all your questions. They will make sure you are cared for and have food. You are safe here. My name is Harper Easton, if you should need me."

"We thank you again, Harper. My name is Lisa."

Harper pulled up in front of the center as people silently and slowly moved from within. "No thanks are necessary. It is what I do and Lisa, I mean it. If you find you need me, ask for Harper or for Frankie, she will know where I am."

"Do you do this for all your rescues?"

"Yep everyone, and so far no one has had to ask for my help but I like to put it out there." She pointed to the people coming closer. "These people are really kind, I suspect more than you have ever known before." The doors were opened, and soft voices urged the occupants out. Harper nodded to Lisa. "Go, get what you need, that is why they are here."

Lisa said quietly, not looking at Harper. "It is hard to trust."

"Then don't, just do the days. Each one will bring something new and trust will come in time."

"Okay." Lisa breathed out on a sigh. "Yeah, we can do the days." With that, it seemed all the females and young gathered their courage and exited her car.

When the last one closed the door, Harper eased her foot onto the gas and moved slowly from the center, and drove to the castle. She knew Frankie and Johner were installed in the family upper level of the castle, as he was a son and brother to the past and present Dragon Lord. Which made Frankie royalty. It amused Harper thinking of Frankie trying to come to terms with that while she'd been away.

She was to live alone in her barn and knew she would love every minute of it. Occasionally she was lonesome for Frankie, not that she would admit that to anyone. Especially not Charlie or Frankie, and never to Reighn, who for some weird reason had decided she needed a big brother. She thought maybe that was why she stayed away, because she was lonely, which seemed weird as she never had been before. Harper got out of the car and gingerly stretched. She had been in her vehicle for a total of nineteen hours this time, and away almost two weeks. She looked up at the sky and saw dragons flying. The sight was enough to catch the breath in her throat.

"You have been away a long time." Reighn said, with his dragon deepening his voice. Harper had known he was there in the shadows. She always knew where dragons were. It was a quirk she had developed since she came to live here.

"I have, it took a while to take down the cartel and fish out the others and then to make this run. But it was time to come home, and this seems to be home."

Reighn laughed softly. "Why the tone of surprise? All know this, but you apparently. Anyway, you have been missed."

Harper debated the wisdom of scoffing at the idea that anyone other than the loved up Frankie had missed her and shrugged. She was tired and too sore to swap quips with Reighn. Instead, she said. "Okay, so what is for dinner? It is Sunday, right?"

"Yes."

Sunday was family day, meaning everyone that was considered family, and that included Harper attended, if possible. Reighn stepped from the shadows. "The usual, you have thirty minutes, then she will come hunting you."

"Yeah, I figured." She hugged him, a spontaneous act, something she had never done before.

Reighn frowned, he adored Harper, she amused and entertained him and his dragon constantly. What she never did was hug. "Harper, little one, what has happened?"

"Music, so sad and graceful it hurt my heart and soul. I have never heard a tune like it before."

"Hum it for me sister."

She did and was amazed the tune came so readily to mind. "Dragon song." Reighn said and laughed softly. "Someone has marked you for their Shadow."

Harper pulled away and laughed. "No way, you are kidding me, right?"

"No." He shook his head. "Sorry Harper, you are officially betrothed."

"No. I refuse."

Reighn walked beside her as they entered the castle. "Is it just because you are contrary or scared?"

Harper growled. "Both and Reighn, you know I am right. Death greets me at every turn. Why would I want to place someone in the middle of that?"

"Maybe because they can stand between you and death, sweet girl. Now I have a question for you, Claire told you of your Shadow, why are you now surprised?"

She shrugged, uncomfortable with the question. "I don't know. I figured she was wrong. I mean, what are the odds, seriously!"

"Claire is never wrong, and the odds were always in your favor. He is here. Think on that as you change for dinner. I will send Ella to you."

"Don't send Ella. I will be okay, give me fifteen and I will be there, I promise."

"As you will, Harper. I wish for you to remain home for a while. You have not worked in your barn for weeks. The family misses you."

"As I have missed them."

"Stay home, do your art."

"I will, I need to. I appreciate it, you know?" She sighed. "More than I thought I ever would."

He ran his hand down her back, feeling the bruises and tenderness of her skin. "I know you do."

"See you soon." She waved over her shoulder as she walked down the long hallway that would cut through the castle to her barn. She could have parked her car closer to it. But she too, needed to be greeted by someone who wanted to see her and would be happy she was home. And she had wanted the hug. *Damn it, she was becoming addicted.* She sighed, she had forgotten to ask him about the song that came from the stones, *friggin hell!*

She left a quietly amused and pleased Dragon Lord behind. He turned his head, acknowledging the fire dragon as he came from the shadows. "She is receptive to your song and hungers for the bond of a Shadow, but she may kill you before you get to the mating."

"It is a challenge." Ace replied in his deep voice, his dragon riding close to the surface with his Shadow now home. "She was hurt?"

"Yes, it is normal for her. Harper fights hard with swords or knives, failing that, hand to hand. She has no half measures."

Ace looked at him as they moved along the wide stone hallway toward the dining room. "You love her?"

"I have claimed her as ours."

"Is this going to be a problem?"

"With any other it would have been, but with you, as I said before, no. Sage believes you are the right male for Harper. You will understand her, and I can already feel the love you have for her."

"Thank you. It is amazing to think she is an artist."

"As you have seen, a brilliant one. Harper is our resident dichotomy, as my Shadow would say."

"Charlie does not strike me as one to allow her to do as she does. She must worry?"

"Charlie most definitely does. I do not think she realized how much Harper would put into this. It worries her, but she will not ask her to quit, as much as she wants her to. They are still working on their relationship. It is hard for them both, betrayed and hunted, alone in the world, believing the other was dead. For many years, they had no one, just their fear and pain to teach them and keep them safe. It is amusing, or should I say intriguing how they both became hunters. Maybe it is in the genes."

"Maybe or perhaps it was a necessity." Ace offered instead.

Reighn smiled and inclined his head. "Yes, there is that. So you will bond with her now she is home."

"No courting?" Ace asked, truly wishing to know. He had thought to court her for a few days or weeks until she accepted him.

Reighn looked out at the night and stated. "Harper will not allow that. I feel she will take what you offer freely. She needs you, probably as much as you need her. I have made it clear she is to remain here for the foreseeable future and that should give you ample time to win her heart."

"She is ours. We have hunted as long as you did for your Shadow. We recognized her as soon as we entered our borders. What is that hum?"

"You can feel that?"

"Yes, it comes from beneath us?"

Reighn nodded. "From the Ancients, they sing every time she comes back. The old ones know she is home. Your song startled her, called to her soul. It is not like you to lose control as you did tonight?"

Ace shrugged. "My dragon was overcome with joy; he is most repentant." He looked toward the ceiling as Reighn hid his laugh at the obvious lie.

Rene` said as he came up behind them. "The Ancients song. I noticed it the first time she arrived at the castle. It is that, I believe, which made my dragon unsettled that day. Ace my son. Harper is your Shadow?"

Ace acknowledged his question with a dip of his head. "She is."

Reighn smiled. "Papa admit it; she is the Seeker; the Ancients sing for her. It means something and you know what it means, the Ancients told me, and the histories speak of it." He quoted for Rene` and Ace. "Only when the Seeker and the Bringer of Justice are together will the wild ones return."

"Unbelievable. That means Charlie and Harper will call all wild dragons home. Are you certain this is what they said?" Rene` asked, thinking of the implications to Dragon's Gap.

Reighn smiled as he said. "Yes, there was no mistake. Keeper has researched the histories and there is mention several times of this possibility."

Ace asked. "So, does this mean there will be no more wild dragons?"

Rene` ventured his opinion. "Who is to say? I would assume that is what it means."

"Well, that is going to grow Dragon's Gap, in a major way. Are we ready for that?" Ace asked Reighn.

"Hopefully, they will not return all at once." Rene` muttered.

Reighn smiled. "I feel they will come as and when they feel the call."

"Lord Rene`." Ace asked. "What are your thoughts on Harper now?"

Rene` rubbed his face. "She is more than a Retriever or half-blood faerie, she is the Seeker. The one spoken about in our histories. We must convince her to remain at Dragon's Gap. You must."

"I will do my best."

Reighn said quietly. "You worry for nothing, Papa. She will not leave. Her home is here, and the people she loves are here."

"She does not seem settled." Rene` said with worry in his voice.

"Ace will see to that as her Shadow, it is how love works, or at least that is what you told me." Reighn challenged his father to contradict him.

Rene` grinned and raised an eyebrow at the neat little trap his son had set for him. "I did, and it does. Believe it or not. I do enjoy her as I do Charlie. She grows on one."

"Yes she does." Reighn agreed as he looked at the male standing next to them and nodded to him and then Rene`, who nodded back. Rene` told him in the voice he reserved for his sons when they had to front up to their mother, about something they had done, and were dawdling over it. "Ace, you had better tell my Verity before she finds out from someone else. She will not be pleased if that happens."

Ace grinned, a look they were all getting used to seeing on his normally harsh features. "I will. In fact, I will tell her now."

CHAPTER TWENTY-ONE:

Harper was tired, deep down, bone tired. Her body ached, her soul hurt, and her heart was just ticking over one beat at a time. She had not seen the inside of her workshop for so long, she could not remember what it looked like. If she could have ducked this dinner, she would have, but a promise was a promise.

She sucked air into her abused lungs, feeling the broken ribs and bruising on her sides and back. If she was lucky, she may be able to get Ella to heal her quietly and quickly before Sage found out. Or Goddess forbid, her over-protective sister- and dragon-in-law Storm. Ever since they had reunited, Charlie climbed all over her ass about her safety.

It was unnerving because she liked it and that told her it was weird and there was that other thing. Who knew she would be the best auntie in the whole of Dragon's Gap? Not her, that's for sure, Frankie said she knew, but she lied and badly, really badly. Harper grinned as she thought about the young ones, and then there was Sage and Reighn. She shuddered to think what would happen if she wasn't here to reel them in on the names they were trying to saddle their unborn or unhatched twins with.

So here she was, trying to walk straight and slip unnoticed into what used to be a state dining hall, but was now the family's private dining room. Called, of all things, the Sunday family room. She just knew Sage came up with that name. Why June and Claire had not stopped her, or even Edith, she did not know. Seriously, she had to stay home just to be the voice of reason, because the others were all falling down on the job. Secretly, she loved family day, not that she would let Verity know. She adored the fact when they were all here in this room with the little ones and the older family members, there were no titles. No lords or ladies, just family, and Harper liked everything about that. She was not the only one who did. Happiness hung in the air throughout the room.

Harper spied Reighn and said as she slipped next to him. "Reighn, call off your Mama. I am here."

"Just in time." He made a pretence of looking at his non-existence watch. Much to Kelsey's amusement, she hugged Harper around the knees. "You sore Auntie Harper?"

After the first few retrievals, Kelsey had learned to ask before she jumped all over Harper. Now she and the other little ones would hug her around her knees unless she had been home for a few days. Then they knew the pain would be gone. She leaned down and hugged her niece, not allowing the groan to pass her lips. "Yeah, just a little."

"Okay, are we painting tomorrow?"

Harper always went to the playroom the kids used for painting when she was home. "We will see in the morning, don't you have school?"

Her sad face, which Harper was sure Charlie was teaching her, hurriedly changed to a smile. "Yep, I forgot."

"Well, next Saturday you can wake me in the morning but not too early." She qualified when she saw her delighted eyes. She had made that mistake only once. Waking one morning not long after she had arrived to find several young ones in her bed at four in the morning had been a shock.

"Yea!" Kelsey ran off. No doubt to tell every child there that Harper was home and they could go see her barn on Saturday.

"They love the barn, not me so much." She told Reighn and Sage when she joined them, who laughed.

Sage snorted, then said. "You know nothing; it is not the barn. They adore you and miss you like crazy when you are away."

Reighn agreed. "As we all do."

Harper looked at Sage, who was literally glowing since becoming pregnant, and said. "No, I dislike every one of them."

She pouted. "How do you know? Some of those names are good. You haven't even heard them yet?"

Harper asked. "Did you think them up?"

"Some, others I found in old books."

Harper nodded. "Then no." Sage stamped her foot and stormed off. Harper grinned and said to Reighn. "Love her so much, she does try hard. You have to be stronger. Some of those names she sent me were ridiculous."

Reighn spread his hands. "How? She is carrying my hatchlings. I do not want to hurt her."

Harper blew air from between her lips. "Yeah, I see that, just as well I am here then."

"It is, isn't it?" Reighn agreed, refraining from telling her Sage and he had spent nights scouring old manuscripts for the worse sounding names to send her. Just so she would return home, it looked like their mission was accomplished. He was pleased, he was becoming worried Sage might actually like some of the recent names they had picked out. He growled now. "You live a dangerous life female, going up against my Shadow."

"Huh! I am doomed for Shadow-hood, apparently. So got to get my kicks where I can."

"Doomed, you amuse me, female."

"I live for that alone." She quipped back. "Oh wait, I meant to ask you. What is the hum I heard earlier when I got home? I do not mean the dragon song."

Reighn rubbed the back of his neck as he told her. "You have been touched by the Ancient ones. This castle is built on the bones of dragons of old and they sing to you. It has never happened before, to anyone, not even me and I am the Dragon Lord."

Harper looked up into the eyes of the dragon, who had broken into her heart and helped start her healing, and asked. "So why me?"

"You are the Seeker, the ghost. The fighter of demons."

Her breath whooshed out of her as her mind wobbled. She struggled to regain her equilibrium as she asked faintly. "Oh, you know about that?"

He placed his hand on her arm, and there came a barely audible growl from Ace standing in the shadowed corner. Reighn raised one brow at the dragon, who sighed and returned to watching the unicorns in the meadow as his brothers surrounded him. Harper, unaware of the silent conversation between Reighn and Ace, regained her balance and looked up at Reighn, who said. "I do. It is not public knowledge. It was incredibly brave of you and Charlie."

"Yeah, maybe, or one could say too young and stupid to know better."

"I think not. You have paid for that decision and you need to tell Charlie why you pushed her away."

"Yeah, I have, mostly. I also need to talk to Scarlett and Elijah. Can you set a meeting up, please Reighn?"

"I am shocked you called them by their names and not those damn faeries."

Harper smiled. "Kelsey growls when I do."

He laughed. "I adore her."

"You adore all the young."

"That I do. I will set the meeting up."

"Thank you, better include Charlie, so she won't yell at me."

"That is what you hope."

"Well, you can come and protect me and bring that crazy Shadow of yours too."

"We will accept your gracious invitation." He half bowed.

"Ha-ha. I laugh at you." She scoffed.

He grinned as he left her to find his Shadow and make a phone call. Harper took a careful breath, looking around for Frankie, when she felt Charlie throw an arm around her shoulders. Which was another thing, they were always hugging. Even friggin Charlie, and she was still not comfortable with it. Although she was a little in awe of Verity, so she sucked it up as that lady had told her too. And did not complain loudly as much as she wanted to. Charlie grinned as she said. "So sis, how's it going?"

Harper just managed to hold back a groan of pain as she hissed. "It's going."

"Good, good, so there's this thing." Charlie hesitatingly said.

Harper sighed quietly. Charlie had officially taken over command of the Retrievers when Sage found out she was pregnant. All about the time she and Frankie had arrived at Dragon's Gap. Fortuitously, some might say, Harper was more suspicious. She believed someone was tampering with her and her family, although she kept her suspicions to herself. The people of Dragon's Gap had absorbed her and Frankie like missing pieces of a puzzle, which still made her scratch her head in surprise. Not so much Frankie, which she understood, everyone loved Frankie, she was weird, but this town accepted that. But, because she had seldom been home, she was still new to the people of Dragon's Gap and yet they accepted her without reservation. She was unsure if it was because of Frankie, Charlie, or because she was an artist. She could not remember actually doing anything when she was home to make an impression on people. So it was always a surprise when Charlie or Reighn told her. Harper the Knife, a nickname she adored, had friends among the warriors and retrievers. And this was why she viewed everything with a healthy dose of skepticism. In her experience, slotting into a situation like a town or family was never this easy. So her conclusion was divine intervention of some sort and one day she would get to the bottom of it. Of course, it was possible the people of Dragon's Gap were just nice, like Frankie said, but Harper remained wary just in case. Eyeing her sibling, she said. "Spill it, don't dither Charlie, it is most annoying."

"I will have you know, I do not dither."

"Yeah, you do, and more so recently. Dear Goddess, has Storm knocked you up?"

Charlie frown at her. "No, even if he did, what is it with the face?"

Harper quickly removed the look of horror from her face and said. "There was no look, and it is obvious isn't it, if you get egged up. Who looks after the Retrievers? It will not be me."

Charlie teased. "But you would be great at it."

"So he got you egged then?"

"No." Charlie snarled. "Don't call it egged, is that what you say to Sage and Reighn?"

Harper grinned. "It wasn't, but it is now." She laughed as she thought of the horrified look Sage would get when she said it. A sight which caused Charlie to just stare at her and then remove her arm. "I will get Ella, never mind about the other matter."

Harper sniffed. "Oh shut up, I laughed. I am not hysterical, seriously Charlie lighten up." She glanced at her and saw the wounded look that came over her face, which was quickly smoothed away when she noticed her looking. She softened her voice. "Charlie, I am thrilled to be home. I have spent the last few weeks thinking and sorting out my feelings. That is all, and truthfully I feel good about my decisions and apparently I am to be bonded to some dragon that sings to me."

"And you are not angry?"

"No." She smiled at Charlie. "If I can be half as happy as you are with Storm, how can that be a bad thing? Now give me the details, so I can go. Is it time sensitive?"

Charlie grimaced. "Yeah, aren't they all?"

They both jumped a little when June stepped up to the two of them and slipped the paper from Charlie's fingers. "I will go. Reighn has said Harper is not to go out again."

Charlie said. "June that is not a good idea."

Harper agreed. "Sage, will be unhappy."

June looked at Charlie and Harper. "Excuse me, I was with Sage when we first started the retrievals and I am quite capable of looking after myself."

"What will Sage and Fin say?" Charlie asked softly. Everyone knew, well everyone but Harper that Fin was trying to court the wily wolf.

"Why will they say anything? I am not a child to be asking permission; I am capable and healthier than Harper at the moment. No offense."

"Oh, none taken, truth is truth." Harper said with a grin.

"Charlie, I will get it done. I will make it okay. I promise."

Charlie smiled, but it did not reach her eyes. She was unhappy, but she could not say no. June was as far as she knew a very good Retriever and, as she said, she was no child. June whispered. "Charlie, I need this. I need to go out for a while. I need to clear my head, please don't make me beg."

"Oh June, never. Go... go and stay safe. Get dead and I will kill you myself."

June nodded, and with a small smile said. "See you in a few days, and Charlie, thank you."

She hurriedly slipped from the room as both Charlie and Harper watched her go. "Do you think I did the right thing?"

Harper whispered. "She is an adult, slightly crazy even for a wolf, but still a deadly female. Yeah, you did okay, why Fin?"

"He is trying to court the crazy wolf. And thanks, now go sit down before you fall. I will send Ella to you."

"Yeah... Yeah, nag... nag."

"Do not make me get Frankie."

"Sure, pull out the big guns."

"So funny." Charlie grinned as she moved off to get Ella.

Harper walked over and eased herself down onto a window seat, and closed her eyes. Letting the moonlight that broke through the clouds soothe her. She was sure she had only shut them for a minute, when she felt her wrist circled by fingers. Not bothering to open her eyes, she just went along with the healing, feeling the warmth from the healing magic flow up her arm and into her body. Finding all the places she had been hurt. She heard a sharp, in-drawn breath and frowned. Sharm never made a noise when he healed, and she knew it wasn't Ella, because like Frankie. Ella had to talk, especially if it was to scold her, which she did frequently. But it had to be someone she knew. Her internal alarm had not gone off, plus the family had not killed whoever it was. Raising her heavy eyelids, because sleep was near impossible when she wasn't at home now, also the weight of her injuries caused her to feel her exhaustion. She was and was not surprised to see her dragon. *Damn it, did I just think, my dragon?*

Ace Battle, the fire dragon she had squared off against last time she was here. The very same one Sage had sent messages about, extolling all his virtues. Apparently, there were many, many virtues, although she never mentioned healing as one. He sat next to her, which showed she must have slept because no one could get that close without her knowing. Dear Goddess, he was beautiful. Short black hair, green eyes that just screamed Irish moss, and lips that begged for her kiss. Harper almost let the moan of desire that trembled on the edge of her tongue pass her lips as she stared into the face of her future. Her voice came out husky, which she would have been embarrassed to know sounded sexy as hell to Ace. "Hello, so you are a healer?"

"No, I can heal on rare occasions. There is a difference because I am a fire dragon. I use a different type of healing."

Harper was positive she was going to swoon and thanks to Frankie, she actually knew what that word meant. Oh Goddess, the voice... that voice just made her want and her knees tremble. There was no way she was going to walk straight now. She cleared her throat and said. "Who knew? So you settled back home?"

"Yes, the family has made me more than welcomed."

"Yep, they do that. Are you staying?"

"I am."

"They must be pleased."

His voice got all growly as he answered her. "Yes, they are. You were hurt and when have you slept last?"

Harper grinned inwardly. Wow, he sounded annoyed, and

when she wondered did she let anyone other than Reighn growl at her. Although Shadows were allowed to, she supposed, at least once. She let it pass, as she was more than likely to growl often at him in the future.

"Bruises and a broken rib or two, maybe a torn kidney. I find I cannot sleep when I am away."

"It was that way for me as well."

Harper sighed as he released her wrist. "Thank you. So I am guessing you know who I am?"

"I do Harper Easton, sister to Charlie, Storm's Shadow."

"Yep, that is me and you are Ace Battle, elder brother of Ash, Ark and Axl."

"I am." He grinned, which just about made her fall from her seat.

"Yeah, I can see that. So you finally came home?"

"Yes, it was time, my dragon, and I found some answers to some very hard questions. We dealt with the darkness that was taking over our souls. Other than that we found we accomplished nothing by shutting ourselves away from our family."

Harper looked out over the room, saw Frankie had returned flushed and happy. She was amusing Johner and Verity with a tale of something she found funny. She watched as Edith and Rene` tried to figure out what it was Frankie had just said. She let her eyes rove over all the little ones walking, crawling, or being cuddled in willing arms and sighed deeply. "It does no good to be away. I get that. They amuse and annoy me when I am here, and when I am away. I worry constantly about them."

"The same for me."

"You sang for me?"

"We did."

"I am a bad bet."

"We will stand with you Harper. We have fought wars and won. We have waited thousands of years for you. Do not push us away. I have learned we will only end up lonely and hurt if you do. I do not know about you, but I am exhausted from feeling that way. I want to demand happiness in my life, to enjoy my family, my new nephews and Ash's Shadow. Your family, and just you."

She placed her hand on his cheek and her forehead against his. Ace felt his dragon recede. The first time he had done so since the trial. She whispered. "I am unsure if I can win this battle, but I will fight hard to make sure I at least give it... give us an excellent shot for the future."

She felt and heard his growl, as did everyone else. Harper pulled away a little, not releasing her hand from his cheek, liking the feel of his skin under her fingers, knowing the entire room watched them.

He promised her. "I protect what is mine. I will be with you to fight at your side."

"I want to deny you, to say this is my fight, not yours, but..." she whispered. "I am frightened. I just made it back last time from that dark place. If I slip again, I know I will never come back."

"It will not happen. I am here and together we fight. The dark side will not win. My Shadow trust me. Trust us."

"I do not want you to think I am bonding with you just for your strength." She told him with raised eyebrows.

He shrugged. "Why not, I am bonding with you for your body?"

Harper burst out laughing. "Well, as long as we are straight on our reasons then."

Ace felt his heart lighten. "Of course, Frankie told me you cannot cook."

"Frankie." Harper yelled, not taking her eyes from the male that her heart had decided to open for. "Did you tell my Shadow I can't cook?"

"Yep, I sure did."

Unsure whether it was her answer or the fact, Harper admitted to Ace being her Shadow. Whichever it was, the room erupted in chaos. Frankie squealed as she ran to Harper and grabbed her in a hug. "I am so excited for you, he is so nice."

Joy hugged him as Clint shook Ace's hand and told him. "We will move out tonight."

Harper cocked an eyebrow at Ace. He said, dragging both teenagers to stand with him. "Clint and Joy live with me, sorry us."

Harper smiled as she looked the two over. Clint, she knew, the girl she did not. "I do not know you?"

Joy ducked her head. "No Lady Harper."

"Oh no, sweet wolf, it is just Harper."

"Oh, okay."

Harper grinned at the young girl, then Ace. She knew there was a story here, but it could wait. She asked Clint. "So you are leaving why?"

Clint blushed. "Oh, umm, you are newly bonded."

"Family stays together, otherwise he will worry, then he will tell Frankie and she will bitch to Charlie. Then I will have to pull my knives and then there will…"

"Yes…. yes dear, we get the picture." Verity hurriedly told her as Clint and Joy's eyes grew huge at her words.

Harper saw first Frankie, then Charlie shaking their heads as they drew the teenagers away. It brought a smile to her lips as Verity hugged first a laughing Ace and then her as she asked him. "Oh, where are we living?"

Verity said. "You have an apartment on the same level as Sage, Edith and Charlie."

"Seriously?"

"What does that mean?" Charlie snarled as Sage crossed her arms with a scowl on her face.

Harper opened her mouth to explain it to them when she heard. "Antee Harper, you live wif me and Kelsey"

"Yes Molly, Uncle Ace and I will."

Kelsey looked up at her. "Can we still come and wake you in the mornings?"

Charlie said. "Of course you can, but same rules apply. You have to knock. Like you do for Mama and Dada."

"Okay."

Harper whispered to Ace. "Otherwise they find you walking around naked."

Ace eyed her, then the youngster. "Yes, do not forget to knock. Now why don't you all come for lunch next Saturday and Auntie Harper will show you her new home and you can help organize the sleepover room."

"We have one of those?" Harper asked over the top of all the childish voices, cheering.

Ace grinned. "We do now."

"Wow, you are the coolest uncle."

"I know."

Ark hugged Harper after the others moved away and told her. "We are pleased he has found someone. We worried no one would want him."

Axl hugged her next, and she noticed the wicked glint of humor in his green eyes that looked so much like Ace's as he said. "Because he is the ugliest of us?"

Harper just stopped herself from choking on her laugh as she replied mournfully. "Well, needs must. Sadly, I will just have to cope."

Axl nodded, the glint of laughter turning into a full laugh. "Well, just grin and bear it. If it helps, lay back and think of England. I have been told that helps."

"Ahh okay, you know he is behind you, right?"

"I run faster than him."

"You would have too." Harper told him, but she was talking to air as Axl was gone.

Leaving an amused Ace behind. He told her. "Ark and Axl will stay with the young ones tonight."

"Uhuh, and where will we be?"

He enfolded her gently in his arms. "Why, I hear there is a very nice apartment in a barn, not a hundred feet from here."

Verity smiled as she took Harper's arm firmly in her hand. "Yes... Yes, dinner is ready."

She dragged Harper from Ace, who told Reighn. "Your

Mama is mean."

Reighn grinned as he said. "Yep, she is."

They both watched Charlie then Storm hug Harper and Harper's face as she tried to scowl at Sage, as she hugged her again.

"She wants and needs this." Rene` said as he gave Ace a quick hug himself.

Ace grinned. "She does. We both do."

Rene` cautioned. "It remains to be seen if she will stay now?"

"It does, doesn't it?" Ace agreed as he wandered after his Shadow.

Rene` and Reighn both sighed deeply, twice.

CHAPTER TWENTY-TWO:

During dinner, Ace and Harper were toasted and a party for their bonding, as well as Frankie's and Johner's, was arranged. After dinner was finished, Ark and Axl gathered Clint and Joy for movies and, with a wink to Ace, they left the family room.

Once they left, there was no reason to linger, so everyone else left to see to their little ones or have a pleasant night together.

Ace and Harper walked slowly to her barn as they moved along the paved walkway and breathed in the night air. Ace asked a silent Harper. "You seem hesitant?"

Harper sighed. "What do you know about me?"

"Mostly what I have gleaned from those that know you."

Harper clicked her tongue against her teeth. "Huh, well okay. So what you do not know because I never ever talk about my personal life with anyone. That means Frankie."

He made no comment, and Harper stopped talking as they moved toward her barn. The night was still, and it seemed a shame to disturb it with talk. Silently, they walked to where her barn appeared. It loomed up like a huge monolith in the soft moonlight. She led him around the side of the building and up a stairway into her apartment.

When they entered, she did not switch on the lights, and could just make out his large shape as he closed the door. Boldly, she stated. "What I was trying to say was, this will not be my first time. I just need you to know that."

Ace grinned, a flash of white in the darkness, as his voice growled out from the shadows. "Just so you know, this will not be my first time either." Suddenly, his arms scooped her up against his chest, causing a small squeak to escape her.

His lips crashed down on hers, making every coherent thought Harper had leave on the last train. She moaned and wound her arms around his neck, returning passion for passion. Slowly, she became aware they were moving. Like a guided missile, he unerringly found his way to her bedroom. He laid her down on the bed, and that was the last clear, rational understanding of where she was for the rest of the night.

This night, their first together was filled with wanting, need and soft loving whispers. Harper and Ace lost themselves in the magic of being together, of finding the one person to fill and heal all the places their souls and hearts had hidden away. Finding and dissolving all the hurts from years of neglect and betrayals. There was no past or future, only what was here and now in each other's arms. And they stayed in that magical place, loving each other until exhaustion drove them to sleep.

Just after dawn broke the horizon, Ace rolled over and hit up against a small, warm body. His dragon purred his contentment. "I can hear you purring." said a sleepy voice.

Ace grinned. "My dragon is content and happy."

That same sleepy voice, which fired his imagination, said. "You know what would make me happy."

Ace thought about that. He could think of several things they had not done last night. The voice, that was not so sleepy now, interrupted his lascivious thoughts. "No, not that!"

Trying not to sound disappointed, he asked. "What did you have in mind, my Shadow?"

Harper laughed quietly to herself at his tone. It was gratifying to know he wanted her again, especially after the wonderful night they had just spent together. She traced a design on his chest and felt him shudder. Before she could change her mind, she said. "I would love to fly with my dragon, just sail through the winds. Can we do that?"

She was in his arms and being carried toward the door

before she could do much more than make a squeaking noise. When they reached the small balcony outside. He placed her on her feet. Somewhere along the way, he had grabbed a pair of her old sweatpants and a tee-shirt she wore when sculpting. Which were covered in dust, but before she could protest. He was shoving the shirt over her head and while she was struggling not to laugh and get her arms through the armholes, he was pulling her pants up her legs. When she was dressed enough, there was a swift flash of air, like a quick puff of warm wind, and a majestic crimson dragon hovered before her. Her eyes lit up with delight as her senses hummed at seeing a beautiful seventy-foot fire dragon gracing the sky in front of her. "Oh my Goddess, you are beautiful, just magnificent. My dragon."

With a hop and shuffle, she was seated at his neck. He shot a tongue of dragon's fire into the sky, causing Harper to make that squeaking noise again, much to her chagrin. Then, before she could scold him, they were swooping high into the sky and what breath she had left she used to laugh with glee.

CHAPTER TWENTY-THREE:

Later that morning, after an amazing flight on dragon back, and a scrumptious breakfast, which Ace's brother Axl delivered. Ace and Harper moved most of her possessions into Ace's apartment.

Luckily, she had not unpacked since moving from the bronze apartment, so it was no hardship to have all her boxes filled with her stuff taken to Ace's place. When he asked her how she had moved the bed to the barn's apartment, she showed him what her magic could do. This earned her an hour of loving on the bed for not telling him sooner she was gifted. In truth, it had completely escaped her mind, but she somehow managed to blame him by telling him his gorgeous body had befuddled her. That earned her another hour of being loved; which she had to admit was delightful.

Eventually, they made it to their new apartment to be met at the door by Joy and Clint. Joy dragged Harper into the apartment, saying. "You are just gonna die when you see your room. It's a turret." At Harper's expression, she said. "I know." Her eyes wide with excitement, she said. "And it has its own bathroom."

Harper grinned at Joy's enthusiasm, apparently having her own bathroom was a big deal. She supposed to a girl who had slept most of her life on the streets or in rat invested motels as Joy had. This would be a slice of heaven. Over breakfast that morning, Ace had told Harper, Clint and Joy's stories as told to him by Hayden and Clint himself and Joy. He had then explained how he first met Joy. When Harper reached for her knives to go hunt down the Prince. Ace pulled her to him and soothed her anger away. The Prince, he told her, was confined to the Grove. Now, as Harper saw the happiness in Joy's face, she could understand how the apartment would be like a dream come true for the girl. Living in the castle would be amazing all by itself. So she allowed herself to be pulled behind an excited Joy as Ace and Clint wandered after the two females. Ace asked Clint. "You alright?"

He nodded. "Yeah, the Queen called this morning. She apologized to Joy and me. We are allowed to go to the Grove next week. Is that okay?"

"Do you want to go?"

He nodded. "Joy is really excited, Commander Sparrow said she would be our guard, so we would be okay. Joy was happy about that."

"It should be fun. Are the others okay?"

Meaning the other youths who had been sleeping rough. Clint nodded. "Yeah, Johner and Claire were really annoyed with me. Healer Sharm said what I was doing was good, but I should have told someone, they could have been hurt."

Ace squeezed his shoulder. "I know sometimes it is hard to know what to do, but you have Harper and me and the brothers now. To help when you get stuck."

Clint smiled. "Yeah, that was what Ark said and Hayden will be home soon too."

"Yes, he will, so you see, you are not alone. Burdens shared are easier to bear. Remember that."

Clint nodded seriously. "I will, thanks Ace."

They followed the sound of Joy's cheerful voice as she said again. "And you have your own bathroom, isn't it magnificent!"

Harper stood just inside the door of their bedroom, looking at the most beautiful bedroom she had ever seen. The room was decorated in tones of blues which was Harper's favorite color, with touches of crimson the color of Ace's dragon. It was easy to see Verity had thought of Ace when decorating this apartment. She wondered if Verity had a touch of the sight or was she just lucky. Either way, the place worked for her with its combination of colors. And it was indeed one of the turrets of the castle. She was amused to see it housed a huge four-poster bed, with bedside tables. As with the bed they were made from, light hardwood, that gave the room just enough diversity to stop it from being opulent. Glass doors led to a curved balcony that Harper fell in love with as soon as she saw it. Her eyes traveled back to the bed. It had to be three times the size of a normal king-size bed.

Ace sighed with pleasure. "I love me a big bed."

Harper raised her eyebrows. "I am going to get lost in there."

Joy giggled, and Clint laughed, more so when Ace said. "I excelled at seek and find."

Harper looked at the predatory anticipation in her dragon's eyes and hurriedly said. "Oh well, okay."

The bathroom as promised, was exquisite with a large shower and bathtub. It boasted twin sinks, all in soft blues and whites. Harper, to Joy's delight, fanned herself as she told her. "This is just amazing."

Joy bounced on her toes. "I know right."

Then she took Harper's hand and dragged her into what Harper thought was a walk- in-closet, but to her surprise, it was a small room. Joy spread her arms out and turned a full circle. "Look at this room. You can get all your clothes and shoes in here and even change your clothes. It is what they call a dressing room, which is why there are mirrors." Of which there were three full-length ones. "Axl said in the old days, males and females had these. Ace has one as well."

Harper was impressed, and tried to work out how she was ever going to fill the room with clothes. Then she looked at the young girl.

"So what is your room like?"

She said shyly. "Umm, we slept in the small lounge last night."

Harper's first thought was, we have a small lounge, meaning we have a large lounge. What came out of her mouth was. "So you looked in all the rooms; what one did you like?"

Joy smiled as she said. "The one with the white four-poster bed, want to see?"

Ace came in and squeezed Harper's shoulder lightly as she agreed. "Definitely, then Clint's room." She asked Ace before they left their room. "Do you like the room?"

He nodded. "What is there not to like?"

"So, we leave it."

"Yes."

Before they got to look at the bedrooms, Frankie arrived. "Hey, I am here, girl. Are you all bonded and everything?"

Harper sighed and said to the two teens. "You guys know Frankie, right?" They nodded eagerly as Harper smiled and said. "She is my friend and pain in my..."

"Best friend." Frankie said loudly, covering Harper's last word. Which made them all laugh, even Harper. She swept Harper into a hug and then Ace, then proceeded to hug both teens. Clint blushed. Joy just soaked it up, which none of the adults missed. Frankie kept her hand on Joy's arm as Harper growled. "Yeah... Yeah, female. Do not hug me."

"Aww, Harper, you know you love it, like you love me?"

Harper sighed as she asked. "Why are you here?"

"To look around with you. I took the whole day off."

"Why?" Harper whined, and she was not ashamed she did. With Frankie here, the quick tour she was thinking of would now be a marathon adventure. As they would have to stop at everything that caught her eye, and there would be so many things that she would gush over. "Did I tour your place?"

Frankie laughed, but Harper could see the hurt in her eyes as she said. "Well, you would have, if you had been home."

Dammit, I am a terrible friend, oops best friend. Feeling bad, she growled. "Did I say I wasn't going to look at your place? No, I don't think I did." Which made Frankie smile and wiggle with pleasure. After that, what was there to say? Harper smiled. "We were going to go look at the bedrooms then lounges."

"Ooh, I love bedrooms and lounges." Frankie said and

skipped off with Joy.

Clint grinned and followed, saying. "Let's check out my room before Joy's."

They heard Joy's squeal of indignation as Ace kissed Harper.

"You are the bestest friend ever."

"Shut up. You will buy me dinner, steak, salad and chips, and I mean loads of chips."

"That sounds great, we are in." Ash said as he walked in with Olinda, followed by Ark and Axl, who both carried babies. There was a quick shuffle as Ace reached for a baby.

Harper asked no one in particular. "Does no one work anymore?"

Olinda said. "Day off, schools are closed for water leaks. We have come to look at your place; you have a turret. Frankie said we are all here for lunch."

Harper sighed. "Of course she did."

Olinda cocked her head to the side as she asked, "Are you annoyed?"

Harper grinned. "Now, what would make you think that?"

Olinda laughed. "Oh, not enough sex. Yeah, I get that, too bad the whole family is coming."

Harper couldn't help herself, especially when she heard Ace or Ash groan at Olinda's outspoken comment. She burst out laughing. "I adore you, never change."

Olinda grinned. "Okay."

Harper said. "They are this way and took her to where they heard Frankie exclaiming over something in Joy's room.

They ended up seeing the entire apartment, which as Harper predicted, took so much longer than she originally hoped it would. Storm arrived with Kelsey, Kammy, Molly, and Cara in tow, just after they had finished in the kitchen.

"Wow! You are busy." Harper said after every little girl had hugged and kissed her.

"I am the designated baby sitter until three o'clock when their Mama's will relieve me."

"So you brought them all here?"

He looked at her as if she made no sense. "There is to be lunch, they are young, they eat."

"Okay, I get that. Well then, you and the brothers are volunteered to go get it."

Storm eyed her suspiciously. "And you will watch them?"

Harper agreed. "Yep."

Storm nodded in agreement and rounded up the Battle brothers, all four of them. Harper saw them leave, and as soon as Storm was gone, she yelled. "Frankie, the girls have come to see you. Girls, go find Frankie."

"Is it a game?" Asked Kelsey.

"Yep, you bet it is, but Frankie is bad at it."

"Yea!" They all yelled and ran to find Frankie.

Harper grinned, pleased with herself, until she turned around and came face to face with Grace and Verity, who asked. "Was that wise?"

Harper replied. "It wasn't unwise."

"And do you know where they are?" Grace asked with a glint of laughter in her eyes.

"Yep, sure do."

"And where is that?" Verity asked in her lady of the castle voice.

"With Frankie, Clint, Olinda and Joy."

"I see, and this is what you agreed to."

"Yep, they are being watched."

"Slippery." Grace said to Verity.

"Very." She answered, as they moved around Harper and started talking about the apartment. Harper breathed a sigh of relief and grinned when she realized she had out foxed the grandmothers.

Frankie and the grandmothers approved Joy and Clint's bedrooms, which escalated Joy's pleasure another degree. Frankie told her when she found her on the floor of the large lounge, the one that came with a fireplace which she knew she was going to love.

"Joy's in heaven."

Harper grinned. "I know, it's nice to see her so happy."

"Sorry I barged in."

Harper grinned. "Nah, it's okay. It was fun. Sorry about your place. I should have been there."

"Nah, all good. We will do it tomorrow, when it is just us."

Harper sighed and held Frankie's hand. "I would like that, best friend."

Frankie laughed. "Good. I called Edith and said I would take Joy shopping this afternoon."

Verity and Grace stepped into the lounge and found seats. "We will accompany you. She needs school clothes and shoes." Verity told Grace.

Grace said. "I should imagine she will be needing school supplies."

Joy told Harper as she entered with the girls and sat on the floor next to her. "I am to go to school."

Kelsey said. "Not mine, she is too big."

Harper said to Joy. "I am happy you are going." She smiled at Kelsey. "Isn't your school attached to Joys? So you can go with her."

"Oh yeah, that would be good. You want to do that, Joy?"

"Yes please."

The guys came back loaded down with food from the famous hamburger place. They had brought Edith with them, who the young girls were thrilled to see, almost as much as the food.

CHAPTER TWENTY-FOUR:

Harper was sprawled on the floor of the lounge with all the young ones and teens around her. Verity, Grace, Frankie, and Edith were on the couches. All the males were on couches or on the floor. Harper was finding it hard to move she had eaten so much. She remembered Joy mentioning school just before the food came and asked. "Joy, did Lord Rene` enrol you in school already?"

"Yes, he put you and Ace down as parents. Was that alright?"

"Well, as we claimed you. I guess that was a good idea."

Joy looked satisfied with the answer, but could not contain her smile. Ace smiled at Harper as Joy's happiness spilled over it was like sunshine filled the room. She jumped up to go see her room again. Harper knew she was still not totally sure the beautiful room with the white four-poster bed that came with its own bathroom was hers.

Verity said. "She shines like her name."

Storm told all four brothers. "Males are going to be panting after that one soon. You will have to be on your guard."

Four growls erupted, and Ace said. "No, she is a baby still."

Harper rolled over and did an eye roll at Frankie and Edith, saying. "Wolves mature faster than dragons. You are going to have to be prepared for that."

Ace's voice became adamant. "No... No males, she is barely a teenager, end of discussion." He pointed at Harper. "You make sure she knows, no males."

Harper looked at Edith, who rolled her eyes this time.

Frankie asked. "Ever? That is kinda harsh. What if some guy, like a dragon, you know, claims her as his Shadow what then?"

Axl said. "He will not."

Frankie thoughtfully said. "Well, there may be someone out there for her. You cannot know there won't be. Maybe another wolf or cat or someone."

Axl once again said. "There is not."

By now, everyone was listening to the conversation and watching Axl become annoyed, which was unusual for the laid-back dragon. Edith placed her hand on Frankie's arm when she went to disagree with him. Softly, she asked. "Axl is Joy yours?"

His eyes elongated, and brown scales covered his arms and neck. His dragon hissed. *MINE!*

Rene` entering the room frowned. "She is too young, you know this. Come with me and we will talk." He looked at Ace and Harper. "Will you allow him to stay near and protect her?"

Stunned at the turn of events, Ace nodded. Harper frowned as she stood, and everyone held their breaths as she said. "There must be rules. You will never be alone with her. She will go to school until she decides she is finished. She will train in whatever she wants to do, and we are her parents and will always have the last say. In saying that you may court her when she turns eighteen."

Axl nodded beyond speech at the moment. He turned to go with Rene`, and came face to face with Joy. She smiled shyly at him and said. "We agree to Harper's terms?"

He nodded stiffly and left. Harper asked. "You do not seem surprised?"

Joy looked after Axl, and then slowly turned to Harper. "Yeah, my wolf has been antsy since yesterday, when he brought the sandwich to me. She decided he brought food he was worthy."

Ace asked. "So you are talking to her?"

"Yes, since yesterday."

"We will find a wolf to guide you."

She nodded. "Thank you."

Harper grinned at Ace as she said. "Who? He will kill any male that comes near her."

Ace looked at Frankie, who said. "I will handle that with Claire, no problem."

Joy hugged Harper and asked her. "Harper, are you okay with this?"

"Yeah... yeah, no hugging. Now go away, all of you. I need a nap."

"She means have S.E.X.Y times with Ace." Frankie told them.

"Frankie!" Harper yelled as everyone laughed.

"What, it is true,"

"Maybe. Leave my home."

Frankie grabbed Joy and left to go shopping with Grace and Verity, who waved Ace away as he tried to give them money.

Clint shook his head and said. "Axl, who knew? I am on duty until four. See you for dinner."

Harper groaned. "I forgot they will all be back."

"More of them probably." Clint murmured.

"Is he necessary?" She asked Ace just before a laughing Clint left the room.

Reighn entered as he left and asked. "Are you going to turn the smaller lounge into an entertainment theatre that would be awesome?"

When Harper groaned loudly, Ace said. "My love, it is a home theater." She could see any alone time with Ace was gone. Sighing in resignation, she returned to lying on the floor with the young girls. Storm, Reighn, Ace, Ash and Ark fell to discussing the merits of a home theatre. Harper asked Kelsey if Dragon Lords were allowed to say awesome. She and the other girls giggled and rolled around on the floor.

Sometime later, Charlie arrived with two faeries. "Hey, your people are here." She called out as she came into the lounge.

Harper asked Ace. "We have people now?" Sage followed Charlie, and Harper asked Ace again. "Does no one knock?"

"Apparently not." He answered as he stood to shake hands with the faeries.

"So grumpy and newly bonded. Sad, not enough S.E.X." Sage sang with a smirk.

"Huh, so speaks the lady with puffy ankles." Harper snarked back.

Charlie laughed as Ace helped Harper up off the floor. Sage snarled. "They are not swollen."

Harper just raised her eyebrows in response. Charlie said to forestall the battle she could see starting. "Let me introduce you. These ladies are both former guards to the Queen of Sands Grove. They have been trained in combat and housekeeping. Echo is a chef, and this is Selby, she will be your housekeeper, organizer and general girl Friday."

"Yeah, but can she wrangle a teenage boy and girl?"

Selby looked at Harper with a glint of humor in her eyes and nodded. "How hard can it be?"

Echo murmured. "They are teenagers, what do you think?"

Harper grinned as Selby said. "Teenagers, hormones and attitude, it's gonna be a bloody nightmare."

"And that is why I picked you two." Stated Charlie to the faeries.

Which had both females laughing. Ace said. "Please come tomorrow, and you can meet Clint and Joy. Also, we will sit down and decide on meals and duties. Ladies, welcome to our home."

After the faeries left with a promise to return. Sage inquired of Harper. "So, did Reighn tell you?"

"Tell me what? He came in and home entertainment sprang up."

"Seriously." Sage looked at her Shadow, who stared back at her, then mumbled. "It is fairly important to arrange it now, my love."

Harper told Sage. "And he said awesome. Kelsey and I are not sure he is allowed to say that, are we Kelsey?"

Kelsey solemnly said. "We are not." This was spoiled when

Reighn picked her up and hung her upside down, causing her to giggle uncontrollably.

Sage shook her head. "Sad my love, just sad."

"So, he was meant to tell us what?" Harper asked as she watched Kelsey dangling from Reighn's hand.

Sage told her. "He arranged the meeting for ten tomorrow morning. Is that okay?"

Ace asked. "What meeting?"

Harper, with her eyes on Charlie, replied. "With Scarlett and Elijah."

"Ahh, I see."

Charlie's head whipped around from her giggling daughter as she asked. "You are just going to talk to them?"

"What is it with that?"

"Well, you know?"

"No, not really. Do you want to explain it?"

"My Goddess, you are so touchy. Did you not get enough S.E.X last night?"

"Why is everyone saying that?"

Ace smiled. "Because you are newly bonded, my heart, and they are nosy."

"Okay, that makes sense." She gave Charlie a hard look and said to Sage. "Tomorrow at ten is good. So, you, Reighn, me and Ace. Charlie and Storm, right?"

"That was what we told them."

"Okay, should be fun." The room went quiet. "What... what. I can have fun without mayhem."

"Well, of course you can. I have seen it." Reighn agreed solemnly. Somehow, no one believed him. Harper sighed loudly at the idiots.

CHAPTER TWENTY-FIVE:

N ext morning, Ace rolled Harper out of bed early. It was Joy's first day of school and she was nervous, evidenced by her plaintive. "What if they don't like me?"

"What is not to like?" Ace quietly asked her.

"My hair, my clothes?"

"Frankie, Verity, and Grace would not have dressed you in something horrible." Harper said, trying to calm the teenager. "You look good."

"Maybe I should change again?"

"How many outfits so far?" Ace asked before Harper could say what she was working up to, which he knew would be along the lines of. I will kill you if you don't shut up.

"Eight."

"You look great." He told her again.

"What if they make fun of me?"

"I will come and kill every one of them." Harper told her with a straight face.

Joy gulped and said. "Oh, well, what if…"

"Jeez, shut up. They will like you. You are likeable, now eat your food." Snarled Clint.

Joy grinned. "Okay." And applied herself to the eggs Ace had cooked.

Clint rolled his eyes and muttered. "Girls."

Harper took a step toward her with a snarl. Ace moved in front of her and gave her a cup of coffee, saying. "Kill? You cannot kill anyone who upsets her and you cannot kill her."

"I beg to differ on both counts."

He sighed. "My Shadow, you must promise you will not."

She sighed as she looked at their faces. Clint looked amused, which she was learning was his normal expression, at least around her. Ace looked expectant, and Joy had a look that wavered between horrified and disbelief. "Fine, no killing, happy now?"

"Immensely!"

Things went smoothly after Selby and Echo arrived. Ace and Harper finally said goodbye to Joy and Clint when Tansy and Molly arrived to go to school. The last they saw of a nervously excited Joy was her holding Molly's hand as she told Joy all about the playground they could play on. A little before ten o'clock, Ace and Harper called the lift to their floor. The meeting was being held in Reighn's conference room on the main level.

CHAPTER TWENTY-SIX:

S carlett was nervous as she asked Charlie. "Will she be very angry?"

Charlie shrugged. "I don't know, she wasn't yesterday, in fact she was happy."

Reighn reminded them. "Remember, she was the one to ask for this meeting."

Scarlett said hopefully. "Perhaps she has forgiven us."

Sage muttered. "Let's not ask for miracles too early."

Charlie snarked. "Well, aren't you just a ray of sunshine?"

Sage shot back. "It's Harper."

Just then, the door opened, and Frankie walked in. "Why are you here? Is she not coming?" Sage asked, worried they had all come there for nothing.

"No... I mean yes, she is coming." She hurriedly said, as Scarlett gasped. "Harper asked me to come at dinner last night. She said I would keep you all calm. Are you all calmed?"

Scarlett and Elijah, along with Sage, laughed at the outrageous female. Charlie grinned. "You are crazy."

Frankie shook her head and said seriously. "Nope, I was tested."

Reighn grinned at her. "Frankie, never, ever change."

"Oh, I couldn't now if I wanted too."

The door opened again to admit Harper and Ace. Sage thought. Harper was correct, Frankie did smooth things over, and she had definitely removed the tension from the room. She looked at Scarlett and Elijah and their guards, and could see they were all more relaxed. Strike one for Harper, she knows her stuff.

Reighn said. "Let us take our seats."

He held a seat out for Sage, as Elijah and Storm did the same for their mates, and then Reighn held a chair for Frankie. Ace pulled a chair out for Harper, who smiled at him and sat. He heaved a silent sigh of relief he had not known if she would understand the gesture.

Harper took a breath and looked around at the waiting people and with a small smile, said. "So good morning. Firstly; do you all know my Shadow, Ace Battle?"

The faeries all nodded, Elijah said. "We do, and please allow us to offer our congratulations to you both. We hope you have many pleasant years together."

Ace inclined his head. "We both thank you."

Harper nodded. "Thanks. So I asked Reighn to set this meeting up so we could talk. I realized my anger toward you." She nodded to Scarlett and Elijah. "Had not so much to do with you but our mother. And what happened the night we fought the shades in the gray mist."

Elijah said. "We would like to say we understand, but in truth we do not. The only other person we have ever known to go there was the former High Queen."

"Oh please do not beat around the bush." Scarlett said, with a little heat in her words. "What my light is trying to say politely, is no half-blood has ever done that. It is supposed to be impossible."

Harper agreed. "You are right, we should never have been able to, but Juna was a Queen. Probably a High Queen and what abilities she was gifted with were only a few of what she carried within her."

"You mean she held the powers of the High Queen in her DNA?" Charlie asked, shocked at the revelation.

"Yep, and passed it on to us, it lays dormant in you but not in me."

"So this is what the darkness has attached too." Charlie asked fearfully as she looked at the pale faced Harper.

Ace took her hand in his as Harper closed her eyes. When she spoke, her voice was a little hoarse as she suppressed long held emotions. "Yes, that was what I believe now. For a long time I thought it was my soul, but it is our mother's powers."

Scarlett said. "No, dear one, they are your powers. You are a High Queen."

Harper let her left hand lay on the table and a blue sword appeared. All the faeries hissed in surprise. The guards went to kneel. "No." Harper whipped. "Do not, I am no Queen.

"I think that ship may have sailed." Sparrow said as they remained on their feet.

"Too bad, I am not going to take that mantle up."

"You may have no choice." Elijah told her kindly.

"I am so not doing any quests for you, Queen Harper. Nope, not happening." Stated Frankie with a scowl on her face.

Harper scowled right back and said. "You would if I asked you too."

"I so would not. I do not have time for quests now." And there was whining. Harper heard it.

Scarlett laughed, as did Elijah. Their two female guards were used to Sage and Edith. So smiled, and the male guards just looked bemused. Sage said. "I am sort of a Queen, you don't do quests for me?"

Frankie snorted. "I run around all day for you."

"Oh yeah, I forgot about that."

"Egg brain." Harper mumbled to Ace, who grinned at her ridiculousness.

Sage yelped. "I heard that?"

"And your point." Harper asked sweetly.

Storm looked at his brother and saw a little vein pulsing in his temple. He hid his smile as he asked. "Reighn, my brother, has that vein always been there?"

Reighn snarled and Storm was positive he saw flame. "Please, for my sanity. May we continue?"

Scarlett said. "I was entertained."

"As was I." Elijah agreed. He, like Reighn, had noticed the sword had disappeared.

Charlie told them. "She was always like this, you get used

to it."

Reighn grumbled. "Do not encourage them. Now Harper, the sword was what you fought with?"

"Yes."

"I do not know what to say." Elijah said as he looked at Harper and Charlie.

Harper nodded. "I know it takes getting used to. I have told Charlie some of this. The darkness I received that night made me push her out of my life. I was terrified I would hurt or kill her. I was so young, and it was so strong, stronger than me. Every day I was losing the battle, and I was scared for you." She pleaded. "Charlie, don't be mad."

Charlie shook her head. "Oh Harper, I am not mad. I am sad you couldn't have told me."

"What could you have done?"

"I don't know, something."

Ace said. "That is in the past, and cannot be changed. Some things we cannot undo, we accept and move forward."

Charlie looked at Harper as she said to Ace. "Yes, you are right."

Reighn asked. "This darkness. What can we do to help you?"

"That is not why I asked for this meeting. I wanted to meet Scarlett and Elijah. I know I judged you unfairly, and for that I am sorry. Our mother loved you very much Scarlett, she spoke of you often to me. Charlie and her..."

Scarlett quietly said. "We know, Charlie told us."

Harper looked at Charlie, who shrugged as much to say it was what it was. "Okay then. Well, Juna missed you more than she ever realized she would."

"Then why did she leave me?" Cried Scarlett.

Harper felt sad for her and closed her eyes on her pain. "She left because your High Queen at the time would not allow her to have children. It was her destiny to have both Charlie and me. We are the future of... No, I am sorry, that is wrong." She took a minute as Ace clasped her hand, and she took a breath, centering herself and said. "We are the catalyst that forces change. Your world has remained unchanged for millions of years. All through the time without magic and now you are here again establishing Groves, but you have not changed. You have been able to have mating's outside your own race for twelve years now, that is a fact. Yet your people do not know this and as far as we know, not one faerie has even thought about looking. Your race, like the dragons, is on the brink of extinction. But again, you would rather that, than have what you call impure blood in your Groves."

"You are referring to the council and a few others?" Scarlett asked her with an edge to her voice.

Harper smiled. "I am, no sister of Juna's could think that way."

"It is not the High Queen; it is the council." Said Elijah. "The High Queen fights constantly for change, ever since she was gifted the title."

Ace asked. "When was that?"

Elijah told them. "The former High Queen went to the High Grove only recently."

Charlie said. "And that is why change is happening."

"Are you saying the former High Queen and the council knew this was to happen?" Asked an astounded Scarlett.

Harper said with a tinge of bitterness in her voice. "Juna told me they had a foretelling. They hated the idea of half-bloods. Pure bloods only is their motto."

Reighn asked. "So Junipa left to have the young the former High Queen disallowed?"

"Yes." Stated Harper.

Charlie asked slowly, like she was waking from a bad dream. "It never made a difference who our father was?"

Harper swallowed and looked at Ace, who nodded, saying. "Tell her, it is only fair, and it was never your fault."

Harper took a breath and said. "Juna told me before she died that the sperm donor, which was how she spoke of him, was unimportant. She knew, as the former High Queen knew, her daughters would always be who they were meant to be. It was ordained, our father had no choice in it."

Charlie mumbled. "That was why he feared us."

"Yes, he knew we were always more than human, that Juna was."

Frankie asked. "So what do we do now?"

Scarlett informed them. "We confront the High Queen and council. Will you come with us, nieces?"

Harper grinned. "I am in, Charlie?"

"Try stopping me; they have ignored us long enough."

Harper told them. "Juna called out to the High Queen on her death bed. She was refused."

"Well, of course she would have been refused, as the council would have ignored her. I bet they hoped she and you would all just fade away. How little they knew of Junipa and her daughters." Scarlett stated with pride.

Ace commented. "If they had looked past their fear, they would have had her give birth to her daughters within the Grove."

Frankie asked. "Why would that have made a difference?"

Reighn smiled. "So they could have directed and controlled the growth of both Harper and Charlie's abilities. They may have had a chance to keep them from doing what they are going to do now. Change the world of faeries forever."

Elijah said softly. "They missed a golden opportunity to control the future course of faeriedom."

Scarlett told them. "I would imagine the former High Queen was terrified of what your birth represented. The council would have been fearful of their position in faerie society. I want you to know I would not have ignored you or your mother."

Charlie said. "We know that Scarlett, and so did Juna."

"I hope she did." She murmured softly.

Harper told them. "Once, I sat and thought about it. I realized I have lived with anger for so long. I forgot who and what I was angry at and why."

Reighn asked. "So Harper, have you talked to the Ancients about the darkness?"

Harper lit up from within, causing more than one person to stare in surprise. "Well, I was saving that for last, but the darkness is gone as of last night."

Ace grinned widely. "It seems bonding with me destroyed most of it and then the Ancients visited my Shadow and removed the last of the darkness residing within her."

Harper grinned. "It could not survive the joining of our souls in happiness. The Ancients said they would not have their Seeker tainted. How would the wild ones return if their beacon was stained or something like that? I got bored and went to sleep."

Ace nodded. "She did. They told me and I wrote it down for you, my Lord."

Reighn shook his head. "Harper, they are the Ancients."

She nodded. "And long winded."

He sighed and said to Ace. "Please give the information to Keeper for the histories.

Charlie asked. "So you are healed?"

"Why would I say I was, if I wasn't?" Harper growled at her.

"Still bitchy, I see?" Frankie retorted.

"Like that would go away." Sage said as Charlie dragged Harper from her chair and hugged her. She then let her go as Frankie did the same, then it was Scarlett's turn.

"Hugging." Growled Harper as she was enfolded in Sage's arms, who she saw had tears in her eyes. "Dear Goddess, do not cry female." Harper pleaded desperately, looking at Reighn for help.

He shrugged and smiled as her eyes narrowed and Sage said with a sniff. "Hormones, it is not because I like you."

Harper grinned as she said. "That is what you say, but we all know you love me."

"I admit nothing." Sage quipped as she released her.

Harper laughed and turned to Scarlett. "Let's go visit the High Queen and councilors."

CHAPTER TWENTY-SEVEN:

T he faerie council sat behind a raised curved horseshoe dais. It was very medieval and ridiculous. Harper sighed with impatience. She was here as a courtesy to the High Queen and her Aunt Scarlett. *And because Charlie has puppy dog eyes and uses them to extreme. So unfair.*

Harper stood in the center of a round room, looking up at the thirteen faeries. Four females and eight males who peered down at her like she was a specimen under a microscope. She looked over at Frankie. *Who was so not meant to be there?* Harper and the others had arrived hours earlier and been shown instantly into the High Queen's chamber, where Harper had once again related what her mother had told her. The High Queen had sat with a sorrowful expression as she said to her Light. "She was very much like that, so positive she was right. She would destroy an entire family to prove it, and the council encouraged her."

"She was your mother. You are not like her, my Light. Remember that. You are your own person and now, more than ever, you need to be who you are. I and my warriors stand with you."

Queen Meadow said. "I will, of course, step down as High Queen."

Harper shuddered at the thought of being Queen and quickly stated. "There is no need for that. I relinquish all claim to the position of High Queen or Queen."

Queen Meadow was confused. "Then why are you here?"

"To explain what Juna told us, life for you has to change. If not, all of faeriedom will be lost and only remembered as a myth, a memory of times past. Right now, there are unicorns at Dragon's Gap, female dragons are talking again, a

Grounder has appeared and the Sun Goddess has gifted sun dragons to the dragons. Elementals walk the Earth. I ask you when before in history, ours, unicorns, shifters, humans, or dragons, has that ever happened?"

Scarlett now added her voice. "I have been saying this for months. We have to make the council look at the signs. You have to look at the portents, they are screaming at you to see we have to change."

"And you half-breed are here to see it happens at the end of your sword, perhaps?" A male said as he walked from behind a screen that hid a secret door.

"My brother Kai." said the High Queen.

Ace and Storm tensed as Harper and Charlie stood shoulder to shoulder. Charlie told him. "Cool the tone boy, or I will."

"You can try." He laughed derisively. "You a half-breed?"

Harper knew a test when she was in one. "You will die where you stand." With a thought, she made the blue sword appear. The tip touched his chest, and she saw him swallow and heard several gasps behind her. "Now I am not as patient as my sister or our Shadows. So you will cease calling us half-breeds. This conversation was between your sister and us. You may stay if you are respectful and to answer your question. No, not at the end of my sword."

Frankie said. "That may have more impact if you were not standing there with one in your hand." She wiggled between the two and held her hand out to the male. Causing Harper to hurriedly remove her sword. "Hi, I am Frankie Kingsley."

The male shook her hand, bewildered by her, as was everyone else. "Hello, I am Kai Rainstree."

"Frankie!" Harper, Charlie, and Scarlett all yelled at the same time. Harper asked. "What are you doing here?"

"How did you get here?" Demanded Scarlett.

"Oh, wasn't I invited. I thought I was?" Frankie asked as she looked around at the people there.

Harper knew, just as Frankie knew, that she wasn't invited.

This was Frankie being Frankie. Harper asked her. "Why would I bring you somewhere if I wasn't sure it was safe?"

Frankie did the lips thing and said. "Charlie is here?"

"Because she can shoot."

"Excuse me, who is this?" High Queen Meadow asked as she looked at her Light as well as her brother.

Harper answered. "Hush, now Queen. In a minute."

"Did she just hush me?" Meadow asked Scarlett.

"Yes."

"But..."

"Oh, please, I need to hear this." Scarlett said as she moved closer to Charlie.

"Did she just hush me as well?" A bewildered and slightly miffed Queen Meadow asked.

"I would say she did my Light." Answered High King Zale, who was thoroughly amused.

"What are you laughing at?" She asked her brother, who just laughed harder.

Frankie crossed her arms and frowned at Harper. "Explain Storm and Ace?"

"They carry frigging big swords."

"Oh yeah. You have a point, but I am here now."

Harper scowled at her and said. "Frankie, I am very annoyed with you."

"Aww, Harper. You say the funniest things. Now where were we?"

"How is that funny?" She asked as she threw her hands up in surrender.

Frankie said. "So, I am Frankie, Harper's best friend. You are High Queen Meadow, and you are her Light, King Zale, and you are her brother Kai, not a prince because you denounced the title."

"Ahh, yes that is so." Agreed King Zale as Queen Meadow stared at her Light, trying to understand what was happening.

Charlie asked her. "How do you know all that?"

Frankie shrugged. "I just do. I am magic."

"Frankie." Harper admonished. "Don't play with Charlie; she has a short fuse."

Charlie snorted, her patience was so much longer that Harper's. Ace and Storm both smothered laughs when Harper turned her gray eyes on them.

"Chickens." Charlie mumbled just loud enough for the males to hear. They growled as she grinned.

Frankie slammed her hands on her non-existence hips, causing Harper to snicker, which Frankie ignored. "Harper, do not ruin my fun. It is not fair, all you guys have stuff."

Harper asked sharply. "Frankie, are you whining? What did I say about whining?"

She mumbled. "Never do it in my hearing."

"And you are doing what?"

"Sorry Harper." Sighing, she told Charlie. "I looked everyone up, before I arrived."

"Okay."

Kai, brother to the High Queen, said into the silence. "Are there more like you, where you come from?"

Ace asked. "Why?"

"I want to go with you when you return. I need a female like these. You are so fortunate." He told Ace and Storm.

Storm said. "When we leave, you are welcome to visit. There are many females at Dragon's Gap. We cannot swear they are like these three though."

"I thank you. I will take my chances." He looked at Frankie. "Are you with a Light?"

Frankie shook her head. "Sorry, I am bonded."

"Oh my Goddess, what did Johner say about you being here?" Harper asked, thinking a dragon invasion was imminent.

"Johner?" Frankie frowned and did the lip thing.

Storm demanded. "You told my brother. Frankie say you did?"

Frankie said. "Umm."

"That means no." Harper said as Storm pulled out his phone and started talking very fast.

Charlie said. "Oh, Frankie."

Scarlett said disapprovingly. "How could you that poor worried male?"

Frankie shrugged. "It just happened, that is all."

Harper told them. "She forgot."

Frankie agreed. "Maybe."

Kai said into the silence. "I so want one of them."

Charlie asked him. "You are not like Tarin, are you?"

Kai frowned, just stopping himself from sneering when he heard the male's name. "Is he being an annoying prick?"

"Yes." Harper said. "He is an ass."

Kai snorted as he looked at his sister. "You will have to do something about him?"

"I know, I will send for his parents, if he cannot control himself even with dragons; he is almost beyond our help." She asked Scarlett. "The young male and the little girl, are they well?"

Scarlett nodded. "Yes, my Queen. Harper and Ace have taken both young ones into their home and are now their guardians."

The High Queen swore silently as she turned contrite eyes to the couple. "I am sorry your young had to suffer Tarin. We are at a loss as what to do with our nephew."

Ace said. "He needs to understand he is not the center of the world, before he ends up getting his guards killed."

She nodded. "It is as you say. Scarlett, we will call his parents, have his guards recalled. I will not have them hurt because of his selfishness."

"Thank you, my Queen."

Frankie clapped her hands together. "Okay, so have we finished with all the threatening yet?"

Kai, amused beyond belief said. "We have."

Frankie looked around as she asked. "Good, what is next? Just you know... I have a Shadow waiting. Apparently he will need soothing to you know... make him happy." She raised her eyebrows suggestively. Which made Harper groan and everyone else laugh.

The High Queen said. "It is time we were in the council room." She asked. Frankie. "I am assuming you will be attending?"

Frankie looked at Harper. "Of course."

Harper sighed. "Of course, it is Frankie."

So here they all were in this farce of a court, Harper felt her patience fraying. As Olinda would say, the needle on her annoyed meter was pointing to anger. Charlie sat with Storm on one side and Frankie on the other. Ace sat between Frankie, Scarlett and Elijah. The High King and High Queen sat together with her brother Kai standing behind them with all their guards. Harper nodded to them all and smiled at Frankie's wave. She stood loosely and waited...

Finally, a tall, lithe female stood and with a nod to the High Queen and King, said in a lilting voice. "We are here today to pass judgment on the one named Harper Battle. Formerly known as Easton. Daughter to Junipa Suntannio."

Harper heard several gasps and Ace and Storm growl. She turned her head a little and saw Frankie frown and Charlie's lips tighten in anger at the word judgment. Like them, she had no idea this was anything other than a question-and-answer session. She should have known they were not to be trusted. From the look the royals passed each other; she would bet they had no idea this was a trial either. The female stated. "Sister to Charlie Kingsley formerly Easton. Daughter also to Junipa Suntannio. Niece to Queen Scarlett Wilde..."

"Point of order." King Zale called. "When did this become an inquisition and trial? This was meant to be a conversation only."

Harper did not let any emotions show, she knew she was being scrutinized from head to toe, and she could feel pressure against her shields. A male stood, and he was not at all like the first faerie he was weather-beaten dark brown with age and had a voice like rustling leaves. Harper thought he may be a forest dweller. "This is not a trial, King Zale. We apologize if it seems that way. We only wish to examine the claims made."

In the face of his words, King Zale could only nod and retreat, although his expression showed his discontent. The old male addressed Harper. "It has been stated by not only one daughter but both daughters of Junipa. That daughter Harper led her sister Charlie into battle against shades and demons of the gray mist. It has also been stated they alone defeated such creatures to end for the next thousand upon thousand years, the threat of their re-emergence."

"Lies... All lies!" Yelled a male from the end of the podium. He stood and looked down at her and sneered. "No one, especially a half-blood, could do what has been reported. If our own High Queen Lorna and now Meadow are unable to. How is it this half thing is supposed to have done so?"

At the insult, Ace, Charlie, Storm and Frankie stood. Harper smiled as the first male demanded in a cold voice. "Councilor Grinthum, representing the Valley Dwellers, it is not your time to speak, remain silent or be dismissed."

The male went red and stared hatred at Harper, his anger was a palpable threat within the room. The older male assured her family. "Please retake your seats, there is no danger to daughter Harper."

They all sat again but remained tense. Ace was unhappy, Harper could tell by the bland face he showed the room.

The older male asked. "How say you, Harper Battle? Was it you and your sister who defeated the foes within the mist?"

Harper stared at the councilor, who had called her a liar as she answered. "If you mean did my sister and I, twelve and half years ago, fight shades and evil demons with swords like these." Instantly, Harper's hands filled with two blue swords that glistened in the dim room. "Then yes."

Suddenly every faerie there went to their knees. Harper's eyes widened as she looked at her sister. Charlie was laughing as everyone rose. The older male said. "We accept Harper Battle's explanation. Council is ended."

All the councilors left the bench, leaving Harper and the others wondering what was about to happen now. Scarlett moved to her side and said. "Dismiss the sword's niece." Which she quickly did. "Now the Queen and councilor Leaf would like a word with you."

"Who?"

Ace whispered. "The older male faerie."

Harper nodded as she asked Scarlett. "What was with the kneeling thing?"

"Respect for the ghost."

Harper nodded, then said. "Oh... okay, we will go and talk to her and him."

Scarlet said. "Umm I think..."

"No, we all go or none." Harper told her.

"This should be fun."

CHAPTER TWENTY-EIGHT:

C harlie watched Frankie and Joy as they sat at a beautiful four seater round table in Frankie's dining room. She sighed when she heard Joy ask Frankie the same question Ace had just asked her. And that was after Fin had demanded to know where June was, because she still had not returned.

They had search parties out looking for her, so far they had not found her. Not only was Sage worried, Charlie was beyond worried. She had not been thrilled having to tell Fin, June was lost. Truthfully, it was something she never wanted to do again. He had said very little, but she would never forget the look he had given both her and Sage before storming from her office. She knew he did not believe that everything that could be done was being done.

Her last recourse was to call Harper back to search for June. And she would do that only if June did not return by the weekend. This was what she had told Fin, he had not been impressed, which was telling by his exit. There was nothing she could do to fix that situation, but what she could fix was this sad situation here.

"Frankie, when is Harper coming home? I miss her." Joy asked as she sat gloomily, doodling in her schoolbook.

"I don't know. Soon, I hope. I miss her too."

"It has been forever." Sighed Joy.

"Only a week. She has a lot to talk about with the councilors and the High Queen. She wanted to show them they are seriously stuck in the wrong century, and that could take a while. They did not seem like they were, move with the times, kind of people." Frankie told her as she stared glumly at the softly falling rain.

"But we need her. Ace is lonely."

"Has he said so?"

"No, but you can see he is. Even the castle is sad."

"Yeah, I know." To change the subject because Frankie's heart was hurting, she asked Joy. "So what do you think of my new bracelet?" It was a chunky silver chain with a sapphire stone.

Joy said. "It is huge. I like it. Did Johner give it to you?"

"Yep, it's my tracker."

Shocked, Joy asked. "He chipped you?"

Frankie grinned. "Yep, something about going off without telling him."

"So, he bugged you. That is wrong, Frankie."

"Nah, this is love, dragon style. He was scared when I went to the High Queen's Grove. This way if I forget to tell him I am leaving, he can find me."

Charlie walked into the room. "Well, as long as you are okay with it?"

Frankie grinned. "I am not, but when Harper gets back and I tell her. Johner will be in so much trouble."

"Devious." Said Charlie with a laugh.

"Hey, he should have told me. Instead of trying to be sneaky."

Joy said. "Oh, so he does not know, you know?"

"Not a clue."

Joy asked Charlie. "Have you heard from Harper?"

"No." At both their sad faces, she said. "Come on you two; it will be only for a few more days."

"Are you sure, Charlie?" Joy asked as she doodled in her book, not looking at her.

"Positive."

"Maybe she will like it there so much she won't want to come home?" Frankie said absently, finally voicing a fear she had since they had left Harper at the High Queen's Grove.

Charlie shook her head. "You know better. You know she will not stay there a moment longer than necessary. Now come on, dinner at my place, Ace is already there." She did not admit that over the last few days, the same thoughts had crossed her mind.

CHAPTER TWENTY-NINE:

L ater that same night Ace woke with sweat soaking his sheets and intense pain locking his body in agony. He threw himself from his bed as he felt like his nerves were on fire; it was so intense he screamed for release. His dragon was under attack it felt as though their souls were being shredded by unseen claws. Together, they went blind with panic as burning slashes of fire seared Ace's body and their souls.

Howling in distress, Ace shifted to dragon and trumpeted his agony and fury as he burst through the balcony doors into the dark skies. His dragon followed the flow of agony as it rose from the castle and landed at the French doors of the medical unit. Ace grunted in pain, then bellowed for Sharm. He trumpeted in despair as he pulled the doors apart and saw Harper's battered, bloody and burned body lying on the floor.

Shifting quickly to his human form, he stepped inside. **"SHARM!"** He yelled as he slid to the floor beside her. "Ancients help her. I am here my Shadow, I am here."

Harper whimpered as she hissed out between bloody lips. "I beat them Ace, you are safe. They can't hurt you ever again."

"Who my heart, who did you beat?"

Then a mist rose around them, and he was confronted by the Ancients. *They lured our Seeker to the gray zone where a demon called from the veil was waiting. She fought well. We have dispatched the demon and told the High Queen. Tell dragon Sharm, demon blood poisons our Seeker. The High Queen has the cure.*

Ace bowed his head. "Thank you, Ancients."

Minutes later, Harper was lifted from Ace's arms and placed upon a bed, and that was all Ace knew as blackness swallowed him whole. Sharm stepped away and gently took Ella's hand in his. "Enough Ella, you will kill yourself trying to heal something we cannot."

"But it is Harper."

"Sad to say we are not enough." He nodded to Keeper, who came and took his Shadow in his arms as silent tears fell from her eyes.

"How is he?" Sharm asked Ash, as he stood beside Ace lying on a bed. "Coming around, I think."

Sharm had flown to the unit when he had heard Ace and his dragon calling him. Only to find Ace and Harper passed out on the floor, blood pooling under Harper's battered body and Ace unresponsive. It was only seconds before everyone else arrived. Reighn had gently lifted Harper to a bed where Sharm and Ella had instantly begun trying to heal her. The brothers and Storm had carried Ace to the other bed. Sharm rubbed his face as Reighn asked. "How is she?"

"The wounds are infected but with what is the problem, they will not heal. I detect poison... but what type is alien to us."

Reighn asked. "Is it like the one that poisoned Storm?"

Ella and Sharm shook their heads. "It is nasty, evil is invading her body and killing her."

"Who is here?" Asked Reighn of Charlie.

Before she could answer, Ace croaked. "Demon blood, call High Queen, she has... cure."

"Who told you this?" Reighn demanded of him.

"Ancients." Then he passed out again.

"What is wrong with him?" Joy asked as she stood in Axl's arms, tears running down her face.

"He is bonded, it is what happens to bonded dragons." Rene` told her. "All of you who are Shadows should know the term 'soul shadow' is not like a mate or wife it actually describes what happens. It is a joining, a bonding when one dies, the other may go with them."

Verity moved to stand next to Ace, her face ravaged with

despair. "Sometimes, if the bond is weak or has been tampered with, Shadows will survive the death of their Shadow's passing. As with Ace and his brother's parents joining."

"It is very rare that happens." Stated Rene.

At Rene` and Verity's disclosure, gasps and cries were heard from all the females in the room. Sage hugged Reighn, and Frankie had her face in Johner's shoulder as she wept silently. Olinda was in Ash's arms. Clint stood helplessly next to Ark as Axl held a crying Joy. Charlie was the only one not crying. She stood within Storm's embrace, her face set like stone, and finally answered Reighn's question.

"Scarlett and Elijah are still at the high court. Only Tarin is here."

This was met with growls and groans of dismay. Reighn said. "He will heal her or die." Then snapped open his phone.

Charlie sobbed back a breath she like everyone else had no faith in the moronic Prince. This was evil she could feel it from where she stood. She had felt its touch once before. It was a vile ooze that invaded Harper's body. Already they could see the mark it was leaving. Fine lines of blue traced her skin.

Verity took Ace's face between her hands and gently told him. "My boy, we have not come so far as to lose you both now. You must fight, fight for Harper, and fight for your family. We need you in our lives. Fight like your Shadow is doing." She asked Sharm. "My son, what do you need?"

"The cure."

Charlie stood, brushing the hair from Harper's bruised and battered face. Her eyes met Reighn's and he could see the knowledge in the look she sent him. She too, knew her sister was dying.

Frankie asked quietly, with tears clogging her throat. "I don't understand. How is she like this? She was at the High Grove. Were they all attacked or just her?"

Charlie said. "I would know if they all were. Daru or Mercca, Tarin's guards, would have raised the alarm. So I am guessing not."

"Well, something happened? Our girl is here, battered, broken and dying. Someone fix her!" Frankie screamed in agony, and the walls of the castle shuddered at her pain.

"Frankie, my heart, please calm. Remember, the castle is hurting. The young will feel your distress." Johner whispered.

"Oh, sorry." She sobbed as she buried her head against Johner again.

"Now, that is power." Whispered Edith to Sage.

"The thing is, what and whose?" Sage muttered in return.

Edith shrugged in reply. Reighn stated in tones cold enough to form ice. "Someone sent our Harper to the gray zone?"

"They must have told her it would help her somehow." Storm said. "There is no other logical reason for her to have returned."

Ash, Ark, and Axl calmly waited as Ash asked. "Who do we kill for this? Our sister and brother lie dying. We are the harbingers of death. Release us my Lord, to exact our revenge."

Reighn said. "When we find out for sure, you are released, until then stand down."

Charlie sucked back a sob as her hand went to her heart. "Oh my Goddess, they made her go back there." Remembered fear and horror shone from her eyes as her voice turned hard. "I will kill them all. They will die. How could they allow this? Scarlett, Elijah. We are... She is their niece." She closed her eyes as she muttered. "The High Queen, how could she do this?" Her eyes, when she opened them, were ghost gray as she pulled her phone from her jeans pocket and snapped it on and hit a button. Storm placed his arm around her, giving what comfort he could. The call was answered as she pressed speaker, but before she could talk, they could hear Scarlett's scathing tones as she snarled. "You lost my niece. Explain to me how you did that?"

A male obviously trying to calm her said, and they could

tell from his tone he was not succeeding very well. "Queen Scarlett, please release Councilor Kildnae."

"Not until he tells me where my niece is and why she was sent back there?"

The same voice said. "I am sure there is a plausible explanation."

Scarlett laughed bitterly. "There better be. You do not understand, because you will not look outside your narrow world."

"This is hardly a time for that old argument now is it Queen Scarlett?" said a condescending female voice.

Scarlett screamed loudly in obvious frustration. "I would shut up Councilor Jasera. You are as much a fool as this one."

"How dare you…"

Loudly talking over the female, Scarlett said. "If my niece dies, you idiot, her Shadow dies. In case you do not realize who that is, his name is Ace Battle, Shield Elite. He is one of four brothers, and their last name should give even you some indication of who they are."

"I do not see how…"

"Be quiet!" ordered a voice that sounded like rustling leaves.

Scarlett hissed. "Her sister Charlie is an Assassin. I know you all know what that is, and her Shadow is a Commander, a killer of rogues. He is brother to the Dragon Lord, who leads the whole dragon nation and is Harper's adoptive brother. They will be on your doorstep when they learn what has happened. And my Grove and I will not lift a finger to help you. So I suggest you answer me **NOW!**" They heard Scarlett's agonized scream, then in a voice devoid of her usual gentle tones, Scarlett said. "You have taken much from me. You killed my sister with your fear and prejudice. If the daughter of my sister dies, I will wipe you and your Groves from this plane of existence."

"Who is this female to have such protectors?" Asked that same male, who was not so calm now. They heard a thump and imagined Scarlett had allowed the male she held to fall, evidenced by someone asking. "Is he dead?"

Then someone else saying. "No, he did not land on his head."

They then heard the cultured tones of the High Queen speak. "The one who you speak of is the Seeker of truth. She is a High Queen. Tell me Councilor Jasera, is that what you, Councilor Kildane and you, Councillor Pearton, are worried about? Is that why you sent her to the gray zone? In the hopes she would be defeated. Was it because she is a ghost or because she is a High Queen without pure blood?"

"Yes." Rasped a male accompanied by a female and other male voices. There were a few rumblings of other voices, whether or not in agreement. It was hard to say without being there.

The High Queen's voice dissolved into anger and disdain. "You stupid, foolish people, you could not leave well enough alone. That sinister, dangerous, unpredictable female, who you sent to her death, had declined my request for her to take up the mantle of High Queen. She said she had a Shadow and a sister, who she loves beyond reason, and a crazy friend who she adores. She told me she was happy living with her aunt and uncle and, most of all, her new family. She would not jeopardize any of them she loves them too much to risk their wrath. You idiots, if you had asked, she would have told you of the promise she made to her Shadow and her brother, before they would consent to her staying here. That she would never leave her home permanently again. She told me they would never forgive her if she broke that promise and you sent her to the gray zone to die."

Then they could hear screams and things falling, then Elijah say. "My Light calm please."

They heard another sound, it was like people choking and King Zale asking. "My Light, do you really want to kill the Councilors?"

The High Queen said in tones never heard from a faerie

before. "Yes, I really do. They took a beautiful, honest, wonderful female and played on her guilt, made her feel she was unsafe and dangerous. They portrayed her as an abomination. She would have gone to save her Shadow, her sister and family, to save us. Especially if they made it seem like she had no choice. You have met her, she would die for those she loves."

"You had no right!" Screamed Scarlett. "She was mine; we loved her." The noises increased until there was nothing but the sounds of death remaining.

The phone fell from Charlie's hand as she said. "I did not get to tell them she is here."

Reighn closed his phone. "I sent a message to Sparrow, she will tell them. She said they will come as soon as the Queens finish killing everyone." They looked at him as he shrugged. "I do not know if she meant it."

They could all tell he did not care. Frankie said. "Did they call me crazy? Because I was tested."

Charlie said. "Oh Frankie, I do love you."

Frankie smiled through her tears. "Oh good, I love you too, don't let her die Charlie."

"I won't, sweet one."

Three faeries arrived. The lead male swaggered in. His whole attitude was one of entitlement and suppressed glee. The other two were reserved, and if Reighn had to guess, he would say they were angry. They reminded him of soldiers on a mission that detested the duty they were forced to do. He bet they did everything they were meant to and not a thing more to discharge their duty to the male they guarded.

Reighn looked at the male faerie who was staying at the Grove. He was the Prince Ace had choked and humiliated when he had threatened Joy. He saw her shuffle behind Charlie, who positioned her further behind Storm and a pale Clint. The movement did not go unnoticed by Axl. Reighn sighed, he would have to address that situation shortly, or the Prince was going to end up dead. Frankie stiffened when she saw the male, she gave a nod to his two guards. Ace was not the only one to have problems with the male. Harper and Tarin had words and threats were said, mainly from Harper. Only the Prince's guards had stopped her killing him. Reighn knew for a fact June had on several occasions smooth ruffled feelings as dragons and shifters alike had been close to hurting the male. He did have the knack, June told Reighn, of upsetting people. Whether it was intentional or by stupidity, she could not discover. He wished she were here now. She would know how to handle the male, because he just knew the fool was going to piss off the Battle brothers or Charlie. Which meant Storm or Goddess forbid Sage, which also meant him.

Tarin looked around at the people in the room and smirked. "Surely, this does not require everyone. It is only a simple matter of poisoning."

Edith said. "Oh, it really does and no, you moron. It is not just poisoning, it is demon blood."

Reighn grimaced because he had just remembered Edith and if anyone was going to get pissed off, it would be her. Tarin ignored her altogether with a sniff of disdain. Then he turned to where Harper was lying, only to be confronted by the three Battle brothers.

"We don't have time for this." Tarin snarled. "If you want the female to live."

Queen Scarlett and King Elijah hurried in with their guards. They were blood splattered and Scarlett had a wild look in her eyes. Kai, the High Queen's brother, said to Tarin. "Leave, if you want to live." With one look at the male, he left. Kai said. "Remain." To the guards, who bowed and stood by the opened door.

Edith smiled and said to Sage. "I like him."

Frankie said. "He is the High Queen's brother, Kai."

Edith frowned. "Oh, another prince?"

"Nope. He denounced his title."

Edith grinned. "Ooh, I really like him."

Scarlett rushed to Sharm and handed him a vial of orange fluid. He immediately filled a syringe and then plunged it straight into Harper's heart, which made most of the females gag at this unexpected action. "Dear Goddess, some warning." Sage moaned as she rushed from the room, her hand over her mouth.

Reighn looked after her. Edith asked him. "You aren't going to see if she is alright?"

He shook his head. "No, she yells at me. I have learned to wait."

"I see." She gave his arm a pat. "Wise dragon."

"We are getting there."

The Queen enfolded Charlie in a hug. "Niece, I am so sorry."

Charlie hugged her back. "I know you are, we all do. We heard you on the phone."

Elijah smiled. "We are pleased she will be well. We were worried."

Scarlett asked. "What phone?"

Loa said. "Oh, so sorry. I bumped my phone... it must have answered without me noticing." Not one person there thought the guard had done so by accident.

Elijah said with a raised brow. "You will have to be more careful in the future."

Loa bowed her head and answered. "I will endeavor to be, my King."

Reighn asked quietly of Elijah as he watched Harper's eyes start to flicker. "Did they leave any alive?"

Elijah turned darkened eyes to his. "One or two, the High Queen was distraught, as was my Queen. There is a need for a new council."

Reighn nodded in understanding. "We are pleased, we do not have to go to war."

Elijah nodded as well. "War tends to put a dampener on friendships."

"This is true." Agreed Reighn. "Will there be repercussions?"

Elijah shrugged. "Confinement to Groves for all Queens until further notice. Our High Queen and King have decided this is an opportune time to update and reorganize Faerie-dom." He smiled as Scarlett came with Charlie to where they stood.

Scarlett told them. "She will be well by morning, well enough to give her Shadow and you Reighn heart palpitations for a while longer." She cupped Charlie's cheek. "They sent her to that place on her own. I will never forgive them for that. She will never forgive me for that."

Charlie hugged her back and whispered. "I know, and she loves you. There is nothing to forgive. This was Harper being noble. She was seeking something to fix when nothing was broken. I think she lost her good sense to fear. Fear she would hurt all of us."

Frankie agreed. "She hates it to be known, but she will die for us all, and they would have taken advantage of that fact. Her problem is she loves too deeply, but as problems go, it is one we can live with."

Scarlett smiled. "Well, it is up to us to make sure she lives a long, long time."

Reighn heaved a deep sigh. "We thank you as well. We all would have missed her. It is hard to remember a time she was not in our lives."

"I know." Scarlett said. "She gave us one of her works. It is beautiful, beyond exquisite."

Reighn grinned. "So you are the ones she gave it to. I coveted it. I am pleased it went to a good home, she is truly gifted."

"In more ways than one." Elijah agreed.

Charlie said to Sharm. "You realize, I will have to listen to Harper bitch forever about that scar you left with that injection."

Sharm spread his hands. "It could not be helped, it is the nature of the antidote, but I have to say I am happy she will be annoyed with you and not me." He grinned widely at

Charlie's frowning face.

Frankie sighed. "Won't matter if it was necessary. Believe me when I tell you that female can bitch, you should have heard her when I accidentally, and it was an accident. No matter what she says, burned my hair off with her blow torch. She never lets me forget it."

"See!" Charlie said. "That was how long ago, Frankie?"

"Oh ages, at least three or four months."

These females. Ace's dragon said, as he listened to the affection and fear lining their words. *They love our Shadow.*

Yes, they do. Ace agreed. He sat up slowly, the pain thankfully was gone. His eyes naturally sought and found Harper and was relieved to see she was breathing easier. He could feel her growing stronger.

"Tell me about it!" Sage moaned as she walked back in from the bathroom. "I asked her once, just once, if I could touch the thing that she was working on and she threw the biggest tantrum..."

Reighn interrupted her. "Because when she let you touch a sculpture the first time, you broke it."

"It was an accident. It slipped from my fingers when she growled and she still pouts."

"You touched her art?" Asked a horrified Edith.

Sage hunched her shoulders a little in defense. "Well yeah, it was there, damn it."

"But her art." Edith looked at her like she was an alien.

"Hey sister, enough, you keep your horrified looks to yourself." Sage said as she pointed her finger at Edith.

"I would have banned you for life."

Reighn laughed as he told them. "She banned her for two months."

"So unfair." Sage looked at Frankie. "How long were you banned for?"

Frankie shrugged. "Still not allowed in."

Kai said. "Wow, she is mean."

Verity scolded them. "Harper is perfectly fine. She is not

mean, I never have any problems with her, apart from Sundays... she will try to get out of them, but she comes when she is home." They all looked at her; she raised her eyebrows and asked. "Why do you look like that?"

Frankie told her. "She fears you. That's why."

"Oh really," Verity smiled. "How delightful."

Rene` said. "Not that scared, she still misses Sunday, if she can."

Ace shook his head as he slipped from the bed and picked his Shadow up, and with her in his arms, turned to see every eye upon him. He simply said. "My family, I thank you. Thank you for my Shadow's life and for my life."

Verity said. "You are loved, both of you. Take her to your home. Relax, be together."

Ace nodded, then looked at his brothers and told them what he should have said many years ago. "My brothers, my love for you grows daily."

All three inclined their heads, Ash said for them all in his quiet way. "For you, we would raze the world."

Suddenly the faeries, and everyone who was not a dragon. Realized how close the world had come to seeing the Battle brothers do what they had been trained for. Rene` said. "If you or Harper need me, call."

"Thank you." Ace bowed his head to Reighn. "My Lord."

"My brother, please be at peace."

Ace inclined his head again in thanks to Scarlett and Elijah and the other faeries. Then included them and everyone else in his warm look as he strode from the room.

CHAPTER THIRTY:

Harper woke and felt like she had been stomped on repeatedly. She groaned as she rolled over.

Ace rose from his chair, where he had been keeping vigil since bringing her back to their home twenty-four hours ago. He sat on the edge of the bed. "Hello, my love."

"Ace, I was dreaming I fought a demon to protect you."

Ace brushed her auburn hair from her face. "I wish I could say it was a dream."

Harper closed her eyes and whispered. "Aww, crap!"

He gathered her in his arms and carried her to the chair he had just vacated. He could feel the castle hum beneath his feet as the Ancients sang. Ace smiled. "It is the first time since you came back that they have sung."

"I am sorry, so very sorry." She told him and did something she had not done since she believed Charlie was dead. She cried as the rain fell outside.

Ace let her cry as he watched the gentle fall of rain against the windows. When she had cried herself out, he handed her a cloth and poured her coffee. She wiped her face and then sipped her coffee and told him how she had fallen victim to stupidity. He listened to her tell how she believed the councilors when they told her she was still infected and that she had left demons in the gray zone. Hearing this, she rushed to kill the shades and demons before they could kill Ace and Charlie and everyone else in retaliation. She laughed bitterly as she said. "Even saying that sounds stupid." She shook her head and said. "When I was in the zone, the demon was bigger and nastier than the previous times I fought demons there. Ace, he was huge and fast, so wickedly fast." Faster than anything she had seen before. She told him how she fought, but every time she cut the demon down, he regrew. Bigger, tougher, nastier. She only had knives, as she could not call her swords to her, and she was losing hope until the Ancients arrived. They destroyed the demon and brought her to the castle, to Ace.

He told her how the Queens found out that some councilors had called the demon using some long forgotten spell. They had also used another spell which removed her ability to call forth her swords. He told her the Queens had killed all but two councilors in their anger and grief. Harper could not find it within herself to feel sorry for them. They almost killed her, which meant her Ace would have died. They rolled the dice and lost.

He then told her how Sharm had run blood tests, as no one could understand how she would have not called him or Charlie. She frowned as she said. "It never occurred to me. That is wrong."

Ace agreed. "They found a hallucinogenic drug designed for humans in your blood. Apparently, you had been ingesting it for days. They probably started giving it to you after we left. It made you easily susceptible to their plans."

"Huh, so I am not stupid."

"Far from it."

She rubbed her chest as he kissed her and then said. "You need to shower, and I need to call everyone and let them know you are awake and well."

"I love you." She told him.

Ace stilled as he said. "That is the first time you have told me that."

"Are you sure?" She asked with a frown.

"Why would I lie?" He asked, the same question Edith asked all the time.

Harper laughed. "Oww! Oh, don't make me laugh."

Ace kissed her neck. "I love you too, Harper. I was scared I thought I would lose you."

She kissed him silent knowing how close they had both

come to dying. Softly, she told him. "We survived and later, when I can move without hurting, I will show you in detail how much I love you. I am an artist and this body of yours is a masterpiece I want to explore over and over."

Ace grinned as he huskily told her. "I will await that time. Now go shower."

She grinned and eased off him, and made her way to the bathroom. He heard the shower turn on as Charlie answered her phone.

"She is awake and sore…"

"Son. Of. A. Bitch. Why is there a scar on my chest?"

"I knew it, she is going to blame me." Charlie whimpered as they heard Harper yell. "What did Charlie let them do to me?"

Charlie hung up as Ace laughed and watched the sun come out from behind the clouds. His dragon mused. *Our life was never this amusing before.*

It definitely is not boring!

CHAPTER THIRTY-ONE:

A few days later Harper was up and walking around and in her barn, it had taken some persuading to get Ace on board with her plan. But she had promised to only make sure everything was in order and not actually do any work.

He was with Rene` and Reighn, trying to decide what to do with his future. Fin had rescued June and was at their home recovering from her adventures. Harper had the feeling she would not be leaving home anytime soon. Scarlett was still confined to the Grove, but as it happened, she was happy it seemed as though Harper and Charlie were going to become cousins. Scarlett was with child or a faerie baby. Harper stood still as she pondered what a baby faerie was called. Something to ask at the next Sunday family day.

"Auntie Harper... Auntie Harper, Grandmama brought me to say hello." Called Kelsey as she and Verity walked in. Following slowly behind was Edith and for some unknown reason, she looked uncomfortable, an unusual occurrence for the bear. The looks she was giving Verity as she walked around the barn had Harper guessing why.

Kelsey was showing Verity things she knew the names of as Harper replaced her tools in the order she liked. Someone or many someone's with sticky fingers had been touching her tools while she was indisposed. Her money was on Sage and Frankie. "So ladies, what can I do for you?"

"I have been to the gallery again and viewed your pieces." Verity told her with a smile.

Pleased, Harper smiled. "Thank you. Did you like them?"

"Most of them, I adored."

Harper raised her eyebrows at Edith. "I see... most of them?"

"Yes, but what I did not like is for another time and not the reason for my visit today."

"It is not?"

"No."

"So what is the reason for your visit, Lady Verity? You know you do not need a reason to visit me here."

"Thank you, Harper. I want two portraits done."

"Okay."

"Yes." Verity walked around knowing Edith had said not to ask Harper, but truly this child was talented and she was family. In another time in history, she would have been considered a Master.

If Masters were allowed to be female, of course. Her dragon reminded her.

Well, that is true. She asked Harper. "I know you do portraits?"

Harper ducked her head to stop the smile from showing as she replied. "Sometimes I take a commission."

"I see."

"I am guessing you want to commission me for a portrait?"

"Yes, I require Rene` and Reighn as Dragon Lords, past and present, to be immortalized."

"Let me get this straight; you want to commission me?"

"Yes, why? What is wrong with that? It is done all the time. What is your problem, Edee? She is an artist. She paints. I want the portraits done."

Edith vacillated between amusement and embarrassment at what Verity asked Harper to do. She considered Harper one of the all-time great artists of this century. She said. "Verity, someone of Harper's skill and tal…"

"So how much you offering." Harper asked, cutting Edith off.

Edith stuttered. "Wh… wh… what?"

"Well?" Harper asked Verity. "I need to know. I am not cheap, you know?"

"What is your normal rate?" Verity asked, crossing her

hands over each other in what she considered the haggling position of a matron when buying fruit. Not that she had ever brought fruit, but the principle was the same.

Harper took up her haggling position, which consisted of leaning against her work bench next to a sitting Kelsey. "Well, it has been a while." Meaning never, she had never accepted a commission for a portrait. The ones she had done were of friends or people she admired.

"And you are asking for two? That puts the price up a lot. Right Kelsey?"

"Yep, Grandmama, we are not cheap, yah know!" Harper high-fived the five-year-old as she grinned.

"Oh I know." said an amused Verity.

Kelsey folded her arms much as her aunt had done and leaned back against the block of wood that was sitting on the work bench. Edith sat on the bench opposite them and asked. "Do you have an agent, Harper?"

Harper scratched at a bit of dust on her cheek. Kelsey followed suit, and she frowned as Harper did. With amusement coloring her words, she said. "No, but I am sure I can get one. What do you think, Kelsey?"

"It's Grandmama Verity."

"I know."

"You should do a drawing of Grandmama, she is pretty."

Harper nodded. "That is true." She looked at Verity as she told her. "So the deal is, you convince Ace to take on the job as Commander for the cadet school and you sit for a portrait. Also, you have to convince Grace to sit for me, then you let Edith show them for a year. Sound good?" She asked Kelsey.

Kelsey thought for a minute, then said. "You forgot cookies and Frankie."

"Oh yeah, of course. You have to swear to tell Frankie you made me do them. And Kelsey and I want six months' worth of cookies for when the kids are all here for art classes."

Edith was smiling with her head bent, so Kelsey could not see her. Verity drew herself up to her full height and said. "Is that your final word on it?"

Kelsey looked at Harper, who nodded. The little girl said. "It is a fair offer, Grandmama. I would take it."

"I do not know, that sounds like an awful lot of cookies?" Verity replied doubtfully.

Exasperated, Kelsey told her. "Grandmama its cookies."

"Alright, I give in. It was a hard bargain. Miss Kingsley."

Kelsey smiled full of pride as she jumped down and ran to Storm when he entered, telling him all about her bargaining.

Verity said. "Are you sure, Harper?"

"Oh yes, Ace really wants to do that job, he just thinks he won't be any good at it."

"No dear, about my portrait."

"No portrait, no deal." Stated Harper sharply.

Edith said. "And you have to promise to let me show it in my gallery. There will be no chickening out."

"Oh... Oh really!" Verity gave her hair a pat. "Well, I suppose so. I will have to decide what to wear and then there is talking Grace into it as well. We may have to buy something new." She muttered to herself as she walked out, followed by Storm and Kelsey, who waved goodbye. "You made her happy." Edith told her.

Harper grinned. "I live to do that."

"Oh, shut up. So sticking around?"

"Four portraits, a Shadow and teenage boy and girl who is going to shift and a friend who is with a cub or egg. What do you think?"

Edith sat completely still. "Sharm is going to scream. How do you know? I just found out this morning."

"Seeker remember?" Harper grinned at Edith's surprised expression.

"Oh, I forgot, we are announcing it this family day."

Harper was going to tell her that hiding secrets among shifters and dragons was impossible, but the excited look on her face made her say instead. "Well, congrats ahead of time. I will say nothing. Now do you think June will be up to coming?"

Edith nodded. "Sharm says she and the babies will be good to go. Fin, on the other hand, well that is debatable."

They laughed, thinking of the dragon who had his life turned upside down. "You happy about the... you know what?" Harper asked as she made round gestures over her stomach.

Edith smiled, and her whole body shone. "You know, I thought I wouldn't be, but I am. I really am."

Harper smiled and hugged her. "I am happy for you. If anyone deserves late night feeds, dirty diapers and crying, it is you."

Edith growled as Harper released her before she could swing at her and ran. Edith laughingly yelled as she jumped down. "Hey girl, if it can happen to me. What chance do you have?"

"Friggin hell!"

EPILOGUE:

Early Sunday morning found Ace standing on the balcony drinking his first cup of coffee for the day. Harper walked out and slipped her arms around him. "What are you staring at?"

He motioned down below to Joy and Axl standing close together. Axl wore his swords and had a bag slung over his shoulder. Reighn stood by an opened portal. "Oh, so he is leaving then?"

Ace sighed. "Yeah, he got into a fight last night."

"So, you guys fight all the time. It means nothing."

"He was drunk on unicorn ale. He lost his shit, or so Storm told me."

"Okay, so yeah, that is not good. Storm doesn't suffer that kind of behavior."

"Reighn is worried. Axl's dragon will find everyone a threat, me, Clint, any male she is around. And she is ready to shift, which for his dragon will signal maturity. He will know she is too young, but her wolf will demand she take him as mate and he will deny her. Because again she is too young and she will pine."

Harper asked. "And she won't now with him gone?"

He nodded as he sipped his coffee. "She will, but it will be a minor ache, so the Matrons tell me. It will be much worse for her, for him and Dragon's Gap, if he remains."

"So he will leave." She asked, feeling sad for Axl, for Joy and for her Ace, who would miss him.

Ace said. "He knows and agrees."

"For how long?" Harper asked sadly, already missing the male that had become her friend. She loved watching movies with him. He was hysterically funny, pointing out all the mistakes.

"He will do a year at a time. We can go visit him."

"But not Joy?"

"No, not Joy."

"He will be missed a lot. It won't be the same without him."

"I know, but it is for the best. She knows that; she is very mature for a twelve-year-old." Ace muttered.

Harper looked down at the couple and said. "We grow up fast, when we have to."

He turned her in his arms just as Axl walked into the portal and Joy fell into Reighn's arms. "I love you, my ghost."

"I love you too, my dragon."

LOVE'S IMPULSE

Fin and June's Story

Authors note:
This Novella is written to coincide with book 5, Ace and Harper's story.

CHAPTER ONE:

June sat in her office and looked around blankly at the walls. She felt like she was living in a surreal nightmare. She did not see the photos of all her nieces and nephews, or the family photos of which there were many. The painting of a lone wolf climbing a snow-covered mountain took all her attention. Harper had given her the painting when she had admired it.

She had been forced to wrestle it from Edith, who was positive every piece of art Harper produced was hers. In the past, present or even the future, it all belonged to her gallery. June took great pleasure in making sure Edith knew she was in possession of several pieces Harper had gifted her. This painting spoke to her, a silly saying, she always thought, until now. The wolf's head hung low, searching for something in the snow or maybe it was just exhausted. June would admit she spent time each day wondering which scenario it was, and if there were clues within the painting to tell her. She knew she could ask Harper, but worried she would say it was just a wolf climbing a mountain in the snow. For her, that did not work she needed it to be more. In truth, she saw herself as the wolf in the painting; it was she that was searching for the love she so desperately wanted. She knew if she could shift to her wolf, she would look like that lone wolf pining for her mate.

Her head was in her hands and as she pulled on her hair, she again asked herself. How was it possible that her mate could just turn up out of the blue and be Ella's uncle, a damn dragon?

Finlay Slorah, a male that took her breath away. The very first time her wolf scented him, she knew he was her mate.

If she was honest with herself, she was not that surprised he was a dragon; it stood to reason; she lived at Dragon's Gap and all her friends were mated to dragons. What surprised her was the male's refusal to bond with her? He had some weird notion that she needed security, as if bonding with a dragon wasn't security enough.

Sadly for June, before she came here having someone have your back only occurred because they were ordered to, or she paid dearly for their security. Never because they felt you were worthy enough to warrant it. But since arriving at Dragon's Gap, she had made friends, genuine friends who had become family. They were people she trusted to have her back, so she had more security than she needed.

The other notion he had was he was supposed to provide a place for them to live? When that was just not true, as she had told him. Sage had told him she had a home already, Reighn had told him, Lord Rene` and Lord Andre` gifted her a property not long after she arrived here. As far as June was concerned, there was no reason they could not live in the house she owned. But he just negated her home and would not listen. Especially when she tried to tell him she was very happy with the property and did not need some kind of enormous estate. She had invited him numerous times to visit the homestead she lovingly restored. So far, he had declined every offer. June sighed she would never admit this to him or anyone, but she and her wolf felt rejected with his attitude towards their den. She had spent months renovating her home, ready for when she would live there, and for some reason, he could not get that.

"Ohh." She groaned and laid her head on her arms as she remembered his other issue, the money. She had a nice tidy bank account, he was immensely wealthy, as most dragons were. She was not concerned about that in fact, she did not care she was house and land rich, and he was cash rich. Seemed fair to her, but not to dragon Finlay Slorah. There was also the little matter of the major hurdle. Employment, he needed to work; she understood that, but he was working. Unfortunately, he wanted to make sure the job was a good fit for him. Apparently, almost three months was not long enough to know, even though he really enjoyed every aspect of his job and was not looking for anything else. He told her the right position made him more worthy, and that was important. How did one fight that? A male's honor was not to be belittled or so Sage and Claire told her and she agreed with that, she really did. Except it was just so unfair. She wanted a home, cubs eventually, she wanted her mate, damn it!

Her wolf was feeling rejected and sadly June was starting to agree with her their dragon was just not into her. The male was everything she wanted. *Well... hell,* she nodded to herself. He was what any female would want, tall, buff, *OMG!* Was the male buff, and he packed serious hardware. June felt herself go warm remembering his hard flat stomach and eight pack that was just such a turn on. Well, it turned her on. Sighing, she stared blankly at the small statue of a female standing with a wolf, her hand on its head, both of them looking into the distance. Harper had given her the statue just before she left on assignment. She smiled as she remembered sneaking it into her bag so Edith would not see it and glare at them both. She had promised Harper not to say anything to Edith, even though she knew Edith would see it the first time she entered her office. She was like a heat-seeking missile when it came to art.

June pouted it was exquisite just like Fin, he was just so handsome, and she wasn't the only one to think so. She had heard there were a few females who thought the same. She was going to have to steer them away from her man, but did he see they were sniffing around him? Her mate was an oblivious male for a hard as nails warrior who was not a babe in the woods. She was honest enough to admit that fact did please her. She was not interested in any young male who was still out to impress and did not know his own mind. But seriously, Fin was as stubborn as the day was long. He annoyed her to her last nerve.

June would agree that some days she was more wolf than human, and she did take on her wolf's thoughts about her mate. They conversed, maybe not in words, but their conversation in emotions was very clear. Her wolf was pining for her mate; she did not understand human relationship issues. She just wanted her mate, June understood that too. Which is why, last night she had given into her wolf's demands and asked Fin when they were going to make this mating happen? He had kissed her and told her again he was working on it. Like that meant anything. When he first said it to her, she had laughed. She did not laugh so much last night, his evasiveness made her see red. So instead of taking the soft approach, June lost her temper. Telling him to get his act together, and until he did, she refused to see him. She had stormed from his apartment, and her last look of him had been him standing in the middle of his lounge with his mouth open in shock. Her anger carried her all the way to her apartment and through a bath and two glasses of wine. When she finally calmed down enough to think, she did feel bad about issuing an ultimatum to him. Which was not helped by her wolf fretting over her demands well into the morning hours.

Consequentially, when she rolled out of bed this morning, she was still tired and hovering close to the days when she used to make decisions she regretted. And to make the day just that much more perfect, it was family Sunday. So when she finally arrived for breakfast, dreading having to see Fin after the night before. She heard not from him, but from his niece, her friend Ella that Fin had left Dragon's Gap to see some friends he worked with. It seemed he had known days ago he would be leaving because he told Ella and Verity he would not be home for family day but he never mentioned it to her. She was devastated, what more proof did she need? The male did not want her.

Glumly she sat now in her office, having to remain cheerful in front of her family was tiring. She just needed time to collect herself, to think clearly before dinner. Depression swamped her, with Fin going away and not telling her he was leaving. It seemed like a big indicator something was wrong. She could only come to the conclusion it was her. Fin had days to tell her he was going or to ask her to accompany him. Was he ashamed of her because she was not a dragon? He never acted like he was, but truth was in the pudding. So Grace would say. Whatever that meant.

Sadly, this weekend sort of said all there was to say about their relationship, and June was tired of feeling like a puppet dancing to his tune. Time to woman up and do some thinking and to do that, she needed to get away from here. She knew Charlie was going to ask Harper to do another sensitive retrieval tonight, but she also knew Reighn was going to order Harper to remain home. So she would do the job, if Charlie would let her. Sighing she admitted it had been a while since she had been on the road. She drummed her fingers on the desk, having second thoughts. Could she do this? Was she prepared to do this? Maybe she couldn't? She straightened her shoulders and flicked her hair behind her ears. She could do this, she was a good retriever, and she always brought her people home. She needed to do this the time away to think that a retrieval would give her would be invaluable. If she had to, she would beg Charlie to give her the job.

With the decision made, June ran to her apartment, which thankfully was on the first family floor of the castle. As it was Sunday, the castle was quiet, not much foot traffic to cross paths with her, therefore she did not have to explain where she was going and why. She loved her surrogate family, but they were slightly overprotective at times and for some unknown reason, they always looked at her decisions with suspicion. But if she was wily as only a wolf could be, she should be able to slip away without anyone knowing, especially. *Mr. Working. On. It, dragon.*

Angry all over again, June quickly packed her retrieval bag, some things she realized as she placed spare clothes and ammunition in her pack, one never forgot how to do. She loaded up on her personal weapons and changed into her old hunting outfit, jeans, shirt, combat boots and leather coat. Ready, she looked around, decided she had forgotten nothing, and quietly left her apartment, running down the wide stone stairs. She stashed her gear in a small closet off the landing and walked into the family room.

CHAPTER TWO:

It seemed luck was on her side. Charlie and Harper were standing together by themselves. June smothered a laugh when they both jumped a little as she stepped up to the two of them and slipped the paper Charlie held from her fingers. "I will go. Reighn has said Harper is not to go out again."

Charlie looked concerned as she whispered. "June that is not a good idea."

Harper agreed, saying. "Sage will be unhappy."

June looked at the sisters, knowing she needed to make this sound good or they would foil her plan. "Excuse me, I was with Sage when we first started the retrievals and I am quite capable of looking after myself."

"What will Sage and Fin say?" Charlie asked softly.

June could see Harper was confused, not realizing as everyone else did that Fin and she were in a courtship of sorts. "Why will they say anything? I am not a child to be asking permission. I am capable and healthier than Harper at the moment. No offense."

"Oh, none taken. Truth is truth." Harper agreed with a grin.

"Charlie, I will get it done. I will make it okay. I promise." June argued, hoping Charlie would not ask Sage's opinion. The last thing she needed was to have Sage demanding to know why she wanted to leave the castle. Charlie smiled, but it did not reach her eyes. She was unhappy, but in truth, she could not say no. June was as far as she knew a very good retriever, and as she had said. She was no child, and well, Harper was hurt more than she was letting on. June whispered. "Charlie, I need this. I need to go out for a while. I need to clear my head. Please don't make me beg."

"Oh, June never. Go… go and stay safe, get dead, and I will kill you myself."

June nodded. "See you in a few days and thank you Charlie." She hurriedly slipped from the room as both Charlie and Harper watched her go. She ignored her wolf's sorrowful howl as she pleaded with her to understand. *We need this to decide what our next step is. Please don't be sad. We will be back.*

Later that night, Fin leaned against the wall outside June's apartment and waited for her to return. He had not attended family day, opting instead to go and see his old comrades. He had received a message three days ago letting him know they wished to return home. His dragon insisted he tell June and even invite her to go with him. But he had been worried, the planet his friends had been stationed on was known as a rogue destination. Finally, he had convinced his dragon she would be safer at home. So he did not tell her he was going, thinking to spare her feelings about being left behind. Ella would say he decided for her and did not give her enough credit to decide for herself. He sighed as he again shifted, trying to get comfortable on the hard floor. Maybe Ella and his dragon were right, maybe he was too protective. June was an intelligent, amusing, gifted female. And he was a lucky male to have her or would be if he could only stop pissing her off as he had last night. His dragon told him. *Because you will not employ the strategy, we agreed on.*

We cannot use that. Our strategy did not take into account shifters. They are all about emotions, not as we had originally thought, dragon rational. Wolves are not dragons, and June is more wolf than human.

So what are our options? Our Shadow is becoming restless and annoyed with our delay.

We are not ready.

His dragon went silent with that, and Fin mentally shrugged. Maybe courting a female wolf differed from preparing for battle. Maybe not all contingencies could be foreseen. He would think on it. But in saying that he knew he was right, he had to make sure he was secure, that he and his dragon could keep her safe. It was something he had learned as an adolescent male. His brother had not done enough for his Shadow or hatchling, and Ella had grown up without him or her parents. He would never allow that to happen to June or any of his young, if he actually had any. *Where was she?*

His dragon murmured. *Maybe she has gone to stay at her home. You are tired. Today was harder than you thought it would be. Settling males that have not lived in civilized society for many years was enough to try my patience. Go to bed, if we are not to see our Shadow. I do not want to be here, where I can scent her anger and frustration. It adds to mine.*

Sighing, he agreed. *Alright. We will find her tomorrow and take her to lunch.*

His dragon grinned, and Fin could almost feel him drooling.

Hamburgers... I like hamburgers.

Yes, you greedy dragon.

CHAPTER THREE:

F in was annoyed, in fact he was beyond annoyed, he was probably closer to incandescent with rage. He walked into the health center where his niece Ella stood talking to an older male; and waited as he paced and felt his anger reach new heights.

He had just been told when he went to June's office to ask her to lunch that she was not there. It seemed she never came into work today, in fact; she was not at the castle or Dragon's Gap. Apparently, his Shadow left last night to do a retrieval. He was here at Ella's place of work because he knew she would know if this was, in fact true. And as she flicked worried eyes toward him and then away, he felt his heart sink. She knew his June had left him.

His dragon moaned pitifully. *Our fault, we took too long. Wolves are not dragons.*

Shut up! The plan was yours as well.

We are doomed to be alone.

Dear Goddess, what kind of warrior are you?

A LONELY ONE! His dragon roared, almost dropping Fin to his knees.

"Uncle Fin?" Ella said carefully after she had finished talking to the male who, with one hesitant look at Fin, hurried away. Ella felt a little sorry for her uncle. He looked like his world had been rocked and not in a good way, as Edee would say. When Charlie told her this morning at breakfast that June had left to go on a retrieval, she wanted to jump up and down with glee. Finally, June was taking a stand, but now, looking at her devastated uncle, she was not sure that was the best plan. She felt her Uncle Fin was being ridiculous; she understood his reasons, as did June. Shoot, everyone did, but there was safe and secure, then there was procrastinating. Her uncle was dithering, as Harper would say, and like June, she did not know why.

"Ella, I cannot find June."

"She is not here. She left Dragon's Gap."

He felt his lungs squeeze his chest in fear and pain. He had known she was not here, but for Ella to baldly say as much, took his breath away. "Why... why would she leave without me knowing?"

"Why would she not?" Ella asked as she led him into an office. Hers by the scent of it. Fin thought as he paced the small room. "She is my Shadow."

"Is she? All indications say you have no claim on her."

Fin growled. "You know I do, we have been in a courtship."

Really, males! Her dragon said. *Why must they complicate everything?* Ella sighed before replying. "You have been in a courtship. June and her wolf have been telling you the courtship was over. They want their mate; you denied her. What did you think was going to happen?"

Fin paced again as he told her. "She understood."

Ella was sure she heard him pouting. Trying not to laugh, she said sharply. "No, she did not, do not fool yourself, she was patient, she was kind and understanding. Now she has lost patience, she is no longer willing to be a doormat, and she does not understand. All she knows is her mate has rejected her."

He slumped into a chair, his chin on his chest. "I do not know what to do. We, my dragon and I, had a plan?"

Sage strode into the room. She hugged Ella, then stood looking at Fin. "Well, you better think of something. My sister left home, without my knowledge and it is your fault." Fin quickly stood, his face a mask of shame and pain as Sage asked with annoyance, coloring her words. "Ella, how did you find out?"

"Charlie told me this morning, when we had breakfast."

"Call her here, please."

Ella inwardly grimaced. She knew that tone, it boded ill for the one she was angry with… and Sage was angry. It was easy to tell by the way she spoke in the voice of the Dragon Lady. "Certainly Dragon Lady."

Sage eyed the male. "Please sit, you and I need to have a discussion." She took the seat next to him. "I am going to tell you a few things about your Shadow." Fin looked at her and said nothing. Sage nodded, *good the male was willing to listen.* "Some of this you may know, some not. There is stuff she will not tell you herself. Her grandmother raised June after her parents left her with her."

Fin nodded. "I know she was a mean, bitter, nasty female who abused my June."

Sage sighed. "Yes, she did, and often. June finally escaped her at thirteen and found a wolf pack, a street pack, in New York. Thankfully, they were good to her. The Alpha believed all pups should be educated, he did not care if the wolves under him were half or full blood. Believe me, that was unusual back then. Sadly, when June was eighteen, her Alpha was killed in a challenge. The new Alpha was not a progressive thinker like the old Alpha, and he hated all half-bloods. The old Alpha feared for June and the half-bloods under his care, so just before the challenge. He made her swear if he lost to take all the half-bloods away. He gave her a lot of money and a list of places she could take them to so they would be safe. As I said, the old Alpha was defeated, and before the new Alpha established himself and his pack. June did as she promised. I am sure you can imagine he did not like that. He hunted her throughout America for months. Probably still is, for all we know. When she had all those under her care safe, she traveled the world doing basically what we do now. Except she took them to my uncle's pack for safety."

Fin looked thoughtful as he said. "I did not know any of that, she never discusses it."

"No, some of those memories are unkind to her and there are some things she did that she would rather forget."

"I can understand that."

"I am sure you can. The thing you should know about June is she can become wolf-crazy."

"What is this term? I have never heard of it before, have you niece?"

"No, I have not. Is it a disease?" Ella asked Sage as Charlie walked in.

"Hello Sage, Fin, Ella."

"Charlie, we are discussing June." Sage told her as Charlie took a seat. She eyed Sage warily, noticing the tight way she held herself. If she was not mistaken, her Dragon Lady was not pleased.

"I see. I am sorry you disagree with my choice but as a retriever she is first class, and she was capable, but most importantly she was willing."

Fin stood. "She is my Shadow; you had no right."

Charlie's eyes went ghost gray as she stood as well. "Stand down Fin or I will put you down."

"You may try Assassin." He growled back at her.

"Stand down, my friend." Storm calmly said as he entered the room.

Fin took a step back and shook his head. "I beg your pardon, my apologies."

"Understandable." Charlie said quietly as Storm nodded.

Sage stood, none were left in any doubt that the Dragon Lady stood before them and she was angry. She pointed at Charlie, and in a voice like ice, said. "I am furious with you. There was no way you should have allowed her to leave for whatever reason without talking to me first. Especially after the last time she did a retrieval. I know you know what happened then." Then she pointed at Fin. "You and your plan of courting have done nothing but cause her to feel rejected. Which has done nothing other than drag up her parents and grandmother's rejection. You have made her doubt herself. She feels as if she is unworthy of being mated. Now your work to convince her otherwise when she returns will be like climbing up a mountain without legs. In fact, that may be easier." She took a breath and said softer, but no one was left in any doubt about how angry she still was. "Realize, I am her sister, so what I am saying now is for your ears only. What June has is not for all to learn about, and it is not a disease. It is something that occurs to wolves that have suffered in their formative years as she did. Wolf- crazy, for you who do not know the term, means she will take chances you and I would never think to do. She will not see the perils because she does not want to, she will willing walk into a trap in the belief she will best it or her opponents. Why? Because when she is wolf-crazy, she never sees the danger in any situation. If people like us get into trouble or feel outnumbered, we will call for backup she will not. She would never even think to do so. It is not a flaw, and it is not because she has a death wish or does not care. She cares, just not about herself, because she believes she is indestructible, she becomes wolf-crazy." She looked at Fin and said quietly. "The last time she was truly wolf-crazy was just after we started retrievals. She rescued three pups from their abusive father. In the process, she killed fourteen wolves before she came home and she did that by walking into their den, knowing she was outnumbered and outgunned with no backup. When I asked her why, she would take such a chance. She shrugged and told me she never once stopped to consider they would win. She believed she had right on her side." Fin and Charlie paled as they stared at each other. Sage told him. "Fin, if she allows you another chance, you will need to learn the signs. For now, I suggest we all sit back and pray to whoever we believe in, that she will come back alive and whole." She looked at them all and bit out. "I am leaving now. Please, none of you see me for a day or two, unless it is about June. I am very angry." Without another word, she nodded to Storm and left, taking a visibly upset Ella with her.

Charlie, with a kiss for Storm and a small smile to Fin, left after she had made sure Sage was nowhere to be seen.

Storm told Fin. "You and I, Broadsword now."

Fin nodded as he followed the male from the room. He was in for a pounding, and sadly, on some level, he knew he deserved it. Maybe he could get some advice from Storm and Lars afterwards.

His dragon snarled. *Now you ask?*

At least I am asking.

His dragon grumbled. *Still lonely.*

Yeah... Yeah!

CHAPTER FOUR:

The music was divine. Heavenly tunes reached out into the night causing the hair on June's arms to rise as she sat in her car. It was impossible not to hear the song carried to her on the breeze and feel anything other than sadness.

It had been three days since she had made her mad dash from Dragon's Gap and Fin. She was on her eighth retrieval, and unfortunately there had not been a day since that her wolf's pining did not make her feel sad. She was no closer to an answer to the problem of Fin. Although she hoped by being out of reach, he may have thought on her last words to him and come to the same conclusion she had. They needed to be together now.

As she listened to the song, she could not help the tears fill her eyes, and wondered who sang with so much heart rendering sorrow. Two rings on her phone let her know her passengers were about to arrive, wiping any tears that may have escaped away. She started the car and unlocked the doors. Listening to the last notes of the song fade away under the purr of the finely tuned engine. She felt regret as sad as the tune was, it was also hauntingly beautiful.

Within minutes, her front and back seats were filled with females that sadly brought with them the familiar scent of fear and desperation. When she heard the last door close, she put the car in gear and reluctantly drove from the small town. Knowing she would be unlikely to hear such beauty again in her lifetime. Sadness washed through her to mix with the fear and anguish residing in the car. Carefully, she let only her eyes travel over the occupants of her vehicle and was not surprised to see the haunted faces of seven under-nourished females and their small children. It had been that sort of town. Even with the beautiful music, there had been an undercurrent of violence and fear in the air that itched at June's nerves. She was relieved to be leaving. A voice whispered from the darkness. "We are grateful for the ride."

June smiled, and it showed in her voice as she answered. "No problem. You are not the first we have taken from around here tonight, and as far as I know you will not be the last. All who need to leave, will be gone before dawn."

"That is a relief, it as a place of horror that I hope we can put behind us." said another more mature female voice.

June told them. "Where you are going, there are people who can help with that, they are good people. I know it is hard to believe there are places and people who are kind and loving to our kind."

The same voice came from the back seat. "That is what the tigers told us. Sad to say, there were some of us who did not believe them, until tonight when you and your vehicles arrived."

June nodded. "Yeah, we get that a lot; it is something we have come to terms with. Oh, by the way, who was that playing and singing in the bar?"

There was silence until a young female squashed in the front seat by the door answered. "There was no music or singing in the bar, just the typical fighting."

June jerked the steering wheel. She had not imagined hearing the music or the singing. To cover her lapse in concentration, she said. "Sorry, bump on the road. Well, it must have been a radio."

They drove so long her passengers finally dropped into an uneasy sleep. She messaged her coordinates and a large oval filled with light opened on the road in front of her vehicle. She drove through the silver doorway. A portal was the quickest way to the drop off point. She had discovered over the last three days, things had really changed since she had done retrievals. A bus sat on the side of the road, with tables and chairs set up under an awning where medical personnel were waiting. Looking around she saw she was one of the first cars to arrive.

She slowed when she recognized a figure detached herself from a table. Faeries, dragons, and shifters streamed out from the darkened bus when her car halted. June gently woke her passengers. "Ladies, we are here. This is the next step on your road to a new life. These shifters and others will see you to Dragon's Gap. Remember you are safe."

There were several quiet words of appreciation, as the doors opened and arms reached for young and adults alike. Soon her car was empty, when there was a tap on her roof she pulled her vehicle around the bus and parked. Just as headlights of another vehicle come through the re-opened portal. Getting out, she reached for the cup of coffee held out to her by the female dragon. "Ella, how are you?"

"I am good, you?"

"Sore, a little too much sitting. I need to be running around the castle. I miss my office."

Ella laughed as she asked. "This is your last run, so I was told."

"Gordon said that, right?"

"Yep."

"He told me the same thing this morning."

Ella blurted out. "Fin, and I have talked?"

"Oh really?"

"Yes, everyone has talked to him. The only ones I think not to have talked to him are Keeper and Reighn."

"Oh dear, that does not sound good."

"So, my friend. Why are you here?"

June sighed. "Your uncle will not commit. My wolf and I got tired of waiting. Wolves dislike uncertainty in their mates." She looked into her coffee and admitted softly. "I didn't know what to do. So I ran."

Ella snorted. "He is an ass! He has been haunting Charlie's office every day, driving her mad, wanting to know where you are, when you will return. She won't tell him, which ignites his temper."

"I am sorry." June mumbled, feeling her wolf's sadness.

"I am not. He is, I repeat, an ass."

June sipped her coffee and smiled at the feisty dragon, then said. "You know, you sound like Edee?" Before Ella could retort, she asked her. "So, why are you here? You normally don't come out. Is Keeper with you?"

"No, he was held up in town. I just wanted to make sure you were okay. You are my friend and soon to be my auntie."

June growled. "See, that is just mean, right there."

Ella laughed as she looked June over. "You look tired."

"I am."

"Are you returning with us?"

"No, I have to go do something."

"Another pick up?"

"Yeah, something like that."

"Would you like company?"

June looked up at the Dragon. "Thank you, no, I will be fine."

"You say that, but you were hurt last time. Sage and Claire have not forgotten and will be annoyed if you get yourself hurt again. Uncle Fin will be obnoxious to live with and a certain dragon will roar which upsets his Shadow. Who is, as we all know, with hatchlings? And Edith is eyeing the art in your office?"

June laughed, then quietly stated. "And yet I am still going." She finished her coffee, and Ella handed her a travel mug with more.

June smiled at the dragon. "Thanks mom, see you soon."

"You have a mean streak wolf. Just keep safe. I cannot listen to another dragon roaring. I am thinking Uncle Fin will be loud."

June laughed and waved to Ella as she jumped back into the car. She stuck her head out the window and called. "Tell that female to keep her sticky fingers away from my treasures."

Ella laugh, as she watched the taillights of June's car become swallowed up by the portal, sighing she went to help the new arrivals.

A minute later, June was through the portal and back on the road outside the town she had left only a little while ago. She wound the window down and sure enough, the music with the haunting song filled her ears. She drove, almost mesmerized by the tune toward a mountain range. With no moon the road was dark, which is why they had done the pickups tonight, undercover of a black sky.

CHAPTER FIVE:

A fter driving for more than two hours, she pulled off the one lane dirt road into a small parking lot hidden behind a line of trees. She sat and listened to the engine tick over and looked out the window, seeing shapes in the distance. Mountains, she thought, and trees, lots of trees, some kind of forest.

It was so quiet and still, it was as though the air forgot to move. She could hear nothing, but she knew something was out there. Her wolf was alert and watching. Taking a deep breath, she could feel eyes on her already, but from what or whom, was something she and her wolf could not detect. She would wait another five minutes, before she chanced leaving the relative safety of her vehicle. At some point, she would find out who or what was watching and waiting for her, but until they revealed themselves, she had something to find.

Decision made, she waited the five minutes then got out of her vehicle. Stretched out cramped muscles, and shrugged into her coat then placed her backpack on. She had filled it with the normal emergency gear, all retrievers carried. Thermal blanket, first-aid kit, flares and a Sat phone, food and water. She hefted it high on her back as she looked up into the mountains. Then she did as she had been taught and checked her weapons and realized she could see better now; it appeared her wolf had come on board and added her sight to hers. Closing the door, she covertly activated her alarms and deterrents. If anyone wanted to tamper with her car, they would end up passed out. She knew from experience Sage's spells were a bitch.

With a grin she picked out a marker in the distance; as it happened, it was a tall tree with wide branches. Starting her hike, she hoped to make good time and figured it would take her ten minutes to reach her target; the terrain was inclined but easy to traverse.

Once she reached the tree, she could hear the song again; she could almost make out words, but the music was so faint it was barely audible. She turned to the right, and the song faded; she turned to the left, and it was louder. She again picked out a landmark to the left and started her trek; it was becoming steeper, and she was having to climb a little more now. But it was not impossible. She knew she would be feeling it in her calves tomorrow. The music and song were her guide, following where it led, traveling over rough ground, climbing rocks. Forever climbing higher up the mountain.

June stopped to drink from another one of her bottles and turned her head both ways, trying to hear the music or song. Only to realize the music was gone, although the feeling of being watched was still there. Now only the song remained, she still could not hear the words. It was as though she was feeling the song, not actually hearing it. When she knew which direction to go in, she walked for another ten or fifteen minutes until she came to an entrance of a cave. Turning on her torch, she shone it down the tunnel which thankfully was head height, maybe five or six inches taller than her and about ten feet long. It looked like it opened into a cavern; she took a gun out, and taking a deep breath, muttered. "In for a penny, in for a pound." She scratched her head and wondered. *Where do I get all these sayings from and what the hell is a pound?*

Moving slowly and cautiously along the narrow tunnel, she eventually came to a relatively large cavern. It was at least as big as a small house. She peeked around the edge of the cave wall and spied a ledge about chest height toward the back half of the cave. She shone her torch and saw a female and cradled in her arms were two small bundles. June rushed to her, shrugging out of her backpack as she went. The female smiled as she said. "You heard our song?"

"I did."

"I was so worried no one would. You are Fae?"

June grimaced. "No, sorry, I am half-wolf. What happened to you?"

She sobbed. "They came in the night and killed my Light. I ran, but the babes wanted to be born. They are early by three weeks, I have given them our light, my males and mine; they will survive. Please take them and keep them safe."

June said. "My name is June Bradly. What is your name?"

"The babies and I called for you, and you heard from all the millions on our world, you heard our song." She whimpered as she looked down at her babies.

June wiped the sweat from the female's face and told her again. "I am not fae."

Without looking at her, the female mumbled weakly. "It matters not, they chose you."

She offered her a drink, which she refused with a smile. June was positive she was fading away as she wiped her face again she felt a tingle on her hands. Quietly she said. "Hush now, I will take them to Dragon's Gap, please what is your name?"

She sighed. "Everything you wish to know is on that." She weakly pointed with her chin to a slip of paper that lay on the stone next to her hand. June picked it up and put it in the side pocket of her pack as the female told her. "We were on our way there, they say it is a safe place."

June nodded. "It is, my family make it so."

"Oh, how fortuitous, that you were the one to come."

"Isn't it, though?" June said with a smile for the ethereal female who she realized was not faerie as she first thought, "Are you an Elf?"

"No Pixie, the girl's father was a faerie."

"Is there someone for me to contact, for the babies on your behalf?

"No, dear one, they will be yours to hold, yours to love and yours to keep safe. Your mate will care for them, hold them safe, he is a good male. I see you as a family, my gifts to you are truly blessed."

June stilled, her body just stopped moving, her mind blanked of all thought as she watched the female kiss each small forehead and fade from the cave.

"Holy shit... I... I..." She took a breath. "Okay, I can do this. So little ones, for better or worse, you called for me. Why, only you know. I really hope she was correct, and Fin is going to be your new daddy, because we are going to need all the help we can get. Now just give me a minute here to sort some things out." With that she emptied her backpack and lined it with the thermal blanket, then she tucked both tiny wrapped bodies within. She looked at each baby, they had green eyes that open and closed slowly, still trying to process what had just happened as she noticed their cotton candy pink hair. She mumbled. "Look, my wolf, isn't this amazing, we have young?"

Her wolf sent her the emotion of happiness and danger: it was a heady combination, which had her reeling on top of everything she was feeling. Her body trembled and she heaved in several deep breaths, letting the sensation wash over her. "You are right my friend, we still have to get out of here. I get the feeling the people who took these little one's parents, will not give up easily." She kissed both of the baby's heads, much as the pixie had done, then murmured. "Well, my pups, we are to leave this haven and go meet your new family. So I need you to just stay in here and remain quiet."

She was amazed at how quiet they were. Maybe she thought half-pixie and faerie babies were quiet. She would ask Elijah and Scarlett. Right now, she had other things to worry about. She could feel the danger her wolf warned her about at her back and knew time and her luck were at an end. Now came the running and shooting stage of this rescue. She quickly zipped the pack almost closed and looped the straps over her shoulders so the bag rested on her chest. With some acrobatic twisting and turning, as well as an almost dislocated shoulder, she finally got the chest straps to snap close across her back securely. She filled her hands with her pistols. There were another two guns on her hips, as well as two more strapped to her thighs, easy to reach and fast to draw. Her pockets were filled with more clips of ammunition.

Leaving her torch off, she eased down the tunnel, when she was feet from the entrance. She leaned her back against the rock wall and took in several breaths. Her wolf gave her the sensation of sniffing, which June did. Drawing in the air and scenting the unwashed stench from the two males just outside the cave, saving her and the babies' lives. She pulled away from the wall and turned so she was facing toward the cavern. Thankfully, her coat was made from thick leather and had a solid lining, which she hoped would protect her body and the babies when she walked or in her case ran backward to the opening of the cave. She crossed her metaphorical fingers and believed it would work. Taking several deep breaths and saying a prayer for luck, she ran backward, toward the cave entrance.

When she broke clear from the opening, swords swept across her back, cutting through the material of her coat. She did not stop moving and passed both males firing her guns as her bullets found purchase in the bodies of her attackers. One attacker was shot in the throat and face, the other in the head and chest twice. She whirled around and just missed a throat cut of her own. She repeatedly shot the unknown attacker in the face and chest as he fell backward. She dropped another male with two bullets to his heart as he rushed her from her right side. Another male fired two shots into her body before she could move out of the way. Luckily her coats protection stopped one, the other grazed her ribs where her coat was flung wide. She swore and emptied the rest of her clip into him. Hastily she buttoned her coat over the pack, then swapped out her guns and ran, shooting both guns continuously. Unfortunately, running and shooting is never a good plan, especially in the dark and on a mountain. Trees hindered visibility and brush and roots had a way of tripping or making her stumble. Her aim was off, and her guns were basically ineffective.

This did not stop the attackers, two more assailants hidden in the brush, rose as she ran pass them. Lashing her with their swords and slicing shallow cuts along her jean-clad legs. Her arms were covered in the armor of her leather coat. The back of her coat, which had been sliced twice already, was open to their swords, and as much protection as her jeans and coat provided her, she still bled. Thankfully, the males were not well versed in the use of their weapon or she was just too fast. She shot and killed at least one more male, but missed others and kept on running, using the trees for cover when she could and when she couldn't. She ran around the trees, hoping to use them for deflection. She heard shots ring out behind her and smiled, she had wondered when they would bring more guns to the party. Several shots, 'thunked' into the trees as she passed them. The first ones were wide of where she was, but luck was on their side.

Suddenly she felt the impact of several bullets hit her coat, which propelled her forward onto her hands. Thankfully, by using the strength of her wolf, she pushed herself upright and forward, saving her life. The bullet that would have hit her spine, instead went through her shoulder. Gritting her teeth to stop the scream of pain, she continued to run. She heard yelling, and then suddenly the guns stopped shooting and as she listened. A male yelled that guns were not to be used. June thought it was a strange thing to say. It was a shame no one told her that before this started. Sadly for them, she only came with guns.

Smiling, she ran a little faster until she sniffed out a hollowed out tree behind a screen of bushes. She lay on her back and wiggled under the brush, hoping she did not disturb the dirt too much or leave a trail of blood behind, giving away her position. She squirmed around enough that she could sit with her back in the tree's hole. Leaning her head against the damp bark and taking in breaths of crisp mountain air. She gave herself a few minutes to settle her racing heart and allow the adrenalin pumping within her system to ease somewhat. *Well, okay, so that was bad.*

She looked in the pack at the babies and softly gasped when she saw they were still asleep. *Amazing!* She re-zipped the bag and knew she could not afford to wait much longer. She was bleeding and the more time she lingered, the weaker she would become, then she and the babies would be dead. She felt her shoulder and was relieved to feel the bullet had gone right through, and the blood had slowed courtesy of her shifter's fast healing. She grinned knowing her wolf was blocking the pain for her. At times like this she loved being a shifter. June looked out into the dark forest and chewed on her bottom lip, thinking hard. How many were left? Unfortunately, she was hampered by not knowing how many there had been to start with, and they were crafty. By not using torches, she could not count the ones still alive and mobile.

She was positive she had taken out ten males, but truthfully had lost count. If they were going to use guns, which she knew they would get around to doing again. Regardless of what the loud voiced male said, she needed an advantage. If she could get to her car, she could stow the babies, then sneak around and take out the others. She thought over her options and decided she liked her plan.

She listened to the fading voices of the males as they moved further away from where she was hiding. When she felt it was safe, she looked out between the bushes and fixed a landmark in her mind. Hoping it was close to where she had left her car. She waited, then checked the babies again. She could feel the blood running inside her clothes from all the cuts. Knowing she would pay for what she was about to do later, if she survived, she asked her wolf to come forth and help her slow the bleeding. Unfortunately, she would not be able to stop the bleeding fully. Because she was also going to ask her wolf to lend her more strength so she could run faster. She changed the clips in her guns once more and scented the air, there was no one close to her. So she heaved herself up, checked her guns again, and then fixed the target in her sights and with her wolf's energy. She took a deep breath and as she exhaled, she broke from her hiding place and ran.

June traveled at an angle to the path she had taken on her way up the mountain. She had almost made it to her car when she was set upon again. Before she realized what was happening, two males rose from behind bushes as she went to run past them. It was a race to see who would recover first from the surprise at her sudden appearance. Twisting left to right, trying to see both assailants in the small clearing. June was slashed with a sword across her back as she was halfway into a pivot, throwing her off balance. So much so that the momentum of the sword scraping against her back made her fall into the other male who stood in front of her. His sword was raised for his own strike. She held securely to her guns as she pushed them against his chest and shot repeatedly. He screamed as he fell away from her and was dead when he hit the ground. She stepped sideways just in time to miss the next sword strike from the first male and twisted half a turn and pulled her triggers. Firing repeatedly into his chest and throat, shredding him as he fell backward. She turned once more, breathing heavily as two more males came into the small blood soaked clearing.

They stood back, away from her. June stood with her guns ready. She was still a distance from her car and prayed these were the last two males that were hunting her. "Give us the abominations and we will let you live." Snarled a tall thin male who stank of alcohol and body odor. His hair hung in long, dirty brown braids and his clothes looked like he had slept in them and were as dirty as he was.

June scented the air between them, and once she got past the unwashed smell, she knew they were both human. The shorter of the two was not as dirty as the male next to him.

His short black hair was clean. In fact, he looked a lot cleaner and only slightly rumpled, compared to the taller male. Unfortunately, the manic look in his eyes behind his glasses bespoke of crazy.

June grinned and knew she looked just as crazy as the male, evidenced by the step they both took backward. "As if, assholes. I know damn well you killed these babies' parents, and for that you deserve to die and you will." She snarled, anger and pain making her normal voice harsher. "Consider this assholes. If these infants are abominations, wait until you see what comes for you next. Now leave. I give you a free pass to say your goodbyes to anyone foolish enough to love you."

They both laughed at her as they looked her over, from the amount of blood covering her she was obviously wounded. With that thought adding to his bravado, the tall male snarled. "You think to scare us, woman?"

June wheezed out a laugh. "I, by myself, have killed twelve of you. How many do I have to kill to drive home the point that you will never lay a hand on these babies?"

The short male who June thought sounded like a fanatical, crazy man snarled. "You are not saving innocents. They carry the gene of the devil within them. They must not be allowed to live."

In answer, June growled deep in her throat, saying. "Exactly how I feel about you. Except I have more of a chance of killing you like I did those others you set on me than you have of taking these babies from me. So choose death or to live another day." She aimed her guns higher, and it appeared as though they both realized she may be covered in blood, but she was still standing strong. They looked at each other and then the impact of what she'd said about killing their fighters seemed to hit them and as one they turned and ran. She swapped out a gun for a small blow pipe and quickly blew two small darts, hitting both males. They screamed and slapped at their necks as they felt the hits, but did not slow down.

June grinned she had tagged both males for the hunters to find later. She took stock of where she was and saw she was only minutes away from her car. Her grin turned into a laugh as she congratulated herself on her plan. She began the walk to her vehicle, but it seemed to take her a lot longer than she thought it should to get there.

When she did finally make it, she was relieved to see it was still intact and safe. She cancelled the spells and unlocked the doors, then spent several long minutes deciding how to get the straps for the pack undone. Finally, she pulled her knife and just sliced them in half. She placed the bag with its precious cargo on the front seat and walked around to the trunk, retrieving the med-kit. Sitting on the edge of the trunk, she saw to the wounds she could reach and stopped the blood which had started seeping from her shoulder and arms and legs. Once she was patched up as well as she could do by herself, she closed the trunk and eased into the driver's seat.

Any energy her wolf had given her was long gone. Exhaustion rode her hard. She unzipped her pack and looked inside to see both babies were still asleep. "If I didn't know better, I would suspect a spell." She bit her lip and mumbled. "Maybe, it is a spell. Whatever little ones, stay asleep a little longer. Mama will get us home. We only have to get to a place where I can activate the emergency signal or bat signal, as Frankie calls it. Then we will be rescued."

Sadly, she had forgotten she did not have her Sat phone or any other way to communicate for help, having left all her equipment in the cave.

CHAPTER SIX:

C harlie eyed the male as he walked into her office and barely kept the sigh from escaping. She had no more news today than she did the day before.

"It has been five days, Charlie. Where is she?"

"Fin, I told you yesterday, we are looking for her. The last one to see her was Ella."

"That was two days ago. She could be hurt somewhere, and no one has found her." Fin tried to keep the snarl from his voice. But his dragon was close to the surface, as he had been since they realized June had left Dragon's Gap.

Charlie stood and just kept the snarl from her own voice. "That is unfair. We are looking for her. I have retrievers out hunting her now, as I told you yesterday. She never told Ella where she was going. Her phone is down or lost and her GPS is disabled."

"That is not enough."

"I know Fin. We are looking. I swear."

He stared at her for several seconds, then nodded and stormed from her office just before Sage walked in from the connecting door between their offices. "We have scried for her without success. We cannot find her, was that Fin?"

"Yes, he is angry."

"Aren't we all? Where can she be?"

"I don't know Sage, but I trust her, she is cunning. She will come home."

"She had better." She held her finger and thumb a little apart. "I am that close to calling out the Hunters and Shields."

"Not yet. Give our people time to search."

Sage nodded. "Twenty-four hours."

"Okay Sage, thanks."

She said nothing as she left, but not before giving Charlie the same look she had been giving her every day since June had not returned. Charlie fell into her chair as she looked at the photo of her kids and Storm. "Where are you, June? Please don't get dead."

Fin strode from Charlie's office. He knew she was doing everything she could but he and his dragon could do more. He made his apartment and kept going, reaching his bedroom, whereby he pulled clothes and equipment from his closet.

His dragon asked. *We leave to find our Shadow?*

Yes, we need a few things first.

Then we go.

Yes, to bring her home.

Good, I want Shadow.

You and me both. Fin shook his head as he packed a bag full of equipment, first aid packs and blankets, food and water. He knew this was his fault. His stubborn refusal to accept June's needs caused her to be out there alone without his protection.

"Are you going to look for her?" Ella asked tearfully from the doorway to his bedroom.

He twisted around at the sound of her voice. He had been so concerned for June he had not heard her enter his apartment. "I am."

"I am sorry, Uncle Fin. I should have gone with her or asked where she was going. I just left her."

He dropped his bag and took her trembling body in his arms. "This is not your fault, it is all mine, my belief I could control everything and look what I did. I drove her away."

"She loves you."

"Does she? I do not know how she could."

"Well, when you find her, ask her."

"I will find her niece. I swear."

"I know you will."

"Thank you, now I must go."

"Take care and bring her home."

He smiled, a quick motion of his lips. Ella could see his dragon in his eyes as he assured her. "We will."

He left the castle and entered the grounds where dragons arrived and left from. Ark and Axl were waiting to secure the bag on his back.

"I thank you." Fin stated, a little taken aback by the brother's assistance.

"We thought today would be the day you would go, if she had not returned."

"I thank you."

They waited for him to shift, then they strapped the bag on his back. Once they moved away, he shook his large body to settle everything. A sixty- five-foot green dragon with purple eyes looked down at the two brothers, who called out to him. "Good hunting."

He bowed his head and lifted gently from the ground, and with one huge flap of his wings, he flew from the castle grounds.

Reighn walked from around the corner as he watched the departing dragon. "He has more restraint than I do."

Ark agreed. "Or us."

Axl asked. "Think he will find her?"

Reighn nodded. "It is what he finds that worries me."

They both grimaced at his words, knowing that for Fin to lose, June would more than likely turn him rogue. Then Reighn would have to issue an order for his death.

Ark stated. "Well, nothing to do now but wait."

"Hate waiting, maybe we should have gone with him?" Axl muttered.

Reighn shook his head. "Fin is deadly, and determined, he will be okay."

It took Fin the rest of the day to track June's movements. He started with the coordinates the driver of the bus gave him. From there he traced June to the carpark where her vehicle had been parked. Next, he tracked her progress up the side of the mountain. It was very difficult. June was immensely talented at leaving virtually no tell-tale signs of her passage.

Whether it was her innate ability as a wolf or just experience, it was hard to say. All he knew was that June was alive and climbing a mountain. Several times he found himself having to backtrack to pick up her trail. He knew he was on the right path when he found the first of several bullet-ridden bodies.

He tracked her to her hide-away, wanting to examine it. He was forced to shift to human; he placed his pack on his back with the simple expediency of shortening the straps to accommodate his smaller human form. Once satisfied, he parted the bushes and crouched down, reading the signs she had left behind. He saw where she had rested, and where she had emptied her guns. Stray casings lay scattered on the ground. He moved the leaf matter away and found small puddles of blood. Despair rode his dragon hard. *We know nothing.*

His dragon fretted. *She is bleeding.*

I would be surprised if she was not. We need to search more, and we need more information.

His dragon did not offer another comment as Fin sighed, then cocked his head to the side as he saw a clear footprint. The first he had found. Either he was getting better at reading her, or she was panicked and did not care who followed her. He thought about that for a minute. It did not ring true. If she was being hunted she would not leave a trail behind her for hunters to find, and he knew June did not panic. He stood and looked around, staying in human form, and began tracking her by reading the signs of her passage through the forest. He found bullets imbedded in the trunks of several trees. Then he started finding bodies. It appeared animals had been picking over the carcasses, but there was enough left to know the males had been repeatedly shot. He walked farther until he came to a place where he scented June's blood and saw where her hands made impressions in the dirt. Looking back along the ground, he found her blood, not as much as he feared but enough to know she had been hurt. He could feel the anger of his dragon simmering. *I know, we will find her. She is hurt, yes, but still alive.*

His only answer was a hissing grunt. His dragon was hunting for his Shadow and the ones who had done this, Fin kept moving and found three more bodies. His June had been involved in a sword and gun fight, evidenced by the dead males with swords by their hands and bullets in their bodies. So far he had counted thirteen dead. It appeared his June was a very good shot. Despite his fear for her, he was impressed at the carnage she caused.

He looked up from a male's body and saw the mouth of the cave and knew June at one time entered there. Bent over he ran through the tunnel coming to the cavern, he saw immediately where she had emptied her bag and as he scented the air. He could smell faint traces of her and something else, something sweeter. It was just barely traceable and was not a scent he had encountered before. He and his dragon were puzzled. *What made June risk her life, and what was it she found that someone wanted to kill her for.*

His dragon told him. *All good questions, which we will ask our Shadow when we find her. But we will not find her here. Standing looking at stone.*

Fin shook himself and agreed. Scooping June's belongings and stuffing them into his bag. He did one more look around then shifted and with a breath of flame destroyed all evidence of her and the sweet scent of the unknown substance in the cave. He then shifted to human and ran outside, where he slipped the pack on and shifted to dragon. He had a trajectory now, all he needed to do was follow it, and he would have his Shadow in his arms once more.

Unfortunately, his tracking had taken more time than he had realised, and he was forced to find a clearing to rest in as night fell along with the rain. Angered at his inability to carry on searching, he curled up in dragon skin and waited the night out. Fear for June uppermost in his mind, neither he nor his dragon had much to say throughout the night. Finally, as dawn crept over the sky and the rain ceased. He took to the early morning air and flew back to the carpark and started their search from there.

His dragon's eyes traced the signature of the car along dirt roads. Many times they had to land and then backtrack to find the trail. Finally, coming to a dirt road that looked like it had suffered severe damage due to the previous night's rain. They landed, and Fin shifted to human and walked along the road, eventually finding where her car had gone off the edge. It looked like she drove down a hill and into a gully; He thought at first she had been forced off the road, but once he shifted back to his dragon and pulled the car from the ravine, he realized she had just lost control.

She was unconscious and wounded, he could scent the infections and dried blood and something else, something sweeter. It confused him and his dragon. Shifting to human again, he pulled open her door to find June was still in her seat belt and the smell of something foul filled the air of the vehicle.

"June, it is Fin. Wake for me, little wolf. Wake!" He growled, fear making his voice gruff.

Her eyes remained shut, but he heard her say weakly. "Fin?"

He held her head back and tipped some water between her dry lips and sharply snarled. "Little wolf, wake up."

June heard him, heard her dragon, and wondered how he had got there. She murmured. "Tired, everything foggy... need to rest, just shut my eyes for a minute." She had pulled off the road to gather her energy and to release the bat signal. She was so tired. Why was Fin here? He had left her, he was gone. Maybe she was dreaming again. Then a picture of the small babies in her bag flashed across her mind and she huskily muttered. "Babies... babies!" As her hands flapped around urgently.

"Hush June, what baby?"

"Bag..." she mumbled, then passed out again.

He saw a black backpack on the floor. Reaching over her he pulled it to him and unzipped it. Looking inside, he saw two little bodies with pink hair. *Oh shit, we have to go!*

No kidding, where did our Shadow get pink haired babies from?

I do not know. At least we know what that sweet scent is.

June roused again, and her hand found his cheek. "Fin... babies... safe... promise."

He kissed her fingers as they curled around his hand and would have promised her the world right then and there. He was so happy she was alive and with him. "I promise little wolf."

But she did not hear, she was unconscious again.

We leave now! His dragon demanded. *Strap pack with hatchlings to our Shadow and we will take her in my claws.*

Right... Right! Said a slightly befuddled Fin, as he hurried to do as his dragon instructed. All he wanted to do was wallow in the relief he was feeling at finding June alive and awe for the two hatchlings.

Were these young ones the reason she had risked her life, what of their parents? He had seen no evidence of them in the cave. Before he realized it, he was dragon again, and holding June in his enormous claws. She clutched the bag with the babies, even though he had securely tied it to her chest. Then he flew like he had never flown before to Dragon's Gap and home.

CHAPTER SEVEN:

F in carried June along the corridor to the castle's infirmary. Still unconscious, she nevertheless held the bag with the two small bundles tightly in her arms. Fin knew he left a trail of blood from her opened wounds as they walked into the medical unit, while his dragon bellowed for Ella or Sharm.

He was surprised at how fast they arrived; he was not to know just then, that they had not long finished cleaning up after Harper's arrival and near death. Fin told Ella as she went to take the bag from June. "Pack, has babies in it."

With a nod, she gently cut the straps tied around June and immediately lifted the bag off or tried to. Ella softly ordered. "June, release the bag sweetie, so I can check the babies, please June."

She would not. Ella was sure her arms held them tighter as she spoke to her. Fin leaned over her. "Little wolf, let them go. Ella has them now; we are safe."

Her hands fell away instantly. As soon as the bag was free from her hold. Sharm started assessing her wounds. Ella laid the bag on the other bed and unzipped it. Just as Charlie hurried in, passing Fin as he reached out for the door on his way to get Sage. His hand had only touched the door when they were thrust open by Sage. She took one look at his face and said. "I was on my way to bed when I heard you calling. How is she?"

Fin shook his head. "Alive, be prepared we brought more than June back."

"What?" He motioned to the table that Ella stood at as she gently removed and unwrapped babies from the bag.

"Oh my Goddess."

Fin told Sage as he stood, hands by his sides, feeling useless and unable to comprehend what he was really seeing. "She made me promise to keep them safe. I believe they are ours, hers and mine. It seems my Shadow has made me a daddy."

Charlie moved next to him with her hand in Storm's as his arm held her securely to his side. So far the last two days had been hard for his Shadow, first her sister and now June. She was feeling vulnerable as she asked Fin. "Do you know what happened?"

Fin turned his black eyes on her and Storm's hand twitched. Charlie sighed and laid her hand over his heart. "Hush, he means nothing by it, you can see he is on the edge."

"Stand down, Fin. I understand how you feel but believe me, this will not help and June will be the first to tell you so. Also, she can yip, it is very annoying." Reighn said as he entered.

Fin growled and smiled at the same time. It was a weird combination, but he knew the yipping could drive a dragon to drink.

Charlie asked. "How did you find her?"

"Tracked her from the point when she entered the portal through our connection, it is very faint. It only got me so far, the rest was luck and hard won experience. Once I found where the portal opened up for her, it was just a case of following the signs. So I had to get real close." They all knew there was far more to it than he was saying, but it was not the time now to examine everything he had done to find his Shadow. He told them quietly. "Her car was off the road, she had gone down a hillside landed in a ravine covered in bush, easily missed."

Charlie's lips tightened as she looked at Sage and said. "We need to teach our people tracking; they rely too much on the Hunters."

Fin heaved in a deep breath and held it as his eyes became wild and he started to shake. Letting go of the breath, it suddenly came to him how close he had come to losing June.

Storm grabbed his shoulder. "I know, old friend, I know. She will be alright, Sharm, and your Ella will make it so."

Fin nodded and Frankie slipped under his arm as Sage did the same on the other side. "Come on Fin; we are here for you." Frankie told the huge male.

"Family." Sage softly said. "We stick together, she will be alright. She is a fighter. You know she is. We all know that."

Hoarsely, he said. "I know... I know."

Ella called to Sage. "Sage, I think the babies are under a sleep spell; they will not wake, and I am sure they will need food. We need Edee as well."

Sage gave Fin's arm a pat in comfort as she moved to Ella, just as Edith arrived. "I am here. Oh my, pink hair."

"That is all you can say?" Sage asked as she turned to where Edith came to a stop.

"Well what else. I mean pink."

"I don't know, something like where did they come from? What species are they, anything other than just pink?"

Edith hummed, then said. "So cute. Molly will be jealous." Sage grinned, knowing it will not be Molly, as much as it would be Cara who will be jealous. It was a well-known fact, Cara thought because she was a unicorn, she should have pink hair. Why she thought this, no one knew. It was what she asked for almost daily, to the point Storm had asked Sage to change the color of her hair. She had declined, especially when Charlie gave her a long look of retribution if she'd dared too. Sage hid a laugh. She knew Charlie was going to have a fight on her hands. Because she was always telling Cara nobody had pink or purple hair other than faeries. She looked over at the worried Charlie and saw she had not realized that yet. Placing her hands over both of the babies' eyes and foreheads, she said a few words. Then a soft, blue mist engulfed her hands and flowed over each little body. Within seconds the babies opened their eyes and cried softly as new-borns did.

"Green eyes, now that is even cuter." Edith murmured as

she placed a hand over each little chest. "Pixie and faerie. Wow, I did not think that was a thing?"

"Not usually." Reighn agreed as he moved to where the young were. "Although Elijah is pixie."

Edith grinned. "Yeah, I forget that. So they are two days old or one day. Fin pick one because of the spell it can be either."

"One day." He said, unsure why that felt right, but it was what he decided, so he stuck with it.

She nodded. "One day it is." Mentally, she recorded the date. Ella and Sage changed both babies into clean clothes while bottles of formula were readied. Sage grinned at Reighn as she told him. "Well... well look at that, I am an auntie and you are an uncle again."

Charlie just stared and slowly lifted her eyes to Fin's black ones saying. "This will not end well."

Fin replied quietly. "I know, they will never let us keep them?"

Reighn rubbed his head as he stared at the babies. "How the hell did our June get them?"

"Does it matter, they are June's and Fin's?" Frankie asked of him.

Reighn looked at her and frowned. "Unfortunately, nothing is that simple." He asked Fin. "Do you want them?"

"My Shadow was bringing them home. This means something. So until she says they are not ours. I will keep them."

Sharm straightened and stretched his back, then walked to where they all stood. "So, it is a good news... bad news scenario."

"Good news first please, my friend." Fin said as Sage braced herself.

"I have healed all her wounds, sword and bullet holes. Someone tried real hard to kill our June."

Sage sucked in a breath through her teeth, then said as Fin's face hardened even more. "Just as well, she is hard to kill."

"Isn't it, though?" Agreed a sardonic Sharm. "Bad news, she

was poisoned, with a type of poison designed to drain the life force of a half-shifter. A human or someone who knows magic has developed this."

"Is it faerie magic?" Fin asked, shocked that faeries would kill one of their own.

"Sort of and yet no, it is magic with a twist and it is the twist I have no cure for."

"Sharm, my brother that is as clear as dirt." Sage grumbled.

"I know." He wiped his face. "So plainly, the poison is draining her life-force, thankfully she is wolf and has the shifter's ability to heal just about anything; this is helping to slow it down. But it will win if we do not find help. I took samples and may be able to manufacture an antidote but do not hold your breath. Dragon Lady, someone is misusing magic. Your department, I think?"

Sage snarled. "It is and someone will pay."

"This may help, it is a variation of what felled Storm."

With a look at his Shadow's strained face and Fin's closed one. Reighn said. "I am tired of this. It seems like every time we turn around, we are confronted with another type of poison. Call the faeries."

Charlie nodded as she pulled her phone out while Sharm turned to the two babies. "Now, who do we have here, it appears as though we have two little faeries?"

Ella nodded in agreement as Edith smiled, saying. "Half right. Pixie and faerie, what a combination. Their parents were brave, very brave to go against the faerie rules, it must have been love."

Fin took his eyes from the green-eyed, pink haired babies and looked at the erected screens where his June was being washed. He looked at Reighn and asked. "What do I do?"

"Well, my friend." Reighn shook his head as he told him. "Your Shadow has brought you trouble. June has taken them as yours, which means before she wakes, we have some decisions to make."

"First thing." Sage said. "Let us get the faeries here. Who is available?"

Charlie grimaced. "Only Prince Tarin again."

"Why, Scarlett and Elijah were here earlier with Kai."

Charlie nodded. "True, but they all returned to the High Queen's Grove before the confinement starts.

This announcement was met with silence until Sage shrugged and said. "Call him anyway; we will do damage control later."

Charlie nodded. "I have already."

Sage told them. "Look, let's see what we are dealing with here, it may not be as bad as we think."

CHAPTER EIGHT:

Fifteen minutes later, Sage's hopes were dashed. "They have to go to the Grove." The Prince announced pompously, putting everyone's teeth on edge.

"Do their lives depend on it?" Fin asked mildly as he watched Verity coo to his daughters in their baskets.

"No, not their lives but..."

"But nothing," Fin answered, "they stay until their mother says otherwise."

Tarin had been at the Grove for almost five months visiting the Queen and King. In that time he had been allowed the run of Dragon's Gap. Fin had heard if it had not been for his personal guards, he would be dead. Reighn grunted and hid a smile. It was unfortunate Elijah and Scarlett were absent when Reighn had asked him to examine the hatchlings after he had seen June. He had taken one look at the babies and started making pronouncements and demands, he wanted to know how June had obtained the twins, which they had no answer for.

Sage had told him it appeared June had rescued two half-blood faeries only a day old, and until she woke, they were still in the dark. Sharm had explained that somewhere between dropping her car load of females and their young off, and Fin finding her. She apparently encountered people with swords and guns who tried to kill her. Tarin nodded several times when Sharm and Sage finished recounting the events leading up to him being summoned. Then he decided he had not pissed Fin off enough and had smirked and said. "Dragon Fin, I do not think you realize the political dilemmas you will cause by not giving the half-breeds to me."

Reighn wondered if the male could get any more patronizing. Fin replied. "You are right, but that makes no difference to what will happen. Especially if you want to remain alive."

Reighn watched Tarin try to bend Fin to his will. He had reports of the male having the occasional temper tantrum that faeries were known for, and he had, of course, had the run in with Ace over Joy. But as he had stayed away from her, and Axl had only threatened to kill him once. All seemed to be settling down. Tarin's guards had made sure he was never in Dragon's Gap at the same time as Joy. The hurt feelings he had caused in the first two months after his arrival had been easily settled by either Frankie or June.

Getting nowhere with Fin, Tarin tried another tactic and decided a better option would be to demand, not persuade or convince. No, just demand that the hatchlings be removed from the castle. Preferably, Reighn was sure before June woke and used her guns. He could see Sage was furious. Her sister lay unable to defend herself or her hatchlings, and this male thought to take them from her. This was not going to end well for the Prince, because Reighn knew, just like he knew, the sun would come up tomorrow. That his Shadow would never allow those hatchlings to be taken. That was, of course, if Fin even thought to allow it. This would not happen regardless of what the Prince said. There was no one more stubborn than his friend Finlay Slorah, who had said only a handful of words since the male arrived, which consisted mainly of no.

Tarin was getting annoyed. His guards, who understood and read the anger in the room better than the Prince, were becoming restless. If the clenching and unclenching of their sword hands were any indication. Any minute now, Tarin was going to screw up, and Reighn was going to let him. He did not like the male and had very little patience for him.

With the next words out of the male's mouth, Reighn was proved right. "I do not think you understand dragon Slorah. These half-breeds belong at the Grove, but under the circumstances, it will have to be the Northern Grove. Where I will undertake their re-education, it is what must happen. You and your female are not permitted to keep what you do not own. If they survive the next few days, which I doubt, as half-breeds do not always survive when they are early birthed. Regardless, we own the half-breeds, as is our right. So I demand you hand them over to me now." As the Prince spoke, his voice had risen enough for all to hear.

Fin straightened from his relaxed pose against the door leading into the utility room. The twins had been fed, bathed and changed and were now resting in baskets Verity and Grace had found for them. They looked adorable. Every now and again, his eyes drifted to them and his dragon crooned in pleasure. All he wanted to do was take his family to the home, waiting for them. So his brogue was more pronounced with the impatience and fear he was feeling. "I understand you are a Prince and that you have only been here a short while. I have been here less, even though it is my home. So I am going to let your poor choice of words pass. Other than to say Dragon's Gap, has no half-breeds, which includes these hatchlings here. So if I were you, I would rephrase what you are trying to say and before you speak again. Think! Now as to the matter of removing my hatchlings to a Grove, any Grove. It will not happen."

Just then, four tiny figures flew into the room. As they landed, they grew and Fin raised an eyebrow in amusement. Prince Tarin swirled around and bowed as Queen Scarlett and King Elijah, with their guards, appeared. Displeasure radiated from the Queen and King, the Prince again unable or unwilling to read the feelings emanating from the new arrivals and thinking he now had substantial backing. As well as ignoring the warning looks his guards threw him, puffed out his chest and said. "Oh please, dragon Slorah, you were saying?"

Fin eyed the male and his guards and then the newcomers, shrugged and said as he straightened from the wall where he had relaxed back too. "I was going to say, I do not know what re-education is, nor do I care to know. What I know is that my Shadow, not my female, as you so eloquently stated. Will not allow her babies to be taken by you or anyone. I, of course, will have to agree with her. They are our hatchlings, not yours, they stay here with us."

Tarin inclined his head in a mocking salute to Fin. "I understand what you are saying, we of course must take into consideration the feelings of your... ahh, Shadow. Maybe we could come to some arrangement."

Reighn stood, head bowed, as Sage looked over at him uncomprehendingly when she heard him mumble. "Do not say it, you fool, it is not worth your life."

Tarin smirked as he said. "We could, of course, offer a monetary compensation for the half... Sorry young."

Every female growled at his audacity, anger swamped Sage, and she threw a blue ball of magic at the male, dropping him to his knees. "You dare! My sister's babies are not property to be bought and sold. You disrespect our young and disrespect our home."

She lifted her eyes to the screen June was behind and found her standing there. Her eyes were on fire as they locked on Fin. He was by her side in a second. "No, my love... No, they will remain with us. I will never allow it. Your family will not allow it. Come, let me take you back to bed."

She nodded and looked at Sage, who said. "I have this, go my sister."

June sighed and her eyes rolled back into her head as she passed out once more. Fin swept her up into his arms, carrying her back to bed. Claire hurriedly went with them. Reighn looked at the male, now on his knees. "Queen Scarlett, King Elijah, explain the facts to the young prince and while you are at it, tell him whose territories these are. It may stop any complications in the future and possibly keep him alive."

They both inclined their heads as the Queen answered. "Thank you for your understanding. We will again discuss the facts with him."

Sage released him and he stood scowling at her. The King looked at Reighn. "She will not heal completely without our help. It is why we are here. May we?"

As the Queen eyed the prince, she said. "One reason. You, Tarin, will stay here until we have seen to our friend." Tarin paled when Scarlett motioned to the four guards. "Make sure he stays." Then she said to the two guards that were with the prince. "Daru, Mercca. I apologize once more for your discomfort."

They both bowed, and the one named Daru responded. "It has been illuminating our Queen."

"I am sure it has been." Was the King's dry response as he and his Queen followed Frankie behind the screens.

Reighn told Tarin. "You are an idiot, aren't you? Is that why you are here?"

"I do not know what you mean. I do not have to answer to you, Dragon Lord." Even now he sneered at Reighn, who took one step toward him only to stop, as Storm was suddenly in front of the male, which may have saved his life. He punched him in the stomach and dropped him to the floor, looking down at him without expression. Storm was Commander of the Shields and one of the most fearsome of dragons. The male made to get up. Storm pointed a finger at him as he said. "Stay down, you fool. You just insulted our Lord, in his home, on his lands. You know you are a guest at his benevolence. You will apologize now." Storm's voice was calm and con-trolled, which made it even more frightening.

Tarin gulped the hot words on his tongue while anger with a healthy dose of fear entered his eyes, sulkily he said. "I apologize for my words, Dragon Lord."

Reighn felt his dragon stir at the look of contempt that entered the faerie's eyes. His guards must have felt it as well, because the guard named Mercca decided it was time to introduce himself. Reighn did wonder if it was to save the Prince from Storm's wrath.

"My Lord, please let me introduce you to our King's guards,

Rumoh and Dumoh. They are brothers and have been with the Queen and King for many years."

They both bowed from the waist and ignored the now trembling Prince as he rose. Tarin finally realized the predicament he was in, when none of the royal guards had stopped the male Storm from hitting him or reprimanded him. In fact, they seemed to radiate quiet satisfaction.

"I am Mercca and this is my partner and friend Daru." They also bowed to Reighn and Sage. The guard, Daru said. "To answer your previous question. Yes, he is an idiot and yes, that is indeed why he is here. It is his last chance, and he has succeeded in making sure it would fail, to what outcome my friends and I have no idea."

The other guard, Mercca told them. "I would also like to apologize for not thumping him in the mouth as I should have or let my partner do it when he was talking earlier. I did not, because Fin was handling it, if I had known June was here. I would not have been so tolerant."

Daru said. "We count both Fin and June among our friends and have spent many delightful days with Fin at Broadswords.

"How dare you?" Tarin spluttered.

Without even looking at the Prince, Daru said. "Shut up Tarin, you are beyond your home borders and in trouble. Our Queen is very tolerant, yet even she has had enough. Your parent's last resort was to send you here. So I advise you to remain quiet."

The Queen and King re-entered the room, and Scarlett enfolded Sage in a hug. "She will be well. Elijah rid her of the remaining infection and poison. It was, as Sharm said, a mix of human and faerie magic. We will send the information to the High Queen, and my people will track down how these thugs got a hold of it. We will need to talk to June when she is well. For now, know she will recover and her daughters will thrive and be well enough to give her Shadow a merry dance."

Sage laughed and hugged her back. "Thank you, Scarlett. I

was worried."

Elijah hugged her as well. "You are welcomed, she is dear to us. Without June, we all would be lost. She is our glue."

"She really is." Sage agreed tearfully.

Elijah said. "Now the young are, as you know, half faerie and half pixie. In as much as I dislike our Queen mother's nephew's words, he is correct in that they will have needs that June and Fin will be unable to manage." Fin walked out from behind the screen. Elijah nodded to him and continued. "Tarin was incorrect as to where they could receive an education. They will be helped and given their normal tuition here. I am a full-blood Pixie. I am sure Tarin just forgot that or he would have told you I am capable of undertaking their education." He held his hand up when Fin went to speak. "It will commence if and only if they show abilities. They are what used to be referred to as gray ones, so abilities can appear at any time."

Charlie said. "So, they do not have to leave our home?"

He smiled. "No niece, they remain with their parents and grace knows they are so very fortunate to have found such wonderful parents and family as sad as it must be. For surely they have lost their birth parents. Fortune shined on them when June answered their call."

Fin said. "June told me they and their mother sung for her to come to them. She was there with the mother when she passed beyond the veil."

Elijah sighed. "That is the way for some of us. She would have been pixie. We are forever concerned with whom to leave our young too if we know we are to die. She would have sung and the young would have joined her to call June to them. Do you know her name?"

Fin said quietly. "I do not, June may. I will ask when she is well."

"Thank you Fin."

Sage asked. "What would have happened if June had not been out there to hear their song would they have reached her here?"

Elijah sighed as he told her sadly. "Maybe, maybe not. Depends how weak the mother was and I think you know what would have happened to the young, dear Sage."

"Oh, it is too terrible to think about." Her hand went to her stomach where her hatchlings rested. From the corner of her eye, she saw Edith do the same action and sniffed back a smile.

Scarlett nodded. "But that did not happen, so this is a good time to rejoice for Fin and June and their new daughters. So my Light, what to do with that?" She indicated Tarin with a nod of her head.

A haughty look came over the Prince's face and as he went to speak. Elijah looked at the male with disgust and flicked his fingers. The Prince's mouth snapped closed.

"I have a suggestion." Charlie said as she moved from her Lord's side to stand in front of the Prince. Storm stood with Reighn, who was joined by Johner, as Frankie was still with June. "First though, uncle, could you release his tongue?"

"Of course."

To the Prince, she said. "I know you know who I am and who my sister is?"

He nodded slowly as Charlie stared at the male faerie and her eyes became distant and ghost hard. "Oh, I see you know who we are. Good. We are the lost ones, which you know of as the gray ones, and all the rumors you have heard about our kind are quite true. So hear and believe me when I tell you this, because I will only say it once. Now that female in there is our friend and as of now her children are our family and they are off limits to you and any more like you. If anything happens to my nieces or if they mysteriously go missing one night or day a week from now, a month, a year or ever. My sister and I will bring a reign of terror down on you and your kind, the likes of which you have never seen before. And if by some miracle you or your kind take us both out, then her Shadow and mine and our combined families, in case you missed that. The Queen and King and their Grove, and the Hunters, the Shields, the Retrievers. Oh hell, the whole of Dragon's Gap will just finish what we started. **Do I Make Myself Clear?"**

"Yes, you do." The shaken faerie replied.

Charlie said to the Queen, who had a very blood thirsty look in her eyes along with a hint of laughter. "So here is my idea."

Scarlett said. "Yes dear."

"Send this one without guards to the castle tomorrow. I think he needs an attitude adjustment."

"How does one go about doing that?"

"Frankie?"

"Yes Charlie." Frankie answered as she came from behind the screen with a pleased look in her eyes.

"You can have him for the first week, then if Sharm and Edith do not mind, they can have him for the…"

"May I make a suggestion?" Reighn interrupted as he too, eyed the hapless male.

"Why yes, dear Lord, you may." Charlie inclined her head.

Reighn sighed, much like his father did on occasion. "Smartass, how about sending him to the ones he thinks are no more than breeders and half-breeds."

"Oh, good idea. Yeah, to the healers he can work on the wards and then to the Retrievers and then the Hunters. Then he can serve in the construction unit for a while."

"Building with his hands may be good for him." Rene` agreed as he and Verity arrived back from making sure everything was ready for Fin to take June and the babies to her home.

Reighn nodded. "Can you manage that, Frankie?"

"I can write a schedule."

Reighn smiled. "Then forward it to me for final approval." He turned to the two royals. "What say you Elijah, Scarlett?"

Tarin, outraged at the proposed plan, spoke for the first time since Charlie had confronted him. "No, I protest. You have no right to enforce your obscene punishments on me. I have said and done nothing to warrant such a..."

"**Be quiet!**" A male voice whipped across his senses and filled the room as two more faeries walked in.

"Mother, Father." Tarin dropped his head into his hands. "Thank your graces; you have arrived. I was to be enslaved." He sobbed into his hands.

The male snarled. "Foolish male, stop this embarrassing display of weakness." He said to the female. "He takes after his Uncle Fregan."

"Oh, I know. It is a shame. I do not know where we went wrong with him."

The male sighed. "It is the problem with the youngest. I suspect we were far too soft on him."

"This could be true."

Queen Scarlett bowed her head slightly when she saw the newcomers. Smiling, she made the introductions. "Dragon Lord Reighn and Dragon Lady Sage, may I introduce you to Queen Isla Ravenswood and King Gideon Ravenswood, the High Queen's sister and brother by marriage. Isla, Gideon, the Dragon Lord Reighn Kingsley and his Shadow Lady Sage Kingsley." They all bowed their heads. Scarlett then said. "Allow me also to introduce Lord Rene` and Lady Verity Kingsley, former Lord and Lady of the castle. Then there is our niece Lady Charlie and her Shadow Storm Kingsley." She continued until she had introduced everyone else. Finally she said. "Isla. I did not know you were coming?"

"Really, and yet we told our son we were."

They all looked at the sulky male. Tarin looked down as he mumbled. "I forgot to tell you."

"Convenient." His father stated. "Well my Light, what should we do with this one. I am out of patience."

"I sympathize with you my dear." She turned her hard gaze on the Prince. "Tarin, we have been informed you are causing problems. You even attacked a young shifter, ward of Scarlett's niece and her Shadow. Is this so?"

He said. "I was misunderstood."

Scarlett growled. "Really, you were caught by her father?"

He protested. "He wasn't then."

"Fool!" His father snarled. "He should have ended you. I would have, if you had done so with my child or Light. Where did you get this idea you are entitled?" When Tarin opened his mouth, he held his hand up. "I do not want to hear it again."

His mother said. "A generous solution has been broached, so you can make amends and you have objections?"

Feeling his mother was softening, he whined. "I do mother, they will turn me into a slave."

Reighn said. "That is not so. You will always be allowed to leave my territories. And if you do not take up the offer. I can have you escorted from my land immediately."

His father smiled with a gleam in his eyes. "Tell me, son. Where will you go?"

Once again, ignoring his father, he said. "Mother, I will go home."

She was shaking her head before he stopped speaking. "No, my son, you will not. I asked Meadow, your aunt, for this placement against your father's objections. I felt the dragons and Elijah would be a wonderful influence on you. I find you have squandered the opportunity to become more than a spoiled child."

His father stood in front of Tarin's mother, so he had no option but to look up at his father. "You may not return to our Grove. In fact, our High Queen has stated because of your outrageous conduct here, all Groves will be closed to you."

Tarin's face paled with horror as he asked. "You would dare to allow this to happen. You could not intervene on my behalf. Am I not your son?"

His father raised one eyebrow at his son as he told him. "We insisted, your mother and I, that your aunt did so."

Outraged, he yelled at his father. **"You have no right. I am not a delinquent. I am a Prince!"**

"Ooh! He really needs an attitude adjustment." His mother snapped, and with a flick of her fingers, he disappeared. "I have sent him to the Groves isolation room."

Amused, Scarlett asked Elijah. "Did you know we have one of those?"

Elijah answered with a twinkle in his eyes. "No my Light, I had no idea." He asked Queen Isla. "We have one of those?"

"You do now." King Gideon said with a smile.

Just then, two tiny cries were heard from within the baskets. Fin stepped over to where his daughters lay. He reached inside and lifted one tiny bundle out and handed her to Scarlett, who along with Isla, had edged nearer to see the babies. Within seconds he had handed the other baby to Isla, who cooed at her then said. "Oh my Light, look at her, are they not both delightful?" And they were, with their tiny scrunched up faces topped by pink hair, and when they blinked, bright green eyes stared at them.

Scarlett fell in love as she exclaimed. "Absolutely delightful."

Elijah said. "You and June are truly blessed Fin."

Fin grinned. "In more ways than one."

King Gideon stated. "So, a little more than faeries when born?"

Elijah nodded. "Much more."

"The High Queen will be happy. Pixies are back on Earth." Isla said.

"Hold on, Elijah, you are Pixie? I do not understand, you just said they were not on Earth." asked a confused Sage.

Elijah grinned as he told her. "I come from a very progressive fraction of pixie. My parents, the Luminary. Which is what we call our monarchs, are very future orientated?"

Reighn and Fin gave each other a look, acknowledging Elijah did not actually answer Sage's question. Charlie asked. "What are a group of pixies called?"

"Luminaries and we live in a Luminia, similar to a Grove. My parents have no problems with mixing races, thankfully, or I could not have joined with my Light. Many Luminaries feel the same." He smiled at Scarlett, who smiled back at him.

King Gideon said. "That could be because often as not pixies always breed true."

Elijah grinned. "That could be true but not always accurate."

"And yet, by the look of these two, it would seem. I am right."

Elijah inclined his head. "I concede you could be right, although I would guess their mother was of high society."

"Is that why you wanted to know their mother's name?" Fin asked.

"Yes, if I knew her name, we would possibly know what other Luminaries are on Earth and where she came from. They will know she has passed, but they still should be told."

"Will they want her young back?" Frankie asked.

"As to that, I cannot say. Our Luminaries would let the calling stand. What they will do is unknown."

"A moot point until we know who she was." Edith said.

Reighn told them. "I agree, and I would not worry too much. The Elementals will impress on all Luminaries to register with us. At some point they will contact us and tell us when, where and how many are here."

Surprised, Scarlett asked. "Oh, did our High Queen do this?"

Reighn smiled. "She did, which is how we were lucky enough to receive a Grove."

Scarlett smiled back. "It was really our luck."

"Shall we agree to say we were both lucky?"

Storm asked Elijah. "I do not understand. I thought you told us that it was against the rules for faeries to bond outside of faeriedom?"

Elijah and Scarlett both nodded as she replied. "That was true, although what I should have said was. A Council and former High Queen, probably in the beginning of time, decided that faeries and pixie were of the same tree."

"So I am guessing pixie do not think the same." Frankie asked Elijah.

He smiled as he said. "We do not, but we do not care for purity like the Faerie council did."

Frankie snorted, then said. "I still think the faerie council was splitting hairs."

"As do our new High Queen and King." Queen Isla told them. "Which is why my sister and her Light are working to change the old ways. It will, of course, go much quicker now after what has happened with Harper and the council."

The babies again cried, which put paid to anymore conversation. Verity had everyone leave, so she could give Fin his first lesson in changing diapers and feeding hatchlings.

CHAPTER NINE:

June came aware slowly. She was in a strange bed, in a strange room. Her first thought was to run, her second was not to move, remembering the pain she had experienced. Her third; was where were her babies? "Babies!" She croaked out.

Fin walked into her line of sight and told her. "You are in our bed, in our house, and our hatchlings are not more than three feet away to your right."

She turned her head and sure enough, there were two bassinets standing side by side. She looked back at him, took in the haggard face, the tired eyes, and saw his slumped shoulders. He was untidy, as though he had slept in his clothes. June wished she was anywhere but here, and whispered. "Pixies and faeries."

"I know my June, someone poisoned you, which is why you feel like a steamroller ran you over. I do not know what that is, but Frankie assured me it was what you will feel like."

She tried laughing and wheezed instead. "Oww, sore."

"I know. I am going to lift you, so you can sit, and then I am going to give you a drink of juice, then water. Sharm's orders."

"Okay."

He helped her sit and passed her a tall glass of juice. She drank half of it, then said. "There is a piece of paper in my pack; it has all their information on it."

Fin said as she started drinking the rest of the juice. "I will give it to Elijah. He says he needs to find out where their birth parents came from."

"Okay, I sort of promised we would keep them." She told him as she reached for the glass of cold water.

Fin smiled. "We will keep them."

It was weird the more she drank, the thirstier she was. She finished the next glass of water he handed her, finally feeling her thirst quench. Then looked him in the eyes. "You do not have to feel obliged, I did not promise for you."

Taken aback, Fin tried to keep the growl from his voice. "June, I know I have been an ass. In fact, I have been more than that, but I have lived in fear that I would fail you, fail any young we could have."

June's eyes remained shuttered as she asked. "What has changed?"

Fin rubbed his hands over his tired eyes and face. "Truthfully, everything, you left me, and I realized I cannot prepare for everything. I thought I needed to make sure you would be safe. That no one or nothing could take you from me." He sighed as he held his face in his hands, then lifted shattered eyes to hers. "You know what happened to Ella's parents. I decided I would never ever allow that to happen to you or our young."

June wanted to hug him, wanted to take that look from his eyes. Instead, she asked softly. "And now what do you think?"

"That I was a fool. I can prevent and prepare for most things, but I did not take into account you. My little wolf... My June. I cannot safeguard against you leaving me." He hung his head, and June's face softened as he whispered. "I swear June. I cannot live these last five days again. Where I did not know if you were alive or dead. I missed you so much, and my dragon pined so much I thought he would die. That is when I realized that was what your wolf was doing. Pining for me, for our lives to start and I am so sorry."

She placed her hand on his cheek. He took it and kissed her fingers as they curled around his hand, his remorseful eyes devoured her face. She glimpsed his sad and fearful dragon looking out at her.

"If I wasn't feeling like a pancake, I would show you how much you mean to me. I am so sorry that you had to go through that."

Fin kissed her hands and her lips, finally resting his head on her shoulder as he told her tiredly. "Sometimes males like me need to be hit with a four by two or so Edee says, to realize what they have to lose."

June grinned, her poor Fin had been hauled over the coals by her family. "Someone hit you?" She asked, a little outraged and slightly amused that someone had attacked her Fin.

He shrugged. "It could have been worse, it could have been Sage or Edee."

At that, June laughed as she asked. "So where is everyone?"

"They were all here, but Verity and Grace chased them all away. Do not leave me my love, we, my dragon, and I will not survive."

"I promise my heart. I will not, my wolf and I found out we love you too much to leave you."

"You love me?"

"Of course, you and your dragon are ours."

"Why... Why, would you love me, after what I have done?"

"Oh, my love. I can honestly say you make me feel like a whole person. I believed my entire life I would never find anyone like you, and yet here you are, all mine. You are my shield or will be once you commit to me."

"I have committed. We are your shield against everyone and everything. You will always be mine."

June brushed his chin with her finger and kissed him softly. "Yep, yours forever. Sleep now."

As he laid down beside her, she rubbed his chest until he fell asleep. June dozed beside him for a little while until sometime later Sage opened the door and looked round the edge. Seeing she was awake, she smiled and drew closer, whispering. "Want to get up?"

"You have no idea. I need to use the bathroom and shower so bad." She whispered back with a grin, still pale, but her strength was returning, making her feel better.

Sage grinned in return. "Okay, I will help you up."

Together they wiggled her out from under Fin, who had

managed to lay over half of her. Once she was standing, she looked down at the enormous male. "I don't think anything will wake him."

Sage agreed. "It has been days since he slept."

June groaned. "Way to make me feel even guiltier."

Sage looked at her with rounded eyes as she said. "Oh, sorry, really didn't mean too."

"Such a terrible liar." June sniffed in disbelief.

Sage shrugged. "Well okay, you sort of deserve it, you know?"

"I know."

"Well, it is justified. You gave us a fright. I worried, and that means Reighn worried and then he roared at Fin. Which made Fin roar, which was not pleasant, just so you know."

June scowled at her. "Got it."

"I was just saying."

"Sage, is there a reason you want to make me roar?"

Sage watched her cover Fin gently with a blanket as June's eyes lifted to hers. She raised her eyebrows. "No, not really, just wanted to make my point."

"Consider it made, sister." June growled.

Then before she could snap at Sage again, she was hauled into Sage's arms and hugged hard enough to crack a rib and Sage whispered. "Wolf crazy, seriously June, I thought you had got past all that?"

June returned the hug, although gentler. "Me too. I think what I considered rejection made me revert to that time in my life when I was just crazy. I am sorry, I swear it will not happen again. I have you, our family, and Fin and the girls now. My wolf and I realize that we have more to lose. Maybe it took this lesson for us I to understand that."

"Maybe." Sage agreed. She honestly hoped so.

They looked into the bassinets at the two pink haired babies. "Like cotton candy." Sage murmured.

June smiled. "I know, we could call one cotton and the other candy?"

"No, Elijah wanted me to ask if you knew who their mother and father were."

"Oh yeah, I told Fin, but..." They looked at the comatose male who snored softly and smiled. June gave her the same information she had given Fin.

Sage grinned. "Thanks hon, now go take your shower. See the alcove?" She pointed to a small room that looked like it could be used for a sitting room. "We have set up a nursery in there, changing table, cupboards with clothes, etc., until they are older. I knew you would not want them away from you. There is a baby monitor as well. So shower, then come down to the kitchen, we will hear them if they wake."

"Sage, thank you for everything" She indicated the baby room knowing it was her idea.

Sage shrugged as she said. "Who loves yah baby?"

June chortled as she walked toward her bathroom. "You do, you big sucker." Then laughed as she closed the bathroom door behind her.

Sage watched her go, then when the door closed she took a breath and let the tears fall as she pushed each bassinet into the newly made baby room. June was okay and she and Fin would finally bond. All that was left was to find out who wanted the babies and if they had a right to them. Olinda and Keeper were pouring over all the information they could find about Pixie Law. Elijah was helping as much as he could. Unfortunately, each Luminia was autonomous. So what he knew about his Luminia may not apply to the girl's birth-mother's Luminia. She had not told June or Fin that they already had a demand for the babies to be returned to their birth-father's Grove. Sage feared they may not be able to stop the twins from being taken. She slipped the paper from the pack into her pocket. She would give this to Reighn and Elijah and hope she was wrong. She had a bad feeling about all this.

CHAPTER TEN:

Deciding to meet June in the kitchen, Sage closed the door from the bedroom and walked down the wide staircase of June's home. Her hand glided over the polished wood of the banister as the stairs curved down to the foyer. This was one of the most beautiful and large entryways Sage had ever seen in a home; the castle did not count. She hurried to the foyer table and placed the paper inside the waiting envelope, sealed it and then whispered a few words and the envelope vanished. Reighn would receive it immediately. She loved being a witch.

She stared at the full-length stained glass panels beside the dragon sized wooden front doors. The colored glass panes had dragons on each panel they were well done and, unless studied, would be missed; she wondered if June knew they were dragons. The home had hardwood floors throughout, which would be good for crawling girls, although she thought maybe the priceless rose patterned rug in the entryway may have to go. Which was a shame, as it was so beautiful. Maybe June could put it in her home office.

Rene` had told June when he gifted the house and fifty acres to her, his mother had always dreamed of a cabin in the woods. This five bedroom log home was the closest his father could come to a cabin. For a dragon, it was considered small. Rene` had said his mother had loved it. Probably because his father built it for her, even though it was a far cry from her simple little cabin she had talked of. Sadly, after his parent's death, he and Andre` had allowed the home to fall into disrepair, partly through youth and partly he admitted because it was painful for them. Memories of their parents haunted the home.

When June had arrived at Dragon's Gap, Reighn had asked his father and uncle ` if they would allow it to be gifted to her. They had immediately agreed, thankful someone would love the house again. In all honesty they were pleased the weight of not looking after it was removed from their hearts.

Sage remembered the day Reighn brought her and June to the house. It was a rundown fixer upper; the yard surrounding it was an overgrown bush land and there was no driveway like there was now, or wrought-iron gates. The place was an unloved wasteland of broken dreams. Panes of glass had been broken or just removed from the windows and the wooden logs that the house was made from were lack lustre and needed repair. The roof needed replacing and the stone fireplace was missing stones and needed cleaning. But in saying all that, June had taken one look at the log cabin and fallen head first in love with the place.

Since then, under her tender loving care, the home had a complete renovation. The yard had been turned into lawns and gardens; she had a driveway as well as walls and gates added. The roof was renewed, and the logs refurbished. Inside saw updated plumbing and electricity and modern bathrooms added and the wooden floors and walls all refinished. The stone fireplace in the great hall or lounge was cleaned and the missing stones found and replaced. The room had cathedral style ceilings with old-fashioned chandeliers, which were cleaned and electric lighting installed, the floors were re-polished, and the chimney cleaned. She had added curtains and rugs throughout the house to make it a home.

Sage was still positive the kitchen was what had sealed the deal for June. Everyone knew she loved to cook and bake. Once Rene` became aware of that, he made sure the kitchen was upgraded for a chef with a six burner stove and large appliances. Granite counters and wooden cupboards with a butler's pantry were also added. A large kitchen table sat before the sun drenched glass doors leading out to an outside patio, which led down and around to a swimming pool and tennis court. There were stables and paddocks that lay empty now, although Sage had heard June allowed unicorns to graze there. She had no idea June had been furnishing her home, but everywhere she looked she could see June had loving found and placed furniture or art all over the house. She just knew Rene` and Andre` would be pleased with the love and attention she had showered on the home their father had built for their mother.

CHAPTER ELEVEN:

S age entered the kitchen and was met with a divine aroma.

"Hello Grace. I did not know you were here?"

"Where else would I be with my girl hurt."

"Ahh, here of course." She agreed and sat next to Molly, who was drawing. Ava was in a highchair, chewing on a cookie Grace had made for her.

Verity came from the pantry. "How is she dear?"

"Dressing. Fin passed out, so she wanted to get up, she will be down shortly."

"Good and the babies?"

"Asleep."

Molly looked at her mother and asked. "Me see Auntee June and babbies?"

"Of course you can. Auntie June will be here soon, and the babies are still sleeping."

"Kay Mama."

They all smiled as Grace said. "Did you tell them?"

"No, I decided to wait. Reighn and the others are looking into it. When they know something, we will know. Until then, let's not borrow trouble." At Grace's disapproving expression, she sighed. "I will if it becomes necessary, before we have a solution or have no choice. I thought dinner here, what do you think?"

Grace accepted the change of subject. If Sage said nothing could be done because they did not have enough information, she would leave it alone. So she said. "Excellent, we have just about everything ready. The roasts will be done about seven."

Sage asked. "Verity, will Rene` come here?"

"Of course, June has changed the house into a home again. It is time for new memories to be made here."

"Oh, okay, maybe we will tell them after dinner if we know anything or Reighn says we need to."

"Tell who what?" June asked as she entered. "Oh my goodness, what is that divine smell?"

Grace hugged her as she asked. "Hello dear, are you better?"

"Still a little weak, but on my feet."

"Good, I have something for you to eat and drink."

Verity hugged her as well. "I am pleased you are well. You gave us quite a fright."

June hugged her back, saying. "I am sorry."

"Never mind, do not let it happen again." Admonished Verity.

Grace cautioned her. "You have more to think about now, other than yourself. You have Fin and those precious girls. You cannot afford to be reckless anymore."

Remorsefully, June told them both. "I know, and I will not allow it to happen again. I am truly sorry, I worried you both."

June kissed Molly, then Ava. "Hello, my girls. Did you miss me?"

"Yes." Molly said. "Isa missed you da most."

"I bet you did, sweet Molly."

CHAPTER TWELVE:

F in and June sat huddled together on a couch. Dinner had finished ten minutes ago, Ella held one twin and Scarlett the other as Grace asked both Fin and June. "Have you chosen their names yet? I refuse to call my grandchildren, twin or baby."

"Yes, Ma'am we have." June answered. She nudged Fin who smiled and said. "Ella is holding Mirren Everly." Everyone smiled and the females all said. "Aww!" Fin squeezed June's hand as he said. "And Scarlett, you are holding Breena Dawn."

Again, all the females said. "Aww!"

Verity asked. "Where are the names from?"

Fin smiled as he told her. "Mirren was my mother's name."

"Breena was my choice." June told them. "We decided we would name one each. So I chose Breena because it is of faerie origins and I thought she suited it, like Mirren suits her name."

Fin, like the males, could not see how the names suited the wrinkled pink haired babies, but no one disputed June's belief.

"Their middle names are courtesy of their Auntie Frankie." June grinned as she nodded to Frankie, who grinned in return as they all looked at her.

"I liked them. They go well with their first and last names." Sage said. "They really do."

"Why do you sound surprised?" Frankie asked her.

"No reason. None at all." Sage quickly assured her she had not forgotten Frankie's display of temper in the medical unit. There was general laughter, then talk turned to other matters as people wandered around the room. Several held a baby or child in their arms as they talked and looked out at the night. Relaxing in the warmth of a home filled with love.

"Rene` are you alright?" Charlie asked as she came to him with Justice on her shoulder. He was making baby noises and taking in everything around him.

"I am." He smiled at the picture she made, a Madonna with child. It was a beautiful memory he would store away, as he would the many he had received since stepping through the front doors of his mother's home. "Did I tell you my Sire built this cabin for my mother with his own hands?"

"Really, I did not know that. Has it always looked like this?"

"More or less, of course we had no indoor plumbing or electricity when I was a boy. It was a vacation home for my mother. We loved being here."

Charlie looked around at the beautiful lounge with its stone fireplace and wooden floors. "You gave it to June?"

Rene` smiled. "Yes." He looked at the happy Fin, who held June's hand like he would never let it go. "Yes, I did, she deserves it, and she loves every bit of this home. Sadly, my brother and I had allowed it to fall into disrepair. We could not face being here, and it weighed heavily on our hearts. It was untouched and unloved until June came and gave it back its heart. She has breathed life back into the very walls and floors and has made it a home for her and her family. It is beautiful what she has done here. There is no better tribute to the legacy my mother and father left. They both would be very happy with who is living here now."

Charlie hugged him. "I believe that this is a home filled with happiness. You can see how in the future we are going to love coming here."

"Yes, I can." He hugged her back. Verity had been right the memories of the past were still haunting the house, but they were happy memories of a loving family. He thought about all the wonderful times he, Andre` and his parents had spent here and thought of the memories to come. He felt the band around his heart loosen as he looked around him. This felt right, and this would make Andre `as happy as it had made him.

Reighn finally sat beside June and Fin on the long brown leather couch. He looked at it and ran his hand over a slightly worn patch.

"Was this in my old conference room?"

"Yes, do you want it back?" June asked with an edge to her voice.

Reighn grinned, he could see the couch in his office. It would be good for afternoon naps, but as her tone impinged on him, he hurriedly disabused her of that notion. And said a silent farewell to the couch. Maybe his Dam could find one for him like this. "Ahh, no thank you. Listen, I need to tell you something has come up."

June nodded. "Someone has made a claim for the girls."

He sighed as he nodded. "Yes, our June, someone has."

Fin asked. "Pixies?"

"No." Reighn said. "Faeries, but I am sure the Pixies will not be long in making a claim."

"What... Why... Who?" A confused June asked, like Fin she had assumed the claim would come from the Pixies.

Fin asked. "The paper with details of the twin's parentage on it. Will that help?

Elijah sat opposite them. "Maybe I have sent it to Keeper and Olinda, as well as to my parents. They are researching the Luminia now."

June asked. "So why are the faeries claiming them, they do not normally? If they breed true, they will be pixie, it seems weird."

"It does," Elijah agreed, "the claim was placed from a Grove on the other side of the world. No relation to the Sire."

"Can they do that?" Frankie asked, as she and Sage joined the conversation.

"It would seem so." Scarlett said, as she sat on the arm of Elijah's chair.

"It is not common." Elijah pondered out loud. "The fact is, they have done so, and we need to figure out why?"

Reighn said. "Someone has decided to go to war."

"Whoa! Big jump there." June almost shouted.

"Hey, how did we get there so fast?" Charlie, like June, seemed determined to bring them back to the here and now, not leaping into war.

"Who and with whom?" Frankie asked, fear shook her voice, she was not happy about her safe world ending.

Fin told her calmly. "With the dragons against the faeries."

"That seems extreme, are you sure?" Sage asked quietly, her eyes on Reighn.

He nodded and said. "Simply put, yes. Several poisonings laid directly at the door of the faeries. One attempt to kill or capture the Shadow of a dragon. Now the claiming of two hatchlings, which have nothing to do with the Grove claiming them. Harper's near death experience at the hands of faeries."

June bowed her head and thought hard. "Is this an ongoing campaign or is it a result of something else?"

The people in the room stopped talking. It was as though the very air itself waited. Sage swallowed and asked. "What are you thinking?"

June looked up. "Well, did this start when we came to Dragon's Gap, or has it been going on for a while? I mean, did it start when the dragons were on their own and dying out or only since we arrived."

"Sela cursed Edith." Olinda said thoughtfully.

"Shit!" Elijah said as he ran his hand around his neck. "I forgot about that, Edith's curse. Scarlett, you always thought Sela was not capable of that spell work?"

"I did, so does the High Queen. We researched her history and found she was ill equipped to manage such intricate spell work."

"So that means someone was behind it." Sage tentatively stated.

"Yes it does." Fin said as he stood up and paced. "Let us recap what we know."

"We need white boards." Frankie told them, "To do this in order and not miss anything."

"Third cupboard in my office." June absently said as she sat, frowning.

Frankie and Johner left the lounge as Grace handed out tea and coffee. Shortly they returned with a stand and a white board. Frankie handed Fin the marker. He raised his eyebrows at Reighn. "Oh, go ahead. You have this."

Fin inclined his head in thanks. "Alright, let us assume the dragons and the faeries are being coerced into a war." He placed both names in the middle of the board. Then, with arrows pointing out from those words, he wrote events and time lines with the help of everyone that were there. June sat and watched the pattern emerge. Claire sat down next to her and murmured. "Your Fin is very good at this."

June smiled. "It is his gift. It is what makes Fin… Fin."

"Harper, honey, are you okay?" Asked Claire of Harper, when she and Ace entered the lounge. They sat together opposite Claire and June. She had her head tipped to the side as she replied. "Yep, sure am. What do you guys see when you look at the board?"

June asked. "Excuse me?"

Harper motioned to the board. By now, everyone was looking between her and the board. "What I see is a concerted attack on the dragons."

"As do I." Reighn agreed.

She asked him. "Do you see when it started?"

Fin stood back and surveyed his board, studied the diagram on it. Then placed his marker on the pivotal point. "Here when this happened."

"When we arrived." Sage stated for everyone.

"Yes, when the dragons opened their doors and minds to the fact shifters could save their race." Grace agreed.

June asked. "Who would do this? Fairies. Pixies. Dragons?"

"All the above." Acknowledged Elijah.

Ace shook his head, leaning forward, his elbows on his

thighs. "No, another, if I am reading this right, we are being played like chess pieces."

Charlie asked. "Are you saying the Elementals?"

"Or the Goddesses." Olinda murmured.

"Ladies please, both of those are not possible." Stated Rene`.

"Why? They both place us where they want us. Make things happen when they want. Look at Frankie and me or Olinda and her Goddess. Do not tell me we are not their toys." Grumbled Harper.

"Wow, bitter much?" Charlie asked.

"Seriously, are you going to tell me it didn't happen?"

"Okay, sure, it seems like that. But do you want to take on the Elementals and Goddesses after the week you just had?" Charlie asked with a smirk.

"Point to you." Harper said with a grin.

Charlie said. "Also remember Sela suggested that there was a male behind her attacks. She implied that he was behind Storm's poisoning."

"But can we trust anything she said or did not say?" Asked Scarlett.

"And therefore we never see the whole." Edith said from the doorway as she and Sharm, Keeper and Ella arrived.

Keeper nodded and told them in his quiet way. "We worry about the parts."

"And look to who is to blame, not to why they are doing what they are doing." Sharm said just as quietly.

Storm asked. "Did we forget the unicorns on purpose or just because we forgot?"

Olinda looked at him. "Never even entered my mind. What about you guys?"

Everyone shook their heads as Sage groaned. "No, I will not entertain that idea. I like unicorns."

Olinda grinned as she said. "I like us too. Well, I like ours."

Charlie said. "Ours are faithful and loyal."

Storm said. "So a possibility then?"

Ash agreed. "Definitely."

Olinda sighed. "I put nothing past that old coot."

"Coot?" Charlie asked with raised eyebrows.

Olinda nodded. "You met him?"

Charlie grimaced as though she had tasted something bad. "True."

Edith looked around. "Well, if we do not figure this out, we are going to be in more trouble. We could get to the point where we do not trust each other." She looked around at each of the people there, her growing family, and said. "I will not allow that to happen."

No one was left in any doubt as to her meaning. Reighn stood with Ava in his arms as he said. "Edee is correct. This is not a way for us to counter this with suspicions and suppositions. That way lies distrust and fractures within our society, within our family. If I am correct, we are under attack. Our very way of life is being corrupted, or at least they, whoever they are, are trying to undermine what we are doing here. I, for one will not allow it to continue. So let us all think about who this could be and why?"

"I think the why is fairly obvious." Elijah answered him.

Claire agreed as she said. "To destabilize the coalition between dragons, shifters and faeries."

"Yes, someone wants to be the top dog. It seems someone dislikes the dragons being the Elemental's shield." June stated.

Reighn gave Ava to Ace as he moved to the board. "I believe June is correct. Although knowing is half the battle, as the saying goes. Now we can guard against them and discover how far into this we are. Fin, I am asking you to take this over. I understand you are working at Broadswords."

Fin shook his head. "My Lord, this is far more important." He looked at June and his daughters. "This affects us all."

With nods of agreement from Storm and Lars who said. "Anybody got any ideas on who we can get to replace, Fin. It will be a hard ask."

Ace said. "Maybe you could recall Hayden." He saw the hopeful look on Clint's face. "It could be the push Master Patrycc needs to return home."

Reighn nodded. "Agreed, Lars, Storm make it so. Fin, what do you need?"

"An office and my old team, this is what we were good at. I know my team members are not fitting into Dragon's Gap as easily as I had hoped they would maybe this will help."

"No one enjoys being cut loose and feeling useless." Verity said she had said little until now. "Are there many others that need help to adjust?"

"Not that I know of Lady Verity, and you are right, we dislike feeling useless." Fin agreed as he looked at Rene ` and Reighn. "We will need him, he has that ability to add two plus two and make five. I feel that this will be required. It is shaping up to be too many pieces of the same puzzle."

Rene ` sighed. "I will ask him maybe we can convince him it is time to come home."

"Who are we talking about now?" Frankie asked of Harper.

She looked at her friend and asked in return. "Why the hell would I know?"

"Why the hell don't you?" Frankie snarled back. Much to Harper's amusement. She opened her mouth to retaliate when Ace cut in before the fight grew legs and involved the entire family, which had happened on more than one family day.

"They are talking about Andre ` Lord Rene's brother."

"Ahh, the black sheep," Frankie nodded, "okay." All the dragons looked at her. Frankie looked back at them as she asked. "What... say he isn't?"

"Well, he is sort of. We just don't refer to him that way." Johner told her, trying to be diplomatic.

Frankie grinned and asked. "Oh, are you scared of him?"

"No, well yes... maybe. He was our trainer and our uncle."

All the dragons looked at him with expressions ranging from amusement to smirks. He growled as he scowled at the males there. "As if you are not ambivalent about him as well."

Grinning at his discomfort, Sage said. "We will still have to have everyone screened."

Rene` looked at Reighn. "I dislike using my gifts for such invasive actions." He held his hand up before Reighn or Sage could speak. "Although I understand the need. Send them to me."

Frankie asked Reighn. "Do you want Fin's office close to yours?"

"I do. Have him, and his team take over the four unused ones at the end of the hall."

"Certainly." Frankie made a note on her tablet. June leaned over and whispered to her. Frankie nodded. "Good idea, never thought of the connecting room between the conference room and the offices?"

"Yes, it will make a good lounge. It also has an exit to the outside patio which they can use as well."

Frankie was tapping on her tablet. "Okay, will do."

Not much more was added after that, in fact the mood plummeted to one of anger. Reighn let them all talk and get the feelings out, eventually bringing the impromptu meeting to a close. "Okay people, we are angry, so let's turn that into productivity. We will find who these people are, and we will make it so they can never play this game again. Now let us leave, June and Harper look like they both need a good night's sleep."

Everyone said their good nights after they had helped put the kitchen to rights and Grace and Verity had seen to the twins. Finally, when they were alone, Fin suggested. "June go up. I will bring you a glass of wine. We will sit out on the balcony like an old married couple."

June hugged him and asked. "What do you know of old married couples?"

He kissed her cheek. "I read."

"Well, it sounds delightful." She slipped her shoes off and ran up the stairs. Minutes later, they were on the balcony, and

June was sipping the glass of wine he had brought her.

Fin leaned against the wooden balustrade as he sipped his whiskey and eyed June in her cream colored dress that complimented her delightful hair. "So, my Shadow, how are you?"

June grinned as she looked into her drink. "I am fine and you?"

"Also fine, quite rested really."

"Well, that is good. I too find I am quite rested."

Fin grinned as he asked. "Not quite the pancake anymore?"

"No, definitely not."

He placed his drink on the table and then leaned a hand on each arm of her chair, caging her in. "What do I have to do to entice you into my arms and eventually our bed?"

June looked up into his eyes and saw his dragon looking out at her. "You could promise me a flight sometime tomorrow?"

"Done!"

"Then you could kiss me..."

He swooped in and dragged her into his arms. Her drink slid from her fingers as his lips found hers, cutting off anything more she was going to say. June had been kissed many times before, but never had she been devoured with such finesse. Her heart beat a quick tempo within her chest as her wolf sang of her happiness at having her mate with her.

June's fingers made quick work of his shirt buttons. In seconds, her hands found the warm skin of his broad chest, and a groan of pleasure escaped her throat. Fin pulled away as he looked down at his opened shirt. June blinked several times and looked at what her questing fingers had done. "Oh my."

He raised an eyebrow as he said. "Let us go inside, so I can discover what is hidden under all that delightful material you are wearing."

She grinned, and he glimpsed her wolf in her happy eyes as she reached up and kissed him. He picked her up in arms of steel and, with his lips on hers, toed the balcony door closed behind them as he moved unerringly to their bed. Where they collapsed gently down to discover why bonding was so very important to wolves and dragons.

CHAPTER THIRTEEN:

I n the two days, since the revelation that there was a campaign to undermine the dragons and their alliances. Fin had established himself in his offices with his four dragon team. Hines Doyle, Karsen Bryne, Casin Kelly and Lock Walsh, his closest friends. They had been together for hundreds of years. June had been introduced to each of the males and had immediately nominated them as honorary uncles to his daughters. Sealing their devotion to her and his hatchlings.

The faerie guards, Daru Senga and Mercca Ware who had been assigned to protect Prince Tarin, petitioned to be assigned to Fin's team representing the Faeries. He had spoken to both males and learned they were normally assigned to their Grove's investigation unit. It was as a favor to King Elijah; they had taken on Prince Tarin's protection.

When Jenny Sanders found out about the task force, how she did was still unclear and a puzzle Fin decided he would look into later. She approached Olinda and asked her to intervene on her behalf; she wanted to be part of the unit. Olinda had agreed, especially when Jordan and Ethan Reading had also asked to be included. So far, Fin had received no word from Lord Andre` about whether he would head up the unit or indeed if he would even return home.

June sat in her home office reading an official request Fin had just given her. It was for them both to attend a hearing on the validity of their claim to the twins. "This is not good."

Fin inclined his head in agreement. "In one respect it is not, in another we knew it was coming so as it is here, the wondering and worrying will stop."

"You were worrying?"

"Were you not?"

"Well yes, but you seemed so calm about it?"

"I was not, but thank you. It appears my mask of indifference is still in place."

June grinned. "You know I was mocking you, right?"

"Really, I had not noticed." They smiled at each other.

Fin said. "So we have until tomorrow to figure out what we should do."

June grimaced as she leaned back in her chair, throwing the papers onto her desk. "Like what, run?"

Fin nodded, he was deadly serious when he told her. "It is an option."

June shook her head, dismissing the idea, even though she knew they could leave and disappear and no one would find them. "No, that is not fair to our families or the girls, especially not to you, my love. You have just found Ella. No, we will fight the best fight we can, then we will surrender the girls if needs must."

Fin stilled as his dragon looked out at their Shadow. Something was wrong this was not his June. The June he knew challenged males that used swords and guns against her to rescue their daughters. She would never think to give them up. Speaking carefully, he asked. "You would willingly give the girls up?"

June's heart broke, but she bravely raised her chin and stared him in the eyes. "For the girls, yes."

Fin stood and slowly walked around to her. She stood as well, her heart racing in anticipation, ready to fight or run. She thought she could hear her wolf howling, but could not make out what she was saying. Fin reached out for her and said. "Well, I am sorry, but we will never surrender our hatchlings."

June asked stiffly. "Do you think I want to?"

Testing her, he said. "I think you are frightened of what you may do. Therefore, you will do nothing."

June's chin notched up more and she snarled. "You are

wrong?"

"Am I? You will hand over our girls when they and their birth mother sang for you."

June sucked in a breath, her eyes widening as her heart slowed its gallop, and she whispered. "Oh, I forgot. How did I forget that? It is so important." Confused eyes stared up at him. "Why did I? Fin my head hurts, what is happening?"

Fin took her hands in his. "Did you forget, or was the memory taken from you? I suspect the headache will tell us." He pulled her into his arms as he made calls to Sharm and Rene`.

June asked, her words muffled against his chest. "You mean someone erased it from my memory?"

"Yes little wolf."

"Who would or could do that?" She asked, then she suddenly went cold all over. "Fin, I can't feel my wolf." Tears entered her eyes. "They hobbled her, they made her silent. I have a mind-shield. I practice all the time holding it in place."

He kissed her cheek and whispered in her ear. "Not when you are poisoned, my love."

"Bloody hell!" He was pleased to see anger spark as she growled. "Someone will pay for this."

"Yes little wolf, they will." Fin agreed as he heard the arrival of the dragons.

Within seconds of Sharm and Rene` arriving. Reighn landed with Sage on his back. Panicked, she flung herself into the house, screaming for Fin or June. When she reached Fin, he scooped her into his arms and cradled her as she sobbed against his chest. "Hush sweet Sage, she is well. Hush you will hurt your young. Calm now."

Sage gulped in a breath as she tried to talk. "Ri... so... sor... worr..."

He nodded. "I know, I really do." Reighn arrived, having been delayed by Claire and Lars, and took his Shadow from Fin and held her close. "My soul, please calm, you will hurt yourself."

"I know... I know." She buried her face in his neck and let the tears fall. "They hurt her again."

Fin agreed. "They did. Lord Rene` and Sharm are looking at her now. It seems when she was poisoned, she was tampered with."

Sage raised her head from Reighn's neck and growled. "Who... who did this?"

Fin smiled. "I think it is time to talk to a certain Faerie Prince."

CHAPTER FOURTEEN:

T arin Ravenswood sat at the table in the interrogation room and felt the sweat run down his back. Fin sat opposite him, his merciless eyes boring into the brown eyes of the Prince.

They had summoned Tarin from the Groves isolation room where his mother had placed him earlier. Guards placed him in silver chains that had been bespelled by the High Queen, so he was unable to shrink and fly away. All this while his parents stood by impassively, with the Groves Queen and King watching. He was then marched from the Grove in front of everyone, and his humiliation did not stop there. Guards then paraded him past dragons who he was sure laughed at his discomfort. Finally, bringing him to this room where he had been shackled to large bolts on the floor and table.

He was told that the Dragon Lord had asked the Elementals to place spells over the chains and shackles to make escape impossible. Once he was placed in this chair and bound by the chains, the dragon known as Finlay Slorah had entered, and they had been sitting like this for ten minutes. Tarin knew because he was counting the minutes as the numbers on the wall clock flicked over. Finally, he could bear it no longer and asked. "Why am I here?"

"To answer some questions." Fin replied, his voice calm and bland.

Tarin raised his hands as far as the chain would allow. "In chains like a common criminal?"

Fin leaned back in his chair. "When one behaves or does criminal acts, then one should accept when caught, one will be in chains like any criminal."

Tarin scoffed loudly looking around at the mirrored wall, he knew the mirror was a two way he had seen enough human cops' shows on the screen. "What crime have I committed?"

Fin kicked up one side of his mouth as he answered. "There are several."

Tarin frowned. "Well, what are they?"

"Impatience will not win you any friends here today, Tarin. I am very close to ending your life as it is. So take care."

Outraged Tarin demanded. "For why would you end my life? I have done nothing wrong."

No longer relaxed, Fin stated. "Really, and yet you removed memories from my Shadow and created two poisons. One that felled a dragon, and another that felled my Shadow. You have consorted with traitors to your realm and mine, and you have helped create a spell that caused chaos to friends of mine. Resulting in the death of the faerie known as Sela Ouster. You have aligned yourself with those that would kill and enslave shifters and have killed a pixie and faerie, a bonded couple, and tried to kill their young. There is also the matter of trying to instigate a war. None of these are minor crimes, I am sure you understand that?" Fin was silent for a moment as he looked down at the opened file in front of him. Finally, he looked up at the worried faerie.

"Yes, I think that is all. More crimes may emerge later, but for now we will deal with only these."

Tarin was worried, anyone of those crimes, if proved, would end his life. He swallowed twice and cleared the sudden fear from his throat before he pleaded with Fin. "You must believe me. I have done none of those things. I do not know how to make a spell or even what would make a poison. As for consorting with people who are doing those things, that is not my fault. I meet lots of people. I cannot be held accountable for what or who they know. I have no idea about a war. You are crazy, you have the wrong person. I have done none of those things."

"Interesting." Fin looked down again at the folder in front of him. "I do not believe you and the reason for that is you did not deny trying to remove June's memories."

"See, if I was that person you accused me of, I would have said something about that." Tarin's voice took on a soothing, dream like cadence.

"Is he trying to beguile him?" June asked as she stood next to Reighn, who smiled as he narrowed his eyes. "It would appear so."

"Amazing." June muttered.

King Gideon looked at his Light. "Did you know he had that ability?"

"No." Queen Isla shook her head. "My dear, I did not, he kept that well-hidden."

"Or it is a recent ability he has acquired." Elijah looked at the parents of the accused male and felt sympathy stir in his heart. To have your only son accused of being a traitor must be terribly hard to swallow.

Tarin's voice rolled over Fin, as his dragon said. *Foolish faerie, we should squash him like a bug.*

Fin responded with a laugh. *I find him amusing and stupid. If he is the leader in this endeavour, we will have this wrapped up in no time.*

He is not. Just another puppet that wished to be someone greater.

Sadly, you are correct. I feel for his parents.

As do I.

Tarin softly said to Fin. "You are obviously too close to this. It was your Shadow that was affected. Maybe you should step away. Let someone of rank who will understand me ask questions, so I can explain it to them. Obviously you cannot understand simple English when it is spoken, all this is above your intellect."

Fin sighed loudly. "Are you finished, because it is becoming irritating?" Tarin's eyes widened. No one had ever dismissed his skill so abruptly before. He was considered above grade when it came to the art of persuasion, and yet it just slid right off this dragon. "Sadly for you, Tarin, your mind tricks will not work on me. I am of rank. I do understand English and worse for you. I do not believe you. Now you may not have realized this, or you did, and in your arrogance thought yourself better than us mere dragons. Lord Rene ` is a Keeper and I know you know what that is. All faerie royalty understand what a Keeper can do. Lord Rene ` searched my Shadow's mind and found the scar left over by your clumsy attempt to remove her memory."

Tarin wiped his face with his chained hands and bluffed as he felt the noose tighten around his neck. "When would I have had the opportunity to do such a thing?"

Fin smiled a showing of white teeth. For a split second Tarin was sure he saw the dragon in his smile. He swallowed nervously again as Fin said. "We narrowed that down to when you were in the medical unit, when I brought June and the babies back here."

Tarin spread his hands. "There you go, with everyone there as well as my parents, unlikely at best. I doubt I would have been able too."

"I do not, that was when you did so."

Tarin felt fear snake down his spine at the dragon's confident tone. He looked at him and was positive the dragon was playing a game.

Fin said, "Now as for the other charges, instigating a war, poison, deaths, spells. I am sure you are not confident or talented enough to do all these crimes by yourself. I want... No, I am sorry, I misspoke. I demand the names of your masters and co-conspirators."

"How dare you?" Tarin hissed. "You accuse me of being someone's puppet?"

Fin looked at the male. "I see."

"What... What do you see, dragon?"

Fin grinned again, another slash of white teeth. Tarin was positive his teeth had grown. He swallowed nervously again as Fin said. "I see that being taken for someone's puppet is more upsetting to you than the actuality of committing so many crimes."

"As it would be to any male." Tarin puffed out his chest as he stated. "I am no one's toy."

Isla and Gideon Ravenswood, parents to Tarin, stood, hands clasping each other's as Isla rasped. "I had no idea. We would never have thought it in a million years. There is no doubt, is there?"

Gideon shook his head. "No, my love. No doubt."

June whispered. "I am so very sorry. This must be a nightmare for you. No parent ever suspects their child of such treachery."

They both looked at her and saw the sincerity in her expression. Isla said faintly. "No, we did not and thank you my dear."

Scarlett said, outraged on her friend's behalf. "Isla, do not take this as your fault. He is an adult and was raised as his sisters were. There was no reason for him to have done this."

Isla held a sob in as she nodded. "I know Scarlett."

Gideon said, his voice hard with hurt and betrayal. "Look at what he did, with all the opportunities we gave him."

Isla looked at his face and saw the same ravaged expression that she knew would be on hers. "Maybe that was our mistake."

He sighed, as broken-hearted as she was. "Maybe, my dear."

Reighn said. "Isla, Gideon, sometimes a bad person is just a bad person. No matter how they were raised or by whom. Remember this as you grieve his loss. At any time he could have come to you, two people who love him. It was his choice not to."

Isla smiled weakly. "You are wise, my Lord, and will make a wonderful father. I will hold to your words."

Scarlett said. "It is not that different to what you told me when I was young and Juna left with that male."

Isla nodded. "Oh, I had forgotten that. There was something wrong with him, always was from a little one."

Gideon said softly. "As was Tarin, we ignored and pandered to it. Hid his quirks from ourselves as well as others, but he has that same wrongness inside of him as Definiao Kiltern had. We just hoped it would go away. In that we are very much like Definiao's parents, who were wrong." He took Isla in his arms and looked at Reighn. "We will do all we can for you, to halt what he has caused, but we cannot witness this. I am sorry for our weakness."

Reighn bowed his head in respect. "There is no weakness here, just heartbroken parents hurting and that my friends, we all understand. Go, do what you must to heal. You are always welcomed here at Dragon's Gap and in my territories." Gideon thanked him as he led his weeping Light away.

Scarlett cried. "I hate this, absolutely hate this."

"I know my Light, as do we all." Elijah soothed her.

"Tarin, I would never have thought he had the balls for it." Harper said as she entered with Charlie who said. "We waited until his parents left, it seemed wrong to add witnesses to their grief."

"Wow! That was very mature of you." Frankie said, as she entered behind them. "Was it Charlie's decision?"

Harper gave her a dirty look as Charlie nodded her head in confirmation. The brief levity helped dispel the despair that had fallen over the room. Charlie stated, "I believe he did it. Weak chins, and beady eyes. Those that have them are nasty, evil people." She looked at Reighn. "You sure you don't want me to question him?"

He grinned. "No thank you. I need him alive."

Charlie shrugged. "I don't kill everyone I question."

"Really?" Frankie asked, "Because I am fairly sure the last ones you asked questions of are dead."

Charlie hunched her shoulders a little at the truth of her statement. "Well, yeah but I did say not everyone." Frankie, along with everyone else looked at her with varying expression of disbelief on their faces. "I have mellowed. I tell you."

Harper snorted as Frankie grinned in disbelief. They once more turned to the window in time to hear Fin say. "Alright, so you take responsibility for all the crimes stated, good to know." Then he rose and started to walk from the room.

Tarin tried to stand and found he could not. "No... no, that is not what I said dragon Fin, you must believe me."

"No faerie Tarin, I do not have to believe you." Fin remained walking. His hand was on the door handle when Tarin screamed and jerked at the chains. "They made me do it!" Fin halted and turned to him, his face without expression, as Tarin sobbed. "I had to do it, I had no choice."

Fin shrugged. "I do not believe you Tarin, you always have a choice. You are a Prince, you had people to go to, your parents, Queen Scarlett and King Elijah. Your guards, the Dragon Lord. Anyone of these people would have protected and kept you safe." He looked at the male and shook his head. "No, you chose to do this."

"I had no choice." Tarin wept openly as he slumped onto his seat. "I was in deep they came to me and told me my life was forfeited if I did not comply."

"Who... who came to you?" Demanded Fin as he stepped closer. Suddenly, the room was swamped with power. Fin felt the hairs on the back of his neck rise.

"What is that?" June asked as she watched her Shadow scan the room.

"Who is that? Is a better question." Harper asked as Reighn walked into the room with Elijah behind him. June and Harper both made to follow, only to be prevented by Charlie, who stood in front of the now closed door.

"Wow! She is fast." June muttered to Harper, who nodded. "Always was."

"Listen up, you two. You stay here, no more exciting times for either of you."

"Spoilsport." June murmured to Harper. "Was she always this bossy?"

"Nope, it is a new thing. I think it is having young that does it."

"Tough." Charlie told the two of them. "You can look from here but no going in."

They all turned back to the window. "Hate it when she is right." Harper said to June. They both missed Charlie's smirk to Scarlett and Frankie, or Scarlett's wink in reply.

Elijah said to Reighn. "I think, my Lord, we are under attack. This is pixie magic. Your magic will not work here, Dragon Lady." He told Sage as she walked in from the hall with blue, glowing hands.

Hers may not, mine will! An Elemental said as he appeared. He placed his hands together as if he was in prayer and slowly drew them apart. And as he did, he revealed two pixies and two faeries standing in the corners of the room.

"Son of a bitch." Harper hissed.

"I second that." Snarled Charlie.

Scarlett mumbled. "Me third it."

The Elemental pointed to a pixie. His voice when he spoke sounded like thunder. *Why are you here?*

With a musical voice, the male said. "We are here to make sure the one who has our young return them."

"Lies." Charlie told the others with her in the room.

Liar. The Elemental stated, and the pixie dropped to his knees. His mouth opened in a silent scream as tears streaming down his face.

The Elemental then pointed to the other pixie, a female this time, standing in the opposite corner. *Speak!* His voice thundered, vibrating the soles of everyone's feet.

She looked at the Elemental, then at the male on his knees. "Our Master sent us to kill this one." She indicated Tarin.

He screamed at her. "Why? I did everything you asked of me. Everything."

She snarled. "You got caught, fool."

She too dropped to her knees, but there were no tears or silent scream as she clenched her jaw shut.

Harper looked at her sister and the other two. "She is

tough."

"Very, but stupid, seriously they want to play here? Foolish, idiots." Scarlett shook her head at the stupidity of some people.

The Elemental pointed to the faeries. *Which of you will answer?*

A male stepped forward. "I will."

Why are you here?

"To discover who was behind the poisoning."

"Part lie." Charlie murmured.

The Elemental flicked his fingers, and the male dropped to his knees. *You play with words. It annoys me.*

The other female moved from the corner and Elijah drew in a sharp breath, when he saw she was half-pixie. She spoke with a lilt that was almost a song. "Elemental, Dragon Lord. I am here to stop the start of the war."

"Who sent you?" Reighn asked, anger in his voice.

She looked at Elijah, who told her. "You should answer."

"I am an agent for the Elturnian."

Sage said. "I would be impressed if I knew what and who that was."

The Elemental said. *As would we all.*

Fin told them. "It is the equivalent of our Shields or the human force known as the C.I.A. They investigate more than they assassinate, although they are trained to do both."

The females in the outer room all turned to Charlie, who shrugged. "Never heard of them. That is not to say I have not worked for them, but if they are as secretive as they seem to be. I would not have known."

"You know a lot about our agency." The female said to Fin, who remained silent, but he did smile a knowing smile.

The Elemental said. *I, like our Dragon Lord, wish to know why you are here.*

"As I said to stop a war."

But agent, you lie.

Charlie said. "One should never lie to an Elemental. Guess

she never got the memo. Scarlett, do you know about these people?"

"Yes, although only in whispers, apparently they are completely autonomous."

"Harmless?" Frankie asked her, and almost laughed when she replied.

"Dear Frankie, no. Anything but, all their agents have innate magic and are taught a good deal more, or so I am told. All three of you would make excellent agents for them and do not be surprised if they do not try to recruit you."

Harper looked speculatively at the female behind the glass as she asked Scarlett. "So they recruit others as well as faeries?"

In answer, Scarlett shrugged. "So I have heard." Then placed her finger against her lips in the sign for silence or secret.

By now the female was on her knees, panting as she begged the Elemental. "Please... Please, Eminence. I came because they were here. I followed them."

Thank you. Is it in your nature to lie? He asked her.

She drew in a deep breath and nodded, not trusting her voice just then. The Elemental mused. *This seems a waste of your talents?*

Elijah said. "All agents for the Elturnian dedicate their lives to the betterment of all races, or so they say. The actual Elturnian council consists of thirteen members at any one time, and they consider themselves above all others."

The Elemental asked. *All others?*

Elijah bowed his head as he said. "Yes Elemental."

I see, Dragon Lord, I will take these with me and we will learn as much as we can, then send you what is revealed. You may keep the Elturnian agent for now. He turned to the female and said. *Do not go far, little agent, we may have a need of you.*

With that, he and the other four people, including Tarin, disappeared. Everyone breathed easier with his leaving. Reighn stared at the female, his mind racing with the implications of her being here. Unlike the others, he knew a lot about the Elturnian. He should, it was his ancestor who originally created the organization. All eyes turned to the female, who was climbing to her feet. She made a motion with her hand and looked shocked, and tried again, then said. "What have you done?"

Sage asked. "Made it so your magic does not work here?"

"Impossible." Agitated now, she flicked her hand several times with the same result. Frankie, Harper, and Charlie, along with Scarlett, entered.

Scarlett asked. "Why are you here, I realized you followed those idiots, but why here?"

The female flicked her hand again, ignoring Scarlett, and asked. "How can you do this? I use Elturnian magic, which is impossible to break or erase?" She looked genuinely upset.

Elijah snapped. "Answer the question cousin."

"Because it is my duty cousin." She snapped back. "The leads led here."

Fin asked Elijah. "You are related."

Elijah shrugged as he grimaced. "Unfortunately. She is from my mother's people. No one has heard of her for years. I guess we know why now."

Reighn asked. "What is your name?"

He pushed Sage gently into a seat as the agent answered. "My name is Faline Lightwind."

"Well, agent Faline Lightwind, you will remain here until you answer all our questions without magic or communications. Unless, you feel inclined to set it up so I can talk to the Elturnian council."

The female was almost six feet tall with well-defined muscle. If she had wings, they were well hidden. Her hair was short and blue, as were her eyes. She was not the most beautiful faerie and pixie he had ever seen. In fact, Elijah was far more beautiful, but then he was full pixie. Still, this female had a certain something that drew the eyes, mystery maybe, Reighn thought.

She looked at Reighn and smiled, a sweet innocent gesture. "It may be possible, my Lord to arrange that."

Charlie looked blandly at the female, then at Reighn. "She lies."

"As I thought." Reighn dismissed her with a flick of his eyes. "Fin, place her in the cells and Charlie, take Frankie and Harper with you. Strip search her, and give her something else to wear. Frankie, do the thing we talked about the other day."

"Oh, do you think I am ready?" She asked him with a worried expression in her eyes.

He smiled. "More than ready. You can do this. I believe in you sweet one."

"Oh!" She smiled at his praise, then shimmed her way out of the room as everyone watched her.

Harper scowled. "Dear Goddess, she will be unbearable now. Thanks my Lord."

"Whatever I can do to make your life interesting, sister. I will."

"Bah!" She said as she strode from the room calling out to Frankie. Leaving Fin and Charlie to escort Faline Lightwind between them. The agent said to Reighn just before they passed through the doorway. "You realize this is in violation of the Elturnian code."

Reighn shrugged. "Who? I have no knowledge of who or what that is." His voice hardened. "Because if there was such an organization they would have asked my permission before sending an agent into my territories."

"Faline." Elijah said. "Cousin, if you have a way of contacting them, now would be the time to share. Do not wait until they come for you. That way ends in blood. You and they do not know who you are dealing with."

She smirked as she said. "Cousin, it is the other way around. Explain to the Dragon Lord who and what we are and how he should be worried for when they do arrive, they will not be gentle."

"Oh sugar." Charlie said, "We don't know the meaning of gentle. Now move your ass."

Fin looked at Reighn. "Tomorrow will be interesting. Where is June?"

Elijah told him. "She went with Sage and Scarlett to see to the babies."

"How did I miss that?"

"Exactly." Reighn said as he nodded at the female walking next to Charlie. Fin grinned as he dipped his head, saying. "Forewarned is forearmed."

Elijah asked after the door was closed. "What is it Frankie can do?"

"Something extraordinary, she can dampen magic. We have calculated she can influence an area up to five miles."

Elijah could not quite keep the laugh from his voice as he said. "So Faline thinks she will be able to communicate once she is in the cells?"

"Yes and she will not."

"Does Frankie have to be close?"

Reighn decided not to tell him everything they had practiced, as he had told Frankie. Sometimes it was better to keep some things close to their chests. "We will see, but we do not think so." He said instead of telling him that Frankie did not have to be anywhere near the place she affected.

Elijah whistled as he thought about the implications of Frankie's gift. "That is amazing."

Reighn rubbed his hands together. "Isn't it, though?"

"Fin knows of this?"

Reighn laughed as he told him. "It was his and Charlie's idea. Now my friend, what do you know about this group known as the Elturnian?"

CHAPTER FIFTEEN:

That night everyone gathered in the large dining room, which was usually used for family days. Harper called out. "Quiet down. I have shit to do tonight."

Reighn sighed as he stood at the head of the table. "Thank you Harper."

Harper grinned. "Not a problem, let us just keep on track tonight."

She looked around as Ace said. "Please... Please let us stay on track, the moaning is annoying."

"Whose Harper's?" Storm asked with a wicked look in his eyes.

"No, his." Johner called out, which had everyone busting out a laugh.

Ace grinned as Harper moaned loudly. "See? This is what I mean about staying on track,"

Reighn raised a hand and the talking and laughing slowed to a stop. "Okay, so this is where we are at, for all of you who have not been directly involved. We have created a task force of specialized agents led by Fin. Sire, have you spoken to Andre`?"

"I have, he said he would think on it and let us know."

"Will he help us?"

Rene` smiled. "Of course he will."

Reighn grinned with him. "So as it stands, the task force will be led by Andre` Kingsley. Second will be Finlay Slorah, who will take lead until Andre` joins us." There were a few smiles at the mention of Andre`. "Fin, tell us who is in your unit."

Fin stood and inclined his head. "Good evening everyone, we are lucky enough to have four of my team with us. Please stand when I say your name, so everyone can meet and recognize you. Hines Doyle, Karsen Bryne, Casin Kelly and Lock Walsh, these warriors are former Shields who worked with me." All four stood and nodded to Reighn and Fin, then retook their seats, four hardened warriors who looked like they had been front and center of too many battles.

"Please stand, Daru Senga and Mercca Ware, who are, as you all know, former guards to the Prince. They are first class investigators who were on loan to the Dragon's Gap Grove, but have moved here permanently. We are lucky enough they have agreed to take a lead with their own teams. We are also fortunate to have Jordan and Ethan Reading. Who, we all know, have unique gifts and are seasoned unicorn warriors. As well as Lady Jenny Sanders, who is well versed in politics? Finally, our ever patient office assistants Lisa Peters and her sister Kera Peters, along with Mike Johns."

Harper looked at the females. She was sure Lisa was one of her rescues. In fact, the more she looked, the more positive she was, although she looked very different now. "Lisa, is that you?"

Lisa grinned, her shiny red hair, and clear blue eyes with a scattering of freckles, belied the sorrowful, frightened female Harper had picked up weeks ago. Lisa blushed slightly as she said. "Harper, it is. I know I look different."

"Wow, you do. I didn't recognize you. We should get together later."

Lisa nodded as she retook her seat. Harper smiled as Charlie asked quietly. "One of your rescues?"

"Yes, I wondered what had become of her."

Frankie leaned over and whispered. "She and her sister are doing great. They have helped Claire and me out a few times, and that was why I thought of them for Fin. They are discreet and very good at what they do."

Harper whispered. "Thanks Frankie."

Frankie whispered back. "It is what I do."

"So now you know my team. Let me tell you what we have

learned so far." Fin explained what took place the previous night and what had happened to June. He told them of the agent still in the cells below the castle and who she belonged to. He asked if anyone had dealings with the Elturnian. It seemed no one had, other than Queen Scarlett and King Elijah. He finished by placing the white board up and explaining the reasoning behind it.

Reighn stood. "So there you have it. What we suspect and what we know. Tomorrow at ten I will convene court. Two petitions have been brought before the Dragon Lord, one by a Grove and one by a Luminia. Each petition wishes to claim June and Fin's daughters, Mirren and Breena."

No one moved or spoke, but the tension in the room ratcheted up. He nodded, then said. "As you can imagine, they will not be leaving here with either of them."

Conor Towers, Leo, and sheriff of Dragon's Gap said in his slow drawl. "If I was a betting lion, I would bet my life savings, which are considerable?" There were a few laughs as everyone knew the lion gave more away than he kept helping the people of his new home. "I would say tomorrow at ten would be an ideal time for an attempt to infiltrate Dragon's Gap and kidnap or kill specific targets in the court. Also, tonight would be an ideal time to break the agent out. I have found organizations like this Elturnian have only two solutions when an agent has being taken prisoner. Rescue or kill." He smiled when he finished speaking and sat as those around him stared at him, then at Reighn.

"If you were a betting lion?" Charlie said. "That would be what you would bet on."

"Yes." He grinned and asked. "What would you bet on?"

"That I would never bet against you."

People laughed at the smug look on the large male's face and the shrewd look on Charlie's.

Ace agreed with Conor. "He is right."

Reighn nodded in agreement. "He is, we have worked out a plan for tomorrow and if Conor and as many of his pride as he can spare would like to be included. We would welcome them."

Conor also nodded. "We would."

Olinda said. "The unicorns are at your disposal, they asked to be included in any plans."

Reighn smiled. "I thank you Olinda and you Conor. Fin, are you commanding?"

"Yes with Ace and Conor." They both saluted, agreeing to the command.

"Good. Frankie, give it out." Reighn ordered.

Frankie stood with a bundle of papers in her hands. "These are magical instructions bespelled by Dragon Lady Sage. Read them, commit them to memory. When you have, the paper will disappear. You have until we leave the room to do so." She passed out the papers to everyone there. Each paper had their duties and where they were meant to be and by what time on it.

Reighn said. "Grace, you and your family will have sole custody of our young. Is that a concern for you?"

"Where?" Ivan asked before Grace could comment.

"Here in the stone apartment, it is reinforced with iron and stone and has magical shielding. Our young, yours included, will be there."

Ivan nodded as he looked at his mother and George. Storm told the bear brothers. "Select your people for inside and outside the apartment."

Ivan replied. "We will have them here by eight o'clock tonight."

Reighn nodded. "Good, Keeper and my father will screen them as soon as you have chosen them."

"Done." George agreed.

Reighn turned to Elijah and Scarlett. "You and your Grove may come under attack."

Elijah nodded. "We have sent everyone to the High Queens Grove. Warriors and guards remain only."

Sage asked. "You will stay here tonight?"

"We will, thank you."

"Johner, Conor, Storm, the people of Dragon's Gap will have to be protected." Reighn ordered.

Conor said. "We have shifters and humans as well as Dragons that have a home they love. No one will willingly give that up to any invaders."

Sage told him. "The young will be brought here along with anyone who wishes to come."

Conor nodded. "We will take the offer for the young. We, the shifters and unicorns can keep everyone else safe."

"You know, the more it looks like we are unprepared, the more likely we can lure them in and grab them. A reverse trap." Edith murmured.

Reighn smiled as he agreed with her. "Edee is right, and we will, but I will not sacrifice our people."

Edith agreed, then asked. "No, of course not, but we could ask them if they will help trap these people."

Conor said. "We will, my pride is doing that as we speak."

"Crafty lion." Harper muttered to Charlie who agreed saying. "And smart… very smart."

Sharm said. "I cannot empty out the medical units, as much as I would like too."

Storm told him. "I will have it guarded and brother, we can mix in Hunters and Shields with your people. No one will tell the difference. As long as all the young are hidden, it will work."

"They will be brought here." Sage ordered again.

Conor told her. "Dragon Lady, they will be here by seven in the morning."

Ace said. "No, tonight, undercover of darkness. It will be safer for all concerned, especially if there is a possibility they will be watching."

Conor nodded. "You are right, if it was me I would be watching."

"As would I. Let's do it as Ace says." Reighn commanded. "So we all know what we are to do. Let us get to it."

"Yes my Lord."

Reighn's commanding voice issued his last orders. "We have eight hours until midnight. We need to have everything and everyone in place by then. Commanders work out a patrol for tonight and the morning."

"Yes, my Lord."

CHAPTER SIXTEEN:

H arper and Ace sat in the dark in the main kitchen of the castle. Their backs against the stone wall. She could feel his warm body next to hers. "You know this is the part I hate, the waiting."

"I as well dislike this part."

Harper eyed her Shadow. "We could make out to pass the time?"

Ace grinned. "We could, but how would it look to your sister if we allowed our quarry to slip by us?"

Harper scowled at the thought. "Yeah, terrible idea."

Charlie and Storm sat side by side with their backs against the stone wall in the medical unit. Fin had reasoned the French doors would be irresistible to the agents. He believed one would at least try to enter from them. "I am bored. I hate this."

Storm smiled as he softly responded. "I can see that, my love. Maybe we could find something to occupy ourselves with while we wait?"

Shocked he would think of sex now, Charlie almost yelled, only remembering to lower her voice at the last minute. "Oh, my Goddess, we cannot have sex on a stakeout."

Storm eyebrows rose as he heard where her mind had jumped to, which was amusing to him and his dragon. "I was thinking of playing cards."

Sheepishly, she mumbled. "Oh, yeah... we could do that."

"Although your idea has merit..."

Axl and Ark sat together, their backs against the wall in Reighn's office. Fin also believed the agents would have instructions to search his office. They would not want to pass up the chance to learn something about the Dragon Lord.

And as the brothers were going to be together, his other brothers had volunteered Ark to ask Axl what his plans regarding Joy were. "So what's up with you and Joy?"

"It is getting harder to suppress my dragon."

"I feel for you, brother. Do you have a plan?"

"No, apart from killing every male here, that is."

Ark smiled. "See, that won't work for me."

Axl rubbed his tired eyes and sighed. "So give me some brotherly advice."

Ark sucked his breath between his teeth and told him what Lord Rene` had advised them to say when he asked. "You know what you have to do. For her, for you, for all us innocent males."

"Shit... that will be so hard to do. I don't know if I am ready yet."

"I get that, but at least you can think about it now. I mean, it is that or kill every male here, right?"

"Yeah... yeah, leaving is such sweet sorrow." He misquoted.

"You know, I know you aced English lit. Why do you persist in misquoting everything?"

Axl grinned, knowing how much he annoyed Ark with his quotes. "Life is too short to be confined by what was written incorrectly."

Ark sighed and shook his head. "You are a fool, brother."

"A fool in love." Axl sang softly.

"Songs you get right."

Fin and Ash sat together, backs against the wall on the level that housed the cells. They were far enough away the agent Faline Lightwind could not hear them. Ash asked. "Are you going to do something about the ones that June tagged?"

Fin nodded. "Of course, as soon as we have this cleared up. Why?"

"Ace came up with a plan to take them out and maybe find out who was behind the attack on the twin's parents."

Fin grinned, just a quick slash of white teeth in the dark.

"Please enlighten me and we can see if it meshes with mine."

Conor and his brother Saul sat together, watching the five agents step from behind a curtain of blackness. Barely moving his lips, Saul murmured. "Neat trick."

"Isn't it, though? Signal Fin."

They watched the five slink on silent feet toward the castle. Conor had guessed correctly that an attempt at a rescue would be tonight. Fin, with careful deliberation, had targeted this location as their starting point. Of course, how they would get here no one knew or could guess. So Conor sent his Pride to circulate within the town while he and Saul elected to remain and watch near the castle. Their patience was rewarded just on two o'clock, five agents arrived, and as predicted they split up.

Ace told them at the final briefing their leader would assume they would have more of a chance breaking into the castle alone. It was no simple thing to slip into a castle undetected by the Dragon Lord or dragons, hence the late hour. So as Conor and Saul watched, Saul signaled Fin, who signaled the teams throughout the castle as well as all the others waiting in town. He and Ace had placed the teams at what they had determined would be the logical points of entry to capture the invaders.

Conor and Saul made their quiet way to where they spied an agent dressed in black from head to toe. She had not disappeared into the night with the other agents. It appeared something had caught her attention. She was looking up at the battlements where Reighn and Sage stood cloaked in Reighn's magic.

She tried to pierce the darkness, positive something or someone stared down at her. Sadly, she would never know as Saul and Conor softly padded up behind her and place a small mask over her face. Inside the attached canister was a potent sleeping gas Sharm had devised with the help of Sage and a unicorn healer. It induced sleep and lasted for three or four hours. Long enough for the other teams to apprehend their targets and place them all in cells.

Charlie and Storm had no trouble taking care of their target. He never even knew they were there. One moment, he was entering the French doors of the medical unit after a cold swim in the moat. The next minute, he felt a hand slap a mask over his face. Charlie smiled at Storm as he lowered the male to the floor. "That was easy. You make a superb partner, my love."

"So can we play now?"

Charlie eyed her Shadow. "We are not talking cards, are we?"

He smiled like the dragon he was as she grinned like the Assassin she was and said. "No, we are not."

At Fin's signal, Harper slipped into the large walk-in pantry, and Ace blended into the shadows. They both knew the agent would not turn on the lights. Harper watched him move stealthily from the door, which had barely opened. He sidled along the wall until he was nearly at the pantry's entrance. Then she jumped out and waved her arms around and yelled as Ace slid up behind the startled male and slipped the mask over his face. He slumped in his arms as Ace asked. "What was that?"

Harper jumped up on to the counter. "I decided to try a new tactic."

Ace moved to cage her body between his legs and arms. "Why?"

She looped her arms around his neck. "It seemed the thing to do."

"Well, do not do so again, my heart cannot take it."

"Oh... want to make out?"

"Of course."

Axl and Ark were more direct. One minute, the female agent was walking down the dark hallway leading to Reighn's office. She felt a wind surround her, then suddenly Ark and Axl were on either side of her. "Greetings!" Axl said as the female's head turned toward him, astonishment on her face. Ark slapped the mask over her nose and mouth and seconds later she was asleep. "Easy as pie." Axl stated.

Ark snorted in disgust. "Truly. I thought these were some type of hardened agents."

Axl grinned as he hefted the dead weight of the female onto his shoulder. "Well, to be fair, they have never come up against us or Frankie's non magical abilities before."

"True, we are unique. I wonder if this stuff gives them a headache."

Axl grinned as he offered. "I could try it on you, and you could tell us when you wake up."

"Brother, I am unamused."

Fin and Ash received confirmation the other agents had been subdued as they waited for their target to arrive. Frankie and Johner stood in a room to the left of the cells. If the male got past the dragons. Johner would drop him with a special blow dart made, just for this sort of thing by Storm and Sharm.

At a signal from Fin, Frankie tightened her sphere of influence to null the magic of the male coming stealthily down the hallway. Fin and Ash moved farther back away from the corridor and the cell they incarcerated the agent Faline in. Fin was sure the male coming toward them was more than likely the leader of the group. It was in the careful way he moved along the dark hallway. Fin caught sight of Faline moving closer to the bars of the cell. They had deliberately placed her in the cell with a barred door, as opposed to the solid wooden ones. He and Ash watched the male slip from one patch of darkness to another.

When he was almost at the cell, he called softly. "Faline Lightwind?"

She whispered back. "London Darkchild, I cannot believe they sent you?"

"And I cannot believe you got yourself caught."

She shrugged. "You have not come up against the Elementals. Until you do, keep your comments to yourself. Now get me out."

London leaned against the bars with his senses ranging out around him. He did not realize Frankie's ability was causing him to read only an area an inch or so from his body. Not sensing any danger, London allowed himself to relax and indulge in some teasing.

Faline demanded. "What are you doing? Release me." London, she knew, could be so annoying, especially if he felt he had the upper hand. It was rare Faline was ever bested by London Darkchild, who was an extraordinary human. Descended, if one wanted to believe the rumors from a great Native American chieftain, not that he would admit or deny the truth. However, he was an exemplary example of the human race with his long black hair and black eyes, wiry, muscled body and sharp, intelligent mind.

He whispered. "All in good time... all in good time. First though, I wish to know how you were caught."

"Why?"

"It is obvious, is it not?" He drawled. "So I do not fall into the same trap, of course."

"Huh, you assume it was a trap?"

"Well..."

"Well what? They did not know we were there. We were completely bespelled until the Elemental arrived, then I could not call my magic."

London stood away from the bars he had been leaning against and snapped out. "Say again!"

Faline said with exaggerated patience. "I said no magic. Now get me out of here."

All his cockiness disappeared. "Yes... yes of course." London touched the lock on the door and pushed with his magic, and nothing happened. He tried again and nothing happened, desperate he looked at Faline, who looked back at him with the same desperation in her eyes.

"Try again."

He did, then asked. "What is going on?"

Faline groaned. "Please say you came with a lock-pick?"

London shook his head. "Why would I? They are only dragons?"

Her head dropped just as a hand grabbed London's shoulder and another hand slid a mask over his face. "Dragons are sneaky. You should remember that?" Fin told Faline as they both watched Ash allow the male to drop to the floor with a soft groan.

Stunned, Faline gasped and asked. "You knew?"

Fin shrugged. "Of course, this is our home. Our Dragon Lord knows whenever a portal is opened. We may only be dragons but we have lived a very long time you may want to remember that, if you survive."

He moved aside as one after the other of his team members deposited the Elturnian rescue team into cells on either side of Faline. Ash picked up the male known as London and placed him in the cell with her. She stood back against the wall while the door was opened. She was no fool, there was no way she would try to run. She knew she would only end up dead if she did. After the prisoners were placed in their cells and the teams had dispersed to their beds. Fin looked at Johner and Frankie. "You will be alright here for the night?"

Frankie had elected to remain close to the agents, as no one knew what their gifts were. She held tight to her dampening spell. "Yep, Johner said we will be."

Fin told them. "Someone will be down to relieve you so you can change for court. Sleep well, my friends."

"You too." They chorused.

Fin nodded to the agent as she stared at him. "Rest, you will need your wits about you for court tomorrow."

She did not answer him. With one more satisfied look at the cells filled with sleeping agents. Fin, his hands in the pockets of his jeans, strolled from her view.

Faline slowly sank to the floor, looking at the comatose male in the bed opposite her. Life she feared was about to change forever. The problem, she worried over, would the change be for the better or worse for the Elturnian, and what changes would come for her, if she survived.

CHAPTER SEVENTEEN:

The next morning June and Fin were up early. Neither of them had slept very much after Fin returned to their bed in the apartment at the Castle. Not that there had been much of the night left. After they had fed and changed the twins, they wandered into the dining room, where June ate her breakfast, or at least tried to. She drank several cups of coffee; she was tired and wired, not a good combination for her or her wolf.

Fin looked at her over the table. "Little wolf, are you with me still?" June took her eyes off the baby in her arms, and Fin could see the wildness in her eyes. He refused to call it wolf-crazy, and as he smiled at her, the look started to fade.

Then she took a breath and let it out slowly, saying. "I am... I am good. They will be safe. No one will die today, or get hurt and we will be a happy family."

He smiled. "Tall order but doable."

She laughed. "You really are mixing with humans and shifters too much."

He shrugged. "I love the way they express themselves. It is enlightening and confuses the Nobles, which as Ace says, is always a bonus."

June shook her head and scolded. "You two really?"

Fin smiled with relief. She was smiling now and relaxing. The feeling of wildness was easing within her as she asked. "So what is Andre` like?"

Fin thought for a moment. "Nothing like Rene` that's for sure. He trained us all at one time or another, and there was no one better. He was tough but fair and mostly patient which, for some recruits, was a blessing. He, like Storm, does not suffer fools easily."

"Uhuh! I meant, what does he look like?"

"Why?" He frowned at her question, seeing no reason for it.

"Well, does he look like Rene`?"

"Oh… I see what you mean. No, he is the light to Rene's dark."

"Oh, different mothers."

Fin smiled at her assumption. "No, just different. They had the same parents. It is just they are visibly different but very much the same personality."

June looked at him and shook her head; she was still none the wiser as to what Andre` looked like. "And you call yourself an investigator."

"I have no idea what you mean?"

"I know." She stood. "Well, we better get ready."

Knock… Knock.

"Who is that?" June asked Fin as he rose with a baby in his arms and went to answer the door. "It should be Harper and Charlie, your escorts for the day."

"My what?" Was all she got out as Harper and Charlie strode in.

Harper cut off anymore talking when she asked Fin. "Why are you still here?" And then asked June. "And why are you not dressed?"

She and Charlie were encased in leather pants and vests with long coats. Harper's leathers were a dark blue, and she wore knives strapped to her thighs as opposed to Charlie, who wore black leathers and guns strapped to her thighs. June asked with a touch of envy. "Wow, you guys look great. Are those outfits specially made?"

"Yeah, Storm and Ace ordered them for us, a while ago." Charlie told her.

"You have guns?" Fin asked June.

She grinned as she said. "You know I do."

"Wear them, and I will also order you a pair of leathers."

June grinned and cheered. "Yippee for me!"

Fin smiled as he handed the baby to Charlie, then shrugged into his sword harness. He, like Harper and Charlie, wore leather armor protection. He kissed June and said. "Take the girls to the stone apartment. I will see you in the courtroom. Do not do anything rash."

She looked up at him. "I will not, I promise."

He looked down into her eyes and said quietly. "Please do not go anywhere without Harper or Charlie."

"I will not."

He looked at Harper. "Keep Claire safe, you know they will be hunting her first."

Harper nodded as she poured her and Charlie some coffee. "We have them all with Sage, they are safe. Edith is with them as well. What did Claire see?"

"She saw a force of fifty to a hundred. She thinks this is only a push, she saw no blood, which she says means they could be scouting."

Charlie grimaced. "It is what I would do to see what our defenses are."

"Yeah, Johner said the same as did Ace." Harper agreed. "It is what I would do too."

"Shit, I hate this." June moaned softly.

"We know, we all do. Stay safe." Fin said as he left.

Charlie nodded to June to hand the baby to Harper so she could shower and change. She told her. "We will get the girls ready."

"Okay, thank you guys."

Harper frowned down at the sleeping baby in her arms. "What we do for family."

Within fifteen minutes, the three females and two babies walked swiftly toward the stone apartment. June carried both babies in her arms as Charlie and Harper escorted her.

CHAPTER EIGHTEEN:

C ourt was quiet, even though over a hundred people were present. So many more than June thought would have been there. She walked between Harper and Edith as they followed Sage, who walked between Charlie and Claire.

When they reached Fin, June stood next to him as Harper, Charlie and Edith went to where their Shadows waited. Claire moved to sit with Jacks as Sage carried on walking to the podium to stand next to Reighn. Stanvis called the court to order. "Court is closed. Guards seal the room."

They waited while the guards closed and stood in front of the doors. Other guards lined the walls and windows. Stanvis, with a nod from Johner, called out. "Be seated." He then took a step back as Lars came forward when everyone had taken a seat.

The pageantry was not lost on anyone as Lars unrolled a scroll and began to read. "We are here today to determine the validity of the claims from Casadaine Grove and Banatorr Luminia, for the young who have been claimed by Finlay and June Slorah. Please come forward representatives from the Banatorr Luminia."

When two females rose gracefully from their seats and walked toward the podium, it was easy to see they were pixies. Both were tall and slim and like the twins, had long pink hair and green eyes, their skin was golden and shone with vitality. They wore light flowing calf length dresses of reds and yellows. Serenity was the only word June could use to describe them. She nudged Fin. "They look like the girl's mother."

He nodded as he watched the females approach the small witness platform. Reighn stood as they greeted him. "Greetings Dragon Lord, I am Mauve Bana and this is my sister Neve Bana. We are the cousins of the one named Marria, who passed through the veil of clouds leaving behind two daughters."

The sister named Neve said. "We come in harmony to petition for the offspring."

Reighn inclined his head. "Thank you. We greet you in harmony. I must ask, why do you have a right to the daughters left behind?"

Mauve replied. "They are of our blood, as distant as that is. We feel the connection as faint as it is."

Reighn asked. "Are they the only reasons?"

Mauve asked. "Is there any other than duty?"

Neve stated. "They are pixie therefore they should be raised as pixie."

"Your petition is denied."

Mauve looked at her sister, then asked Reighn. "May we have clarity on your decision?"

Reighn waved his hand over to where June sat by Fin. "There is your reason. June Slorah answered the song of the mother and daughters. She suffered life-threatening injuries caused by those that took the lives of the twin's birth parents, to fulfil her promise to the one you call Marria. To bring her daughters to her Shadow and Dragon's Gap."

The two females bowed to Reighn, then turned and bowed to June and Fin. "We withdraw our petition there is no better mother and father for the daughters of Marria than the ones they have now."

June and Fin stood and bowed back. "We thank you."

When Reighn excused them, they silently walked to the door that was opened by a guard and escorted to a portal.

June blew out a breath as Fin murmured. "One down, one to go."

Lars called out. "Casadaine Grove, please step forward and state your petition."

Two faeries, male and female, stood and walked to the

small platform. They were dark in coloring, it was as though they had both been dipped, clothes and all, in chocolate. Both of them bowed to Reighn, then the male introduced himself and the female with him.

"Dragon Lord Reighn, may I introduce Councilor Carmel Waysong, adviser to Queen Mist Mesa. I am Montel Mesa, brother and adviser to King Palto Mesa of Casadaine Grove."

Reighn inclined his head, then asked. "Why has your Grove laid claim to the hatchlings?"

"On behalf of our Queen and King, we bequest the infants be given into our care to be raised as faerie."

Reighn frowned as he said. "Yet you heard the evidence of the call the birth mother made, along with the infants, to Lady June. You also know of the trials she endured to rescue both young?"

"We did."

"You still wish to proceed?"

"We do."

"Why?"

"I beg your pardon, Dragon Lord."

Sage stood and walked to stand beside Reighn. "I, as Dragon Lady, ask why? Your petition is frivolous at best. Downright insulting at worse and so I ask why?"

The male inclined his head as the female remained silent. "It has come to our Queen and King's attention you have harbored gray ones. They feel the infants would be unsafe to remain here, because of the inherent dangerous nature of those types of half-breeds."

Harper whispered to Charlie. "Does he mean us?"

"He does."

"Well, that is rude. Should I explain to him how rude that is?"

Ace said without taking his eyes off the male and female. "Do nothing, yet my soul, let us see what the Dragon Lady does."

"Okay, but any more slights and my feelings will get hurt."

"I am aware."

Sage asked the couple. "Can you explain that?"

The female finally spoke. Her voice was cultured and very refined. "Dragon Lady, our Queen rightly worries about the infants. It is a known fact, gray ones are notoriously unstable."

Sage raised an eyebrow. "Really? We have not found that. I was assured the new understanding of the gray ones was sent to all the Groves by the High Queen and King. Are you saying that your own Groves Queen and King are spreading misinformation or are you implying the High Queen and King are lying?" The male went a shade darker as the female drew in a sharp breath. Sage tipped her head to the side. "You cannot have it both ways. Both your Groves Queen and King are trying to embarrass the High Queen and King by challenging for infants that do not belong to your Grove. Or your Queen and King are just misguided and need the High Queen and King to send a recall and close your Grove."

"You have no right to make such scurrilous supposition." Stated the female.

"She may not, but I do." The High Queen said as she was escorted into the court by King Zale, and followed by Scarlett and Elijah. The faeries dropped to their knees. "High Queen, High King."

Reighn and Sage smiled as Reighn greeted their guests. "Queen Meadow and King Zale, we welcome you to our court."

Meadow smiled as she said. "We thank you, Dragon Lord and Lady, for allowing us to attend today. If we may, we will take the representatives and their people to your conference room. Where we can discuss this petition and talk about politics and their Queen and King."

"By all means Queen Meadow and please will you and your Light, as well as Queen Scarlett and King Elijah, join us for dinner. If Queen Isla and her Light are well enough, please convey our invitation to them as well."

"We would enjoy that very much Lord Reighn. Will the Lady Frankie be there?" King Zale asked.

Reighn inclined his head. "I believe she will be."

"Outstanding." The King said with a twinkle in his eyes.

"Dragon Lord, the petition for the infants is withdrawn." Stated High Queen Meadow.

"We thank you, High Queen."

Meadow bowed her head to Reighn. She looked at the faeries, still on their knees. "Rise my people; we will depart. With your permission, Dragon Lord and Lady."

She and her Light left the court with the faeries as several others rose from their seats and joined them. Sparrow led a contingent of guards that surrounded the visiting faeries as they walked through the opened doors. Reighn remained standing. "Come forth Finlay Slorah and June Slorah."

They moved to stand in front of Reighn. "Your claim for the two hatchlings known as Breena Dawn and Mirren Everly is granted from this day on. They are yours to love and cherish for as long as you live."

"We thank you Dragon Lord." Fin said as June hugged him.

She smiled at Reighn and Sage. "Thank you all." She looked out at her friends and family. "Everyone, we thank you."

Sage called out. "Bonding party next Saturday everyone book babysitters."

There was general laughter as June and Fin went back and sat with everyone else. Reighn let them all talk for a minute, as Sage said. "So Frankie made an impression on the King."

Reighn laughed. "She did, they adore her."

"Is she alright?"

"Apparently, she is thrilled her damping spell works so well." Reighn grinned with pride for Frankie. "On the other hand, the agent Fin and Ash caught is furious, and the others are not too happy either."

"Too bad they broke the rules; they pay the price." Sage looked at her Shadow. "You are angry?"

"Very, this is not how the Elturnian should operate."

"Well Fin, enjoyed himself, Frankie told me."

Reighn stared out at the smiling male and said. "Practice, he and Ace are very good at this kind of thing. Those agents had no chance. His talent is strategy when he turned his mind to the Elturnian, wishing to rescue the agent. It was, he said, a simple matter of logistics."

"Whatever, it seemed to work."

"That it did my love... That it did."

Lars arrived. "My Lord, I know you will be surprised to hear that there is a Councilor from the Elturnian waiting to see you."

Reighn grinned as the court went silent at Lars' announcement.

"You know I don't think I am." Reighn murmured to Sage. "My love, please take Mama and sit with the others. Let us not allow him too much information."

Sage smiled and agreed, then with Verity left the stage. Rene` said. "He will know me so I will stay."

When Fin came closer, he said. "As he will know me."

Reighn nodded. "In truth, he probably knows all of us, but why let him know we suspect?" He then said a little louder. "Alright Lars, remain with us, but all others fade into seats and guards into the shadows with you, please."

Fin and Rene` stood with Reighn and Lars as Stanvis announced. "They are on their way. Frankie is with them."

Reighn nodded. "Johner, place her with Harper and Charlie. Let's not let him see her."

Johner looked relieved when Frankie slipped through the door ahead of the prisoners and called out. "They are a minute away."

Johner hugged her, and she whispered. "I am okay, I promise."

"Good, go sit with Harper and try to look innocent." She laughed up at him, and he could see the tiredness in her eyes. He nodded as she went to where Harper and Charlie sat.

Harper moved over a seat for her. "You look tired,"

She nodded as she whispered. "It becomes a strain, but it is like a muscle, that just needs strengthening." She smiled at Harper's concerned gaze. "I promise I am alright."

"Good, because the High King and Queen are here and they specifically asked Reighn if you would have dinner with them."

Frankie squealed in delight, Reighn laughed. It appeared Harper told her of the King's request.

Just then, the side door that led to the hall that led to the cells opened and the six Elturnian agents entered. Faline Lightwind stood in the middle of the other five agents. Reighn noticed she was not as defiant as she had been before. Perhaps learning there were others more capable and better equipped than the organization you belong to, sapped the arrogance right out of you. Or maybe it was the easy capture of the other five agents the Elturnian had sent to rescue her.

As he watched them walk to stand in front of him, he sighed. These agents seemed like ordinary people he even spotted humans among the faeries, pixies and shifters. All of them were species that could easily slip into Dragon's Gap without raising any suspicions. Anger pulsed the room as he thought about how easily they may have done so. How many times over the years had they infiltrated his innocent town and befriended his citizen? His eyes elongated, and his voice deepened as his dragon rose to the surface.

Stanvis opened one of the court doors and a male walked in. He was tall and carried himself with arrogance and self-confidence, as some royalty did. Everything, from his bright blue eyes and slicked-back golden hair. To his black suit and deep blue cloak, said there was not a being in the world that was better or more justified in being alive than him. He was the master of power. No one moved in his world without his permission. He was Quin Nightcall, First Councilor of the Elturnian. He strode into the court as though he owned it, looked around as a sheen of amber covered his blue eyes. He used his power to catalogue and store away the information of the abilities of each person in the room. At least, that was what was supposed to happen. Fortunately, with Frankie there, he was rendered impotent, his abilities nulled. His eyes widened in surprise as he felt the power of the field dampening his abilities, and he had no idea of how far it covered. Was it just confined to the courtroom or all of the castle? The possibilities fascinated him. How wonderful it would be to bring into his fold the one with this skill. He almost salivated with anticipation, imagining rubbing the other councilor's noses in his new acquisition. They had been against him sending in agents to Dragon's Gap. If they knew, he and his hand-picked agents had not only gone against their wishes, but also failed. They would surely end his position on the council. If they discovered he was actually here now, his life would be worthless. The Elturnian did not suffer fools easily, and as it was turning out, this endeavor was proving to be a very foolish mistake. But when he took this null back with him, as well as the two Assassins that lived here. He would again be hailed as the only true Elturnian, and they would never question his decisions again. With those thoughts, he almost lost control of the rage that was building within him. How dare this Dragon Lord have the audacity to keep these talented people from him? Especially this null, it was outrageous. With enormous strength of will, he throttled back his rage, as he looked again for some sign of the null.

Reighn saw the male glance right over Frankie, as if she was not even there. And watched as his eyes almost lit with fire when he saw Charlie and Harper, who stared at him with blank expressions.

Quin lifted his top lip in a quirk of a smile at their expressionless faces. He would change that attitude with training. His eyes lit on Fin, where they stopped as a frown marred the perfection of his face as he tried to remember where he had met the dragon before.

The male is certainly beautiful. Sage thought. Like a shiny gold coin, he made her powers twitch with irritation. *What is he?* She asked Reighn through their bond.

He replied, not taking his eyes from the male. *No one knows.*

She laughed back at him as she returned. *I bet you do?*

That would be a sure bet.

Sneaky dragon.

Yes, let us hope it is enough.

Quin Nightcall finally strode to where his agents were lined up. Anger made his voice sharper and his eyes bluer as he addressed Reighn. "Dragon Lord, I thank you for the invitation to your court." His voice was like a winter's night, with a faint accent of something other worldly. It sent shivers down the backs of the shifters and humans alike.

Conor Towers, who was in his massive lion form, rumbled out a growl that vibrated against the stone floor and into everyone's bones. Causing the hair on the arms of most people to rise with the knowledge danger lurked in the shadows. Reighn inclined his head, ignoring the grumble from the lion. "I am pleased the Elturnian received my invitation. I would have thought the council would have come themselves and not sent the First Councilor."

Quin bit back the angry retort hovering on his lips. No one sent him anywhere. Instead, he bowed his head slightly. "I deemed it unnecessary to trouble the council with this matter."

"I see. So I am to assume you are willing to explain your decision?"

"What decision are you referring to?"

"The decision to invade my territories."

Quin spread his hands. "I am here to collect my wayward agents. Not to answer inane questions."

"Take care, Councilor. You are here at my invitation, it does not give you the right to be disrespectful to my court or me."

"A misunderstanding only." Quin hurriedly assured Reighn.

"Lie." Charlie said, loud enough for all to hear.

Quin spun around but he could not see who had spoken. Every face looked only interested, not suspicious. Reighn became tired of the males posturing and demanded. "Explain to me, Quin Nightcall, why I do not end your life and the lives of your agents now. You sent operatives into my territory without my knowledge or permission and sent those same operatives into my house. What part of that is not a violation of our trust?"

"Dragon Lord, we answer to no one. You are treading close to lines of enquiry that you are hardly privileged to."

Reighn's eyes misted red as his dragon raced under his skin, and the room shook with his anger. In that moment, the benign ruler had vanished and in his place stood the Dragon Lord, whispered about in stories of mayhem and bloodshed. Every dragon there shifted with unease. Everyone else held still, not wanting his gaze to find them.

His voice when he spoke was as smooth as silk, with an edge of death sliding along the vowels. "When did the credo of the Elturnian change?"

Quin sounded almost bored as he answered. "They are as they always have been."

Reighn's voice became colder. "No, First Councilor, trespassing into a kingdom or world without the consent of the ruling or governing monarchs or government as far as I know, were never in the rules of the Elturnian."

The Councilor said nothing as some of his confidence seeped from his bearing at Reighn's tone. He knew he had breached protocol and possibly exposed the Elturnian to scrutiny. Reighn could see when he decided to exert his position once more. It was when his chin lifted and his face became harsh with the stamp of arrogance that seemed to be a habitual expression. The male was out of his depth and if he had looked to his left and seen the look of shame and anger on the faces of his agents. He may have thought twice about what he was about to say. But unfortunately, his arrogance and belief that the Dragon Lord had no power over him or his role as First Councilor to the Elturnian would be his failing. "Better to return to your ignorance and leave the Elturnian to our own agendas. Dragon Lord, go back to governing your corner of the world and let us look after the rest."

Reighn's dragon entered his voice as he told the councilor. **"Quin, you have no idea what you have just unleashed. You had no right to usurp the Elementals or my rule."** Before the male had a chance to speak, Reighn's dragon released his voice, and he stated.

"The Elturnian code is to do no harm, and their mission is to only interject when a country's governing body calls for help. Or the government is out of control and the Elturnian have no choice but to step in and help the citizens. You had a choice, First Councilor. No one was under duress here. Dragon's Gap is not ruled by a tyrant. Dragons are the arm of justice for the Elementals, and you should have listened when the councilors advised you to refrain from sending agents here without my knowledge. In essence, Councilor Quin, you should have talked to me."

"What benefit to the Elturnian are you, Dragon Lord." Quin Nightcall sneered as he felt the hand of trepidation slip over his skin.

"As of five hours ago, I am the Elturnian."

"How is this possible? You speak lies." Quin Nightcall snarled.

Reighn shrugged as he told him. "Very easy, I assure you. You and the councilors made two mistakes. Firstly; my Ancestor gathered together a specific number of species to watch and help the world when needed. It was not always good, honest people that were given power to rule worlds or countries, so ensuring, no one stepped outside the rules set down by the Goddess. As well as stopping rulers thinking they could become gods unto themselves. He put in place the Elturnian, you First Councilor, have overstepped your own tenets. So as stated in the Elturnians' own laws. I am now required to step in and take over control of the Elturnian. Your second mistake; was to exclude the Elementals. You again, First Councilor placed the most powerful beings in our Universe, if not all Universes on bypass. One has to ask. Why you would do this?"

Yes, Quin Nightcall, explain to us and our Dragon Lord how it is you think your society has the right to do so. I like my brothers are very interested to know. In the room stood all four Elementals, the one who had spoken stood slightly in front of the others as universes swirled in his eyes. Quin Nightcall could only stand there, shaken from his normal arrogance and unable to utter one word.

Little agent explain, please.

Faline Lightwind swallowed and bowed. "Please Elementals, I do not know. I am an agent, not a councilor."

But are you not an intelligent agent?

"I am."

We await your answer.

Faline looked at the Dragon Lord's hard face and swallowed the bile that rose in her throat and started talking. "From all that I have observed and read, also with a fair amount of supposition. I would say the council felt they did not need to explain their existence to the Elementals. Because they consider themselves long lived and far cleverer, and their reach far greater than the Elementals or the Dragon Lord."

As we thought. We are not pleased, Dragon Lord.

"As, I am not."

We extracted much from the ones we took with us. A pile of folders appeared in Fin's arms. *You will find everything in there that they knew, dragon Fin.*

"We thank you Elementals."

Do with these others what you wish, Dragon Lord. We will take the one called London Darkchild, and this one called Faline Lightwind. When we have schooled them, they will return. You may place them as trainers of the new Elturnian society.

"Thank you once more, and I will see to the new society."

Choose your new First Councilor wisely.

Then they were gone, taking the two agents with them. Only one Elemental remained, he said. *Dragon Lord, do not take too long. They are an invaluable tool. Erase the corruption within their society as you will.*

"I will not." Reighn looked over the remaining agents and Quin Nightcall. "Johner, remove them to the cells. They can join the other councilors until I can talk to them. Frankie, you are released with our thanks. The Elementals placed a dampening field around the cells."

"Okay, thank you."

Reighn could hear the relief in her voice. The doors opened, and the guards entered to escort the agents and the bewildered Quinn Nightcall out. An agent asked. "My Lord, will Faline and London be alright?"

Reighn nodded. "Yes in time, they will be better than ever. Go now, I will see you all tomorrow."

"Thank you, my Lord." He bowed as the others did. Except for Quin who looked as though his world had been removed from under his feet. By the time his brain started working again, he would be in the cells with the other councilors, answering some hard questions.

Once they had left the courtroom, Reighn told the remaining people. "Our Seer was correct, we arrested forty-nine infiltrators. They are being questioned off world by the Shields now. Thank you everyone for your participation, you all worked well."

There were a few smiles but more worried frowns as they all rose from their chairs. Lars called out as Reighn and Sage stepped down from the podium. "Court is dismissed. Go with peace in your hearts." They all looked at him, some with surprise and others with amusement. "What? I am trying something new. It was a friendly way of saying, get the hell out."

"Well, it was nice but weird." Harper told him as she stood and stretched. She was still tired from her late night.

"Creepy." Charlie commented.

Olinda smiled at him. "I liked it Lars, it was kinder."

Frankie agreed. "Made me feel all warm inside."

Claire shook her head at him; he raised an eyebrow in return. "You heard them; it made them feel warm."

"And creepy and just plain freaked out." Edith called out, causing several people to laugh.

"None of you have a soul." He retorted as he stormed from the room, which caused more laughter.

Claire declared. "So easy."

"He really is." Reighn agreed with her as Sage hugged him. June was hugged by Frankie as Fin handed off the folders to his staff. June finally made it to Reighn and Sage. "Thank you both."

"For what, those babies are yours. You were always destined to be their mother." Sage told her softly. "I am proud of you. There was no wolf-crazy."

June blushed. "Well, it was tough there for a minute but my Fin and babies deserve better than wolf-crazy."

"Well, they have that." Reighn assured her.

"Yep," Sage said, "you have finally grown up."

"See, that is just mean." June pouted and spoiled it all with a laugh.

CHAPTER NINETEEN:

Later that night, Reighn stood on his balcony with a drink in hand as Sage slipped her hands around the hard plains of his body. "What is it?"

"We know the name of the one who has orchestrated the war against us."

"Is it war?"

"It is a kind of war."

"Who is it?"

"The male that enticed Charlie and Harper's mother from her home."

"Oh, my Goddess, does Scarlett know?"

He shook his head. "No, just Fin and I and you now."

"Will you tell Charlie and Harper?" And just like that, he fell in love with her all over again. Asking rather than demanding he tell them, he knew if he chose not to speak of what he knew to Harper and Charlie. She would go along with his decision. If he told the sisters, she would be right by his side. He hugged her to him. "I will have too."

Sage felt a shiver of something roll down her spine as she whispered. "This is bigger than them though, isn't it?"

"Yes, he has spent years planning. Fin says we are playing catch up and we need to do so fast."

Sage held him tighter. "How do we fight someone we cannot see?"

"We fight as we always have, with intelligence and patience."

"But dragons are not alone this time. You have shifters and faeries, all of us to help."

He smiled grimly out at the dark night as he murmured. "And for better or worse, we have Andre`."

EPILOGUE:

A portal opened in a small town in the mountains of the Ouachits. Fin read the sign that spanned five feet across.

"Mason Town. Population 355. Mayor and owner Jacob Mason. Only Humans allowed within the town limits."

"Seems rude." Johner said as he, Ash, and Fin stepped over the imaginary town line.

Fin looked at him and said. "You sound like Frankie."

"It is catchy but still rude."

"True, we should educate the people of this quaint town on rudeness."

Ash advised. "It is our civic duty, to not do so would be just plain rude ourselves."

"Are you studying law?" Fin asked the male as he strolled between him and Johner.

Ash grinned. "Olinda likes law shows."

Several shadows flew overhead as Reighn and Ace led twelve dragons in formation over the town. Fin saw a church like building that seemed to be filled with townspeople. They stopped outside and listened to a male as he thundered about abominations and the power of the sword. He seemed to be getting worked up over what he deemed the corruption of the world because of shifters. He told the congregation that a good shifter was a dead shifter, which was met with loud cheers and foot stomping.

Ash rumbled. "Seems intense."

"I have heard some preachers can be like that." Johner said. "Frankie told me where she came from, this was normal on a Sunday."

Fin grunted. "Seems a stupid way to ruin a Sunday."

June stepped in front of the three males. "Hey, are we doing this?"

Fin grinned. "My love, we only awaited you."

"Okay, let's go." With that, she walked up the steps and entered the church and started walking between people. She was sure these people had not seen a bath for days, if not weeks. The stench was overpowering.

Her mere presence made people make way for her, or it could have been the three large males holding swords following behind her. As she walked down the aisle of what had been a church at one time, she was unsurprised to see the two males she had tagged standing on the stage. She stopped and called out to the short male, who seemed to be preaching to the masses. "Hey dude, do you remember me?"

The male, who she now knew was Jacob Mason, stared at her as his face paled. "Go away, you are not allowed here."

The taller male who had been standing behind Jacob, as he loudly spoke of the evils of shifters, stepped forward and stilled on seeing who was with her. June noticed he was still in need of a bath. His hair, if possible, looked dirtier, and she just stopped the look of distaste crossing her features as he growled out. "Leave, unless you brought the abominations back?"

"Nope, I told you, if you thought they were abominations. I would show you some real ones." She smiled at the people there and motioned to the windows. "Look about you Preacher."

"I am the mayor and owner of this town."

June shrugged. "Don't care, look up." She told him.

He stayed where he was, Fin thought he probably assumed the stage protected him. He was so very wrong.

Jacob Mason watched as people rose from their seats and looked out the windows. Soon, the screaming started, and people began pushing and shoving as they ran over each other to leave the building. Ash was amused, wondering where they thought they could go to be safe. When fire dragons flew, nowhere was safe.

"Foolish humans." Murmured Johner.

June grinned at the two males on the stage as she said. "I told you to say your goodbyes to your love ones. I hope you took my advice, because it's too late now to do so."

She turned and kissed Fin as a portal appeared, then she stepped through and turning she waved at the males that stood opened mouthed watching her. Once Fin dismissed the portal, he looked at the fifty males gathered around the stage, where the two males June had tagged days before cowered. He asked in a voice that froze their blood. "Which one of you thought it was a good idea to try to kill my Shadow?"

Hours later, Fin held June in his arms as he asked her. "Are you happy, little wolf?"

"More than I ever believed I could be. If this is a dream, may I never wake up?"

As his lips lowered to hers, he whispered. "This is no dream, my June. This is our life."

BOOKS IN THE DRAGON'S GAP SERIES

Dragon's Gap: Reighn & Sage
Dragon's Gap: Sharm & Edith
Dragon's Gap: A novella Love's Catalyst
Dragon's Gap: Storm & Charlie
Dragon's Gap: Ash & Olinda
Dragon's Gap: Ace & Harper
Dragon's Gap: A novella Love's Impulse
Dragon's Gap: Thorn & Ciana
Dragon's Gap: Conor & Ocean
Dragon's Gap: A Christmas Surprise for Dragon's Gap

I hope you enjoyed this compilation of books 4&5 plus Love's Catalyst

Time for the final three books:

Dragon's Gap: Dragon Shifter Romance Stories 6-7 Plus A Christmas Surprise

Printed in Great Britain
by Amazon

11117963R00323